INNOCENT BYSTANDERS

By Sandra Scoppettone

SUZUKI BEANE (with Louise Fitzhugh)
BANG BANG YOU'RE DEAD (with Louise Fitzhugh)
TRYING HARD TO HEAR YOU
THE LATE GREAT ME
SOME UNKNOWN PERSON
HAPPY ENDINGS ARE ALL ALIKE
SUCH NICE PEOPLE
LONG TIME BETWEEN KISSES

INNOCENT BYSTANDERS

SANDRA SCOPPETTONE

NAL BOOKS
NEW AMERICAN LIBRARY
TIMES MIRROR
NEW YORK AND SCARBOROUGH, ONTARIO

Copyright © 1983 by Sandra Scoppettone
All rights reserved
For information address The New American Library, Inc.
Published simultaneously in Canada by The New American Library of Canada Limited

 NAL BOOKS TRADEMARK REG. U.S. PAT. OFF. AND FOREIGN COUNTRIES
REGISTERED TRADEMARK—MARCA REGISTRADA
HECHO EN CRAWFORDSVILLE, INDIANA, U.S.A.

Library of Congress Cataloging in Publication Data

Scoppettone, Sandra.
  Innocent bystanders.

  I. Title.
PS3569.C58615   1983   813'.54   82-14270
ISBN 0-453-00422-9

SIGNET, SIGNET CLASSICS, MENTOR, PLUME, MERIDIAN and NAL BOOKS are published *in the United States* by The New American Library, Inc., 1633 Broadway, New York, New York 10019, *in Canada* by The New American Library of Canada Limited, 81 Mack Avenue, Scarborough, Ontario M1L 1M8

Designed by Alan Steele

First Printing, April, 1983

1 2 3 4 5 6 7 8 9

PRINTED IN THE UNITED STATES OF AMERICA

PUBLISHER'S NOTE

This novel is a work of fiction. Names, characters, places, and incidents are either the product of the author's imagination or are used fictitiously, and any resemblance to actual persons, living or dead, events, or locales is entirely coincidental.

For Darly...(as always) of course and naturally

PART ONE

Ruined Hearts

1955

ONE

The checkered taxicab was new, a smell of fresh leather was unmistakable. Danielle Swann tasted this essence on the back of her tongue as though she had sampled a bite of the sleek, burnished interior. She swallowed, trying to chase away the flavor; she could not help thinking of the animals who had furnished their skins to create this environment. Yet she ate meat, wore leather belts and shoes, carried handbags made from hides. Never, however, would she wear a fur coat: it was one principle she still embraced.

After a while the odor of new leather diminished; cool air from the open windows flooded the back of the cab. Her children, one on either side, sat on their haunches, clutched the window frames, and watched the buildings and stores of Fifth Avenue pass by as if the tableau might have changed since the last time they'd made the trip uptown, three days before.

"This corner will be fine," Danielle said to the driver as the light changed to red.

The cab swung to the curb and stopped with a jolt; her outstretched arms protected both children from lurching forward. The abrupt stop had been unnecessary, but when Danielle saw the inexplicable hostility in the cabby's eyes, she decided not to mention it.

On the sidewalk, still puzzled by the burly driver's demeanor, Danielle watched the cab peel away as if there might be an explanation in its exhaust, like skywriting. Fifth Avenue, bathed in an early evening June light, was strangely still. The block between Sixty-eighth and Sixty-ninth seemed placed under a giant bell jar. In this rarified atmosphere the sudden shrill scream was even more discordant than it might have been elsewhere.

As Danielle, terrified, whirled around, the wordless shriek turned intelligible: "Mom-mee," the child cried. Galvanized by her daughter's call, she was quickly kneeling by Cristina's side. "It's all right, honey, it's just a scrape." Relieved, Danielle chastized herself for drifting and abandoning her usual perfect vigilance. She kissed her six-year-old's cheek, stroked her hair.

"It hurts," Cristina said, small hands encircling her knee, an isolated island of pain.

"Don't be a baby," said Claude, the four-year-old.

"Shut up," Cristina snapped.

"Can you get up, honey?"

"It hurts awful, Mommy."

"I know it does," said Danielle soothingly. "But you have to get up so we can make it better at Grandmaman's."

The boy, shuffling a sandled foot near his sister's rear end, said, "Get up, Tina."

She ignored him. "I don't know if I can walk."

Danielle held her smile and asked seriously, "Do you think you need an ambulance?"

Silent seconds passed before Cristina replied, equally seriously, "I think I can make it." She offered her small thin arms to her mother, needing, at least, to be lifted to her feet.

As she helped her daughter up, Danielle was struck, as always, by her height; she would favor Martin in this respect and Danielle was glad of that. It was better to be tall, she believed. She'd spent a lifetime looking up, reaching. "Okay?" she asked.

Cristina took a step, faltered, winced with pain. "I can do it," she said bravely.

"Good girl." She circled the little girl's waist with one hand, and with her other she engulfed Claude's hand, the fingers so small and delicate they stirred a place within her to ineffable joy. "Not much further," she said.

Danielle smiled at the little stoic beside her. So far, Cristina's height was her only inheritance from her father. Otherwise, she looked exactly like her mother, a miniature Danielle. Her black hair was cut in a way identical to Danielle's and fell to her shoulders in the same wavy fashion when it wasn't held back on either side by two small barrettes, as it was now. Like Danielle's, Cristina's eyes were almond-shaped and the color of a good, dark Italian leather. Her straight, thin nose was delicately flared at the nostrils, her mouth was full, the upper lip two even arcs, the bottom perfectly curved, a tiny indentation at each corner. She had a strong, rounded chin with the hint of a dimple in the center. Here they differed: Danielle's dimple was prominent, startling.

"Evening, Mrs. Swann," Howard, the doorman, said, touching the brim of his gold-braided gray cap. "Oh, my, what've we got here?" his eyes on the wounded knee.

"A very bad fall," answered Cristina.

"Practically fatal," Danielle said.

At the elevator, Cristina pressed against her mother's hip while Claude, perhaps to emphasize his lack of injury, hopped on one foot, then the other; his yellow hair, growing like a buttercup over his brow, flopped in time with his jumping. As she often had, Danielle wondered if the pale complexion and light hair came from her mother's or father's side. There were no blonds in Martin's family.

The door slid open and Paul, the elevator operator of the past twenty-five years, stood smiling at them. Cristina limped in, emphasizing her injury.

"Got a bo-boo, huh?" he asked.

Cristina nodded and nestled into the folds of her mother's lavender skirt. At the tenth floor, Paul stopped, cranked open the gate, released the door.

Claude ran to the apartment door, slapped his hand against the wood to be let in. From her purse Danielle took a key and unlocked it.

The children's shoes clacked across the white marble foyer as they ran to find their grandmother. One of the three cats, Danielle thought it was Pia, streaked from the library and down the main hall.

"Evening, Mrs. Swann," said Wallace, the Dudevant maid.

Danielle smiled. "Hello. Where's Mother?" She knew she was in; Thursday was the night the family always had dinner and tonight was special.

"She's in her bedroom." Wallace had a fragile, pointed face, brown eyes a shade deeper than her skin.

"Thanks." On a petit-point hall chair, Danielle placed her summer straw handbag, a sweater, and a second bag filled with the children's things. She walked the long hall to her parents' room. The door was ajar and she could hear voices: the children and Maman. She pushed open the door and entered the large room; it was decorated in shades of blue, the furniture, like the pieces in the formal living room, were Louis XVI, the walls painted a rich cream.

"Maman?" Danielle called, seeing the empty room.

"In the bathroom, dear. Medical emergency," answered Amelia Dudevant.

Danielle crossed the Persian rug; Maman would give Cristina the proper attention, create a sense of seriousness. She poked her head round the bathroom door.

Cristina sat on the closed toilet seat while Amelia, bent over the cut knee, gently swabbed out the dirt with a wet ball of cotton. Claude, his chin in his hands, elbows resting on his thighs, sat on the edge of the tub, watching.

"Dreadful, dreadful," Amelia said.

Cristina wrinkled her face in fear. "Will it hurt?"

"Well," Amelia said, "to be honest, yes, it probably will. But it must be done, my darling. Isn't that right, Danielle?" she asked without turning to her daughter.

"Grandmaman knows best," Danielle replied, believing it. She had unusual respect for her mother.

"Unfortunately, we don't have anything but iodine, and that does sting. Be brave, Cristina." Amelia dabbed the red liquid on Cristina's knee.

"Ow-eee!"

"Big baby," Claude said.

Danielle sat next to him on the tub, put an arm around his tiny shoulders. "No, Claude, she's being a real soldier."

"Good girl," said Amelia. "Now the bandage."

The rest of the operation took only a few seconds and then the children were allowed to go to the kitchen for some homemade Wallace cookies.

"Hello, my darling," Amelia said, kissing Danielle on the lips.

"Maman."

"Such a ruckus," said Amelia, putting away the medicinal paraphernalia.

Her mother was an extremely good-looking woman for fifty-eight, Danielle thought. Her gray eyes were large, clear and lightly made up, a touch of shadow, a slight darkening of brows and lashes. Lines had begun near her nose, deepening around her rose-colored mouth, and there were cross-hatchings at the corners of her eyes, but her forehead and skin in general had a moist, luminous cast to it, free, for now, from the aging process. Her auburn hair had turned gray years before, but Amelia kept it dyed, natural looking, stylishly coiffed, maturely molded around her heart-shaped face. Amelia's only problem was her weight; she loved to eat and was about twenty pounds heavier than she should be. Still, Danielle hoped she looked as good as her mother when she was her age.

Slipping her arm through Danielle's, Amelia led her from the bathroom to the delicate tulipwood table beneath the windows. "Shall we have a drink before the others arrive?"

"Fine," said Danielle, as though it were a first, rather than what they did every Thursday, part of the reason she came early: to have this time alone with Maman.

Amelia reached out a ringed finger and pushed a buzzer. Almost immediately, Wallace, who knew the routine, entered with their drinks: an old-fashioned for Amelia, a martini for Danielle. Paté on toast was also on the tray. They clinked glasses.

"*A votre santé*," said Amelia.

"*Santé*." Her mother's use of French words amused Danielle, but she remembered how it had irritated her, the way it did her brother now, when she was a teenager. Thinking of Guy, she asked, "How was the graduation ceremony?"

"Oh, well, lovely I suppose. Those occasions always make me cry and I hate to in public. I wish you could've come, dear."

She had very much wanted to go to Guy's graduation but, without her knowledge, Martin had arranged a matinee date for her with the wife of a colleague and refused to let her out of the engagement. Tickets to *Cat on a Hot Tin Roof* were not easy to get, he'd said, pretending the tickets, rather than impressing his colleague, were the issue. She'd acquiesced, as always.

Amelia knew the reason for Danielle's absence (her daughter told her everything) and although she believed a wife should obey her husband, she thought sometimes Danielle went to extremes. She also understood that not having attended Guy's graduation caused her daughter some pain, so she changed the subject, filling her in on the latest gossip.

Danielle sipped her drink, lit a Pall Mall, and thought of how much Martin hated her smoking. She blew a plume of silvery smoke into the air, enjoying the taste and the gesture thoroughly. Martin said people used cigarette smoking as a cover for their feelings. He never let his patients smoke during a session. Dr. Offenbach allowed her to smoke and she was grateful for this meager concession as she was convinced he gave her little else and was seriously considering quitting. Martin would be enraged, of course, if she made such a decision independently. For that reason alone, the idea intrigued her:

it had been a very long time since she'd done anything without consulting him.

"Mmmm, this paté is lovely, dear. Have some." Something was troubling Danielle; it was time to press. Amelia cleared her throat as if to empty it of idle chatter. "What is it, darling, you seem upset."

Maman knew her well, too well sometimes. Occasionally Danielle resented having nothing of her own, not even thoughts. It crossed her mind to dismiss her mother's insight but, instead, she said, "I was thinking about Martin."

Martin Swann had never been a favorite of Amelia's, although on the surface she could find nothing really objectionable about him, at least not in the beginning. Certainly the ten-year age difference was nothing she could point to: her own husband was nine years older than she. "What about him?" she asked.

Dr. Offenbach said it wasn't healthy that her best friend was her mother, that the things she confided in her were often inappropriate. She'd never told her about Brian, though. But what, really, was there to tell? Perhaps the innocence of it all was why she'd kept it to herself, and not because she was having a fling at autonomy. "Sometimes," she found herself saying as though she were a ventriloquist's dummy, "I wish I'd never met Martin. That's terrible, isn't it, Maman?"

"No, not terrible. Sad. It makes me very sad to know you're so unhappy. Oh, Lord," she said, sounding suddenly angry, "I wish Pierre had never brought him here."

Danielle would always remember the first sight of Martin. On her entrance into the library, he had risen from the midnight blue velvet chair he occupied, facing her father. She hadn't known there was to be company and was as much surprised by that fact as she was by the tall, craggy-faced man who smiled affably and whose eyes, pearl-shaped and pervading, were the color of carbon. He extended his hand, long thin fingers drooping, and took several steps toward her. It was then she was finished. Martin Swann had an unmistakable limp. It was as though her heart had been sliced neatly in two: she could have been mourning a summer's eve, with everyone in white, waltzing; or glimpsing a magnolia tree in full bloom, the petals dripping slowly onto the greenest of rolling lawns. When he locked her small hand in his she knew her life would inexorably change from that moment on.

And of course it had. In the beginning he was supportive, encouraging, eager, he said, for her to become the lawyer she had studied so assiduously to be. When she passed the bar, the only woman to do so, he was ecstatic. She remembered being made uncomfortable by his enthusiasm; it was as though, through osmosis, he had added a law degree to his medical one. And for a tiny flash in time she knew that Martin would absorb her, an insight she denied so quickly that the thought skidded off her brain, leaving no impression.

"I should have been more perceptive," Amelia said.

"No, Maman, *I* should have."

"But you have the children," Amelia said, granting her the universal consolation for a bad marriage.

She accepted her mother's offering, smiling. "Yes, I have the children." It was true, of course. They were central to her life, but children, no matter how sublime, could never make up for adult company.

Careful to word it as a question, not an admonition, Amelia asked, "Are you thinking of a divorce?" There had never been one in her family or Pierre's.

Quickly, Danielle shook her head. "No, no, I'm not." But why wasn't she? There was virtually nothing left of their marriage. Was it because she knew her parents would disapprove?

"You were happy once, weren't you?" asked Amelia, implying the answer rather than waiting for it.

Good daughter gave the proper response: "Yes, of course." But were they?

Their honeymoon had been a Grand Tour and on their return home, Danielle, preparing to begin practicing law, was suddenly faced with pregnancy. Her mind flew immediately to a night in Florence. They'd been married only three weeks and since they had agreed on no children for at least four years so she could become established professionally, Danielle always used a diaphragm. But on this night, she recalled, after a particularly delicious meal and perhaps a little too much wine, Martin had, upon entering their room, almost roughly pulled her to the floor. She'd whispered that she wasn't prepared, but he'd ignored her. She hadn't known whether he'd heard or not.

When she told him she was pregnant, however, she knew. Of course he feigned surprise and even sympathized with her dismay. But his eyes and mouth betrayed him: his eyes turned a raven-black and a twitch forced his lips into a trembly smile. A child *now* had been his plan; there was no doubt in her mind. The thought of an abortion rose momentarily before her, then collapsed.

This knowledge of Martin's manipulation was the first chip in the disintegration of their marriage. But Danielle denied, then buried, what she so chillingly knew. Before long her pregnancy and the coming birth of her child occupied her completely. And for a while she and Martin became close again, enjoying the child, enjoying each other. It hadn't lasted.

"We were happy for a while," Danielle answered her mother. "You and Papa have always been happy together, haven't you?"

In the face of her daughter's admission (not really a surprise), Amelia found it uncomfortable to admit that she and Pierre had had an exceptionally satisfying marriage. "Oh, there are always problems, little things," she said not able really to lend it weight, not even for Danielle. Should she encourage her daughter to rid herself of Martin? Amelia knew the influence she wielded and although divorce was an abhorrence to her, Danielle's contentment was essential. She drained her drink, placed the glass with the perfect imprint of her lips on its rim, back on the table.

"Darling," she said, "if you believe it's best to. . . ."

"Ah, my two *petites femmes,* swilling it down in private, eh?" Pierre stood in the doorway, smiling.

Tomorrow, thought Amelia, I'll tell her to leave him.

Danielle rose and crossed the room, meeting her father halfway, kissing him. "Hello, Papa." She adored him and knew, even though he was often shy and reticent with her, that he loved her profoundly. Sometimes she wished she'd never left home.

Pierre squeezed his daughter's shoulder before crossing to Amelia. *"Ma petite souris,"* he said, touching his lips to hers.

Amelia sighed. She'd been telling him for years not to call her his little mouse: it did no good. "How was your day, darling?"

Pierre began to recount a story. Danielle envied her mother this: Martin never told her anything about his work. He refused her passport to his professional life and she absorbed the denial as diminishing. Her eyes rested on her father.

He was the epitome of the distinguished older man. His hair, though sparse, was white as milk, and with the exception of a tonsured spot at his crown, was kept short and combed neatly in the conventional American style, parted on the side. Eyebrows, like two small silver shelves, protruded above cadet blue eyes which were as clear and alert as a youth's. His skin was stretched tautly across the narrow bridge of his nose and his high cheekbones, creating a lustrous sheen, as if he'd been sprayed with an evanescent coat of varnish. A white toothbrush mustache completed the picture.

Wallace knocked at the door; Amelia gave her Pierre's drink order and her own. "Danielle?" she asked.

"No more for me now."

"Well," Pierre said, "tonight we celebrate an ending and a beginning. Before long we shall be toasting the younger Dr. Dudevant." He smiled and touched the mustache, smoothing it down although not a bristle was out of place.

Danielle felt terrible. Guy had no intention of becoming a doctor. He had asked for her intervention with their father some time ago, but she'd yet to speak to him; it was not a discussion she looked forward to.

"Is something disturbing you, Danielle?" Pierre asked.

"No, Papa." She smiled, touched her father's hand. "I should see about the children."

"They are fine. I saw them when I came in."

"Run along, darling, if you wish," said Amelia. "Pierre would keep his two women here with him alone all evening if he had his way."

Danielle walked down the hall toward the kitchen. The children would be in Wallace's bedroom looking at television. The Dudevants refused to own a set, as did Martin. Television was an extraordinary treat for Cristina and Claude. She supposed Martin was right about this, but sometimes, when friends spoke of programs they'd seen, she found herself feeling deprived and knew the children felt the same with their small friends.

Guy stood at the sink, finishing a glass of water. "Hey, there you are." He came to her and enveloped her in his thin arms.

"Hello, graduate," she said looking up into those incredible eyes: they were a vivid violet with long, thick, black eyelashes.

"Harvard, here I come."

"Guy, I'm sorry about not coming to your graduation, I. . . ."

"No sweat. I understand."

"Do you?"

"Sure I do." He kissed her on the forehead, put an arm around her and led her out of the kitchen.

She could hear the television blaring from Wallace's room; the children were fine. They made their way back down the hall to the library, the only room considered casual in the Dudevant residence. She had never confided in Guy about Martin, her dissatisfaction with her marriage, but in these last two years they'd become quite close despite their sixteen-year age difference. Guy had, she knew, observed her relationship with her husband. Sometimes she'd been embarrassed in front of her brother, his scrutiny and perception forcing her to view things through his eyes even though he said nothing judgmental.

"Want a drink?" he asked.

"Not now, thanks."

"I think I'll have one."

She couldn't help smiling. Guy was asserting his graduate status: a grownup making his own drink. She wondered how old he looked to others. He was still a baby to her, in a way, so little definition in that handsome face. He'd been through minimal stress in his eighteen years and life had yet to register. Guy was still innocent.

He sat across from her in the blue chair, his gray suit giving him a stolid, stiff appearance. Amelia insisted on suits and ties at dinner. "You okay?" he asked.

She was surprised. "Yes, why?"

He shrugged. "I don't know, you seem quiet or something."

"I'm in a reflective mood. It's the marking of time, I suppose. Your graduation from prep school is one of those markings."

Guy nodded. "It's a helluva marking for me, I'll tell you. Getting out. God, I can hardly wait for September."

Danielle suddenly felt sorry for her parents. "Honestly, Guy, you'd think you lived in a prison."

A sense of disappointment that Danielle was, after all, not completely in his corner, invaded him. "You know what I mean. Like this damn tie, for instance."

"Well, yes, but it's not that awful." She didn't like the way the conversation was going, didn't wish to seem in opposition to him, taking her parents' side. It wasn't true, really; she did understand his need to be on his own. "Honey, please don't get me wrong."

12

He took this fragile moment to ask: "Have you spoken to Papa?"

"Not yet. There's plenty of time."

"I'll have to register for classes and then he'll know. I mean, there's no point taking premed stuff, Danielle. It'd be a waste."

"All right, I'll talk to him this week, I promise. But don't count on my making the slightest difference."

"Oh, come on, he dotes on you." The implication was clear: Danielle was the favorite.

If only Guy knew how wrong he was. Perhaps it was time to tell him. A graduation present? Something held her back, as if to part with a knowledge she shared only with Maman and Papa, would decrease her sense of worth. Was this why she'd never told her husband, children? "You're the boy," she said. "Boys are always the favorites."

"Maybe. Anyway, are you afraid to talk with Papa?"

"A little, but I know it's silly. He'll rant and rave, that's all. But I honestly don't think it'll make a damn bit of difference what I say, Guy. I hope you understand that."

"Yeah, I know." He took a long swallow of the gin and tonic. "But I can't be a doctor. Last week Fred Van Iderstine cut his dumb finger, a tiny cut, and I was standing there and guess what?"

"You threw up?"

"I almost fainted," he said weakly, and looked down at his knees.

Danielle gazed at the crown of his head, black curly hair neatly slicked down; she felt the urge to cry at the sight of his unnecessary humiliation. "It doesn't make you any less of a person . . . a man," she said.

His head remained bent, the long outstretched legs slowly dragged in as if he were reeling in fishing line, giving up.

"Guy? Did you hear me?"

"I heard." His voice was muffled.

"Lots of people feel that way about blood."

At last he looked up at her. "But *he* doesn't know that. He won't understand. To him I'll be a failure."

"And to you? Will you be a failure to yourself?"

He was thoughtful for a moment. "No, I don't think so. It'd be worse if I put myself in a premed course and flunked out. And I would."

"Then that's what's important. Guy, listen, we'll make Papa understand together. I promise. Don't ruin tonight. Whatever he says, well, just smile and go along with it, okay?"

"But it's so hypocritical."

Absolute truth was essential at Guy's age, she remembered. Only later did the compromises, the accommodations, the desertion of principles begin, all necessary but sad. "It may be hypocritical in a way, but it's also kinder."

"To whom?" he asked ingenuously.

"To everyone," she answered selfishly.

"I guess it would be pretty lousy to make a scene about it tonight. Anyway, who am I kidding? Here I am hiding behind your skirts and pretending I'm going to stand up for my rights. What a phony I am."

"No you're not. I think you're terrific." And she did. He was an adorable boy, soon to be a fine man, she was sure.

Guy smiled, uncurled himself, limbs loose again. "You know, I think I'm a really lucky person to have a sister like you. I used to hate it that you were so much older, but now I'm glad."

"Why?"

"Wisdom."

The word startled her, then made her giggle. "Oh, sure."

"No, really. If you were twenty or something you'd be just as big a jerk as I am. I'm very glad you're an old lady." His eyes changed to lavender, sparkling.

"Thanks, bud."

"Welcome."

"I think I'll have that drink now."

"You've got it!"

Danielle and Martin still shared a bed, although it had been a long time since they'd made love. She barely remembered what it had been like with him, but when she tried it was the night of Claude's conception that she unfortunately recalled. She tried to bandage her memory, covering over the nasty parts, but here were moments when the tape slipped and she was forced to confront the truth. Could you really say your own husband raped you? She had hinted at this to Dr. Offenbach, but he hadn't picked up on it. Still, there was no other name for what had happened. It was all too reminiscent of the honeymoon night in Italy which had produced Cristina.

She'd felt frightened, as if she were suddenly with a stranger whose hands were huge paws, whose eyes were menacing, whose mouth was mean, lips drawn tight across the teeth. Of course, she knew it was Martin. Yet something goaded her to resist; she crossed her arms over her breasts and tried to pull up her knees. But he was too strong. He managed to flatten her legs, spread them and, while holding both her arms above her head at the wrists, to enter her harshly. Oh, yes, it had been rape.

They'd never spoken about it, but it changed everything. Sex, which had been good for them, dwindled to a perfunctory, once-a-week union with little or no passion and, finally, into extinction. Now she couldn't even remember the last time and prayed there would be no future time. But she was thirty-four! Was this to be how it ended, a sexless life causing her to shrivel and shrink until her skin was as dry and crumbly as her spirit?

Martin, in paisley pajamas, climbed into bed. He smoothed down the sheet over the summer quilt with long fingers, nails carefully rounded and white. "Well, that went all right, don't you think?" he asked, as though they'd been to a lecture.

"Why shouldn't it?" She wished they had a larger bed: the heat from his body annoyed her.

"Oh, I don't know," a touch of asperity in his tone. From his bedside table he took a book.

"Do you think Guy liked the watch?" They had given him an Omega for graduation.

"He should, it cost enough."

"Oh, Martin, really." Everything was always reduced to price for him; another difference between them. She was accustomed to luxury, but it was still new to Martin, even after many years.

"Well, it did," he said, looking at her.

"Yes, I know. Do you resent it?"

"Of course not. I like the boy. He'll make a splendid doctor."

She took her book from her table, casually opened it to her place. "No he won't."

His book, resting against his bent knees, fell shut again. "Why do you say that?"

"He has no intention of being a doctor. The sight of blood makes him faint." She often told him things this way. Knowledge she'd had for a long time she'd finally drop, uncushioned. The suddenness of it irritated him.

"But Pierre thinks . . . I mean, Danielle, the man is sending him to Harvard."

It was the expense he was thinking of again. "Well, there are other things one can study at Harvard. Anyway, he's not going to be a doctor."

"And when does the little bastard intend to tell his father?" He turned in the bed, facing her, insisting with his position that she look at him.

Languidly, she turned, eyes meeting his. "*I'm* going to tell him."

"You certainly are not."

Was she really surprised by his response or had she known and fashioned it? "And just what does that mean?"

"I think it's clear. I don't want you involved in a thing like that."

"Martin," she said as if she were speaking to a small child, "it's *my* father and *my* brother."

"And it is *their* problem. You mustn't become involved, Danielle." He slid closer to her, draped an arm over her waist. His voice changed, softer now. "Darling," he crooned, "please understand."

"Understand what?" His arm felt heavy across her.

"It's important, first of all, for Guy to fight his own battles. I think you've become much too entwined in the boy's life."

"I love him," she said simply.

"Of course you do. That's not the point."

He was stroking her, the satin of her nightgown against her skin creating sensations she'd rather not feel; not induced by Martin. She slid her hand under his, pretending to hold it. "What *is* the point?"

Voice silky, free from the New England accent he'd once had, he patiently explained. "It's essential that Guy deal with Pierre on his own. And it's also essential that we stay out of matters that don't concern us if we wish to continue on good terms with your parents. Do you see, dear?"

She supposed there was some validity to what Martin said. But she'd promised Guy, and she had no wish to let him down. His friendship was of value to her; the closeness she felt with brother and parents somehow innured her to the harshness she suspected in the rest of the world. Dr. Offenbach had suggested it was time to move out of the family and into the real world of friends and acquaintances, but she'd yet to see any reason to try. She was content, in a sense. Her children, her parents, her brother. There was, of course, a missing link: a husband, a man whom she could love in the truest sense. Martin was good to her in his way, but his center was glacial. The discussion bored her now, it would lead nowhere, help nothing. Only she could change the life she led. A matter of courage.

"Danielle, do you understand what I'm saying?"

"Yes, Martin," she answered, "I see your point." How many times had she capitulated in this way?

"Good." He squeezed her hand. "Then you'll stay out of it?"

"Yes, all right."

Martin lifted himself onto an elbow, bent and kissed her with his frosty lips. He didn't say *good girl*, but he might as well have. Moving away from her, he settled back into his pillow and lifted *A Stillness at Appomattox* from the bed, opened it, and began to read. Another idiotic issue settled.

Lips chilled, Danielle opened her book, but the print blurred. Why was she crying? Something inside her had shifted as though a sudden gust of wind had rearranged her soul. A new beginning. Tomorrow evening she'd visit Papa and tell him Guy would not be a doctor, firmly and convincingly. It felt right, easy. And when she was finished, she would tell her husband what she'd done. Offenbach said she must take actions on her own behalf. Is this what he'd meant? Somehow she doubted that defiance of her husband was what the good doctor had had in mind. Too bad. It was what she was going to do. At last.

TWO

The Peacock Café on West Fourth Street in Greenwich Village was a favorite of Hedy Somerville's; it was, in fact, the *only* coffee house she frequented. She had discovered it several years ago when she was scouting the neighborhood and aquiring information. Now her knowledge of the area, bounded by Fifth Avenue, Washington Square Park, Sixth Avenue, and Tenth Street, was comprehensive. Had anyone asked Hedy a question about any store or building within those confines her answer would have been accurate; of course, no one ever asked.

This was a special day to her. She had been planning it for a long while; it was hard to believe the time was at hand. But here it was, that Friday in June she'd dreamed about. She was going to change the shape of things and finally get something she wanted. There was no one, she was sure, who was more deserving.

The waitress placed a cup of cappuccino in front of Hedy. Steam rose from its foamy surface, carrying the scent of cinnamon and coffee to her nostrils. Lifting the sugar shaker, she carefully measured out her ration: three heaping teaspoonfuls. She stirred the cappuccino three times, sweeping her spoon around the edge of the cup. With her tongue she licked the lingering froth from the spoon; then, before laying it to rest, she used it as an instrument to tap the saucer surreptitiously three times.

Hedy looked down at her small, stubby hands. The fingers were short and blunt, the nails casualties of her chewing. They were the hands of a peasant; her father had told her this millions of times. But her mother had told her she was related to royalty. It was just one of the scores of arguments her parents had had. Hedy remembered them all, even though her mother had been dead for eighteen years. The diamond Hedy wore on the ring finger of her right hand was proof of her heritage, her mother had said. She stared at it now, casually moving her finger to catch the sun as it shone through the café window.

The largest diamond was a hexagon in a silver claw setting, surrounded by smaller diamonds on all sides.

The ring had been given to her great-grandmother, maid in a royal household, as compensation for producing a royal, though bastard, child (Hedy's grandmother), thereby making Hedy a direct descendant of Queen Victoria. This story was apocryphal, her father said. That judgment caused the most aggravated fights of all. The ring, her mother said, would always be Hedy's insurance against the poorhouse. Typical thinking, her father said, of the peasant mentality. He insisted the ring was glass and platinum and repeatedly challenged her mother to a day at the appraiser's, later offering the same contest to Hedy who, like her mother before her, refused. She needed no appraiser. Her mother had never lied to her, and wasn't Hedy's resemblance to Queen Victoria proof enough?

Mainly it was her cheeks: they hung down like two wobbling pouches framing her thin straight lips, her receding chin. The upper part of her face was no more attractive than the lower. Her blue eyes seemed faded, as if they'd been in the sun too long, and even though they were behind glasses, one could tell they were small, set too close together, giving her a pinched, peevish appearance. Today she wore a wide-brimmed straw hat, her hair, thin and the color of dead leaves, drooped from beneath it like long well-worn fringe.

She was short, although she avoided a dwarfish look by several inches. Her breasts were ample and almost always concealed, as they were now, by a loose blouse buttoned to the neck. A long peasant skirt, ruffled at the hem, fell to just above the ankle. Her feet, in a pair of brown sandals, were short and wide with stumpy toes.

Hedy glanced at her small lady's watch and saw that she still had plenty of time. Her father had given her the watch for her high school graduation present. She remembered how joyful she'd been, planning her escape to college from the house in New Jersey; but, always diffident, she'd viewed the change with some trepidation. Still, anything would be preferable to continuing to live in the small house in Irvington with her father and brother.

But it was not to be. In August, her father had had a stroke, leaving him paralyzed on one side. There was not enough money for a nurse or housekeeper and her brother,

Ralph, was not expected to give up his last year of college at Seton Hall. It was presumed, however, that Hedy would forfeit *four* years, not to mention the rest of her life. She was, after all, only a girl and the probabilities and plans for her life were more easily dismissed. But not by Hedy. Even though she agreed to stay home tending her father, the time she had alone, when he slept, or the rare moments she stole from her assiduous daytime schedule, she spent dreaming of her future, which included something just for her.

When Ralph graduated, he immediately got a job with an insurance company and became the family's sole support. To continue to be in the house with Ralph, her room separated from his by a thin wall, was almost more than she could endure. Even though, at first, he no longer bothered Hedy, the memories did. Then, later, he started again. He couldn't afford other women, he said; his income was needed for his father's support and hers as well. She owed it to him, he said; it was her duty, her obligation.

She knew this was wrong, nonsense. But Ralph was stronger both physically and mentally and, as he had when they were children, he eventually wore her down.

Perhaps if she had not given in to him the first time, when she was ten and he was fourteen, her life would have been different. But it was only days after her mother's death and her defenses, as well as her spirits, were depressed.

She was lying in her bed, trying to read a Nancy Drew book, her mind wandering, seeing the face of her mother in those last days of her illness, then, again, in the coffin, looking totally different, not asleep, as Hedy's aunts had said she would, but rather like one of Hedy's dolls, shiny, waxen, unreal and, in a way, better than she'd looked in a very long time. The images were confusing, disturbing, and Hedy's book was not obliterating them. When Ralph came into her room, she was glad for the distraction even though he always made her feel slightly uncomfortable, as if he saw food caught between her teeth or a patch of petticoat dipping below her skirt.

He plunked himself down on the bed, facing her, his hand on her calf. "What're ya doing?"

"Reading, can't you see?"

He began to rub her calf, his fingers making headway up her leg. "You miss Ma?"

She nodded, swallowed, not wanting her eyes to fill with tears but unable to stop them. In a moment her vision was blurred.

"Ahh, don't cry," he said, and moved up on the bed, his hand going under her skirt and resting on her belly.

"Don't," she said through her tears.

"Don't what?" He was all innocence.

"Don't put your hand there," Hedy said. She knew this was wrong, improper. No one had ever told her (she couldn't remember her mother saying, "Never let Ralph put his hand on your belly"), but the warmth and tingling it caused her made her know.

Instead of withdrawing his hand, Ralph began to move it, slowly, rhythmically, his fingers trailing into her crotch. "I'm just comforting you," he said. "Doesn't it feel nice?"

It was impossible to argue with that. It was very nice and not an alien sensation, although somewhat different from the feelings she caused in herself. This was better. Still, she knew it was wrong.

"I don't think you should, Ralph," she said.

"Why not? It'll make you feel better."

"It's wrong."

"Who says?"

Now he had her. Who indeed? But she persisted, calling up her last shred of resistance. "Mommy."

Ralph smiled, knowing this couldn't be true, knowing that his shy and retiring mother would never have spoken of this or any other matter relating to sex. "No she didn't, Hedy, you're lying. Anyway, Mommy's dead."

The word *dead* reduced Hedy to a completely vulnerable state and Ralph, guiltless about his duplicity, quickly moved in on his prey. Lying next to her, his hand in a better position, he inched his way under the elastic of her cotton pants.

"What about Daddy?" It was Hedy's last semblance of protest.

"Out," he said, his voice strange, hoarse.

Weeping, Hedy succumbed.

It had gone on for years, at least once a week, Ralph always embroidering the occasion with new and fancier tricks, but always stopping short of intercourse. Hedy lived in a sea of guilt and remorse, but was never able to stop him or even

21

put him off, for the waves of pleasure she experienced superceded everything else.

But it was different now. Now she hated it; she hated him and herself. Why had she allowed it to begin again? There had been that long interval from the time Ralph went off to college until 1949. They'd both been at home, but he'd suddenly stopped coming to her room. While there was a part of her that felt forsaken, in the main she was relieved. The pardon, however, was not to be permanent. It was only a respite, a temporary reprieve, lulling her into a sense of security, which at the end of seven years, was demolished by just one visit from Ralph. He cajoled, pleaded, demanded, and finally, using some force, prevailed. And now the weekly visits included intercourse. It was an act Hedy found so violent, with its thrusting and ramming, that she could not take any pleasure from it whatsoever. Throughout Ralph's performance, she gritted her teeth and gripped the sides of her single bed, her knuckles growing white.

Then why the collaboration? In this part of her life, as well as in others, Hedy felt she simply had no rights. Who was she to say no to the man who put food in her mouth, who bought her clothes, who kept a roof over her head? As Ralph had suggested, she'd better do something to earn her keep. Taking care of her father was only part of her service; sex was the other. Something given, something taken.

She had told no one. There was no one to tell. Even when she'd gone to Dr. Swann, she hadn't mentioned the sex with Ralph. It was too humiliating, too mortifying. Besides, she couldn't have weathered Dr. Swann's disapproval. Instead, she spoke of her breathing problem. Hyperventilation, he called it, a symptom of anxiety. He urged her to tell him more about her everyday life, but what was there to say? The life she led was so circumscribed.

Unknowingly, Ralph paid for these sessions, Hedy told him she was seeing a doctor about liver problems. She hinted that if Ralph didn't pay she would reveal to their father the true nature of their relationship. Ralph also paid for several courses at New York University, where Hedy first saw, heard, and met Dr. Martin Swann.

He was delivering a lecture on schizophrenia. Hedy found him intelligent, articulate, impressive. She knew immediately he was the only person who could help her. The rapid breathing which caused her to feel faint and produced prickly sensations in her hands and feet wasn't the only thing that bothered her. She also had a twitch in her eye. It resembled a wink and often, in public, led to misunderstanding and embarrassment.

When the lecture was over, she approached Swann and arranged to see him privately. For three months she had a session once a week. He urged her to reveal herself in more detail, but she steadfastly refused. At the end of 1951, he suggested that they terminate. Perhaps when she found herself more forthcoming they might resume, he said; perhaps another doctor might be more suitable. But Hedy knew the truth and vowed to herself that she would help them both some day. Dr. Swann hadn't needed words to communicate his desires to her and she certainly was not one to ignore any man's wishes. Of course an exchange was in order. Naturally.

Finishing her cappuccino, she smiled, knowing soon everything would fall into place. She lifted her large, black patent leather handbag from the floor, where it rested against her leg, and placed it on her lap. As she unclasped the snap and peered within, a sense of felicity filled her. There, at the bottom of the purse, lay her purchase of the day before. She could see it gleaming. Reaching inside, she gained a feeling of power and courage from its cold metallic feel. Then she withdrew her hand, closed the purse, and called for the check.

Now it was time to watch and wait.

It was a sharp day. Or so it seemed to Danielle. The air had an almost acrid taste to it as though someone had overdone a spice. And the sun, vivid and glaring in an all too brilliant blue sky, illuminated everything in Washington Square Park in an angular fashion. All of it was too much for her and she inwardly swore at herself for forgetting her sunglasses. Cristina and Claude played in the cement circle so she couldn't close her eyes against the intruding blaze of midday. She watched as Cristina arbitrated between Claude and another small child. A toy truck was the object of the argument. Danielle was almost sure, with Cristina as their counsel, it wouldn't come to blows.

On the grass behind where Danielle sat, someone had switched on a portable radio. Joni James was singing "Little Things Mean a Lot." Cristina, having settled the dispute, looked up at her mother. Danielle waved, smiled, nodded, acknowledged her daughter's accomplishment. Cristina waved back, unsmiling, fiercely proud.

Danielle felt someone sit down on the bench next to her. Turning her head, she saw an obese woman, a brown shopping bag snared between her small, black-booted feet. Her meaty forearm disappeared into the bag, swirling and swishing through its contents, finally emerging with a dried-out cruller hanging from the tips of her forefinger and thumb like a dying fish on a hook.

The woman's rooting about seemed a private affair and to sit and watch her felt like a breach of etiquette so Danielle looked away. Yet, after a moment or two, she found herself staring again, but this time in a less blatant fashion, her head turned only slightly, her eyes peeking from their corners.

Beginning to eat, the woman tipped her head backward and still holding the cruller between her two fingers, she dangled the sweet over her open, waiting mouth. Then, bit by bit, she lowered it, taking small, delicate bites. It reminded Danielle of a baby bird being fed by its mother. But the thought of the massive woman resembling an infant bird was obscene and made Danielle queasy. Still, she was unable to turn away.

When the woman had devoured her snack, she licked each finger with quick, darting movements of her tongue, like a snake with its prey. Finishing this, she dried the fingers on her huge thighs, which were encased in a pair of old brown trousers.

Turning somewhat more toward the woman, Danielle was suddenly struck by the possibility that this was a man, not a woman after all. Was it possible? Why not? And why did the idea frighten her so?

She tried to take in the details, the features. The hair was shoulder length, straight and dun-brown; it was clear it had not been washed in a very long time. Danielle's eyes snapped to the chin, searching for signs of a beard. There were none, but somehow that didn't resolve the question of sex. The olive-drab jacket was of military origin and the sleeves were much too short, revealing the mammoth size of the forearms. The hands, which resembled two inflated rubber gloves, now lay unmoving on the lap; nails on both hands had been left to grow long, hard, and yellow, some of them bent and sharply pointed. Danielle's stomach lurched and just as she was about to dissolve her gaze, the fat person turned in her direction, smiling, exposing tiny needle-like teeth. Caught, Danielle grimaced but the woman/man didn't notice.

"Nice day, huh?" the androgynous voice asked, and went on not waiting for an answer. "I like days like this. It's the same kind I always liked when I was little. Were you ever little? Some people were never little I've noticed, have you noticed that? When you're little they love you or so they say, I've never noticed that myself. Elvis the Pelvis says they never do, but I've seen some." She/he laughed, short, staccato type sounds almost like an attack of hiccups.

Danielle was mesmerized, neither able to turn away nor to get up from the bench. The fat person went on, running sentences together, never taking a breath. "Oh, yes, some of them definitely have had a time of it. My landlady, for instance. I've noticed her time of it. Howdy Doody says it doesn't matter what time it is, but I've noticed the time makes quite a difference. The difference is that some people haven't got respect and that's what my landlady dismisses and so does the man she goes 'round with, the one with no head. I've noticed him a lot, have you noticed him? He comes 'round mostly on Tuesdays and sometimes...."

Jarred by the image of the man with no head, Danielle forced herself to rise and, stumbling, went toward her children.

Cristina, seeing her mother, rose, too, waiting expectantly.

"Come, darling," Danielle said, offering her hand. "Let's get Claude."

"Are we going home?" Cristina asked.

Danielle looked over her shoulder and, discerning that the fat person was still on the bench, said, "No, just moving to another spot."

"The swings?"

"Yes, if you like."

"Oh, good." Cristina clapped her hands together and gave a small jump. "Claude, come on, we're going to the swings."

Pretending not to hear, Claude went on playing with the truck and his small dark companion. Cristina looked at her mother and shared a knowing viewpoint: two females bound in understanding of the difficult, exasperating male.

"Claude," Danielle demanded.

Raising his large brown eyes, his brow furrowed with annoyance, Claude said, "What?"

"We're going to the swings," said Danielle. "Come along now."

"I wanna stay here."

"Come along, I said."

"Oh, Mommy, I'm playin' with Raymond."

Slipping her purse over her shoulder, Danielle clapped her hands together making a sharp, cracking sound. "At once," she said.

The sound reached him in a way her words did not and reluctantly he got to his feet, said a leisurely good-bye to Raymond, and, as though he were doomed, climbed woefully over the outer rim of the circle to the pavement. Danielle tried to give him a steadying hand, touching the tips of her fingers to his shoulder, but he shook her away in defiant independence and walked several steps in front of her. Cristina took her mother's hand as they walked toward the swings.

Checking once more, Danielle looked back at the crazed, gross figure, and seeing that "it" hadn't moved from "its" place on the bench, slightly relaxed.

"Is something wrong, Mommy?" Cristina asked.

"No, nothing, darling."

They walked hand in hand toward the swings and slide, Danielle feeling a kind of comfort from her daughter's small hand in hers. When they reached their destination, the children ran off to play and Danielle, feeling safe again, found a particularly green and inviting spot on the grass and eased herself down onto its solid snugness, once more to be the watching mother.

June Allyson, smiling coquettishly, looked down into the awakening eyes of Guy Dudevant. Groaning, he turned over on his bed, face into the pillow. It was the only safe place. If he cast his gaze anywhere else around his bedroom, he was bound to see the long profile of Gary Cooper or the red hair of Rita Hayworth, the legs of Grable, the toughness of Bogart. Not an inch of wall or spot of ceiling was unadorned by some forties movie star. Seven years earlier, while his parents were away, he and a friend spent a weekend redecorating the room.

Maman had not been happy with what Guy thought of as an improvement, and the punishment was that he still lived with his handiwork. He found it excruciatingly embarrassing; but then, so many things were. Still, to have his bedroom completely papered in movie stars made him a Number One Drip!

Guy flipped over on his back and placed a pillow on his face, thinking: I-am-free. A summer filled with endless free days stretched ahead. No dumb job for him. The old folks at home had agreed that this transitional summer between high school and college should be his without responsibilities or cares, and with a hefty allowance. It was his main graduation gift from his father, and Guy thought it was great. Working was for the birds, loafing neat. Soon enough he'd have to settle down to hard work at Harvard. Harvard. A sinking feeling stole over him; what would Papa do after Danielle spoke to him? He couldn't believe his father would deny him a Harvard education because of his refusal to become a doctor, but you never knew what a father might do. The hell with it. He wasn't going to think about that now. Now he was going to think about *The Grand Seduction,* starring Guy "Ladykiller" Dudevant and Susan "Vestal Virgin" Phillips. Opening night: Tonight!

Sex in itself was no particular big deal to Guy; he had gone through that rite of passage two years earlier. But sex with Susan Phillips was a big deal. Nice Girls Don't, was Susan's motto, and he thought he might go nuts if he heard it one more time. The truth was that sometimes Nice Girls Did and he thought they were nice even so. Some guys, of course, were just as drippy about it as Susan and dropped a girl after they got her to go all the way, but Guy couldn't see doing that.

Susan and he had been dating for about a year and although they petted, she'd never agreed to go all the way. But tonight was the night, or else. He was sick to death of this baby stuff. Now that he was a Harvard man (well, almost), he was either going to have a steady girl he did it with or he and Susan were going to break up. He grabbed his pillow from his head and threw it to the end of his bed. Swinging his long legs over the side, he planted his big feet flat on the rug, looked down at his thighs, sighed, and shook his head: no matter what he ate he remained thin. Feeling scrawny, he rose and made his way across the room to his bathroom, narrowly escaping the grinning face of Glenn Ford, and turned on the water for a shower.

Guy ran a comb through his hair and thought that there was no reason on earth why Susan would ever go to bed with him. He had never seen anyone worse-looking in his life! A cloud of loathing opened above him and torrents of self-doubt descended. For sure, he decided, he looked like a girl. If only his hair was straight, smooth, and blond. And what kind of nose was that? Turning his head, he tried for a profile. Jimmy Durante had nothing on him. Or maybe it was Bob Hope. Jesus! Danielle had reassured him it was a very small bump, aristocratic and sexy, but he had his misgivings. Could you really trust your sister to see you accurately? His mouth was all right, but his eyes were the bane of his existence. Amazingly, girls said they liked them. The truth was, Guy was stunned by how easily he attracted the opposite sex. Once, at a dance, he'd overheard several girls talking, using the words "dreamboat," "doll," and "gorgeous" to describe him. He'd learned, sometimes, to integrate this sort of information with his assessment of himself, having moments of great self-assurance, certain that he radiated an air of insouciance. But he also had days when the only way to survive a crisis of confidence was to summon up a remembered glaze in one girl's eyes, the overheard compliment of another. This was one of those days; the smallest curve could throw him. It came in the form of a pimple.

To Guy, it was as large as a tomato, as bright as a beacon. It nestled in the crevice next to his nose and only death would relieve his embarrassment. How the hell could you be a neat lover with a dumb pimple on your face? It could mess up the whole plan, which was to get Susan to a room he'd booked at the Earle Hotel and sweep her off her feet. But who'd want to go anywhere with a person who had this enormous pimple? He could see Susan now, her eyes riveted to the side of his nose, thinking: *Yuch!* What the hell. There was nothing he could do about it now. It was getting late and he had no intention of letting Susan stand around Washington Square Park waiting for him.

Quickly, he turned away from the mirror, took his wallet from the dresser, shoved it into his back pocket, and left the room. As he walked down the hall he hoped, actually crossing his fingers, he would manage to get out of the house without running into his mother. Nearing the end of the hall he gasped, stopping short as he spied a dead mouse on the floor. Immediately, he realized it was a horrible hairball thrown up by one of his mother's cats. After all this time, he thought, I should know what it is. He was always seeing them like miniature mummified creatures planted in his path by some unseen, unknown curator. He kicked it aside with his loafered foot and continued down the hall. His mother's voice called out from the library.

"Is that you, Guy?" She gave his name its French pronunciation.

No, he wanted to answer. "Yes, Maman."

"Come in here," she demanded.

There was no use arguing. Knowing what was ahead, he took a deep breath as though having more oxygen would prepare him for the interview.

Amelia Dudevant was seated on the Oriental rug, her legs tucked under her. She was brushing her favorite gray Persian, who stood on newspaper, peering, angry and outraged, from squinting eyes and pushed-in face.

"Doesn't Pia look beautiful?" she asked.

"Mmmm," he muttered. "Did you want something?"

"She's Maman's baby."

Guy ground his teeth together, knowing there was nothing he could do to rush her. He wished she wouldn't go on about her cats as he wished so many things about his mother; he especially wished she weren't so old. Guy hated having such old parents. Most people his age had grandparents that old. His friends' parents were in their early forties, a few in their late thirties. And they were fun. His parents were definitely not fun. They were old-fashioned, crotchety, and a pain in the ass, as far as he was concerned.

"I think Pia's coat is much shinier than it was a few months ago, don't you, dear?"

"Much," he said, shifting from one foot to the other, waiting for her to get on with her inquiry.

"There she is," Amelia said, letting go of the cat and putting down the soft brush. She looked up at her son. *"Mais, non!"* She clapped a bejewelled hand over her mouth, closed her eyes, slowly shook her head.

Guy hated it when she used French expressions, even one

so prosaic. Amelia was not French. Her maiden name was Taylor; she was a mixture of English, Welsh, perhaps a little Irish. No French. He knew what was coming, had known from the moment she'd called out to him, but gave his line like a good participant. "What's wrong, Maman?"

"Where are you going dressed that way this lovely afternoon?"

"Downtown to meet Fred," he quickly lied.

"Downtown?" she queried.

To Amelia, as their apartment was in the sixties, downtown was the fifties and forties: the Plaza, Bendel's the Waldorf, the Blue Angel, Lord & Taylor. Greenwich Village was an outpost, a suburb, and a highly unsavory one. It was also where Danielle and Martin had elected to live and Amelia had still not recovered from their choice, although they'd lived on lower Fifth for nearly three years. Greenwich Village in her mind was synonymous with evil.

"I'm going to the Village," Guy said.

"Greenwich Village?" she inquired, her lips turning downward in distaste.

"Yes, Maman." He glanced at his new watch. "I'm already late." He hoped she'd show him mercy.

Ignoring this, she went on: "Are you going to visit Danielle and the children?"

"No, I'm just meeting Fred."

"And what will you do down there?"

"Oh, walk around, look at the shops." He tried his best to sound like Archie in the comics.

"I suppose," she sniffed, "you *are* properly dressed for that area."

He was wearing khakis, a white button-down shirt, sleeves rolled above the elbows, white socks and loafers.

"I'm dressed just fine."

"You'll be home for dinner?"

Pia brushed against Guy's legs, leaving streaks of gray hair Amelia had missed. He leaned down and pulled the offending fur from his pants. "No, I won't be home for dinner," he said, his head upside down.

"I see. When *will* you be home?"

Rolling the hair into a ball, he answered, "Maman, please, I'm eighteen now. In the fall, I'm going to college. I'll be home when I get home." He dropped the furry ball onto the newspaper.

She stretched out her two arms in a signal for him to help her up. Taking the cue, he leaned down, clasped her hands in his, and lifted. Although he was slender, looking at times like a stalk of bent wheat, he was strong and, balanced properly, Amelia's one hundred and sixty pounds did not daunt him.

Clinging to his hands, she stood close to him, her peppermint breath fanning his chin: "Be a good boy." She turned her cheek for a kiss.

Guy bent his head and kissed her lightly.

In the foyer he heard her call *"Au revoir."* At the door he had to move aside Françoise and Andre, the two Siamese, before he could exit.

Walking down Fifth Avenue toward the subway stop at Sixtieth, he tried to shake his feeling of fury. *Be a good boy.* What did that *really* mean? It was if she were prescient, her crystal ball flashing pornographic pictures.

Desperate to regain his earlier mood, Guy looked skyward. The sun was like a perfect egg yoke, its glare almost garish. Instantly, it infused him with feelings of lightheartedness and buoyancy. Be a good boy? Not a chance!

It was growing warmer, but the trees cut down on the glare from the sun as Guy entered Washington Square Park. Whenever he came to the Village, which was as often as possible, it always amazed him how many people seemed to be idle during the day. How did they live? The idea of a life in the Village was very seductive to Guy. It was a life he wanted, though he had no real talents. The thing was, he was creative in an oddball kind of way, like what he'd done in junior high with The Moogies. He smiled, remembering.

Guy reached the statue of Garibaldi. Susan was late. He leaned against the statue, crossing his feet at the ankles. Ah, yes, The Moogies. He'd begun the whole crazy thing by handlettering posters and small signs and placing them strategically around his school. They said things like: THE MOOGIES ARE COMING or LOVE A MOOGIE TODAY or MOOGIES ARE BEAUTIFUL. Stuff like that. No one knew *he* was doing it, but after a few weeks other signs began to appear that he was not responsible for and within a month almost everyone was wearing MOOGIE buttons cut from cardboard and someone had even written a Moogie song. Yet by the time the craze ended, no one knew what a Moogie was, including Guy.

He had loved the experience of feeling a sense of power: getting others to think and act the way he wanted them to. Still, he couldn't imagine how he could use that talent (if indeed it was a talent) in his adult life. And there had been other times he'd accomplished similar things. Of course, they were all stupid and silly, like the time he got all his friends to put one bare foot in the toilet and then flush it. He'd told them it was a fab experience and loved watching them pretend they got something out of it. Really dumb. But it tickled him. How could you translate something like that into real work?

Guy wished he'd stopped to buy cigarettes, but he hadn't wanted to keep Susan waiting. They both smoked Pall Malls, so at least he'd have one as soon as she arrived. Glancing down one of the paths he saw a small boy in a Davy Crockett hat and, beyond him, Susan. He felt a mixture of excitement and anxiety. a million *what ifs* caroming through his brain. She spotted him, waved, and he walked toward her. When they met he kissed her on the lips quickly and then they looked at one another. She's staring at my pimple, he thought.

"Got a cig?" he asked, hoping to distract her from his face.

"That's a swell greeting." She rummaged in her handbag.

"Sorry. I'm having a nicotine fit, that's all. I would've bought some, but I didn't want to be late."

The dig was not lost on Susan, who snapped, "It wasn't my fault, Guy. The tube just wouldn't come. God, you're a pain."

Oh, great, just great. They were off to a really neat start. "I didn't mean anything," he said, looking down at her. He was about a foot taller and she always complained of a crick in her neck when they danced.

She offered him the red pack of cigarettes. "Oh, sure. Well, what are we going to do today, huh?"

There was definitely a challenging note in her voice. Guy lit his cigarette. "Let's sit for a minute, okay?"

They walked to a bench. As always, Susan looked wonderful to him. Her blond hair was smooth and shiny and she wore it midway to her shoulders, where it curled under. She had big blue eyes, a turned-up nose, and a small soft mouth. Her lipstick was a medium red and today she wore a yellow sleeveless dress and pearls around her bare neck.

"Why are you smiling?" Susan asked.

"Because I love you."

She gave his arm a small tap, almost a push, and fussed with her skirt. "So what are we going to do today?"

"Well, I don't know. I mean, I have a surprise for later . . . tonight, you know . . . but I didn't really plan anything for today. I thought we'd sort of play that by ear."

"What's the surprise?"

A lump of guilt plunked itself down in the middle of his chest. He prayed she wouldn't think it was theater tickets. "You can't tell a surprise, you nut." Guy thought Susan seemed awfully distracted today. There was always a remoteness about her, but this was different. "Something wrong? You seem weird."

"Thanks. Hey," she said, leaning forward, "isn't that your sister over there?"

"Where?" He looked in the direction of Susan's pointing finger.

"Sitting next to that fat woman."

Guy saw that it was indeed Danielle. The fat woman was talking to her.

"Should we say hello?" Susan asked.

"No, I don't think so." He didn't like the idea of seeing his sister when he had sex in the forefront of his mind. Maybe it was dumb, but it embarrassed him.

"Why not? I like her."

"Look, I don't feel like family, okay? Anyway, I just saw her last night."

"You know what?" Susan said, squinting her eyes. "I think that's a man, not a woman."

"Who?"

"The person Danielle's talking to."

"Nah." Guy wondered whether the fat woman was someone Danielle really knew or just a park acquaintance. Although it was hard to tell from this distance, she didn't seem like Danielle's sort of person. Suddenly his sister rose and seemed to stumble toward the circle.

"Hey, something's going on," said Susan.

Guy watched as Danielle gathered Cristina and Claude and walked off; they were not headed home, he noticed.

"You think she's okay?"

"Sure. Why not?" Guy was used to Susan seeing drama in the slightest shadow. Her penchant for the theatrical was the one thing he didn't like about her.

"I just got the feeling that that fat man upset her."

"Fat woman."

"How do you know, bigshot?"

"I have eyes."

"You just don't think a man could be that fat, do you?"

"What's that supposed to mean?"

"Nothing. Never mind."

Looking back in the direction of the obese person, Guy decided he was no longer sure if it was a man or woman, but he'd be damned if he'd tell Susan that.

"I'm starved," she said.

He stood up. "Good. Let's have lunch."

"Italian?"

"Sure. Aldo's?"

"Neat."

Guy put his arm around Susan's shoulders as they walked to McDougal Street, Beginning with the warning from Maman, to Susan's strangeness, to seeing Danielle, this day looked like a bust. That dumb glimpse of his sister was the last thing he wanted or needed. Danielle wouldn't care if she knew what he had in mind for that night, but still, it gave him the creeps. A sister was a sister, no matter what. And then there was the nagging thought that the fat creep *was* bugging her. Maybe he should have gone over and made sure she and the kids were all right. God! Life was hard. All he wanted to do was to make love to his girl, and everything seemed to be getting in the way. Was that really true? he wondered. Had anything *really* happened or changed? No. The hell with Maman's *be a good boy* and the hell with Danielle. She could take care of herself, for God's sake. Guy smiled as two silly lines ran through his head: *"Toujours Amour.* Tonight for Sure!"

You bet.

Claude wrapped himself around two bars of the jungle gym and although he was merely inches from the ground, Danielle, watching, felt anxious. If he fell, nothing serious could happen—a scratch or bruise at most—but the possibility of any injury to her children always alarmed her. There was nothing seasoned about her motherhood and she feared she would always be delicate in this area: overprotective and fussy. But as long as she checked herself, made sure she didn't convey unnecessary fearfulness to the children, it would be all right. She had no desire to infuse them with her own neurosis.

A young boy and girl stood nearby, shaking out a green and black plaid blanket, carefully placing it on the grass. They carried with them a radio which they immediately snapped on, the dial speedily turned, producing an eerie squawking sound.

Danielle watched and waited, hoping these were classical music lovers, knowing instinctively they were not. She winced inwardly when the boy settled on a station playing the new sound called rock and roll. To Danielle's ears it was abrasive and unmelodic and she hoped the fad would die soon.

She looked away from the young couple and back at her children. Cristina was swinging, her long legs, toes on point, stretched out in front as she came forward, then tucked back and under the wooden seat in a determined effort to gain more speed and ascend even higher. Danielle tried to blot out fantasies of flying falls and bloody heads.

A man walked by, absorbed in his thoughts, and something about the tilt of his head, the droop of his shoulders, reminded her of Brian. Remembering her conversation with Martin the night before and her resolve, she wondered if she'd been a fool to let Brian go out of her life. But at the time there was no other way.

Claude was only months old, Cristina two, when Danielle met him here in the park. He was younger than she by five years, a poet, a drifter, but kind and gentle, understanding. They'd shared picnics and poetry as if they were teenagers. And then, inevitably, he'd wanted to make love with her. But she simply couldn't be adulterous; it was alien to her nature and the immorality would have destroyed her. Eventually, he'd gone away, dear Brian. She used a panoply of devices to forget him, to excise him from her mind and heart. Still, thoughts of him crept back into her consciousness from time to time, like today.

Behind her the sounds of a commotion made her turn her head. Two men were arguing over what looked like a bottle in a paper bag. She turned away and, as she did, she saw the androgynous fat person headed down the path in her direction. Quickly she jumped to her feet, calling the children as she walked toward the swings.

"Oh, Moth-er," Cristina whined.

"I'm playin'," said Claude.

Looking over her shoulder she saw the lunatic bearing down on her. "Please, kids," she urged, "don't make me say it again." Authority rang in her voice and the children slowly climbed down from their respective perches.

As the fat person approached her and started to speak, Danielle could see there was no sign of recognition; the stream of consciousness began as if she were a brand-new person.

". . . and then I said to Ike and Mamie, why not take a whiff of this, garbage and perfume are the same, you know, but they weren't having any because it was their turn for the Salvation Army and if you can believe it they wanted me to join the Army, well why not, I thought, they're all in it for the money so why shouldn't I get some and maybe. . . ."

Danielle, impatient, stamped her sandaled foot and called the children again. She noticed Cristina eyeing the creature behind her and then she felt something warm and wet on her leg. Looking down, she saw a black and white mutt who was just finishing peeing on her bare leg. "Christ," she said, "this just isn't my day."

Cristina couldn't help giggling as she looked at the dog pee-pee on her mother's leg; Claude, too, was dissolved in laughter.

"Very funny," Danielle said, swabbing at her leg with tissues.

But Cristina knew she wasn't mad at them for laughing; there wasn't that bad sound in Mommy's voice. When Mommy got mad, she could tell. And Poppy too. It was worse with him because his voice was louder.

They stood under the arch as Danielle wiped her leg. She'd taken their hands and run with them to this spot before she stopped and took the tissues from her big green bag. Cristina wondered why. Had Mommy been afraid? Was it because of the funny fat lady?

They crossed the street and started up Fifth Avenue toward their house. Cristina liked holding her mother's hand. It never got all wet and sticky like Lolly's. She liked Lolly, their maid, but she wasn't Mommy. Nobody was. Only Mommy was Mommy. And there wasn't anybody Cristina loved better. She loved Poppy, but he wasn't around much. She loved Claude, but he was only a baby and sometimes he was a pain.

In front of the apartment house, Danielle let go of their hands and Claude ran ahead. Cristina stayed by her mother's side.

"Mrs. Swann?" a woman's voice inquired.

Both Danielle and Cristina turned.

Cristina saw a lady with glasses who was wearing a big hat.

"Yes?" her mother said.

"Are you Mrs. Swann?" the lady in the long skirt asked again.

"Yes, I am," said Danielle. "Is there something I can do for you?"

Cristina watched the lady's hand go into her black bag and then come out again. Something shiny was in her hand. The lady winked and said:

"This is for——"

A loud bang like an explosion blotted out every other sound. Cristina saw the lady's mouth move but didn't hear the word. She also saw a flash of light from the shiny thing. The noise frightened her and she turned to huddle into her mother's skirt. But her mother wasn't there.

There was another loud bang and Cristina screamed. Where was Mommy? Then she saw her. She was lying on the sidewalk, her eyes closed. There was red wet stuff all over her blouse.

"Mommy, Mommy," Cristina shouted. "Get up, get up."

Arms circled Cristina's waist and someone was dragging her away from Mommy. "No. Noooo."

Suddenly there were lots of people all around. They were screaming and yelling. And she was screaming and yelling. She looked up at the faces. Some she knew from the building; some were strangers. None was the lady with the hat who had winked.

Most of the young interns at the hospital venerated Dr. Dudevant, but some thought he was an old fogey and should retire. He was sixty-seven and surely that was time to step aside, make room for other, more modern doctors. But Pierre Dudevant had no intention of retiring—ever. "They will," he often said, "have to carry me out." He was not insensible to the negative thoughts and feelings about him: he simply didn't give a damn. As for the idea of "modern" doctors, he thought it ridiculous: medicine was medicine. And he kept up. He read the journals, attended conferences and lectures (gave some, too), and spent time with his colleagues in discussion. Pierre believed the phrase "modern doctors" was really meant to describe a certain kind of bedside manner.

This manner, which some of his young colleagues had adopted in the last ten or so years, sickened him. He felt it was important to maintain a kind of distance between doctor and patient, nothing too lofty but rather as though there were a scrim between them. Not only was the "modern doctor" a pal to his patient, but the degree of intimacy exceeded good taste: all that sitting on the edge of the bed and holding the patient's hand. Pierre found this type of behavior inexcusable, indefensible. As a doctor, he was meant to minister to his patients, not to mollify them with conviviality like an old woman at a quilting bee. If his bedside manner was considered archaic by the interns, it was just fine with him.

Nearing the end of rounds, Pierre turned to Jackson, a limp and delicate looking young man.

"Well then, what have you to say about Mrs. O'Donnell?" The day before, Jackson had made a mindless error in diagnosis and Pierre wished to give the boy another chance, although he believed he was quite untalented.

Pierre listened attentively as Jackson listed Mrs. O'Donnell's symptoms, his analysis of same, treatment, and prognosis.

"Very good, Dr. Jackson, very good." Why not give the boy a little approval? Pierre loathed the attitude of other doctors, who found it rewarding to make interns squirm.

At the door of the ward, he nodded perfunctorily to the interns and walked off down the corridor, his thin arms swinging as if in time to marching music heard only by him. In his office he exchanged his white coat for his gray pin-striped suit jacket, donned his Homburg, ignored the persistent ringing of his phone, and set out for his luncheon appointment.

After giving the address of his destination to the cabdriver, he settled back, prepared to be patient with the city traffic. He hated to be late for anything but if he was, he knew she would wait. She, of all people, was aware of his antipathy toward tardiness and would realize that it must be through no fault of his own.

Pierre stared at the back of the driver's head. Who did it remind him of? There was something about the neck, which was long and thin like the stalk of a dandelion, the head too big for it, blond curly hair thick and swirling. In a flash, Pierre knew the neck, hair, curls reminded him of his brother, Robert, who had died more than fifty years ago of tuberculosis. His mother had never really recovered; she'd taken to her bed and he'd never again had her to himself. And his father, a doctor, had become an even more shadowy figure than he had been. Seldom home, when he was, he wafted through the hollow rooms of the house, wraithlike.

A shrieking horn rent Pierre's memories.

"Goddamn idiot," his cabby shouted at the offending driver.

"Blow it out your ass," came the reply.

"What'd ya say, buddy?" Angrily, the cabby shifted into park and reached for the door handle.

Leaning forward, Pierre said, "Please, I am late for an important engagement."

The delinquent driver gunned his motor. "Asshole," he shouted, speeding away.

Pierre watched his cabby's neck turn a frightening purple.

"Goddamn nigger," the man growled. "Oughta send 'em all back to Africa where they belong." He put the cab into drive again and headed downtown. "Bunch a junglebunnies," he muttered.

Pierre, who was feeling slightly nauseated from the fumes and heat, was further sickened by the driver's ravings. He would not, he decided, give the driver a good tip. Why should he reward such conduct?

"These boogies just don't know their place."

Pierre realized the comment was directed at him. In the rear view mirror, his eyes connected with the driver's. They were mud-brown, dull, and stupid. Speaking of knowing one's place, how dare this cretin think Pierre would share his views? The suggestion of camaraderie was presumptuous and Pierre considered, for a moment, telling the swine just that. But he decided his silence would be statement enough: like a slap across his cheek with a pair of gloves.

Oblivious, the cabby went on: "They're tryin' to take over,

ya know. In twenty years they'll turn this city into a dung heap. Animals."

Seeing that he was a block from the restaurant, Pierre said: "This is fine. I will get out here."

The driver pulled over to the curb and flipped his flag. Pierre got out and, standing next to the yellow car, he extracted his long thin wallet from his inside breast pocket. The driver would never understand that an improper tip was Pierre's way of chastising him for his bigotry; he'd merely think Pierre cheap. And there was no time now for a lecture nor for any contretemps. Pierre concluded by handing the man what was expected.

Walking toward his destination his mood sagged, but he told himself it wasn't his place to educate every narrow-minded person who crossed his path. And by the time he entered the resturant, cool air engulfing him, his dispirited morale of moments before had vanished.

"Good afternoon, Dr. Dudevant," the maitre d' said, displaying a small bow. "Madame is already seated."

Pierre nodded his thanks for the information and followed Marcel to the interior dining room. Approaching the table his heart thumped in his chest, as it had for thirty-seven years, at first glimpse of Amelia.

Marcel pulled out the table and Pierre joined his wife on the plush maroon banquette, his eyes brightening, a handsome smile creasing his cheeks.

"Ah, *ma petite souris*," he said, his lips pursed for a kiss.

Amelia, not wishing to smudge her lipstick nor redden his mouth, returned his kiss lightly. "I am not your little mouse," she said reproachfully, yet with a teasing tone. Wagging her forefinger, which was almost dwarfed by a large black opal ring, she added, "I think you call me that to annoy me, Pierre."

He slapped his hand against his chest and drew back in surprise. "*Mais non*, Amelia. I would never do anything to annoy you."

She took a surreptitious glance around the dining room, then pinched her husband's cheek, lovingly. Amelia was not callous to Pierre's devotion to her; she knew all too well, having observed her friends' marriages, that she was in a unique situation. There was nothing spurious about his affection for her—or hers for him, for that matter—even if he did have other women here and there. Of course she had no proof of mistresses; it was just that he was French and Amelia could not believe that a Frenchman of Pierre's generation would not have had an inamorata or two or three over the years. The idea of this did not bother her at all; she thought her women friends who wailed and raved upon discovery of some alien perfume on a handkerchief or a passionate note stuffed in a pocket were insane to remonstrate. It was so much more dignified and wise to ignore such evidence. But when she gave that sort of counsel to her friends, they always told her she didn't understand. She had no idea how lucky she was to have a man like Pierre, so loyal, so faithful, so steadfast. But she did know. What *they* did not know, however, was that that kind of dedication from a husband could, at times, become a burden.

"Would you like a cigarette, *ma chérie?*"

"What are those?" she asked.

"Tareytons. Something new." Pierre flicked his gold Dunhill and lit her cigarette. "You cannot imagine how much I need a drink." He motioned for the waiter.

Amelia raised her eyebrows, making deep furrows in her forehead. She disapproved of anyone's *needing* a drink.

Seeing her censorious expression, Pierre quickly reversed himself. "Well, I do not really *need* one, *ma petite*. It is just that I had a most trying experience on my way to meet you."

Smiling, she whispered, "I knew there was a good reason for you to be late for *me*."

"Of course." He took her hand in his, squeezed. Then he gave his drink order to the waiter who had suddenly appeared at their table.

"Tell me what happened, darling," Amelia crooned.

Absorbing the look of adoration in Pierre's eyes, she was reminded again of the demands his undying love made on her. It might seem that if a man loved you the way Pierre loved her, that you could become casual in attitude and appearance. But Amelia felt it was incumbent upon her always to look her best because if love was so generously given, the giver deserved reward. Besides, he was her darling boy.

When Pierre finished the story of the cabdriver, Amelia asked: "And what did you do?"

"I gave him a piece of my mind and when I paid the fare I tipped him only a penny."

"So brave, so principled," she said, looking up into his face, her eyelashes rapidly tapping a message of worship.

"Oh, well," he murmured demurely.

Pierre looked down at his drink. He hated telling these lies, even little white ones. But when one had a wife like Amelia, so glamorous, so gorgeous, so enchanting, it was, he believed, his duty to be worthy of her. And what would she think if he told her the truth about his encounter with the cabby? No, it was best to embroider here and there.

He placed his hand on her ample thigh and almost imperceptibly they moved closer to one another, their shoulders grazing, as they began to study the menu. They were, each thought, the most fortunate of people.

The chair Martin Swann used in his office was far too comfortable; he must change it soon. He'd get Danielle to pick one out for him that wouldn't promote sleep. Not that he'd actually ever fallen asleep while in session, although he often felt on the verge of it. But it wasn't just the chair; the patient had something to do with his concentration and efficacy as well.

Aaron Waldman did nothing to keep Martin alert. He'd heard everything Waldman had to say time and again. After almost nine years of treatment, nothing had changed. And the truth was, Waldman bored Martin; he viewed the therapy as strictly a maintenance measure.

While Aaron droned on, Martin regarded his office, eyes browsing here and there. Danielle had wanted to redecorate the moment she saw the office, but it had been the same for ten years by then and he was quite comfortable with it. Now it was seventeen years old and perhaps it did need overhauling. The heavy brown velvet draperies at the two sets of windows were showing wear; they were badly faded and the nap was thin and separated like the coat of an old animal.

Opposite the black leather couch, which had held up well, was his massive mahogany desk, the only surviving piece of a long-ago life. It had been his father's, although Martin had never once seen the man sit behind it. Even when Martin was a child, it seemed queer that a man in his father's occupation would have such an imperious desk. Why did a chimney sweep need *any* kind of desk? Martin remembered, as a boy, seeing his father in his black top hat, thinking surely he was at least a duke. Later, when the other boys made fun of "your dirty, filthy old man," he'd wanted to crush the hat; he'd had fantasies of jumping on it until it was completely flat, useless.

Looking away from the desk, a sadness sweeping over him, he gazed down at the pallid gold rug and saw that the pile was worn like a recently mown lawn. It was odd that he hadn't noticed the patent shabbiness of the room before; clearly a case of taking one's surroundings for granted, he decided. Martin realized it was not a decorous office for a fifty-dollar-an-hour Park Avenue psychiatrist. He must have Danielle do something about it immediately.

Or perhaps Lynn. His deep-set eyes grew brighter, their midnight color turning blue-black and becoming almost opalescent. Of course, he thought. It was because of Lynn that he was noticing his dingy office; she had awakened *all* his senses.

The first time Lynn Cunningham walked into his office, more than a year ago, he'd been immediately attracted to her. That had happened with female patients before, but he'd always been able to control his feelings, eventually expunging any residue of the sexual, making it possible for him to continue treatment. In the beginning he tried to tell himself he'd done that with Lynn and, for short terms, he did. Then, suddenly, after a quiescent period, his desire would break out again like an uncontrollable rash. After three months of treatment, he found himself torn between professional and human behavior and finally accepted that he could no longer treat her. He'd been clumsy and stupid in his dismissal, interrupting their session.

"Miss Cunningham, I think I must refer you to another doctor."

Lynn sat up, swinging her long lithe legs over the side of the couch, and looked at him with discomfitted eyes. "I beg your pardon?"

"I can no longer go on treating you," he said bluntly.

He watched while her chin flattened against her neck as though he'd slapped her. Unable to arrest what he'd begun or even to modify his words, he went on. "We must terminate the analysis at once."

Her mouth opened as if to speak, then snapped shut.

"There are several good doctors I can recommend," he said. "Dr. Ambler is one of my colleagues and has a fine——"

"Please, please don't," she murmured.

". . . reputation," he finished. It was only then that he seemed to notice her pain, and it brought him suddenly to his senses. "My God," he said, rising, "I'm terribly sorry. I guess I've been awfully. . . ." he trailed off, not knowing what to say.

"Cruel," she filled in. She grabbed her purse and started toward the door.

"Oh, no," he blurted, "don't go."

His voice, like a frightened schoolboy's, she said later, stopped her and she turned to look at him.

"I think . . . I've fallen in love with you," he said.

Her sharp intake of breath was the only sound in the room.

"Believe me, I know how unprofessional this is. I should have dismissed you months ago, but I couldn't, you see. I didn't want to lose you and it only just occurred to me that if we terminated perhaps you'd consent to see me and. . . ."

She had begun to laugh. Noticing the wounded look on his face, she said, "I'm sorry, I'm not laughing at you. I'm laughing at myself. Just now, when you started all this, I was sure it was because I bored you."

"God no," he said. And they laughed together.

It had taken him a number of weeks to convince her to see him. She was a forty-year-old widow with two sons, one twenty, another eleven, and the idea of beginning an affair with a married man was not particularly appealing. But after sedulous attention he eventually wore her down. And since then he'd been a new man: passionate, sensitive, alive. He wouldn't relinquish this, yet something had to give.

His marriage to Danielle had been one of convenience; he'd never been in love with her, although he liked her very much. At age thirty-seven, he'd decided it was time to marry and a union with the Dudevant family could only enhance his ascending career; the right connections were important. Dudevant had been one of his professors at medical school and later a colleague. For years he'd wanted to be invited into the small coterie of doctors Dudevant cosseted and when, finally, the invitation to dinner was extended, Martin swore he'd make the most of it. He had. The look on Danielle's face when she first saw him imparted everything he needed to know.

There was no question that Danielle would be an asset;

beautiful, intelligent, rich, and well-connected. Yet with all she had to offer, Martin could not find within him a proper passion for her. Having never experienced that kind of ecstasy, he assumed he was incapable of it, devoid of the kind of ardor that had infused other men for centuries. It was as though some feeling part of him had been excised; or perhaps he simply did not have access to a particular sort of desire. So it had seemed, at the time, perfectly sensible to marry Danielle Dudevant, for there could be no one who could possibly offer him more. Besides, he wanted to have children before he got much older.

But he'd had no idea how really significant they'd be. Now he couldn't imagine how he'd endured his existence before them. Claude was still too small to be truly interesting; but Cristina was infinitely fascinating and made living a sparkling affair, filled with joy, exhilaration, and pride. If he divorced Danielle to marry Lynn, he knew he would lose the children. Yet he couldn't think of sacrificing Lynn; she was the final part which made him whole. Could he have it all? How long would Lynn consent to being his mistress?

Martin looked at his desk clock. The session was over. "It's time, Mr. Waldman." He rose and, limping, ushered Waldman to the door.

Back at his desk, he dialed the answering service for his morning messages and, while he waited for someone to pick up, he wondered once again what in his life would eventually give and knew in his heart of hearts that only Danielle was expendable.

THREE

Danielle died in St. Vincent's Hospital at two twenty-one P.M. No one she knew was with her. From the time she collapsed on the pavement in front of her Fifth Avenue apartment house until she died, she never regained consciousness. A team of doctors worked very hard to save her. She was young, a victim of violence, and a doctor's wife. She died anyway.

A little over six hours later, Detective Lorenzo Campisi sat in a midnight-blue velvet chair in the Dudevant's oppressive library, waiting. The room, with all its expensive period pieces, colorful hanging Tiffany lamps, its hundreds of books, seemed shrouded in darkness, the lights illuminating only what lay directly beneath them. Zo Campisi felt as stifled as if he were sealed in a tomb.

He unbuttoned the top button of his shirt and pulled down the knot of his patterned tie. It wouldn't really do to look sloppy with these people, but better that than choking; he could always adjust it later. Only the husband, the father, and the maid were available to be questioned tonight; the mother and the victim's children had been sedated and were, presumably, asleep. The brother was out: whereabouts unknown.

Instinctively, Zo knew this was going to be a tough case. He'd already come away from the crime scene feeling defeated: no one had seen anything. Oh, yes, there'd been those "eye-witnesses," four at least, who described the assailant as: a man, a woman, tall, short, blond, dark, fat, thin, old, young. But when pressed, none of them could be really sure and their descriptions disintegrated like crushed moth wings. Nine out of ten times this was the way it went. Often it didn't matter: no one cared. Zo always cared. Color, wealth, age had no bearing on his tenacity. Sometimes, on his own time, he followed leads; in a few instances he'd solved what had been considered insoluble. This was why, at age thirty, he was a Third Grade Detective, having only been a member of the New York Police force for six years.

His superiors were delighted with him; he made them look

good. But his colleagues resented Zo; often he made them appear incompetent or indolent. This didn't bother him. He was far more interested in his work than he was in winning a popularity contest. With his job, his wife, and the two friends on the force he did have, he was a man fulfilled. Children were to play no part in his life. He and Helen had agreed his profession was too dangerous; it would be irresponsible and unfair to have them.

Zo paced. He was a big man, almost six three, and his broad shoulders suited him. When he walked he dipped his head, leading with his brow as if he were anticipating a sudden gust of wind. Slightly slanting brown eyes were set deeply in his face. His black hair, strawlike, stuck out from his head in careless angles, exposing lighter streaks like the striated underside of a mushroom. A clear olive complexion was studded by black stubble on his strong jaw and square chin; he could almost never keep ahead of his unruly beard. Strips of pink lips struggled to close over large, slightly protruding teeth. But his straight nose brought the rest of the irregular features together, forming an appealing, comfortable face.

He was unused to rooms like this, cases like this. His was the Sixth Precinct, the First Detective Zone, which did not take him above Thirtieth Street. Most of his cases were in the Village, Little Italy, or on the Lower East Side. But this Swann case was upper class stuff. Zo thought he would have been somewhat more comfortable sitting in the Swann apartment; at least it was in his Zone. However, Dr. Swann had brought his kids and the maid to his in-laws. It was understandable.

The library doors opened and Zo expectantly turned toward them. It was J. J. Kelly, his partner; he'd been in the kitchen interviewing the Swann's maid, Lolly Washington.

"Anything?" Zo asked.

"Nah." Kelly plopped down on a brocaded settee and found it uncomfortable. "Shit, what do they use this thing for, torture?" He switched to an easy chair.

"What about the maid?"

J.J. ran a large hand over his ham-pink face as if he were an impressionist about to come up with a new character, but when the hand slipped off his chin it was the same old face: large and puffy from too much alcohol with watery blue eyes and eyebrows so pale one had to look hard to see them. The veins across his nose were beginning to show like intricate map lines and his lips were thin and pallid like an old scar. J.J. was twenty years older than Zo and he was tired; two more years and he would retire. He could hardly wait. He was going to open his own bar.

"The maid don't know nothin'. According to her, the victim was a saint." He rolled his eyes in disbelief. "No enemies. Loved by one and all."

"How about the marriage?"

J.J. lit a Camel. "Perfect."

"What do you think?" asked Zo.

"I think she wants to keep her nose clean and maybe she's a little afraid of Swann."

Zo nodded. He trusted Kelly's instincts and had learned a lot from him even though the man was a drunk. Zo knew J.J. sipped all during work hours but waited until he was off duty to really knock them back. Sometimes, walking beside him, Zo imagined he could hear the liquid sloshing around inside J.J. But Kelly was a top-notch detective, so no one said anything, least of all Zo.

"This is some joint, ain't it?" Kelly said.

"Pretty neat." Zo thought of his own place on Thompson Street below Houston. Four railroad rooms, a tub in the kitchen, a w.c. in the hall they shared with another couple and an old man. But it was forty-eight dollars a month and Helen had made it comfortable, home.

The doors opened and a tall, thin man limped slowly toward Zo, extending his hand. "I'm Dr. Swann," he said.

Zo took the proffered hand, felt the long bony fingers, the assertive grip. "I'm Detective Campisi and this," he gestured toward J.J. who was standing now, "is Detective Kelly."

Martin shook Kelly's hand, too. "Sorry to keep you waiting so long." He shrugged his thin shoulders as if to say, I know you understand. "Sit down, please."

Turning toward a chair, Zo slipped up the knot on his tie. Scrutinizing Swann's face, he saw tension and shock but failed to detect signs of grief; sometimes it took a while. "We're sorry to bother you, Doctor, but it's important."

Martin nodded, a quick, perfunctory signal of agreement.

"Do you have any ideas as to who could have killed your wife?" Zo noted the involuntary jump in Swann's cheek on the word *killed*.

"No, I don't. People liked Danielle. It must have been an accident . . . I mean some random violence."

"How long had you been married?" asked Kelly.

"Seven years."

"Would you say you had a happy marriage?" Zo knew no one ever said: "No, it was a nightmare," but you could tell something from the way they said yes.

"Very," Martin answered.

There was the slightest beat of time before he responded and, like a computer, Zo picked it up, as did Kelly.

"How about you?" Kelly asked. "You got any enemies, Doc?"

Zo noticed a line of distaste around Swann's mouth when Kelly called him Doc.

"Well, I don't think I do. Not to my knowledge. But does anyone ever think they have enemies?" He tried a smile, failed.

"You'd probably know the answer to that better than we would. Your profession, I mean." Zo implied that the doctor was sagacious.

"Yes, I suppose," Martin said. "Well, then, I know of no enemies." Now he was definite, sure.

"How about your patients, Doc?"

Martin sat straighter in his chair. "What about them?"

"Could any of them——"

"No, of course not."

"Why, of course not? These are . . . ah . . . sick people, right?" Kelly persisted.

"They're neurotics, not psychotics."

"What's the difference, Doc?"

"It's too difficult to explain," he answered pompously.

"Wouldn't you say anybody's capable of murder, Doc?"

"That's not my conviction. As for *my* patients, none of them would be capable."

"Yeah, well, we'll see about that," Kelly said contentiously.

Martin sighed in exasperation and turned to Zo. "I agreed to this interview tonight because I obviously want to assist in finding the . . . the person who did . . . who murdered my wife. But I feel this line of questioning is out of order."

"I'm sorry you feel that way, Doctor, but it's a natural assumption for us to make. You see, one of your patients might be mad at you . . . that happens, doesn't it?"

"Well, yes, that's common in analysis but——"

"Then we'll have to interview them all," Zo concluded.

"Interview my patients?"

"Naturally," Zo answered, as if surely Martin would have expected this.

Martin stiffened. "I can't permit that. It might upset some of them terribly."

"But they're just neurotics," Kelly said, lighting a cigarette. "A little conversation ain't gonna make 'em go to pieces, is it, Doc?"

Martin ignored Kelly and went on addressing Zo. "I'm not even sure you have the right to ask me their names."

Zo nodded up and down, slowly, as he answered, "Oh, yes, Doctor, we do, you can rest assured about that. And you have to tell us. What you don't have to do, I guess, is tell us anything *about* them. That's what's called privileged information. Sort of like a priest."

"Well, that's debatable."

"Beg pardon?" Zo said.

"I'm certainly not giving you any names until I check this out."

"Tomorrow will be fine," said Zo. "Now, Dr. Swann, did your children tell you anything?"

"Tell me anything?"

Why, Zo wondered, did he have the impression that Swann was stalling. "They witnessed the shooting, didn't they?"

"Yes, apparently my daughter Cristina did. I believe Claude had gone into the lobby. Then he came running out with the doorman. He saw his mother lying there. Some neighbors grabbed the children and took them away."

"So your daughter was an eyewitness?" Zo said.

"One would believe."

"Believe?"

"Look, my daughter was in shock. This is going to be a damaging trauma for her . . . for both of them. I didn't interview her in her condition. I gave her a Miltown and put her to bed."

"What's Miltown, Doc?"

Martin set his gaze on the burly Kelly in an openly hostile way. "It is meprobamate."

"A tranquilizer," Zo said to Kelly. It was a fairly new drug and Zo only knew about it because it had been prescribed for his brother. "Thanks very much, Dr. Swann. We'll talk again."

He offered his hand, but Martin ignored it. "Do you think we could see your father-in-law?"

"I'll send him in." Martin limped to the door.

Zo wondered about the limp and made a mental note to check it out. "Dr. Swann, do you know when your brother-in-law is expected home?"

"I don't know. He's eighteen now." His answer implied that Guy's age explained everything.

Kelly's eighteen-year-old had strict curfews, so it explained nothing to him. "Yeah, so?"

Martin's voice rose in aggravation. "The boy doesn't have time limits. I don't know when he'll be home. Is that all?"

"This boy," Kelly went on, happy to irritate him further, "did he like your wife?"

"Yes, of course," Martin answered tersely.

"What Detective Kelly means, Doctor," said Zo, "is what was the relationship between brother and sister? There was a big age difference, wasn't there?"

"Is that a crime?"

Zo smiled sweetly. He was aware that there'd been a substantial age difference between this husband and his wife, as well. "No, no crime. Interesting though. Were they friends?"

"Yes. Very good friends, I'd say."

"Thank you, Doctor."

Martin pushed at the door as if it were an opponent, then slammed it shut behind him.

"Nice guy," Kelly said.

"Well," Zo said slowly, "how would you feel?"

Kelly cocked his big head to one side, smiling, and said: "You kidding?"

"Ah, J.J." Zo waved a hand in dismissal.

Kelly hated his wife. The enmity that existed between the two of them was something Zo found difficult to fathom. On the other hand, he understood that it was requisite for their relationship; their loathing of one another made them flourish in an ugly, distorted way. In the early days of his partnership with Kelly, Zo and Helen had tried several evenings with J.J. and Betty, but each one had been disastrous. The game the Kellys played was war. No subject was safe. The choice of a restaurant or the color of someone's eyes could be the platform for a scabrous, nearly interminable, altercation.

"My time," Helen said one night after a particularly un-

51

pleasant evening with the Kellys, "is too precious to me to waste one more minute with those people."

And Zo knew she was right; it was one of the reasons he loved her. Helen had a very staunch sense of her own worth, her own rights, and seldom did things that made her uncomfortable. She offered to tell the Kellys the truth the next time they extended an invitation. But Zo was not quite up to that and opted for making excuses until J.J. took the hint and finally stopped asking.

It was after the final refusal that J.J. began to speak openly to Zo of his hatred for Betty. And when Kelly implied that he'd be delighted if somebody killed *his* wife, Zo knew it was part of the game.

"Maybe he didn't like her," Kelly said of Martin.

"I don't think it's hit him yet."

"Yeah, maybe."

But Zo did find Swann's reaction odd. It was nothing he could pin down, just a tension he couldn't identify. Perhaps it was the natural superiority all doctors seemed to project. Or maybe it was Zo's own response to them, especially psychiatrists. He automatically distrusted them. What good had they done his father? But maybe he would have killed himself anyway. Even at the moment of death, his father had been deeply enmeshed in his deviation. Powdered at the final powder, Zo thought cynically.

"I got the feeling Swann was hidin' somethin'. You?" Kelly asked.

"Yes, now that you mention it, maybe that was it."

"You don't think it was a hit, do ya?"

Zo shrugged. "Wouldn't be the first time."

"Or the last. He could afford it, all right. These guys get thirty, forty an hour."

"Well, we'll get a line on him and. . . ."

Pierre Dudevant, shoulders slumped, entered the library. Seeing the two detectives he straightened, readjusted his slack mouth into rigid lines of implied strength, and offered a steady hand.

Taking it, Zo felt the gelid touch of shock and grief, its iciness betraying the feelings of the father for the dead woman. Why, Zo wondered, did men think it admirable to dress despair in party clothes? Women were so much wiser there. Poor bastard, he thought, and gently motioned Dudevant to a chair so they could begin.

Hedy sat at the white enamel kitchen table sipping a cup of Lipton tea, waiting for the eleven o'clock news on the radio. She stared at the old maroon Motorola on the sideboard as if it were a tv set. Music was playing; some women singing something about a sandman. In the living room, Ralph, her father, and his best friend, Father Frank, watched the end of a television drama. She could hear shouts coming from the set. Usually she watched with them, but tonight she'd claimed indifference to the war story and revulsion for a particular actor. Father Frank, in his usual maladroit way, said that Hedy probably had a crush on the actor and couldn't bear to look in case he ended up with some woman in the story. Whenever possible, Father Frank made sexual allusions which sent him into paroxysms of laughter, his wattles as springy as if they'd been vulcanized. The priest particularly liked to involve Hedy in his lascivious banter. She never participated, not even so much as a blush, but Father Frank was unstoppable, enjoying his games as if Hedy were an ardent accomplice. She loathed Father Frank, but she kept that emotion neatly submerged.

Looking into the white Staffordshire cup, a remnant of her mother's reign, Hedy saw that the tea, cool now, had left brownish stains in its wake. She wondered if the stains of blood on the sidewalk where Mrs. Swann had fallen would resemble these? Surely there would have been bloodstains. Hedy had not seen any blood at all. After firing the second shot, she'd scudded up Fifth Avenue toward Tenth Street, turning there, making tracks to Sixth Avenue, then fading into the crowd while she threaded her way toward the Path Train at Ninth Street.

Riding the tube toward home, she'd put her hands in her capacious handbag and, with one of her brother's handkerchiefs, which she'd secured and stored for just this purpose, she wiped the small gun clean of fingerprints. In the Hoboken station the other passengers hurried to their trains and buses while she lagged behind, slowly making her way to the end of the platform where it was dark, covertly dropping the gun to the tracks.

When she got off the bus at Irvington, she was feeling quite secure. Not that she'd been especially nervous, but a sense that the deed was behind her, a herculean task accomplished, was almost complete. The last link in the chain would be the news report.

Now, as the clock struck eleven, accompanied by the bong of the time tone on the radio, Hedy readied herself to receive the news.

It was not, of course, at the top of the report. Hedy chewed at the skin of her fingertips and tapped her sandal against the leg of the table. Finally it came:

"*In Greenwich Village in Manhattan this afternoon, the wife of a prominent psychiatrist, Dr. Martin Swann, was shot and killed by an unknown assailant,*" the newscaster said. "*Mrs. Swann, thirty-four, was returning to her home on lower Fifth Avenue from Washington Square Park with her two children when she was gunned down at the entrance to her building and died later at St. Vincent's Hospital. The motive is unknown.*

"*In sports tonight. . . .*"

Hedy turned off the radio. She heard the men talking in the next room, Father Frank getting ready to leave. It was imperative that she join them, act normally. She poured out her muddy tea and gave the cup a cursory rinse, storing it in the sink for a proper scrub later. Every detail of the news item was squirreled away in her mind ready to be brought out and chewed over when she was alone. Now she must say good-bye to Father Frank.

"Ah, Hedy girl," the priest said, "you missed a good one. And that actor ended alone after all." He screwed up his face in what passed for an elfin grin, his eyes disappearing behind folds and puffs.

Hedy, winking, smiled enigmatically.

"I think our Hedy has a crush on that fella, what d'ya say, George?" he asked Mr. Somerville.

George Somerville sat in his swivel chair, the tan leatherette worn and chipping, his rheumy eyes fixed on his daughter. When he opened his mouth to speak only the left side moved; the right side, stiff from his stroke, stayed stationary as if glued in place.

"She only loves herself," he eked out of the bleak half-hole of his mouth.

Hedy, used to unfair slurs from her father, said nothing, felt nothing.

"Ah, now, George, our Hedy's a grand girl and good to you. Some girls would have gone off and led their own life. You don't know how lucky you are. You don't see, like I do, how these modern girls behave." Father Frank shook his large head. "They just go off, leaving their old parents to suffer, not caring a fig. Hedy here's a devoted daughter and you should be grateful, George." He patted Hedy at the waist with his massive brick-red hand, then slowly let it slip to the small of her back and down to her buttocks.

Hedy watched Ralph's eyes narrow as he took in the priest's grazing hand. As much as Father Frank's attention to her posterior enraged Hedy, the look of jealousy on Ralph's face made it worthwhile. So she remained where she was, allowing the liberty. Anything that caused Ralph pain was pleasure for her. She wondered if the priest's daring and unusual sortie were the result of one ale too many.

"Our Hedy's a decent Catholic girl, George." His hand trailed off her body and he ran a sausage-sized finger between his collar and neck.

"She goes out and leaves me for hours and hours," Somerville whined. "Like today. Gone all damn day."

Hedy felt a nervous dance in her belly. "I had errands," she said. Her eye winked.

"Leave her alone, Dad," said Ralph.

Father Frank went on. "You've got both your grand children at home, George. You're a lucky man."

"Lucky?" George squawked, screwing the good side of his face even with the twisted side. "You call this lucky?" he gestured with his good arm at the wreckage of his left side.

"Could be worse," Father Frank said cheerily. "Could be paralyzed totally. Could be you couldn't move a thing but your eyelids . . . not hands or feet or mouth or bowels. Still, absolutely still. Only the flick of your lids to communicate, once for yes, twice for no, three times for maybe." The priest's eyes had a glossy look as he became more and more enthralled with his description. "Imagine that, George, not even to move a toe. God spared you, fella."

"I wish he'd struck me dead."

"Now you don't mean that. You'd better say some Hail

Marys tonight before you go to sleep. You see to it, Hedy, when you undress him and put him to bed, that this boy says his prayers."

Primly Hedy said, "I don't undress him and put him to bed. Ralph does that." She enjoyed pricking the balloon of Father Frank's image: the daughter with the naked father.

There was not even a beat of embarrassment as he said: "Then *you* see he says his prayers, Ralph."

Bored and disgusted, Ralph said, "Will do," shifting his gaze toward the front door, hinting that the priest should leave.

"All right now, I'll be going." His cassock skirt swishing, Father Frank trod to the door where he turned to face the three Somervilles, Hedy and Ralph standing on either side of the old man's chair like two sentinels. He raised his hand and made the sign of the cross. "God bless this grand family." In a move that was meant to approximate gracefulness, he pirouetted to make his exit, but his rosary looped over the doorknob and he remained caught, straining against the beaded lasso like a hapless animal in a snare.

Ralph, smiling disdainfully, moved forward and unhooked the fretting father from the doorknob.

Sputtering, the priest said, "Thank you, boy," and scuttled out into the night.

"Damn ass," said George.

As always, Hedy was startled by her father's epithet. He was a master at feigning friendliness, respect, and admiration. Even though George considered Father Frank his best friend, he took great pleasure in maligning him. His misanthropic nature had been exacerbated by the stroke, and the incapacity seemed to have served as the final catalyst for the full flowering of his hatred.

"Fat hypocrite! Stupid Mick!"

"Time for bed, Dad," Ralph said, reaching under his father's arms and easily lifting him to his feet.

"The man's mind has fermented like rotten fruit," George croaked.

"Put your arm around me," Ralph directed.

Following the orders of the nightly ritual, George leaned on his son and, as they made their halting way up the stairs, he continued to fulminate on the subject of his good friend, Father Frank.

Hedy, picking up the Pilsner glasses, full ashtrays, and the plates studded with discarded fruit pits, successfully blotted out the sound of her father's dysphonic speech.

As she washed the dishes, she allowed the earlier news report to filter back into her mind, bit by bit. So the woman was dead. Well, it had to be done. Hedy musn't give shelter to the smallest amount of regret; she hadn't any choice in the matter; she'd only done what Dr. Swann wanted her to do. Her hands submerged in soapy water, she wondered what Ralph and her father would say if they knew? Maybe Ralph would be afraid of her. After all, who was to say she wouldn't do the same to him? This thought imbued her with a viscous warmth, as if honey were pumping through her veins. But there would be no admitting that she'd killed Danielle Swann. No one could know. Except for her mother, to whom she told everything. That would come later.

She dried her hands on a red and white checked dish towel, then snapped it back in place through the refrigerator door handle. Reaching up above the table she pulled the long brass chain, plunging the kitchen into darkness. In the living room, she clicked off the lights before ascending the stairs to the second floor.

In her room she switched on the overhead light, illuminating a dreary, colorless place stuffed with dark overbearing furniture. Squeezing down the aisle between bed and armoir Hedy bumped her hips against the furniture. On a mahogany nightstand stood a metal lamp, which she turned on, the green glass shade harboring the light and emitting an eerie glow. She turned around in the cramped space and sideswiped her way back to the end of the bed, then to the wall where she switched off the overhead light. Instantly the room was in semidarkness, its massive furnishings casting gloomy shadows.

Hedy began to undress. She wondered about the Swann child who had been a witness. From her research she knew the child's name was Cristina; she was six years old. How much could the eyes of a six-year-old see? Surely the child wouldn't be able to describe Hedy accurately. And what if she did? Where would that get anybody? It wasn't as if there were a picture of her on file somewhere; her face hardly adorned post office walls. Would Martin Swann recognize the description? Impossible. She pulled the orange cotton nightgown over her head. Even if he did, why would it matter? Martin would never betray her. He would thank her when she let him know. How happy he must be tonight.

Crablike, she scrabbled to the bed and pulled down the pink spread, revealing sheets grown thin with use. She propped up her pillow against the chestnut headboard and leaned against it, crossing one hand over the other on her sheet-covered lap.

How surprised Martin would be to hear from her after four years. She would wait until the furor died down before she contacted him in person. His routine was as familiar to her as her own; she'd had him under surveillance for the last three months. She knew about the woman, Lynn Cunningham. That discovery had been Hedy's final encouragement. When their relationship had been disclosed to her, all the pieces had fallen into place. As she'd suspected four years ago, Dr. Swann had released her to do important work for him. It was simply a matter of things unfolding. When she divulged to him that she had removed his wife, there would be no question of his acquiescence in her request. After all, one favor should be rewarded by another.

Holding out her right hand in front of her, Hedy stared at the diamond ring. She'd never told Dr. Swann of her royal heritage. But when she presented her plan, it would be an integral part of her discourse. If he had any reservations, her lineage would allay them. Then there would be a merger of the highest order.

Ralph, in pajamas, interrupted her thoughts. "Jesus, it's taking longer and longer to get the old man to bed." He sat on the edge of the bed, his inimical blue eyes staring at his sister. "What are you doing?"

"Nothing. I'm doing nothing," she answered, winking.

"Stop that," he demanded.

"Doing nothing?"

"Winking."

Behind her glasses her eyes took on a minatory expression. "You know I can't help that."

"It's creepy."

"Then leave." She knew he wouldn't.

"I hate that pig of a priest," Ralph said. "He had his hands all over you."

Hedy grinned.

"What's funny?"

"You. You have a nerve, don't you think?"

His white skin flushed. Ralph's face looked unformed, as if nature had quit the process too soon. Thin, lank brown hair lay on his scalp like burned grass.

"Turn out the light," he commanded.

Waiting a moment, forcing him to remain exposed even for that fraction of time, gave her intense pleasure. Then she reached out and snapped off the light.

Ralph drew down the sheet and pulled up her gown. Hedy closed her eyes and prepared to converse with her mother. It was the way in which she endured.

By two A.M., when Guy emerged from the Sixtieth Street subway station, the weather had changed. A fidgety wind flicked at his face like small ineffectual whips and across the black sky the clouds seemed to be dragging the jaundiced moon as if it were a burden. He was a solitary figure and the clacking of his heels against the pavement emphasized his aloneness and provoked the quickening of his step. Never before had he come so late; he silently prayed that no one would know.

After putting Susan on the train, he'd gone to a bar on Eighth Street and had several rye and gingers. His aim had been to get drunk, to drown his sorrows the way they did in the movies, but it hadn't worked. He might as well not have bothered; it was a waste of time and money.

He felt like a complete fool. All his plans right down the old drain. Not only hadn't he gotten Susan into bed, she had dumped him! "I'm sorry, Guy," she'd said, "I don't want to hurt you, but I've fallen in love with a man." The man turned out to be twenty-one . . . three years older than he was. When Guy had pointed that out, Susan said the new one was very mature, implying that Guy was not. Was he immature for his age? Or was Susan just using the maturity thing as an excuse? He needed to talk this over with someone and there was only one person he could think of: Danielle. Even when she didn't solve a problem, she always put it in a new light: asking leading questions, opening new doors.

The midnight-to-eight doorman, Dudley, was seated just inside the door reading *Reader's Digest*. As Guy approached he snapped to his feet and opened the door.

"Ah, there you are, sir," he said.

"Hello, Dudley." The stocky, beaky-nosed man sounded odd, Guy thought, as if he'd been waiting for him.

"You all right, sir?"

"I'm fine," Guy answered, puzzled. "Why?"

"Well, sir, you know, I mean . . . considering."

Considering? Guy thought. Considering what? But he didn't stop to ask, the horrible thought that somehow Dudley knew of the fiasco with Susan propelling him onward to the elevator. He pushed his floor and, as the doors closed, he realized it was crazy to think Dudley knew. So what had he meant?

When he entered the apartment he saw an arrow of light from the library slanting across the marble foyer. Someone was waiting for him. Well, he'd have to endure a dopey lecture.

Guy pushed open the library door. The shock was immediate. There was his father, looking crumpled and soiled, like old laundry.

"Papa," Guy said feebly.

"So late," the old man muttered.

"I'm sorry, I. . . ." Something told him not to go on; he knew it was unnecessary. There was another, larger matter hanging in the air between them. And then he knew as surely as if his father had spoken. It was so obvious he couldn't believe he'd just thought of it.

"Maman," he whispered.

"Pardon?"

A chill circled his throat like a necklace of ice. "Is it Maman?"

"No. Sit down."

His legs wouldn't move. "What is it, Papa?"

"It's Danielle."

Guy's mind jumped to images of his sister, Cristina, Claude, the fat person in the park. "What is it?"

Pierre opened his mouth to speak, but the words wouldn't come. His mouth closed, the lips two bloodless bands in his gray face.

"Papa, please," urged Guy.

Again the lips separated, forming a small dark cavern, and this time he emitted a sound as if he'd been struck. "Dead," Pierre said.

One moment Guy was standing, the next he was lying on the rug, his father holding his wrist, fingers on his pulse. Guy's eyes fluttered open and rested on Pierre's face.

"You fainted," he said.

"I'm sorry."

He waved a wrinkled hand in dismissal. "Sit up, can you?"

Pierre helped him from a sitting to a standing position and carefully, arm around the boy's waist, led him to a chair. Then he went to the mahogany bar and poured each of them a Courvoisier.

Pierre handed him the brandy, their eyes meeting, then skidding away as if they were ashamed of something.

Guy spoke first. "How?"

"Murdered. Shot," the old man answered, the words themselves like bullets.

"Who did it?" The shadowy image of the fat woman appeared before Guy.

Pierre lit a cigarette, then, as an afterthought, offered one to Guy. "We do not know."

He took the proffered cigarette. The ghostly fat woman began to emerge from filmy focus, a simulacrum slowly forming.

"We do not know," Pierre said again. Then he told Guy all that *was* known.

Guy listened, detached, as if he were hearing about a novel or a play. He couldn't relate the words to himself or his family. He visualized Danielle as he'd seen her the day before, moving away from the fat woman in the park. Or was it a fat man? Desperately he tried to fill in the still indistinct lines of the man/woman who had been talking to Danielle. His memory rose to the occasion and at last he had a full picture. Should he tell his father?

"Were the police here?" asked Guy.

"Two detectives. They will be back to see you tomorrow . . . this morning. You had better have some sleep."

He would save his information for the police. What good would it do his father? "Will *you* sleep? And what about Maman?"

"Amelia has been given a tranquilizer by Martin. He and the children are here. Sleeping, I hope."

Unsteadily, Guy rose.

"Are you all right?" asked Pierre.

He nodded. "Will you sleep?" he repeated.

"Later I will go to the room and lie on the bed." He shrugged. "Who knows what will happen."

In his room, Guy fell across the bed. He knew he hadn't the energy to undress. He felt he'd been scooped out, left hollow. His mind was flaccid, unable to center on any one thing.

Thoughts came and went, flying into one another, crashing, splintering as if he were, after all, dizzy and drunk.

And then the knowledge of Danielle's death surfaced, slamming into him like a wave, dragging him under, scraping him raw. "Oh, my God," he whispered into the bedspread. "Oh, my God."

Helen Campisi was reading *Bonjour Tristesse*. The novel was by a nineteen-year-old French girl and a substantial fuss had been made over it the year before. She supposed it was quite remarkable for someone so young, but she enjoyed a book with a little more depth. Unless it was a mystery novel.

Zo was very late tonight; he was always late when there was a murder. He'd called about seven and given her a sketchy version of the case. When he got home he'd fill her in more completely. Unlike many police husbands, he shared his work with her in detail. They agreed that the idea of protecting the woman from the so-called sordidness of police work was nonsense. What happened on Zo's job was three-quarters of his life; if he kept it to himself, that would be three-quarters of him lost to her. Too much. Besides, it fascinated Helen. Sometimes she wondered if it wasn't his work that drew her to him in the first place.

She marked her spot in the book, got out of bed, slid her feet into her open-toed summer slippers, and walked to the kitchen where she poured herself a glass of orange juice and sat at the painted wooden table.

After Zo's call she'd changed her plans for the evening. Whenever she knew he'd be late, she went to bed by nine, knowing she'd wake like this in the middle of the night. That way she wasn't completely exhausted for work in the morning. She genuinely liked working; the job itself wasn't particularly engaging, but she enjoyed the companionship of the other women and being out in the world. And what would she do at home all day with no children?

The thought of their infrangible agreement depressed her, as always. It was the only true defect in their marriage. When she'd agreed to not having children she thought it would be all right, that she wouldn't mind, that having Zo would be enough. And it was, in a way. But now she desperately wanted a child. She'd discussed it with her mother and Laura James suggested she simply not take precautions. The recommendation appalled Helen; she couldn't imagine engaging in that kind of duplicity. She'd made an agreement with Zo and she would keep it. Her only recourse was to pray that he would change his mind, and she did so each morning and night.

At twenty-eight, Helen Campisi was turning into a very pretty woman. She had always been attractive, with her translucent skin and her cheeks so red they seemed permanently stained by raspberry juice, but now her features were becoming more defined as life registered in her face. Her eyes were blue and her hair, impossibly fine, was the color of sunflowers. She wore it short in a gamin cut pointed in the middle of her forehead and curving sideburns arrowed toward each cheek. She was small and delicate (a size five) and people kidded her and Zo about looking like Mutt and Jeff.

It had been the same with her mother and father. Sometimes she wondered if she was trying to recreate their marriage, which had been inordinately happy, according to the party line given out by her mother. Helen's father died when she was eleven and she didn't have a clear recollection of her parents' relationship. But she believed what her mother told her. To Laura James, her dead husband was the apotheosis of manhood, and more than sufficient reason to remain a widow. Helen and Catherine, her younger sister, believed their mother was simply not keen about sex and used her *reason* as an excuse. If they were right, Helen wondered how happy the marriage really could have been? But did anyone ever understand their parents' marriage?

Helen drained the glass of orange juice and rinsed it, leaving it in the sink. Would Zo want anything to eat? Often he and J.J. stopped at a diner for something. But sometimes he arrived home hungry. She opened the refrigerator and looked in as if it might magically be filled with an abundance of delicacies: tomorrow was her shopping day.

Hearing Zo's key in the lock, she closed the refrigerator and walked to the living room, framing herself in the doorway to the kitchen in a mock model pose: one hip thrust forward, knee bent, arm raised above her head touching the woodwork.

"Hi, big fella," she said as he entered.

Zo smiled and looked her over appreciatively. "Seymour sent me."

"Seymour?"

He shrugged and ran a hand through his shaggy hair. "First name that came to mind."

"Honestly, Zo," she said laughing. "Seymour." She opened her arms to him and he to her, his embrace dwarfing her like a bear with a cub. They kissed.

As their lips parted, Zo said, "Nice girls don't French kiss."

"French girls aren't nice."

"You French?"

"Sure, can't you tell?"

"Well, I. . . ." He couldn't go on; the French allusions brought him thoughts of the Dudevants. He shook his head. "Depressing case. The people are French."

"Ah." She understood. "Hungry?" She hoped he wasn't.

"Had something. Any beer?"

She took his big hand, leading him to the kitchen where he sat at the table while she got him the beer.

Zo rubbed his eyes, feeling exhaustion spread through him: his arms and legs ached and pulled, hands and feet pulsated. Helen stood behind his chair and helped him off with his jacket, then she poured the beer carefully to give it a good foamy head the way he liked it.

"Want to tell me about it," she said.

"Yeah." He took a sip of the beer. "Good. The victim had two kids. A girl and a boy, six and four. My God, it's an unfair world."

Helen knew, on some level, that Zo was responding to his father's death; he always did when children were involved. She knew, too, to say nothing about that and urged him to go on with the details of the case.

He told her all he knew, which wasn't much.

"Tomorrow . . ." he looked at his watch, "this morning I'll see the kids, I guess. And the mother and brother."

"You'd better get some sleep." She patted his hand.

Arms around each other, they walked down the narrow hall to the bedroom. In bed, they held each other, legs overlapping, arms encircling bodies. He rested his head on her shoulder until she fell asleep and pulled out from the tangle they'd created, turning her small back to him. Moments later, he was asleep and dreaming: *he* was the child on lower Fifth Avenue and his father was falling, falling, falling as bullets were pumped into his body.

Zo's eyes snapped open. His sense of loss was profound. He felt an old hollowness as if everything within him had dried up. He was sure if someone shook him, his shrunken sorrow would rattle inside him like withered seeds in a desiccated gourd.

Carefully, he got out of bed and went into the kitchen where his jacket still draped the back of a chair. From a pocket he extracted his crumpled pack of Chesterfields and went on into the living room to sit in his favorite easy chair. In the dark he blew out a puff of smoke. Going unseen into the air, it was curiously unsatisfying.

He stretched out his long thin legs and wondered how he'd make it through the day. He knew he wouldn't sleep again tonight: he never did when dreams of his father woke him. Would it never end? Would he carry his father's life and death forever with him as if it were an inoperable hump on his back? No one else bothered him about it. The few scattered relatives who were left never knew the truth, not even Marius, his brother. Only Zo and his mother knew. So the continued cradling of the past was his own choice. Fourteen years later the ghastliness was as vivid as it had been on that cool October day.

He had expected the house to be empty. It was his mother's bridge day and his father, a lawyer, was at his office or in court. Marius was a marine, fighting in Germany.

When Zo closed the front door behind him, he experienced a strange sensation. At first it was unidentifiable. But in moments it was clear, intangible but undeniable: he was not alone in the house.

"Mom?" he called. No answer. He called again. "Mom, you home?" Silence.

Was he crazy? No. He knew someone was somewhere in the quiet house. Slowly he opened doors, crept into rooms. There was no one, nothing amiss on the first floor.

He climbed the stairs, the creaks and groans in the wood needling his insides. At the top he surveyed the hall and noticed that the door to his parents' bedroom was closed. This was uncustomary when the room was unoccupied. Someone must be on the other side of the door. Quietly, he crossed the hall and stood in front of the closed door, listening. His heart tripped when he heard the sound. At first he thought it was someone sighing. Then he recognized it was something moving, blowing, rocking. He balled his hand into a soft fist, two knuckles slightly protruding, and gently rapped on the oak door. There was no response.

Holding his breath he grasped the porcelain doorknob and turned it to the left. Then, circumspectly, he pushed open the door. Almost immediately he pulled it shut with a crash, his back against it as he faced the hall, his eyes wide and stunned, the scene etched on his mind as if burned there with acid.

But who *was* she?

He'd seen a woman hanging from one of the beams in the ceiling, a chair lying on its side on the floor. It wasn't his mother; he'd caught a flash of her hair and it was red, orange really, and his mother had black hair. Besides, his mother was under five feet tall. This woman was big.

Who *was* she?

Zo searched his memory for a name to put to the swinging woman on the other side of the door. The idea that he might know her was just as disturbing as the idea that, hanging from a beam in his parents' room was a complete stranger. Eventually, he decided, he must look again.

Twisting the knob, he inched open the door. His head was bent downward so his eyes viewed the large wooden planks of the floor, the edge of a braided rug. Timidly, bit by bit, Zo raised his head: more rug, the legs of the white iron bed, the curved rococo end piece, the blue bedspread, the spectator pumps! He gasped for breath.

The large feet in the brown and white shoes swayed gently. Zo's eyes traveled up the nyloned legs and reached the hem of a pink skirt, stopped, then continued upward, taking in the silk dress until he again arrested his gaze at the neck which was festooned with jewelry, pearls and something gold, and, of course, the rope. Now came the really difficult part, that last glance up to see the face.

Delaying, he shifted his eyes first to the right hand, which was unusually large, the fingers long and attenuated, blazoned with rings, and then to the left, adorned at the thick wrist with a simple gold bracelet. Was there something familiar about those hands? A flicker of recognition slammed his heart against the wall of his chest and he looked away, back toward the neck. Where had he seen those hands before? He couldn't place them. The time had come. He must raise his eyes to the face. And he did.

Her features were distorted: the eyes bulged and the tongue hung out and lolled over the lower lip which was painted with a bright red lipstick. The cheeks were powdered and rouged tastefully and the orangey hair was curled and puffed into bangs on the forehead, pulled up on the sides and hanging down, long and curly, in the back. Claudette Colbert had worn hers like that in *The Palm Beach Story*, which he'd seen two days before.

There was something about the nose. It seemed familiar, like the hands. It was long and narrow, a slight bump in the bridge like his father's. When Zo made that connection, the rest fell into place like a photograph coming up in its acid bath, clearer and clearer, sharper and sharper. It *was* his father! It couldn't be. But it *was*. Now he saw his father's eyes and mouth, the delicate line of his chin, the hands.

By the time his mother arrived home, the police had cut down the body and placed it on the floor. Zo could see the shock in the men's eyes, the pity when they looked at him and his mother. Two of them accompanied her upstairs to confirm the identification. When her scream didn't come, Zo somehow knew his father's costume was no surprise to her.

His father had left no note; there'd been no need. The dress, jewelry, makeup were like a splashy mordant document. But why had he done it that way? Was the blatant hostility directed at Zo's mother? Perhaps Alberto Campisi resented his wife for her natural femaleness. Perhaps he intended a final jab at her, a whip of contempt. Or was his female facsimile directed at his son? Was he saying: there's no use to manhood; we are, finally, reduced to skirts and powder and frippery; we are, finally, powerless?

Or was there still one more possibility? Had his father's last, acerbic declaration been: this is who I am and the hell with everyone? Yes, that was much more like it. The quiet, considerate man in life had, in death, splenetically sallied forth for his finish: fuck all.

Fourteen years later, mulling over once again why his father hadn't cared that Zo would probably discover him, the answer remained the same as always: he hadn't given it a thought. The ultimate selfish act, as suicide invariably was.

Zo hadn't always known that. There had been years of confusion, guilt, terrible pain. Only when he'd become a policeman and repeatedly come up against suicides did he finally understand and at last absolve himself. But still, he couldn't forget or completely forgive, although he tried. He was the one detective at the Sixth Precinct who never made cracks about the transvestites who were pulled in.

After the funeral, Zo had gone to his mother's room where she lay on top of the blue spread, her eyes swollen, face puffy. He hated going into that room and wondered how she could lie in there.

"You okay, Mom?"

She nodded and held out a hand to him, indicating he should come to her, sit on the bed. Her usually springy black hair seemed limp, framing her small face, which had the off-white color of skimmed milk.

Staring into her hazel eyes, he said, "I gotta talk, Mom."

She patted his hand encouragingly.

"I gotta know."

"Know?"

"Mom," he said, studying his big hand beneath her frail, tiny one, "you have to tell me about the dress and all."

"Ah," she sighed. But said nothing more.

"Mom? You hear me?" He wanted to scream, to shake her petite body, which appeared boneless to him now.

"He had a secret life, Zo, that's all."

"What d'ya mean, *that's all*, for God's sake?"

She flinched as if he'd struck her. "Don't."

"I'm sorry, Mom. I just gotta know. Was he a queer?"

Gloria Campisi rose up and slapped her son across the face, her hand leaving reddish marks on his cheek.

"Never, ever say that again," she commanded, eyes glittering.

Zo, stunned, touched his stinging cheek. His mother lay, once again, back against the pillows, appearing fragile and delicate like a transparent piece of china.

"I'm tired," she said.

He'd left the room no wiser than when he'd entered, at least not about his dead father. About his mother he'd gained an insight: she wouldn't be forthcoming about her husband's proclivities. And Zo must ask no more.

He hadn't for years. Then, when she'd remarried, he'd tried again but found her as inaccessible as ever. When her second husband died of cancer and she brought Marius home from the V.A. hospital to live with her, Zo tried one last time.

"It's no use," she'd said flatly.

And she was right. It was no use trying to understand the motivations, the secrets of another person. What for? What would he gain now if he knew or understood why his father wished to wear dresses and stockings? Or why he'd married and had two children? What possible use could it be to him? Still, he felt thwarted. He was a detective, after all. But he tried to accept that this mystery would go unsolved. No amount of pleading would change his mother's words, her sentiment. *It's no use* would be her epitaph.

Zo rose, stretched. When he raised the shades, he saw that night had changed to day and rain clearly threatened.

In the kitchen, he put on the coffee water and picked up his jacket. The back of it was covered with small white hairs, discards of the Dudevant cats. The sight brought him into the moment and he shifted his thoughts to the grim day ahead. At least it held a mystery which could be solved.

FOUR

Rain ushered in the new day, seedlike drops splashing the windows of Amelia's bedroom. As she slept, the dark sky was brightened only for a second by serpentine lightning, followed by the crack of thunder. Water sloshed through the half-screens, spraying the sills, dribbling down and spotting the parquet floor beneath the windows.

When Amelia woke, she was thinking of her mother who had been dead for more than twenty years. Had she been dreaming of her? She couldn't remember. Sleep, drug-induced, had been flat and black and unencumbered by emotion. Still, here she was, thinking of her mother. It was not unusual for her to conjure up the small, sanguine woman who had lavished love upon her. But she found it curious that she would awaken with these thoughts. And then she remembered, the knowledge coming with full force, a cataract sluicing its way through her brain. Danielle. Her darling girl. Dead. Now she understood the need for her mother, Mama. But *she* was the Mama. And her child was dead. This unacceptable knowledge immediately yielded to thoughts of her mother again.

During the first months after Marjorie Taylor's death, Amelia continuously reached for the phone to call her, or thought *I must tell Mama, she'll love this* or *Maybe Mama will know what to do.* Gradually, those impulses were reduced to wishes that her mother still lived and only occasionally did Amelia forget and begin a call or a thought. But she never stopped missing her, not even after all these years.

She remembered thinking at the time of her mother's death that one didn't really understand the loss and the inevitable feeling of mortality until it happened to you. And mother was far deeper a loss than father. She had loved her father, but when his death came it was not the wrenching experience her mother's death had been. When he died she'd felt sorrowful, dolorous. When her mother died, it was as though the umbilical cord had been given a final painful snip, leaving her floating in space, alone, desolate.

And desolation was what she felt now. Turning her head

toward Pierre's bed she saw that it was still made. She had known, without looking, that he wasn't in it, the feeling of aloneness palpable. At least, she thought, we have each other, a cold comfort wrapping around her like a wet towel.

Amelia, he gray eyes still clouded with drugged sleep, watched the dripples of rain ooze across the windowsill and slide over the edge. She should do something about the seepage, at least ring for Wallace. But she couldn't; a lassitude replaced her usual peppery arising. Today was different; today, wet and bleak, unfolded into a world minus Danielle. There was nothing to get up for.

Even the sound of her door opening didn't cause Amelia to move. Pierre's footsteps, ordinarily springy, now slow and plodding, came toward her bed, stopped, then continued on until he stood next to her, his trousered thighs even with her eyes. She fluttered her lids and with effort raised them, taking in his caved-in face, eyes dull like beach glass. For seconds they stared at one another.

"Are you awake?" he then asked stupidly, looking into her open eyes.

She understood, didn't deride him for the foolish question. "Yes," she answered huskily.

Pierre backed away then, slowly widening the gulf between them, and with the backs of his legs felt the edge of his bed and lowered himself. She was surprised that he'd moved away, but found she was relieved.

"Did you sleep?" he asked.

"Yes."

"*Bien.*"

"What time is it?"

"Eight-thirty."

Amelia's eyes widened, alarmed. "Guy?"

"He is having breakfast."

"Having breakfast," she repeated as if it were an act new to her, established only that day, something she'd yet to try. "He knows?"

"Yes. I met him when he came in. He took it well."

She wondered what it meant that he *took it well*. How did one take death well?

"Will you eat something, Amelia?"

Her stomach rebelled at the suggestion and she closed her eyes in answer.

"We must keep up our strength," said Pierre automatically, without conviction.

Why? she wished to ask, but her lips wouldn't form even that single small word. If only he would tell her it was all a dream, a nightmare; couldn't he at least do that?

"The police will be back today. They will want to talk with you. If you cannot, it will be simple to put them off, *ma cherie*. I will say you are under sedation. And that reminds me, would you care for some more of the Miltown?" he asked, as if it were a party and he was offering her another cocktail, a canape.

Amelia could not answer; her mouth, the lips tenaciously bonded, would not move.

The report of a thunderclap cleaved the silence and Pierre, a small frisson of fear surprising him, drew in his breath. He turned to look out the windows and saw for the first time that the rain was splashing the sill, trickling downward. Stiffly, he rose, lowered the windows, then returned to his place on the edge of the bed. He'd forgotten what they were saying before the thunder sounded. The rain came in torrents now, beating against the closed windows like the wings of giant birds begging for admission.

Again Amelia stared at her husband's face. It was as white as a stripped stick.

"What shall we do?" she said at last.

"Do?"

"Aren't we to do something?" she asked ingenuously. "I can't seem to place what comes now. It seems one must be expected to do this or that."

He realized then that no funeral arrangements had been made. Or perhaps Martin had seen to that. Where was his daughter's body? And then he remembered that under the circumstances an autopsy would be performed. His mind instinctively closed against picturing the mutilation he knew so well. For a second it opened again, like the lens of a camera, and he saw the cavity of her chest stuffed with newspaper. Quickly, he canceled the image, grateful it was not one Amelia would have to deal with.

"Yes," said Pierre doggedly, "I suppose there are things." He couldn't for the life of him begin to imagine what they were. Surely, someone would inform them.

"What things?" she asked.

Almost imperceptively, his lower lip begun to quiver and his blue eyes misted. He felt frightened and inadequate, as if he'd lost his place or forgotten his lines, and for a moment he shivered with animosity toward Amelia, who clearly expected him to know the answers, and he wondered why it was always that way. But immediately he buried those feelings, so deeply. in fact, that there was not the slightest sign of them when he spoke.

"I shall find out," he said, and rose like an intrepid knight.

When he was gone and she again felt relief, Amelia was stunned. It must be that she was simply glad to escape the demands of conversation, she rationalized. But when she found herself longing for Guy's comfort, company, she knew it was Pierre she wished to avoid.

Martin sat in the library, one hand draped over the telephone receiver, the other pleating and unpleating his chin. He must call his parents in Maine; he should have done it last night, but there'd been so much confusion he'd forgotten. He hadn't even called his sister. Lynn was the only one he'd told.

His hand fell from his chin and joined the other on his lap, flopping over it like a protector. How strange the call to Lynn had been; had anyone overheard, Martin might easily have been misconstrued as guilty. He'd sounded as if he were, in some way, responsible for Danielle's death and he wondered if Lynn had heard that in what he'd said. Or was he confusing grief with guilt? Grief was alien to him. It seemed impossible that a man of forty-four could claim such an omission in his life, yet it was true: both sets of grandparents died before his birth and no other relative or friend had died since. Now grief was expected, demanded. Was it possible that he felt he didn't deserve to grieve because of Lynn?

Even though he'd never really been in love with Danielle, he'd liked her, respected her, and she was the mother of his children. Hadn't he just that afternoon been thinking . . . oh, yes, that was it: he'd thought of her as expendable! But death had never crossed his mind. I'm glad it wasn't me! Martin sucked in his breath. That was the source of his guilt. He wanted desperately to live: to love Lynn, to love his children and watch them develop, to pursue his work. He understood this response was normal, but Danielle had wanted life too. Grief would come; he was sure of it now. It would arrive soon like an unwanted guest, capricious and guileful, insinuating itself for a protracted stay.

Now, while he was still able, he must call his parents. As the phone rang, Martin pictured his mother, her old, thin form bent over her garden, weeding with arthritic fingers. His father would, most likely, be on the wooden side porch, the long, sad face buried in the morning paper. Who would answer? It was she. Martin stood up as if this would give him strength.

"Halloo," came Elsie Swann's unmelodious voice.

"Ma," he said, the boy in him rising to the surface, "it's me, Marty."

The line was crepitant with static. "Who's theah?"

"Marty," he repeated, annoyed.

"Mahty!" Then, away from the phone, she called, "Thaddeus, come on in, it's Mahty on the phone."

Her voice sounded, as always, like a gnat's. He imagined her standing in the hall, shoulders slumped, wisps of gray hair, like cobwebs, creeping away from her bun.

"I have news," he said dully.

She shouted again: "The boy has news, Thad, come on in."

Now they would think he was reporting some accomplishment, although they'd never really understood any of his except the birth of his children. He shouldn't have put it that way.

"Ma, listen, it's not good."

But she didn't hear because she was still shouting for her husband. Then she said, "He's comin', Mahty," and dropped her voice to a conspiratorial whisper. "He's old, ya know, it takes a minute," as if she were speaking of someone generations older instead of her senior by only two years.

Martin saw the old man as clearly as if he were there: body bent at the waist, sloping shoulders, his head thrust forward on a long wrinkled neck like a turtle poking out of its shell, his sparse hair, thin and gauzy looking, hidden by his ubiquitous red hunting cap, the flaps tied on top, his hooded eyes a faded green, the face weather-worn, deeply creased, perennially brown.

"Thad's heah now, ya can tell us youh good news," said Elsie.

His heart fell. "It's not good news."

"He says it's not good news, Thad."

"It's Danielle," Martin said softly.

"He says it's Danielle."

To say the words frightened him, as though in saying them he was making it real, final, and if he just kept it to himself Danielle would remain alive, walk into the library any second. What he really wanted to do was hang up.

"Danielle is dead," he suddenly said, surprising himself.

"What's that?"

Hadn't she heard, or couldn't she believe what she'd heard? "Dead," he yelled, unable to control the volume of his voice. "Danielle is dead." He was shouting.

Again the verbal silence, the open line snapping with dissonance.

Then he heard her say: "Thaddeus, Danielle is dead." Back into the phone: "What happened, Mahty?" Her voice was hollow now, the stridency muted.

Forming the words *she was murdered* in his mind, Martin almost laughed. Ridiculous. That was how they sounded to him: ridiculous. He said it aloud.

"Murdered?" came the expected reply.

"We don't know who or why."

"How?" she asked.

"Gun."

"Gun," she repeated. "When's the funeral, Mahty?"

This shocked him most of all, and he reeled slightly as if he'd been pushed. He sat again. The funeral. Had anyone made arrangements? Pierre must have called the funeral parlor. "I'm not sure."

"Prob'ly Thusday, wouldn't ya say?"

"Yes, I guess so."

"When do you want us, Mahty?"

"Want you?"

"To come down theah."

Never, he thought. He saw his parents as seldom as possible. They depressed him. Why on earth would he want them with him at a time like this? But that was what people did; families gathered at funerals to console one another. He tried to envision his mother giving him solace, but the image, totally unfamiliar, wouldn't materialize. And his father, remote and elliptic, presenting the unaffable, frosty picture of a typical New Englander, was an equally impossible candidate for that role. Still, how could he say don't come?

"It's a long trip," he said lamely.

"Mahty says it's a long trip, Thad."

In the background, Martin heard his father say: "Know that."

"Mahty, youh fathah says he knows."

Did that mean he was willing to make the trip? Martin felt having his parents with him at this time would be impossible. He was needed by his children, his in-laws. And that would be another problem: his parents and the Dudevants had never met. He hadn't invited his parents to his wedding, implying that it was informal, and telling the Dudevants they were too unwell to make the trip. For the Swanns and Dudevants to meet now, under these circumstances, seemed unthinkable. Martin had always cared too much for the opinions of others, and he suspected this deficiency would plague him all of his life.

"You don't have to come," he said in a pleading tone.

"Mahty says we don't have to come, Thad."

Martin felt his craven behavior pull him into the quicksand of despair.

"Well, Mahty," his mother was saying, "if ya don't want us ta come——"

"It's not that I don't want you," he quickly interjected, sweat dotting his forehead like seed pearls. "It's just that I know you don't like to travel." It was as if he were speaking of a vacation they might consider.

"That's true," she said. "Just a minute, Mahty." Again the buzzing in the background. "Youh fathah wants to speak to ya."

He listened as the phone passed from her hands and he pictured his father standing there, readying himself for the enormous task of speaking.

"Mahtin?" The sonorous sound shuddered through the line. "Sorryboy."

"Yes, Dad, thank you, I. . . ."

"It's me, Mahty," Elsie said.

The man was gone. That was all. *Sorryboy*.

"Well, yull let us know if theah's anything we can do, won't ya? Have ya called Carol?"

"Not yet."

"She'll come." Implicit in those two words was the knowledge that Martin wouldn't try to discourage his sister from attending.

"Well, take cauh, Mahty, and give ouh love to the children."
"Yes, yes, I will."

They said good-bye and Martin, soaked with sweat under his jacket, slumped in the chair. He closed his eyes and listened to the steady hammering of the rain, interrupted occasionally by the clap of thunder. *Sorryboy*. He'd heard it before, those two words run together as if they were one, as if that took care of everything, the final balm to all ills. Martin glanced down at his legs stretched out in front of him, the one leg so obviously shorter than the other, and his mind floated back in time.

He was fourteen, still growing even though he was already five eleven, and this was the day he was going up on a roof to help his father, to begin his apprenticeship as a chimney sweep. Only once had he hinted to his father that being a sweep wasn't what he wanted to do with his future, and the look he'd received in reply was so baleful he'd never broached the subject again. It wasn't just that Martin wanted more out of life: to get out of Maine, to go to college, perhaps to be a doctor. He was afraid of heights. He'd never told his father this; fear of any kind was unacceptable to Thaddeus Swann.

In the truck, riding to the job, there was silence. When they arrived at the Crockett house, Martin thought he might vomit. He'd seen the house before, but today it looked as tall as pictures he'd seen of New York skyscrapers.

After they'd set the ladder against the house, his father went back to the truck for the equipment and for his black top hat which he ceremoniously placed on his head. Gesturing with a jut of his chin, Thaddeus told the boy to begin the ascent.

Slowly, Martin began to climb, each rung like a step toward death. He'd certainly entertained the possibility of plunging from the roof to his destruction more than once as he'd contemplated this day. Halfway up his booted foot slipped back to the rung below, his hands slid down, and his bowels churned. From behind him he heard a gruff: "Keep movin'." And he did.

Once on the roof, sweat, like mist, covered his body. He knew he mustn't look down and stood, his legs apart and aching from the tension within, waiting for his father. Like crabs, sideways, they made their final approach to the chimney. Martin grabbed a corner of the brick structure, trying to hide the tenacity of his white-knuckled grip.

As concisely as possible, Thaddeus began to explain the procedure. Then Martin felt his body begin to tremble, his feet began to slide. His fears had not been chimerical after all.

They said blacking out had probably saved his life, making his body less rigid. Still, he'd broken several ribs and his right leg. He would always remember the painful ride home, stretched out in the bed of the truck, every bump in the road causing him to cry out. He'd assumed they were heading toward the Bangor Hospital, so when the truck stopped in front of his house he was confused.

Martin was in too much pain to question this and now assumed that his father would send for Dr. Perkins even though he hated him, distrusted doctors. But he'd been wrong.

Inside, lying on his bed, he'd watched in horror as his father prepared to minister to Martin himself.

"Thad, please let's get the doctuh," Elsie begged

"Quiet."

"You don't know what youh doin'," she ventured.

For a moment Martin thought his father might strike her, though he'd never known him to. But his voice was the only thing he raised.

"I'll say this once. Doctuhs are fools. I can do it bettuh."

Resigned, Martin allowed himself to sink into the texture of his pain; his physical misery was somehow easier to concentrate on than his mental torture, his awareness of his father's intervention. Soon he lost consciousness again.

His leg had never mended properly, of course, and two years later, when it was obvious that the left leg had grown and the right had not, his father, watching Martin limp into the kitchen one day, looked him in the eye and said: "Sorryboy."

And that was that. It had never been referred to again. But Martin knew that although the old man *was* undoubtedly sorry, he really had never forgiven Martin for falling from the roof. That, in his mind, had made it impossible for his son to join him as a sweep; the bad setting of the leg was only an ancillary act.

Tears streaked Martin's cheeks, the sound of *sorryboy* still in his ear. In a moment he found that he was sobbing and wondered why he was crying, all these years later, having never cried about the fall or his leg before. His sobs were wrenching, from deep within, and as he gave way to them he knew, finally, that he was crying for his wife. Grief had arrived.

At first the sound seemed to be part of the storm, but almost immediately it became clear that it was coming from within the Fifth Avenue apartment. It was shrill and sharp and inhuman. Then it altered. A bellow, like the cry of a wounded elephant, filled the rooms. Again it changed, the vociferous noise rising now to a wail all too human.

Everyone rushed into the main hall: Martin, his eyes red and puffed, came from the library; Pierre emerged from the living room, two white smudges across his cheekbones as blood drained from his face; Lolly appeared at the end of the hall, her dark skin almost a match for the doors and woodwork; from the kitchen Guy, still in his rumpled, limp-looking clothes of the day before, staggered into the hall as if he were drunk. There was no sign of the children but two of the cats, their ears flattened against their heads, tails huge, bellies low to the floor, bolted from one end of the hall to the other, disappearing into the library.

The sound was ululating now, but there was no longer confusion as to where it was coming from and what it was: Amelia.

Pierre was the first to move, his thin, tired legs taking him in a trot down the long hall. The others followed; Lolly, too, though she didn't enter the bedroom, but hung back, her shoulder slumped against the wall.

Inside the room, Amelia, sitting up on the bed, her back rigid, arms crossed over her bosom, her fingers digging into her shoulders, screamed. Her eyes were wide, the pupils large and annular. A fear, as if she'd just witnessed some unspeakable act, hung in her eyes. Her cries came in short bursts, like bleating.

Pierre stood at the edge of the bed, shouting at her: "Amelia, Amelia, stop!"

She went on as if she hadn't heard, didn't see.

Martin approached and Pierre, beseeching with his eyes, waited for assistance.

"Amelia," Martin commanded.

The howling continued.

Martin glanced at Pierre quickly, as if to apologize, and then slapped Amelia hard across the face, twice. Instantly, she ceased her screaming. It was ironic, Martin thought, that with all the medical knowledge he and Pierre shared, he was reduced to using blunt brutality.

Pierre's uxorious nature rebelled against this violence toward his wife and he grabbed Martin's arm, quickly dropped it, and leaned over, placing a hand on each of Amelia's shoulders, his eyes searching her staring ones.

"We must cover her," he said.

As the two men eased her down and back under the covers, Guy, shivering in the doorway, began to feel the full force of what had happened. It was shocking to see his mother this way. She tended to be excitable, but he'd never seen her toally and frighteningly out of control. He watched as Martin took her pulse.

"Not good," Martin said to Pierre.

Guy backed out of the room. He was simply extra baggage there. In the hall he confronted Lolly, her thin, six foot frame, hovering like a phantasm.

"How is she?"

"Not good."

"Oh, Lord, Mr. Guy, how can it be?"

"I don't know," he said.

"It was my day off," Lolly said, as if had she been there it might have been she who'd been murdered and that would have been fine.

Guy said, "It's not your fault, Lolly." But was it his? he wondered. If he had gone over to Danielle in the park, might she now be alive? The fat woman loomed up in his mind like the rising of a full moon. Solitude was what he needed now. Moving down the hall toward his room, he was interrupted by the appearance of his niece, looking so much like a miniature Danielle he felt he might dissolve.

Cristina wore a pink cotton nightgown, its hem brushing the floor. Guy leaned down and picked her up, kissed her cheek, and gently pushed back a strand of hair from her eyes.

"You sleep, honey?" Lolly asked, touching the child's hand.

She looked stricken, dazed, as if she had no idea where she was. "I slept. Claude's still sleeping."

"Well, c'mon into the kitchen and we'll get some breakfast."

Lolly held out her arms to take the child from Guy, but he shook his head and started toward the kitchen.

Sitting at the round table was Wallace; her brown eyes glittered as if she had a fever. Her skin was lighter than Lolly's and Guy had come to know it was an issue between the two women.

"How's your Mama?" Wallace asked.

He shrugged. "She'll be all right."

Wallace clucked her tongue.

Guy's breakfast remains were still on the table, eggs congealed on the plate, bacon cold and crumbly. The sight of it turned his stomach and he looked away.

"Cristina's gonna have some breakfast, Wallace, okay?'" Lolly knew her place.

"Sure thing. You wanna make it, or should I?" It was hard to know whether this was an honest inquiry or a challenge.

Lolly said, "Whatever you like," and smiled knowingly, placing the decision firmly in Wallace's scrawny lap.

Wallace narrowed her eyes, nodded. "I'll do it." What could have been a defeat was quickly turned into a victory and making breakfast for the child was the reward. "What you like, honey?"

"Cereal," said Cristina, still in Guy's arms, her head on his shoulder.

"Comin' up."

Guy walked to the table and deposited Cristina in a chair, then sat down himself.

"Uncle Guy?"

"Yes, honey?"

"I had a bad dream."

All activity in the kitchen stopped. The three adults shared the same thought: did Cristina believe the murder of her mother was a dream?

"It was about this terrible fat lady," Cristina continued, twisting the collar of her nightgown.

"What else?" Guy asked.

"I can't remember. But it was bad." Her lower lip trembled. "It scared me."

Guy scooped her up and planted her on his lap, his arms engulfing her. He had so many questions he wanted to ask her but was afraid to. Maybe she didn't remember; maybe she *did* think it was a dream. But why hadn't she asked for her mother? Why hadn't she said anything? He wished Martin were here; a psychiatrist would surely know how to handle this. The fragility of the situation frightened him. What if he did or said the wrong thing? And what about the fat . . . lady? He could feel his insides fluttering like blowing leaves.

Wallace placed a bowl of cereal on the table. "C'mon, child, eat now."

Ready to lift Cristina back into her chair, Guy stopped as he saw tears brimming over, rolling down her cheeks. "Oh, Cristina."

"Mommy," she blurted. "I want my mommy." She flung herself against his chest, sobbing.

He held her tightly, his face buried in her hair as his own eyes filled and sorrow began to erupt inside him.

"Mommy, Mommy," she sobbed, "I want my Mommy."

"Me too, me too," he whispered, crying, astonished to realize he meant Amelia, a longing he'd thought he'd left in childhood.

Clinging together, they cried, uncle and niece, both yearning for the mothers neither would ever have again.

The Dudevant living room was formal, the furniture all Louis XVI with its classical forms and motifs. The two divans, which faced each other, were upholstered in blue silk and embroidered with caryatid figures in gold. The chairs had the square, tapered and fluted legs of the period, the backs rectangular at the bottom, rounded on top. The mostly blue Aubusson rug had a three-dimensional effect and the wall panels were papered.

Filling out the rest of the room were cabinets, tables, desks, all enhanced with gilt, marble, ormolu, brass. Every available surface was covered with objects d'art in china, glass, porcelain, enamel, jade, ebony, ivory. The room was the envy of many a collector.

To Zo it was a nightmare, an obstacle course. The delicacy of the pieces made him feel awkward and titantic and he feared any movement of his might result in massive damage. Although he did not know the period or value of the objects and furniture surrounding him, he did know they were antiques, precious. He sat primly on a sidechair, feeling oafish, and took a puff of his cigarette, his first, even though he'd been in the room almost an hour: he had waited until Guy and Pierre Dudevant lit theirs. Now, the ash growing too long to wait any more, he searched the satinwood side table for an ashtray. Were any of the items on the densely covered tabletop ashtrays? His hand hovered above a jade bowl.

"The small one," said Guy, coming to his rescue.

Zo nodded and flicked the ashes into the porcelain dish Guy had indicated. The boy, who seemed to him truly shattered, had given him his first break. A fat man or woman, Guy hadn't been totally sure, seemed to have been harassing his sister on the day of the murder. Zo had relayed the information to his precinct and, even as he sat here, men would be combing the park for suspects who fit the description Guy had given him.

Now they waited for Martin to bring in his daughter, apparently the only eyewitness. Kelly, meanwhile, was interviewing Dr. James Offenbach, the murdered woman's psychiatrist.

"Do you think," Zo asked Pierre, "your wife will be better later today?"

"I do not know," he answered tersely. "I do not understand why she has to be questioned. What can she possibly tell you? Surely, you do not suspect *her*?"

"No, sir, I don't. But sometimes mothers and daughters share confidences." He recalled the momentary jealousy he always experienced when Helen spent time alone with her mother; he imagined exchanged secrets, cryptic confessions, none of which he'd ever know.

Haughtily Pierre replied: "I do not understand."

Feeling empathetic, Zo tried to explain. "Maybe your daughter mentioned something to your wife of a private nature. The name of someone she'd met in the park, let's say." This still implied secrecy; Dr. Dudevant remained extraneous, excluded from the arcane conversations of women.

"My wife and I have no secrets. She would have passed on any information Danielle gave to her."

Zo crossed one ankle over the other, and felt the bottoms of his trousers, still not completely dried, flap against his nylon socks, damp and clammy. He separated his legs, sitting more stiffly than before.

"It could be something she didn't think was important enough to pass on," he said gently.

"To us, everything about our children is important. Do you have children of your own?"

Zo never got used to the question. Perhaps because it was never asked without an acrimonious edge, as though, if his answer were no, he was not really an adult or, worse, somehow subversive.

Readying himself for the inevitable response, he replied, "No, I don't." He watched Pierre's blue eyes shift from suspicion to congratulation, then alter further, dismissing him, at least in the matter of parents and children, his acumen here a washout.

"Well, then," Pierre uttered, as if that said it all.

And it did. Still, Zo had to persist. "I'll have to speak to Mrs. Dudevant at some point, Doctor. I'm sorry, but I just have to."

"It's his job, Papa," Guy said.

"Yes, yes, I know." Pierre slumped as if air were leaving his body, a rubber dummy deflating.

Zo daubed out his cigarette, holding the ashtray in his hand, then gingerly replaced it in the space between a gold and enamel snuffbox and an ornate figurine of gilded china.

Martin Swann appeared, holding the hand of one of the most beautiful little girls Zo had ever seen. There was something about the child which touched Zo; the sensation was tangible, piquant, and disquieting. He rose from his chair as if he were unfolding.

The child, still holding her father's hand, turned her head toward Martin's leg but kept her eyes on Zo.

His mouth felt dry. "Hello, I'm Zo."

Something registered in Cristina's eyes and around her mouth, amusement perhaps.

"I'd like to talk to you," he said.

"I've explained it to her," said Martin briskly.

Zo nodded. "It would be easier, I think, if we could be alone."

"Completely?"

"Well. . . ."

"I think *I'll* stay," Martin said, looking at Guy and Pierre.

"C'mon, Papa." Guy held out a hand to his father who, surprisingly, took it. The touch of his father's hand, as dry as if there were no more sap under the skin, caused Guy to flinch, but Pierre didn't notice. Quickly, Guy slid his hand up the man's arm and escorted him out of the room.

"Why don't we sit down," Zo said. He waited until Martin and Cristina were seated on one of the silk sofas before taking a position on the one opposite. Zo desperately wanted another cigarette, but he'd noticed that Swann didn't smoke.

In Zo's years on the force he'd never interviewed a child in quite these circumstances and he had to push himself to begin. "Cristina, I understand you were in the park yesterday. Is that right?"

She nodded, head still turned toward her father, eyes on Zo.

He wished Swann were not there and that he could have the child on his lap. Even though she sat close to her father, Zo felt she was not comfortable, secure.

"Did anything happen in the park different from other times there?" He leaned forward, hunching over, elbow on his knee, his chin in his hand.

Turning, she moved away from Martin and looked directly at Zo, her almond-shaped eyes seeming to brighten. "You said, hello, my name is Zo." She smiled. "That's a poem."

Zo smiled back. "Yes, it is, I guess."

"Cristina," Martin said sharply, "this is no time for games. Try to pay attention. This is very important."

"Yes, Poppy." Her eyes dulled and she seemed to sink into herself.

Zo wanted to shake Swann; what was wrong with him? Then he felt a small pang of guilt. The man had just lost his wife. What if Helen had died? Would Zo act normally? Still, something persistently told him that this *was* Swann's normal behavior.

Softly, Zo said to him, "It's all right."

Martin pressed his lips tighter.

"Now, Cristina, do you remember if anything odd or different happened when you were in the park yesterday?"

Zo thought she might start to cry, but then it became clear she was suppressing a smile.

"Well," she said, "there was the dog who did pee pee on Mommy's leg." Her small hand flew to her mouth, covering it, and her eyes puckered at the corners. Zo could see she was trying not to laugh.

Smiling himself, Zo tried to convey to Cristina that she

wasn't bad to find this funny, that every moment did not have to be solemn. This attitude wouldn't sit well with Swann and Zo felt he'd risked further alienating the man. But it was worth it. Not only did it dissipate the canopy of tension that was descending over them, but it brought him closer to the girl, and that was the main objective now.

"Go on," he urged. "I bet your Mommy didn't like that much."

The hand dropped and the smile burst through. "She didn't. She said, 'Christ, this isn't my day.'"

The words flashed in the air like tiny exploding rockets. Glancing at Swann, Zo saw that color had drained from his face. He shifted his gaze back to Cristina. The irony of the words had obviously penetrated even that six-year-old mind. Zo watched as her smile slowly drowned in sadness. Desperate to save the interview and to ameliorate Cristina's pain, he asked about the fat woman . . . or man.

"It was a fat *lady*."

"You're sure?"

"Well, I . . . she had long hair."

"Would you know this person again?"

"Yes." Then, startling both Martin and Zo, she said: "But she isn't the one who did it."

They'd leaped miles ahead of where Zo had planned to be at this point. Carefully, he phrased his next question. "Do you know who *did* do it, Cristina?"

"You mean her name?" she asked, sounding frightened, as though she might be about to fail a test.

So it was a woman, Zo thought, surprised, and watched Swann cover his daughter's hand with his own. He saw in Martin's eyes an unbelievably soft light: solicitous, devoted. Although Zo would have sworn this man was incapable of such a feeling, he had to admit now that Swann clearly loved his daughter.

"No, honey, not her name, unless you know it," Zo answered.

She shook her head.

"Did the lady say anything?"

"Yup."

"What, honey? What did the woman say?" His heart was flapping wildly in his chest.

"Well, she asked if Mommy was Mrs. Swann." She pulled

one leg up under her and began to fiddle with the hem of her yellow organdy dress.

"And your Mommy said yes," Zo supplied.

"Yup."

"And then?"

She was silent a moment, then shrugged. "I dunno."

"Did the lady say anything else, Cristina?"

An expression crossed her face, almost imperceptible, but one Zo was familiar with. He'd seen it hundreds of times when questioning people. It said one of three things: I know but I can't remember; I know but I won't remember; I know but I won't tell you. There was no way of being sure, at this stage, which of the three this was. He would try only once more now.

"Cristina, did the lady say anything else?"

Her eyes glazing over, she answered, "I don't know."

He would have to wait, perhaps forever. It depended on the depth of the trauma. "Can you tell me what the lady looked like?"

Totally engrossed now in the folds of her dress, Cristina ignored the question. Zo felt panicky, he couldn't afford to lose her now. "Cristina?"

She didn't answer or look at him.

Zo, meeting Swann's gaze, silently implored him to help.

Martin slid Cristina onto his lap and her head fell against his shoulder, resting in the crook of his neck. "Sweetheart," he whispered, "you must try and answer. The detective needs your help."

Zo wondered where this verbal tenderness had been hidden earlier. "Can you tell me what the lady looked like?" he asked.

After a moment she said: "She had a big hat."

"A big hat?"

"Yup. Like that," and she drew her hands around her head, indicating a wide brim.

"And what else?"

"A long skirt and sandals."

Zo felt the clicking inside, something he always experienced when he knew he was getting warm. "What was her blouse like?"

"I dunno."

"Did it have long sleeves?" he prodded. He could see in Cristina's eyes that now she remembered.

"No, short. And it was white." There was pride in her voice and Martin rewarded her with a stroke of her hair.

"This is very good," Zo said, not wanting to be outdone. "And the skirt. What color was it, honey?"

Warming to her task, Cristina seemed to recall more and more. "It was long, to here." She ran a finger across her ankle. "And it had pictures on it and . . . and that stuff around the bottom." Her face twisted into a frown as she tortured her memory. Now she desperately wanted to be best girl. "You know that stuff?" she asked Zo. She was opening and closing her hands.

The gesture told him nothing, but he took a guess. "Ruffles?"

"Yeah, that's it," she said, a luminosity in her eyes. "One. One big one around the bottom."

A peasant skirt, thought Zo. "That's great, honey, just great. I know exactly what you mean."

She sparkled. Martin brushed his lips against her temple.

Inexplicably, Zo felt jealous, but pushed the feeling aside and went on. "Anything else you can remember, Cristina?" He watched the recollection hit her, as evident as if the words had flashed cogently in her eyes.

"Glasses," she fairly yelled, thrilled with her own recall and brightness.

Zo was overwhelmed by the observance of this six-year-old and, although he doubted whether her description would stand up in court, it was definitely holding up with him; his gut told him, for sure, it was correct.

"Now, sweetheart, this is going to be hard. The glasses, were they round, or shaped like this," he drew harlequins in the air with his forefinger and thumb of each hand, "or something else?"

"Round," she answered. No doubt.

"Oh, that's terrific." He glanced at Martin and as he did she said:

"She winked."

"Huh?"

"Winked. The lady winked just before. . . ." Her face crumpled, this memory devoid of fun.

Although Zo noted Cristina's pain, he was focused on what he'd seen in Martin's eyes when she'd said *she winked*. Again, it was almost imperceptible, but there had been an alteration in the man's eyes: a flicking of the pupil, as if an infinitesimal shade had snapped up, rolled around its dowel, then snapped back down. He stored this away to deal with, examine and analyze, later.

"The lady winked?" he asked Cristina.

But she was lost to him now, her painful recall obliterating any need to go to the head of the class. "Poppy, I'm tired."

Martin stood up, holding his daughter in his arms. To Zo he said: "That's all for now."

"Thanks, honey, you did real well," he said patting Cristina's hand.

She didn't care and lowered her head onto Martin's shoulder, a cheek against his jacket, a finger in her mouth as she tumbled backward in age to a safer time.

When they'd gone, Zo allowed the excitement at what he'd learned to amplify. Even the oppressiveness of the room couldn't squelch his high. He picked up his trilby from beneath the chair where he'd stashed it, plunked it on his head, and walked to the front door.

Outside, the rain had stopped. The sky was clearing and the buildings crowded against it like bodies. Wet heat rose steaming from the pavement, instantly enveloping him in clamminess. He lit a cigarette and flipped the match into the gutter, a rivulet of dirty water sweeping it south. He thought about Cristina's last description: *the lady winked just before.* . . . Jesus Christ. What a memory to grow up with. But why had the woman winked? And what had that statement meant to Martin Swann? For now, Zo had no answers, and until he did those questions would live in his mind like fluttering wings of a captive butterfly.

He opened the top button of his shirt, pulled down his tie, and headed for the subway.

Poppy had told her that Mommy was never coming home. Dead. Mommy was dead. Cristina knew about dead because a year ago she had had a kitten who died. He was black with white feet and a big white splotch on his face. One day he was fine and frisky and the next he was . . . dead. They told her he got a disease named distemper and he died. She'd cried a lot and told everybody she saw that Gordon had died. All the people looked sad when she told them and patted her hair or squeezed her hand and a couple even kissed her and told her how sorry they were. She had liked that a lot. Now she wondered if they would act the same way when she told them Mommy had died. Mommy was dead.

Cristina turned over on her side and looked across at Claude in the other bed. In the dark she couldn't tell if he was asleep.

"Claude?" she said softly.

There was no reply.

She listened carefully for the sound of his breathing, but she couldn't hear it. Maybe Claude was dead. When you were dead you didn't breathe any more.

"Claude?" she said louder.

Nothing.

What if Claude *was* dead? Sometimes she had wished he was dead and now that she thought he might be, she felt scared.

"Claude?" she demanded.

"Wha?" he answered sleepily.

Relieved, she asked, "Do you remember Gordon?"

"Huh?"

"Gordon. The kitten. Do you remember him?"

"Oh, yeah. Sorta."

"Do you think Mommy is with Gordon now?"

"Huh?"

Sometimes she just hated Claude. Sometimes he was so dumb. She had to explain everything all the time.

"When Gordon died, Mommy said that he went to heaven and now Poppy said that Mommy went to heaven. So do you think they're together?"

"Mommy and Gordon?"

Cristina sighed. "Oh, Claude, never mind."

"Well, what?" he whined.

"It doesn't matter. Go to sleep."

"I hate you," he said.

"I hate you too."

There was a long silence and Cristina thought about hating. Mommy said it wasn't nice to hate people but sometimes Cristina couldn't help it. Sometimes she just did. She had even hated Mommy once in a while. And Poppy. And Lolly. She couldn't remember ever hating Grandpapa or Uncle Guy or Grandmaman. She thought of Mommy again and said:

"Mommy's never coming home."

"Don't say that," Claude said.

"It's true."

"Don't."

"Poppy told us."

"I don't care."

"What's that mean?" He was always saying *I don't care* to everything.

"Shut up, Tina."

"Shut up yourself." Dumb. He was just dumb. Suddenly the fat lady appeared in her mind. Cristina's brow creased. That man who had asked her all those questions said the fat lady was maybe a fat man. But she had long hair and men didn't have long hair. Mommy had been scared of the fat lady and then the dog peed on her and then the other lady said, *This is for* . . . and there was the big noise and Mommy was on the ground with blood and people were pulling her and. . . .

Cristina could feel her heart all jumpy in her chest as if it were trying to get out. And she could hear it, too. Her ear was against the pillow and when you did that you could hear your heartbeat. She remembered the first time, a long while ago, when she'd heard it and not known what it was and it scared her so much she'd started to cry and then she screamed for Mommy and Mommy came and held her and kissed her and told her what it was. And everything was better. Mommy *always* made it better. The knowledge that Mommy would never make anything better again hurtled through her small body as if it would tear her apart.

"Claude?" she asked.

"What?"

"You don't think Mommy's in heaven?"

"Nope."

"Well, where is she then?"

"I dunno."

She started to feel mad, hating again, because she'd decided to believe whatever Claude told her. She didn't like what Poppy told her. Now she hated Poppy.

"Tina?"

"Yeah?"

"I think I know," he said, sounding very serious.

"Know what?"

"I think I know where Mommy is," he said, a certitude in his voice that was unusual for him.

Seconds ticked by before she asked: "Where is she?"

"I think," he said, "Mommy has gone to the store."

Cristina absorbed this information for a moment and then she said: "I think you're right, Claude. I think that's where she is." And she pictured Mommy in that big store, Bloomingdale's, looking at pretty sweaters. "Bloomingdale's," she added.

"Yes, Bloomingdale's," he chirped.

Cristina nodded her head, smiling. But it didn't last long, that smile, that sense of security, of Mommy safe and happy, shopping in Bloomingdale's. It faded from her mind just like when you turned off the television, leaving only a white glaring spot and then nothing.

Mommy was not at Bloomingdale's. Mommy was dead, like Poppy said. And she was never, never, never coming home again. Cristina wished she didn't know it was true, but she did.

The lady said *This is for.* . . . Cristina tried hard to see the lady's mouth, to picture the word she said next, but the mouth blurred, went fuzzy. *This is for.* . . . No use. She couldn't hear it, couldn't see it. She hadn't told Zo the lady said *This is for.* . . . Maybe she'd never tell him and then he wouldn't be mad that she didn't know what came after *for.*

"I'm goin' to sleep now, Tina."

"Night."

She thought about telling him that Mommy wasn't at Bloomingdale's, then decided against it. He was just a baby. He'd know Mommy was dead soon enough, when she didn't come back from Bloomingdale's. He wouldn't be able to pretend for very long. The truth, Mommy said, was always best, even if it hurt. Now she could hear Claude's breathing and knew he was asleep. She turned over, faced the wall, and took a deep breath. A hard thought came into her mind: Claude believed Mommy was at Bloomingdale's and he was sleeping; she *knew* Mommy was dead and she was awake. Which was better? Pretending Mommy was at Bloomingdale's had felt good for a minute, but then it didn't. Mommy said it: *The truth is best even if it hurts.*

So this was best. Mommy was dead.

FIVE

On the morning of Danielle Dudevant's funeral, Lynn Cunningham greeted the day with uneasiness. She was not, of course, attending, although a part of her wished she could be there: invisible. As a child she'd often fantasized such feats: being an ant in her parents' bedroom at night; a mouse in the corner of the room when her teacher spoke of her; unseen when a certain boy discussed her with a friend. Martin had been so peculiar, so strange, in the two phone calls she'd had from him since the murder that her return to childish invention almost seemed appropriate. She wished to view Martin at the funeral.

The first call was, understandably, muddled, incoherent. Still, the note of fear she'd detected in Martin's voice had surprised her. The second call had come last night.

He'd filled her in a little more, although she knew almost all there was to know. The New York papers, with the exception of the *Times*, had slapped it across their pages, wringing every bit of sensationalism they could from the little they had to go on; the class of people involved made good copy. Martin had also informed her that they mustn't see each other for a while, that he was calling from a pay phone. In short, he was behaving like a guilty man. Obviously, he hadn't pulled the trigger himself. The latest report was that the killer was a woman. But the idea that Martin might have hired someone nagged at Lynn like a persistent mosquito.

When she'd asked him how long he had in mind for their hiatus, he'd faltered at first, then said he honestly didn't know but could foresee a few months or at least until things were settled. Did he mean, she'd asked, until they caught the murderer? Yes, he'd said. He didn't think it would look good for him to be seeing another woman so soon and he didn't want to involve *her* in any way.

So what was wrong with that? It was thoughtful and considerate. Did she really want policemen swarming all over her apartment, questioning her child? Why had she twisted concern for her into something portentous?

She could even understand why Martin would be anxious about being seen with her so soon, making it seem he'd picked up with a new woman immediately after Danielle's death. So she'd suggested that he tell the police about her. He'd responded hysterically: voice rising, inveighing against her as if she'd gone mad. To her, the proposal had seemed sensible; why conceal it unless it could be construed as a motive? But it was absurd to think Martin had hired some strange woman to kill his wife. Ridiculous. Still, as Lynn sipped her morning coffee, the presage deepened.

The feeling of fear, of things askew, had been exacerbated the day after the murder when she'd picked up a copy of *The Daily Mirror*. On the front page was a picture of Danielle and Martin in evening clothes at a fundraising ball the year before. Seeing Martin in grainy black and white was stunning enough, but what really caused her shock was the photograph of Danielle. She was absolutely gorgeous.

Lynn, like other women in her position, had often conjured pictures of her lover's wife. Basically, she'd imagined her as quite ordinary, having nothing to go on except Martin's lust for herself, Lynn. Based on that, she couldn't believe his wife would be in any way exceptional. *She* was, she knew, no beauty. Her face was long, her nose slightly crooked, and she wore glasses. She was narrowly built and her hair, light brown, thin, formed curls like tiny watch springs. From the beginning, as she had with Whitney, she'd wondered what it was that Martin saw in her. But when she actually viewed Danielle, she almost dropped the paper in the street. Why in the world would a man with a wife who looked like that want her?

Ross, still in pajamas, interrupted her thoughts.

"Hi, darling." She kissed her son's cheek and smoothed his tousled, brown hair. "Breakfast?"

Ross wrinkled his nose in distaste. "Like what?"

It was the same each morning; Ross was a picky eater. Whitney Jr. had eaten everything and anything but then, he'd been a breeze straight down the line. Lynn had a sudden rush of missing him. But Whit was twenty now and if he chose to go to summer school to speed up his education, how could she complain?

"What about some nice eggs?"

"I hate eggs." Ross slumped into the breakfast nook his father had built, brought his bare feet up to the bench, and pressed them against one another, sole to sole. "Can I go to the movies today?"

"Let's decide about breakfast first. Cereal?"

"Phoo!" Tiny speckles of spit sailed from his mouth.

"Please, Ross," Lynn said, "just say yes or no, all right?"

"Orange juice."

Grateful, Lynn got the juice from the refrigerator. "What else will you have?" These morning games were enough to send her back to bed. She set the glass of juice in front of him. "Bacon?"

"Canadian?"

"If you like." It wasn't much, but it was something; protein at least.

"Can I go to see *Rebel Without a Cause* today?" He finished the juice and licked the clinging pulp from the inside of the glass.

"Well, no, Ross. I think you're too young for that picture."

"What d'ya mean?" he squeaked.

"I think that's clear. You can't go."

Ross banged the glass on the table. "Why not?"

Lynn turned away from the hissing bacon and looked at him. "I just told you. You're too young."

"I wanna see James Dean," he screamed, face turning red.

"Stop that, Ross."

His mouth formed a defiant smile. "If you don't let me go, I won't eat that bacon."

She began to feel the panic but remembered Martin's words: "You mustn't let the boy blackmail you with threats of not eating. Don't give in. He'll eat eventually."

"All right, don't," she said.

Ross was shocked. Maybe he hadn't heard right. "I-won't-eat-the-bacon," he said again.

Lynn reached over and turned off the jet. The sound of bacon frying slowly died. "Then don't eat it, Ross. I don't care. You're not going."

"I'll die if I don't eat. Is that what you want?" he yelled.

So there it was, blatant at last. This refractory child had held her hostage for years; thank God for Martin. She had to bridle her smile.

"No, Ross, I don't want you to die. I love you. But it's up to you if you want to eat or not. I won't be blackmailed any more." Lynn watched as his astonished expression turned to pain, then frustration, and her first impulse was to take back everything she'd said, beg him to eat, promise him the movie. But she held on.

Rising from his place in the breakfast nook, Ross uncurled his body like a snake ready to attack; this was war.

"You hate me," he accused through his even white teeth.

"I love you." She desperately wanted to touch him, to hold him in her arms, but she knew he'd throw her off and she wasn't sure she could endure that.

"You hate me and I hate you, you . . . you lamebrain." The second he'd hurled his pathetic epithet, he ran from the room, bare feet slapping against the floor.

Lynn started at the sound of his slammed door, then, relieved, poured herself a fresh mug of coffee and took her place at the table. Martin had told her it would be difficult the first time. She was quivering inside and her hand shook as she lifted the coffee to her lips. She always paid, it seemed, for any gain, no matter how small. Her nervous system was her worst liability; her body never failed to betray her. Why should this foray into parental control prove any different? If only Whitney. . . .

A tiny arrow of anger pierced her; her resentment that he'd died and left her in charge still lingered, though, of course, it diminished daily. And after three years she still couldn't help, at times, missing him, though she was never sure that it was Whitney, the person, she missed or simply the husband, caretaker, manager.

She *had* loved him; eighteen years of marriage had not been worthless. Although the early passion had fizzled, a kind of comfort had taken its place; sex was no longer magical, but it served to relieve and affirm. The rest of their relationship—daily life, raising the children, companionship—was even but not boring. It had seemed to Lynn just right. One couldn't expect the scintillating times of youthful love; continuity had a way of blunting the sharp edges of romance. And what was all that, anyway? Insanity. She wouldn't have remembered had it not been for Martin.

Experiencing the madness of love with him reminded her of the early days with Whitney, and at times her feelings fused, confusing her. Still, there was a difference: no matter how beguiled she became, she was forty now, not nineteen. The echoes of foolish, youthful love hovered, but the mature woman waited in the wings as if she were a thresher removing the grains and seeds from the straw and chaff.

And now a new reality superseded everything. Death. Murder. She had been mad to think Martin had any connection to his wife's death. Surely his behavior, his desire to hold their affair in abeyance, was for the sake of privacy, to protect them from speculation. It was, she had to concede, sensible. Typical of Martin, who was a remarkably sensible man. Her earlier doubts dissolved now like romantic summer promises.

She drained the last sip of coffee and put the mug in the sink. In a day or so the police would surely have this thing solved and, in a matter of time, in an appropriate manner, she and Martin would reveal their liaison to their respective families and then. . . . Then what? Would they actually marry? Again, insecurity overwhelmed her. Could a man like Martin Swann really love her, want her, desire marriage, if circumstances permitted? Or was she still a child, who hadn't grown, living in a world of fantasy, expecting miracles?

Suddenly she felt ill and disgusted with herself. Danielle Swann was dead, being buried this very day, and here she was wallowing in self-obsession: invention, fiction. Today was not her day: it was Danielle's. And Martin's. Accepting that, Lynn felt something lift inside her. Perhaps she had grown up a bit, after all.

The Campisi bedroom faced Thompson Street and at night the streetlamp shone through the window, bathing the room in a tender blush; Helen and Zo said it was their private moon. When they slept, they closed the cream-colored wooden shutters, but when they made love they left them open so they could see one another without a garish light.

Helen lay on top of the white sheet and watched as Zo undressed. When he removed his undershirt and turned to toss it on a chair, as always something in her stirred; the huge purple birth mark which stretched from just under his neck to the small of his back and widened below the shoulders to a half foot in diameter was clearly delineated in their "moonlight." She remembered their wedding night, how Zo had hidden it, backing into the bathroom.

When Zo had folded his trousers over the chair and tossed his underpants into the laundry basket, he joined her on the bed.

"Where'd ya get my name?" she asked.
"Tough Tony."
"Some stud."
"You ain't seen nothin' yet."
"Oh, yeah?"
"Yeah. Get a load of this, toots." And he kissed her, his tongue investigating her mouth, contacting her tongue.

When their lips parted, she whistled softly. "Not bad."

"Not bad yourself." He smiled, his voice changing. "I love you, Helen."

"Oh, Zo." She drew him down on top of her.

Their bodies pressed together, skin silky, electric ripples running the length of them. Moving against one another, hands and mouths exploring, searching, Zo and Helen quickly soared to an almost unendurable pitch of sensation. He stroked her breasts, then teased the nipples with his tongue, mouth. She ran a hand over his lower belly, inside his thighs. Sometimes they went on like this for long periods, playing, caressing; tonight urgency was their dictator, the need to join, immediate. Slowly Zo entered her and, rhythms in accord, strove to find the pinnacle of pleasure.

Afterward they lit their ritual cigarettes, lay on their backs holding hands, and blew plumes of smoke into the air where some of it disappeared into the dark and some was caught on pendants of light: swirled, fuzzed, melted.

"It just gets better," said Helen, squeezing his hand.

"I know."

"If it's this good after five years, think what it'll be like after twenty!"

"I don't know if I could take it," Zo said, laughing.

"Oh, you'll manage."

For a few moments they were quiet, smoking, enjoying the liberation of their bodies from daily tensions. Then Zo cleared his throat and said:

"I guess there's something I should talk to you about."

Helen stiffened. To her those words signaled danger.

Understanding the tightening of her body, quickly Zo said: "It's nothing bad, honey."

Delivered, she relaxed.

"It's about a house."

"A house?"

"Yeah. In Long Island."

Helen extracted her hand from his, pulled herself up, and leaned on one elbow, looking down at him. "Zo, what are you talking about?"

"There's this house for sale in Bellmore on Long Island. Three bedrooms, two-car garage, finished basement, for under twelve thousand."

Helen stubbed out her cigarette in the black ashtray they'd taken from Sammy's Bowery Follies, a crazy club on the Bowery, and said impatiently: "Yes, so?"

"Well, we could buy it." His voice sounded as if he were sinking inside the center of the mattress.

"Buy it? For what?"

Zo looked up at her. "For what? To live in, dope." The skin at the corners of his eyes crinkled into small pleats, his mouth smiled. "Like normal people, you know. House, car, yard. . . ." His voice trailed off.

The obvious next word was *kids*, and they both knew it. Zo turned away. Helen lay back on the pillow, stared at the ceiling. A silence, saturated with unspoken accusations, desire, filled the room, their separation as real now as if a bundling board had been inserted between them.

"Listen," he said, "if I ever had any doubts, they were wiped out when I saw those Swann kids. They're devastated. They'll never get over losing their mother."

"I didn't say anything, Zo."

"I know what you're thinking."

Of course he was right: he did know. But it was the invidious subject of house-owning which had caused their minds to turn toward children, a subject *he* had raised. She felt resentment well up within her.

"I'm not interested in buying a house, living in the suburbs with a lot of other cops and their wives and *brats*," she said.

When Zo didn't respond after a few moments, she went on. "What would I do there? I'd go nuts. You want me to sit around coffe-klatching all day?"

"You could commute with me," he said sullenly.

"No thanks."

"You could get a job there. It's not Mars, you know."

"Might as well be." She jammed her pillow up against the brick wall they'd spent days exposing, lit another cigarette, and roughly grabbed the ashtray from Zo's belly where it bounced when he talked. She flung herself into the pillow, sucked on her cigarette, and hissed a stream of smoke into the air.

"Damn you," she said.

He sat up, the sheet dropping to his waist. He faced her; his eyes, lit by the streetlamp, were angry and bruised with distress.

"You knew. You knew from the beginning how I felt about having children."

"Lorenzo, the only person talking about having children is you." Her voice shook. "What did you bring up this house thing for, anyway?"

"I didn't think I should make a unilateral decision, that's all." With both hands he attacked the sides of his unruly hair, smoothing to no avail. "J.J. told me about it and I didn't think it would be right for me to say no without asking you."

"To say *no?*"

"Yeah." His mouth suggested a grin, then settled down. "I mean, what would *I* do there? I'd go nuts. You want me sitting around looking at football games all day?"

"You're a bastard, you know that?" she said, trying not to laugh.

He nodded.

"What would you have done if I'd said I wanted to buy the damn place?"

"Tried to talk you out of it." He was openly grinning now.

"You're really something."

"You think so?" He reached out and touched her shimmery yellow hair.

She took his hand in hers. "Ah, Zo, sometimes you're bad." She kissed his palm.

They moved toward one another, their arms slipping around their naked bodies, flesh touching, melting, pressing hard in loving affirmation, the allusions to children sliding into their unconscious minds, where the subject would lie in wait, ready to erupt at the next opportunity.

But for now it was good again.

Joe's was a luncheonette on the corner of West Fourth and Jones streets in Greenwich Village. Zo and J.J. often had breakfast there before starting their day; it was a good spot to exchange notes on whatever case they were working on. Besides, the food was fair, and the waitress, Rosalie, resembled Gina Lollabrigida. Occasionally, they had lunch there when the special was Chilichow: half chili, half chow mein. It was so awful it was good.

Rosalie, in a tight green sweater and a tighter gray skirt, came to their booth. "So, yeah, what?" She held her stubby pencil poised over her order pad.

"How's my best gal?" J.J. asked, the ever-present cigarette bobbing between his lips as he spoke.

"Yeah, fine. You eatin', or what?"

Zo, sensitive to the fact that they weren't the only customers in the place, gave his order but J.J., undaunted by Rosalie's pruned replies, pressed on.

"When are ya gonna give me a tumble, Rosalie, huh?"

"When hell freezes over, bigshot. So, yeah, are ya orderin' now, or what? 'Cause if ya ain't I'm movin' on."

J.J. laughed, pale blue eyes blithe, as if her brusqueness were an invitation. J.J. was relentless, his ego as big as his belly. Finally he gave his order, then crooked his neck to watch her swish away from the table.

Turning back to Zo, he said: "That's some can, ain't it?"

Zo grunted noncommittally and lit a Chesterfield. Sometimes he wondered how it was possible that J.J. could be such a cliché cop. It was as if he'd stepped full-blown out of a forties B movie: the inevitable smart-mouthed, hard-drinking, two-fisted, womanizing dick. Actually, Zo suspected, where women were concerned, J.J. did more talking than acting. He liked to play the games, give the impression he was a skirt-chaser but, Zo thought, boozing was really more important to him and he preferred ending his nights with a bottle rather than a babe.

"So what've you got?" Zo asked.

J.J. took a pad from his inside jacket pocket, flipped it open, consulting it. "Still no make on the fat woman. She seems to have disappeared into thin air."

"Could be a fat man, you know."

"Yeah, a he-she."

Zo's inner guard went up. He knew J.J. meant a transvestite. "No, not a he-she." He tried to keep his voice even. "It's just that there's confusion about the sex because of the long hair."

"Well, no fat guy's been seen either."

"I don't think it matters much. Fat man or woman's not the killer."

"You believe the kid's description total?"

"I do." He was anxious when he thought of Cristina and what was going to happen in a few hours. Swann had finally given permission for Zo to go to the park with her and see if she could spot the woman who'd killed her mother. He didn't want to think about it. "What else?"

"I saw Offenbach again."

"You get something this time?" Dr. Offenbach had claimed privileged information during the first interview.

J.J. smiled, forcing the broken veins across his nose and cheeks to stretch. "He decided to be more cooperative."

Zo knew J.J. wanted him to ask how this came about, but Zo had no interest in how his partner operated; in fact, he'd rather not know.

"What've you got?"

Checking his notes, he said: "She wasn't happy at home. The marriage stunk. Surprise, huh?"

"Yeah, big surprise."

Rosalie appeared and, like a circus performer, slid plates and cups from her arms and hands onto the table, the collision of china against the linoleum top making thudding, whomping sounds.

"Eat," she instructed, as if without her directive they wouldn't know what to do. She was gone before J.J. could reply.

Zo sipped his hot coffee, careful not to burn his mouth. "What else?"

"She had a boyfriend."

Zo's cup hit the saucer hard. By now he knew a lot about Danielle Swann and this surprised him; he simply couldn't see her as an adulteress. In fact, he couldn't see her as anything but beautiful, intelligent, fascinating; he was, he knew, a little bit in love with her and that was dangerous on many levels. It had never happened to him before. He felt like Dana Andrews in *Laura*, only in the movie Laura wasn't really dead and the detective wound up with her. Danielle Swann was really dead. And besides, he loved his wife. The small obsession he'd developed about this victim would soon dissipate, he hoped.

"What boyfriend?"

"His name was Brian O'Connell, a drifter. It was three and a half years ago." J.J. shoveled a wedge of dripping buttered toast in his mouth.

"What happened to him? You mean, she didn't see him since then?"

The sound of toast crunching filled the booth. "Right. They never screwed or nothin'. She wouldn't."

As J.J. went on to explain about the platonic relationship between Danielle and Brian, Zo felt a surge of relief and a sense of exoneration for her. But how could he have thought, even for a moment, that Danielle was that kind of woman? He hoped she'd forgive him, immediately recognizing how crazy that thought was. He'd better watch it. His eggs were growing cold and he pushed them around on his plate, his appetite fading.

"So ya think we should follow up on this O'Connell?"

"Run a check on him. Won't hurt." He asked J.J. to give him what else he had. Rosalie poured them each another cup of coffee and took away the other dishes. Zo lit a cigarette, listening to J.J.'s information, none of it very illuminating.

It was more than two weeks since the murder and Zo knew that each day that passed without any real leads made the odds higher that the crime would go unsolved. Unsolved crimes were always unacceptable to Zo but this one, in particular, distressed him and he found himself chafing against the possibility of defeat. He knew this had to do with the children, bereft and alone. Of course, even if he solved the murder, found the killer all by himself, it would change nothing for them. But for him it would restore a kind of balance and that's what his job really was, after all: equalizing good and evil. He was, in the end, a bookkeeper, forever tallying credits and debits, but instead of numbers he dealt in lives and if he didn't keep a check on himself he drifted into a feeling of omnipotence, reeking of sanctity, the hangman's noose dangling from his belt like an aberrant pocket watch.

"I'm gonna check out Swann in detail now. Fitzgerald's been tailin' him, but so far nothin'."

Zo returned his focus to J.J. "Anything turn up in his files?"

"Nah. But they only went back three years. After three years he destroys 'em."

"Why three years?"

"Beats me. They're nuts, these guys, ya know. You shoulda seen that Offenbach. Looney tunes."

"I think the answer's with Swann. He might not even know it now, but something tells me he holds the key."

"He's a creep." J.J. sloshed down the last of his coffee, wiped his mouth, and picked up his check. "So what about the house, Zo?"

"We decided to stay in the city."

"You're crazy. It's a great buy."

"Not if you don't want it. Look, J.J., we just don't like the idea. I mean, it's not for us. We're city types."

"It's all right now, but when you have kids of your own. . . ."

"How many times have I told you we're not going to. . . ."

"Yeah, yeah, I know." He waved a big hand in dismissal.

J.J. didn't believe Zo wasn't going to have children anymore than anyone else he told did. Angry, Zo slid out of the booth but, as usual, J.J. was oblivious to his partner's mood and slapped him on the back as they stood at the counter waiting to pay their checks.

"You'll change your mind. There's nothing like having kids."

Zo said nothing.

On the street in front of Joe's, they went their separate ways. Zo walked down West Fourth toward Sixth Avenue. He was still feeling annoyed and tried to shake it. What difference did it make what J.J. or anyone else thought about his not wanting children? The important thing was how he and Helen felt about it: resolute and firm. But for a moment the truth surfaced like a swimmer coming through the crest of a wave: Helen *wanted* children, deferred to him. A new wave swallowed the swimmer.

The day was growing increasingly humid and Zo's shirt stuck to him. He glanced at the sky. The sun was a pale yellow disk and in the distance there were dark streaks like long thin bruises. He hoped it wouldn't rain.

At Eighth Street he turned east. Had the killer run down Eighth after doing what she had to do? Had she fled down Fifth to the park? Turned east or west at Ninth? At Tenth? Why hadn't anyone seen? Was it just one of those things?

The Eighth Street Bookshop was on the corner of McDougal and Eighth streets and Zo stopped to look in the window. Near the front he spied a new Agatha Christie, *Witness for the Prosecution*; he'd have to buy that for Helen, who loved Christie.

Continuing down the street, he bent his head as if he were

ready to butt a challenger, his hat controlling his mutinous hair. At Fifth, he turned north.

He was glad Swann had moved his family back to their own apartment; lower Fifth was Zo's turf and he felt comfortable and in command.

The Swann apartment house was red brick, built in the twenties and in good repair. Boxwood framed the small plots of grass at either side of the entrance. The doorman, small and gray and looking ridiculous in his blue uniform, blazoned with gold braid, opened the door and eyed Zo suspiciously.

"Yessir, can I help ya?" His shoulders slanted downward as if the big gold epaulets were too heavy for him.

"The Swann apartment. Detective Campisi. I'm expected."

The little man seemed to snap to attention, going for the buzzer system immediately. Zo wondered if he was the replacement for the doorman who'd been on duty the day of the murder. He'd been fired, the poor bastard, as if he could have done something.

"You can go up, sir. Seven C."

On the seventh floor he rang the doorbell and in a moment Lolly, tall and regal, stood in the open doorway. "Come in." She stepped aside as he entered. The foyer was large, the floor tessellated in black and white tiles. Lolly ushered him into the living room, spacious and light and appointed with bright, soft, comfortable furniture.

"Dr. Swann has patients this morning. I'm gonna go with you."

"Don't you think that'll look funny?"

"Meaning what?" She straightened her shoulders although it seemed impossible that they could become any more square.

Zo realized she might be thinking it was a racial slur and perhaps, indirectly, it was; they would make an odd couple with the child. He chose his words carefully.

"I mean, we might draw attention to ourselves. We're both so tall and handsome."

She laughed, knowing exactly what he meant. "Well, Dr. Swann insists I go along. But I don't have to walk or sit with you. I could walk behind," she said pointedly.

"Or in front," he said, grinning.

She nodded once, acquiescing, but there was no obeisance in the gesture. "Sit down. I'll get Cristina. Claude's with his grandma." She started from the room, then stopped, a hand on one hip. "Speakin' of lookin' funny . . . the hat, the jacket, the tie. I'd leave 'em here if I was you."

"How come?"

"How come?" She gave a hoot of laughter. "How come is because with 'em you look about as much like a father or a uncle or whatever as I look like Snow White."

"Thanks for the tip, but I got to keep on the jacket. My gun," he said, patting his hip.

Lolly turned down her lips in distaste.

"Regulation," Zo said apologetically.

"You know best." But clearly she thought he didn't, and left to get Cristina.

Zo undid his tie and placed it on a table along with his hat, pulled at his jacket as if to make it more casual or father-like, whatever that meant, then sat in a square, plush orange chair and waited. The anxiety he was experiencing reminded him of the days when he dated, feeling like an oaf in the living room of some girl. But he was a grown man waiting for a six-year-old girl who had witnessed her mother's murder.

When Lolly returned with Cristina, Zo leaped to his feet, as if, indeed, his date had at last entered. "Hello, Cristina."

"Hi," she said shyly. Her skin was pale, accentuating the deep brown of her eyes. She wore blue shorts and a lime green ruffled top, the neck low and scooped, her arms bare. Small leather sandals adorned her feet.

Jesus, thought Zo. This is a nightmare. He didn't have a clue as to how to begin.

Lolly, taking pity on him, came to the rescue. "Cristina's Daddy explained what we're doin'."

"Oh. Good. I guess we might as well go."

At the door, Cristina slipped her small hand into Zo's. He was shocked at first, receiving a jolt that ran the length of his arm, then almost at once he settled into the odd comfort, reassurance, it gave him. Then he returned to protector, his confidence solid, a modern paladin.

In the park, Lolly sat across from them, knitting. Zo and Cristina talked, their conversation desultory, but he felt he was getting to know her. Although he wasn't acquainted with many children, he instinctively knew she was special: bright, intuitive, sweet.

"Zo?" she said. "I need to ask you something."

"Anything."

"I heard these two ladies talking about my mommy and they said it was Mommy's fault she got killed. That she brought it on herself."

He could have wept. Blaming victims, particularly women, for their own murders, wasn't new. But it was unfair and absurd and, he'd come to believe, a way for the onlookers to remain aloof, innocent and safe.

"Honey," he said, touching her lightly on the knee, "pay no attention to stuff like that. People say all kinds of things that don't make sense. Your mommy had nothing to do with . . . it . . . her death. It's nonsense what you heard."

She looked up at him, the eyes blinking in the sun. "Do you think I could play in the circle?"

"You understand what I just told you?"

"Yup."

He wasn't convinced, but decided not to belabor the point. "Sure, you can play, honey. But keep your eyes open, huh?"

"Okay," she answered distractedly as she left the bench, but she knew what he meant: watch for the lady in the big hat who winked.

Zo followed her to the circle and sat on the cement lip. It wouldn't be safe to allow Cristina to play too far from him. The Winking Woman, as they'd come to call her, could appear out of nowhere and unless he was close there could be disaster.

"Excuse me," a voice said.

He looked into the freckled face of a woman. She seemed familiar.

"You're a cop, aren't you?" she asked. She had a narrow nose and a sharp mouth.

Feeling like a fool, he said: "Why do you ask?"

"I was a friend of Danielle's."

Now he remembered. He'd seen her at the funeral. Perhaps someone there had told her who he was. He felt better.

"What can I do for you?"

"Look, I think Martin did it," she said bluntly.

"What's your name?" He turned back to Cristina, needing to keep an eye on her.

"What difference does that make?" she asked.

"None. I just thought. . . ."

"Look, I don't want to get involved. My husband would kill me if he thought I was talking to you."

107

He glanced at her, taking in two huge, pale green eyes, then looked back at the child. "Why do you say Martin Swann did it?"

"He was having an affair."

Zo felt something click and surge inside. Was this it? Was this the break they'd been waiting for? If it was true, it would establish a motive.

"How do you know?"

"Look, I don't want to get involved."

"You *are* involved. But you have nothing to worry about. You have information, so give."

"I don't want to go to court or anything. My husband's going to kill me."

Zo ignored the irony of the statement. "I won't tell him. How do you know about Swann's affair?" His eyes were on Cristina again.

"My husband. He works in the same place *she* does. He heard her telling another secretary."

He couldn't believe his good luck. "What's her name?"

"Lynn Cunningham."

"Are you suggesting this woman's the killer?"

"Arthur, that's my husband, says it's impossible. But the description, well, it could fit."

Sweat ran down Zo's back, his excitement blending with the heat. "How long have you been a friend of hers?"

"Danielle? Years. We're park friends, or we were," she said sadly. "We didn't socialize. I never even met *him*. But even so, I didn't like him."

"Did she know he was having an affair?" He hoped not.

There was no answer.

Zo turned and saw that the woman was gone. Then he spotted her titian hair as she ran from the park. It didn't matter. If he needed her, he could find her; she'd given him plenty of clues to her identity. He called to Cristina. At last he had something concrete. Lynn Cunningham. Jesus. Maybe by nightfall the damn case would be solved. He felt elated.

Cristina came to him and took his hand. His elation vanished. If the case were solved he'd never see this kid again, never feel her silky hand in his. Well, maybe that was best. Too much exposure to this child might weaken his resolve.

"Where we going, Zo?" she asked.

"Home," he answered, and wished that it were true.

SIX

The air in the library was suffocating. It was six thirty in the evening and the thermometer hovered at eighty-five degrees. Guy clawed at the knot of his striped, silk tie. The lack of air-conditioning was part of his father's stubborn refusal to accept technical home advancements. As far as Guy was concerned, August, not April, was the cruelest month.

Pierre, who was now two minutes late, had requested an interview with him and he hadn't a clue as to the topic. Since Danielle's murder, nothing was predictable. Guy was beginning to realize that you could count on, plan, nothing. The wonderful, free summer he'd looked forward to had turned into a joyless, depressing interval. But there were only fifteen more days left. Even though some of the excitement of going to Harvard had been diminished by the tragedy, leaving home and parents was really all he lived for. His mother, it seemed, was beyond comfort, and his father, remote. Not that Guy blamed them; it was understandable that they'd drifted into regions of their own. He, too, had become isolated. For him, at a time like this, the only person who might have consoled him was Danielle.

And then there was Susan. The two events, Susan's dropping him because of his lack of maturity and Danielle's death, had a way of fusing in his mind, forming one reality. But when he separated them, like a beachcomber sorting through flotsam and jetsam, he found that his reaction to Susan's rejection was also one of grief: two deaths instead of one. Guy had been unable to talk to anyone about it. Although they'd never been close, he had toyed with the idea of confiding in Martin. But before he'd thought it through, his brother-in-law's scandalous affair had surfaced, making that impossible.

In the Dudevant household, Martin had become a pariah. Both parents damned the man and Guy shared their view: Martin had cheated on his sister and he loathed him for it. When the picture of Lynn Cunningham appeared in the paper, Guy was astonished. How could Martin have had an affair with *her*? Danielle had been beautiful and this Cunningham woman was very plain. And it wasn't as if Danielle had been some sort of harridan or something; she was kind and gentle and . . . oh, Lord, he thought, I've got to stop this or I'll start to cry.

Pierre arrived, his usual shiny skin lusterless, as if he'd been powdered. "So sorry to be late." He offered no explanation. "Would you care for a drink?"

Guy declined. Was his father drinking more since Danielle's death, or was it his imagination? When Pierre's martini was prepared, they sat facing each other in the blue velvet chairs.

"I suppose you know why I wish to speak with you," Pierre said, licking a drop of liquor from his upper lip.

"No, I don't know, Papa."

Pierre took another sip of his drink, then placed it on the marble-topped table next to him. "It is your maman."

"What's wrong with Maman?"

"Do you not understand her suffering?" he asked, shocked.

"Oh, sure. I mean, I thought you meant something else."

"What else? The murder of her daughter is not enough?"

The terror in Guy's stomach felt as if a tiny ratlike animal were trying to chew its way out. "Please, Papa, I only meant. . . ."

"Do not interrupt. I have something of a serious nature to tell you."

"Yes, Papa." He prayed tears wouldn't fill his eyes.

"All your maman has left is us. Her devoted son and her devoted and adoring husband. She has lost her son-in-law as well as her daughter. And there is the utmost possibility that in a short while her grandchildren may be lost to her as well. There is no telling what Martin Swann might do. Do you comprehend this?"

"Yes, Papa." Yes and no, he'd decided, were his only safe responses.

"*Bien.* Maman needs you here at home."

"Yes, Papa."

"You understand this?"

He couldn't mean. . . . "I . . . I'm not sure."

"I have canceled your admission to Harvard and enrolled you at Columbia."

"But you can't," Guy blurted.

"I beg your pardon?"

"Papa, please. Harvard. No." Guy's mind spiraled downward as if his brain was falling in on itself and capacity for understanding was lost to him.

"It is all arranged. Fortunately, I have friends at Columbia or it would have been too late. Your maman needs you here at home this year. You are an only child now. Perhaps next year you will be able to transfer to Harvard. We will see."

There was nothing to say, no argument to raise. His father was paying for his education and the choice of where Guy went was, in the end, his. All arranged.

"I'll live here at home?" he queried softly.

"But of course. That is the whole point."

Guy had felt anger for his father on many occasions in his eighteen years, but never anything approaching what he was harboring now, his resentment as palpable as if it had a shape and a color.

Finishing his drink, Pierre placed the glass back on the table. "I know you must be disappointed, but that is part of life. You will survive this setback, but I am not sure your maman would survive the loss of you too."

"But I wouldn't be——"

"It is settled, Guy."

A long silence ensued, the boy and man immobile, a deadly quiescence, like a third person, present in the room. Pierre stared at a crease in his trouser leg; Guy scrutinized his feet. Minutes passed, then Guy lifted his head and, with his eyes, bridged the gap between him and his father. Dr. Dudevant, as if receiving a signal, raised his gaze to meet his son's.

"It's not fair, Papa," Guy said, almost inaudibly.

"I did not say it was fair," he responded. "Where is it written that life is fair or just? The sooner you understand this, the better you will make your way in this life." He touched the hairs of his small mustache, patting them into place as if they were wildly askew. "Was it fair or just that Danielle was murdered?"

Guy's head slumped in answer.

"Is it fair that. . . ."

There was a soft tap on the library door.

"Yes?"

Wallace peered between the double doors. "Dinner is served."

"Thank you, Wallace. Come along, Guy."

Rising as if he were a robot, Guy fell into step behind his father. They traversed the long hall to the dining room where Amelia, thinner now than in June by twenty pounds, was already seated at the table.

"Good evening, *ma petite souris*," Pierre said, and kissed her sagging cheek.

Amelia did not respond.

Guy kissed her as well.

She stared at her plate.

Pierre seated himself at the head of the table and Guy across from his mother. Wallace began to serve. Tonight's meal began with a cream of sorrel soup.

"Ah, *très bien*, Wallace, *très bien*," Pierre complimented.

"Thank you, Doctor." Wallace stalled, waiting for Amelia's assessment, but her mistress failed even to raise her spoon. Each evening along with the meal, Wallace, a superb cook, brought new hope with her into the dining room; inevitably, she had to content herself with the doctor's praises, for Mrs. Dudevant barely ate and never commented any more.

When Wallace left the room, Amelia said: "If only we'd insisted Danielle live in a more sensible area. We knew. Oh, yes. We warned her. Clearly we were not assiduous enough. We failed our child."

Inside, Guy screamed, then prayed, as he did at each meal, for control. This was how it always went. She began with "If only we" and moved gradually into "*If only you*," blaming Pierre.

"Now, now, *ma chérie*."

Guy felt as if he were in an insane asylum. Nothing seemed real to him. No one even looked the way he thought they should. Balance was a thing of the past. Estrangement and isolation, constant.

". . . and *you* brought Martin Swann into this house," Amelia was saying. "If she'd never married him. . . ."

No exit flashed through Guy's mind. At least a year of witnessing violation upon violation. Would he really survive? A feeling of rightness with the world was unavailable to him now, as if he hung by the tips of his fingers from an unseen ledge.

The soup plates were cleared and eventually the table was adorned with new and more brilliant creations: chicken broiled with mustard, herbs, and bread crumbs; green beans *gratiné;* cucumbers *à la Grecque.*

None of it appealed to Guy but, unlike his mother, he would eat.

". . . why did you allow her to marry the adulterer? Why did you. . . ."

Guy waited for the inevitable moment when Pierre would throw down his napkin and storm out of the room. A short reprieve from Amelia's diatribes would follow; then, slowly, she would turn her gaze on Guy. And although blame was not hurled his way, the litany of failures and *if onlys* would continue.

For the next year this hapless triangle was doomed to life under the same mantle. After all, they were his parents, and he supposed he owed them something. Attending Columbia and living at home for a year, he decided, was his punishment for surviving. He would, somehow, endure.

"*Mon Dieu,*" Pierre shouted, slinging down his napkin and overturning his chair. "Enough, enough, I have had enough."

Amelia raised her irreparably damaged eyes. She looked, to Guy, so old and brittle that when she moved he imagined he heard a crackling sound. Despite his anger and disappointment, to view his mother this way shredded his heart.

"Go on, Maman," he encouraged gently.

"Perhaps," Amelia said, "if on that day I'd invited Danielle here. Perhaps, if she had. . . ."

One year, he thought, a long, long time. But when it was over, no matter what the situation at home, he would have to get out. His sanity was at stake: perhaps his life.

Parting the lace curtains, Hedy watched Father Frank patiently, slowly, usher her father down the front walk. Once a week the priest took George Somerville for what he called "a little outing." It was not clear what they did on these occasions, but when they returned Hedy always noticed the smell of alcohol on her father's breath. She wondered if they drove up to the Orange mountains, perhaps to Washington Rock, parked, and passed a flask back and forth between them. Or did they go to some iniquitous bar, hiding themselves away in a back room in order to swill down drink after drink? She wouldn't ask her father how he and Father Frank spent the three or four hours each week; to do so might encourage an intimacy she would detest. The important thing about these excursions was that they took place: Hedy lived for them. It was the only time she was in her house alone.

Father Frank propped George against the back of the black Buick while he opened the passenger door. Then, pushing and pulling, he managed to get the crippled body into the front seat. George lifted his good right leg inside and Father Frank closed the door with crisp attendance as if he'd successfully completed the packaging of a fragile cargo. From the window, Hedy could see that the man's florid face was even more blowzy than usual, his efforts with her father causing his aging heart to pump harder and faster, shooting blood into the wormy veins that crossed his face so near the surface of his skin. She continued to watch as the priest withdrew a large white handkerchief from the pocket of his skirt and wiped his shiny brow, returned it to its nesting place, then made his way around the front end of the sleek car, trailing a flat hand across the metal hood. A moment before his jowly face disappeared below the horizon of the roof, he waved a hand at Hedy, knowing she would be watching. The gesture made her hiss between clenched teeth and she dropped the curtain, continuing to peer through its gossamer fabric until the car was gone.

Finally and truly alone, Hedy luxuriated in the feeling of space and air surrounding her even though the living room, where she stood, was dense with massive pieces of mahogany furniture. To be the sole person in the house gave her the illusion of lightness, freedom, independence, and not even the huge credenza or the towering pot-bellied curio cabinet could dwarf her sense of liberty.

In the kitchen she poured herself a cup of coffee and sat at the table. After the ritualistic three times stirring and tapping of the spoon, making the coffee safe, Hedy drank. Tomorrow was the last day of September and this was the first time in three weeks she'd had any sense of relaxation; even on the other occasions of her father's absence she'd been unable to unbend from her constant vigilance. Her body had felt coiled, ready to spring at the slightest unfamiliar sound; her brain had been abraded by the daily news reports.

She had known immediately that the gun which had killed a twenty-six-year-old policeman had been the gun she'd used to kill Danielle Swann. The boy who'd committed the murder stated he'd found the gun near the Path tracks at the Hoboken exit. Surely there wouldn't have been more than one gun tossed or lost in that spot. It was, she had thought, reading the newspaper, only a matter of time until the knock sounded on her door. What a fool she'd been. If she'd been wise enough that day to have taken the ferry and thrown the gun into the water, this could never have happened. It did not occur to her that if she had, a man might still be alive. She thought only of herself and how soon they would catch her.

But yesterday, relief had finally come. The paper revealed that the boy had filed off the serial number of the gun, not realizing that a serial number could lead only to the purchaser. Now there was no way to trace the gun, which the ballistics department said was the weapon used in the Danielle Swann murder. Hedy was free again.

The coffee, she decided, was particularly good today. She twisted her diamond ring around and around on her finger and thought of her mother when she had been beautiful: tall, thin, and rosy-cheeked. She remembered her sitting at this table, sipping coffee, a pinky extended.

"Never forget who you are, darling girl, no matter what your father says. He's jealous because his heritage holds nothing special. We, you and I, are descended from royalty and you mustn't ever let that float from your mind." Her eyes, unlike Hedy's, were definite, vivid, their hue like the deepest blue in a Wedgewood plate.

"Isn't Ralphie like us?" the small child asked. He had not become her tormentor yet and she was more than willing to align herself with big brother.

Mary Somerville's mouth moved into a pursed position as if she was readying herself for a kiss, then drifted open as she spoke: "Yes, of course he is, but he's male."

"Oh," little Hedy said. But she didn't understand.

Mary held out her right hand, flattening it against the white enamel tabletop, the long thin fingers splayed; she lifted only her ring finger, up and down, up and down, the diamond glinting. Hedy was mesmerized by the moving finger, as if it had a life of its own, a little person willing to impart the wisdom of a lifetime.

"Your great-grandmother was given this ring by a member of the royal family. It will keep you from the poorhouse, no matter what happens."

Hedy wasn't sure who the royal family were or what the poorhouse was. But in the next four years, before her mother died, the tale was told so often and refuted so noisily by her father, that she came to understand every nuance as if it were a bedtime story read each night.

"When I am dead and gone," Mary Somerville intoned, "this ring will be yours and you'll pass it on to your daughter unless fate forces you to sell it." She took Hedy's little hand and ran the small pink fingers over the hexagon stone, the silver claw setting. "Never, never part with it, Hedy, unless your destiny brings you to a place where food and shelter are yours only if you sell the ring. Do you understand?"

"Yes, Ma."

And she did. Living in her father's house, supported by her brother, she'd had no need to sell the ring. It had occurred to her, however, that it might be a way out: she could take the money she gained from the ring and go to California where she'd buy a house and live on the beach. But when she thought it through, saw herself boarding the train and so forth, panic forced her to abandon the idea. Any plan to leave, as sparkling as it might be at its inception, eventually tarnished, finally turning black. The truth was, it was becoming more and more frightening out there for Hedy; she left her house as seldom as possible, going only to the grocery store and back. She knew, of course, that another trip to New York would be required when the time was right, and she hoped she would be able to make it without too much inner fuss.

Hedy drained the last of her coffee. There was no question in her mind that when she had her child it would be a girl. Mary had told her just the night before that this was so and Mary never lied to her. She wondered what she'd name her. Mary? No. There could be only one Mary in the house; it would be entirely too confusing. Danielle? She smiled. It might be fitting, and then again it might give someone a suspicious idea. Lucy? Oh, no. Now why had she thought of her?

Annoyed, she climbed the stairs and entered the bathroom, which had always been her sanctuary, the one room in the house with a lock on the door. It was not a particularly spacious room, but it gave Hedy a sense of order. The large white tiles on the lower half of the walls had a luster to them she experienced as calming; the floor was tiled also, but with small white octagons and in some places the grout had been disturbed; tiny indentations and missing pieces gave testimony to this. It had been Hedy who, in younger days, had lain on the floor and with a nail file had chipped away at the thin coarse mortar. She'd spent hour after hour this way, as if it were her life's work, and in a way she missed this activity which in the past had filled her with a strange sense of accomplishment.

She stared at herself in the mirror, the fluted light above casting a bluish glare, deepening shadow, emphasizing protuberances, elongating planes. Unable to look any longer, she opened the medicine cabinet and removed a tube of Preparation H. She closed the cabinet, unscrewed the black cap, squeezed the shiny sand-yellow salve into her hand, and began applying it to her face. It had occurred to Hedy some time ago that this particular ointment would be good for keeping the skin tight, thereby avoiding dreaded wrinkles and creeping creases of age and, although she was only twenty-eight, it was never too soon to ward off, or prepare for, what was coming. She'd treated herself with this agent for years. It had come into the Somerville household during Lucy's reign and been used, presumably, as intended: to treat hemorrhoids. Nevertheless, it had made perfect sense to Hedy that it would do as well on the face and so far it seemed to be working, as she hadn't a line in her peaches and cream complexion. This beauty treatment was one thing for which she could thank Lucy.

As always, when thoughts of her dead stepmother entered her conscious mind, Hedy's winking eye became riotous and her hyperventilation erupted. She hated thinking of Lucy and even though there were many reminders around the house, such as the toothbrush cozies she'd made (little faces on white felt which were now gray and nubby), she was almost always able to forget they were Lucy-fashioned by the simple process of denial. Even the kitchen ceiling still harbored the Lucy-mark. One afternoon the woman had tried to paint clouds on the ceiling; the end result was a sky blue background with streaks and curls of white bearing no resemblance to clouds. But George had thought it adorable, as he did everything his new wife produced. Surely, had she lived, he would have adored the baby she carried at the time of her death.

More than once Hedy had begged to repaint, but her father remained steadfast in preserving this homage to Lucy. So Hedy no longer raised her eyes upward in that room. She had her ways, her tricks, to avoid the memory of Lucy Allen Somerville, but once in a while, like today, the image of the woman sneaked in, flooding her brain with thoughts she'd rather avoid.

After capping the blue and white tube and returning it to the back of the cabinet, she washed and dried her hands, and viewed her face in the mirror. The oily sheen seemed to emphasize the scope of her pouchy cheeks as if she had stuffed them with balls of cotton. More and more, she thought, she looked like a chipmunk.

In her bedroom she sat, eyes closed, head back against her chair, unable to think of anyone but Lucy.

Her father had introduced the woman into the household a year after Mary died, but he hadn't married her for another year, when Hedy was twelve.

The first thing Hedy noticed (and hated) about Lucy Allen was that her hair and face, both red, clashed. Her lips were full and brightly colored still another red. She wore wire-rimmed glasses, but instead of producing a prim expression they made her appear surprised. She was a small woman, no bigger than Hedy, who had reached her full height by that time, and her build was slight and wiry. Lucy wore her red hair coiled in two braids at the sides of her head, covering the tops of her ears. It was a long time before Hedy could look at her.

When Lucy and George had been married six months, and after Lucy had tried every imaginable ploy to gain the child's approval and been rejected, Hedy decided to seek refuge from Ralph's advances by telling her stepmother. Mary said it would never work, but she disregarded her mother's warning and went ahead. She might as well try to get something out of this intruder, Hedy thought.

It was a Saturday morning in November and her father and brother were out; Lucy was in her bedroom when Hedy knocked on the door.

Invited in, Hedy pushed open the door to find Lucy tucking in the sheet, making a hospital corner. She was wearing one of her usual cotton print dresses, topped by a royal blue cardigan. Hedy had observed that Lucy always wore one of three cardigans, no matter what the weather; she had never seen her stepmother's bare arms and wondered if there was something wrong with them.

"Yes, dear?" Lucy said, straightening up.

"Could I talk with you a minute?"

Behind her glasses, Lucy's eyes brightened as if lit by tiny inner bulbs. "Of course, dear. Sit down." She gestured toward a chintz-covered chair and, leaving the bed unfinished, she perched on her vanity bench.

Sitting there, staring at Lucy, whose hands were folded in her lap like some pious receiver waiting for her confession, Hedy was already sorry she'd begun and tried desperately to think of a way out: some other problem to reveal, perhaps, but she could think of none.

"Cat got your tongue?" Lucy asked, giving a good imitation of a kindergarten teacher.

"It's Ralph." She blurted it out.

"Your darling brother?"

To Hedy, this response bordered on betrayal. How could she possibly go on?

Lucy helped. "Is something wrong with the sweet boy?"

Hedy thought she might vomit. A kind of perversity took over and although originally she had wanted help for herself, she now wished only to crucify Ralph. She was uncertain whether the exposure of his base nature or the puncturing of Lucy's idea of him was more important; either way, she could hardly wait to see that face turn an even deeper red.

"Ralph makes me do sex things with him," she stated with no further ado.

As if something had pinched Lucy through the vanity seat, she popped up, her face coloring, complying with Hedy's wishes.

"What's that?" she squeaked.

Hedy controlled the smile dancing dangerously at the corners of her mouth. "Dirty things. He makes me do all these dirty things with him. He creeps into my room and. . . ."

"Stop," Lucy demanded, holding up her palm like a traffic policeman.

Hedy, warming to her subject, barreled on: "When no one's home, Ralph comes into my room and makes me take off. . . ."

Clapping both hands over her ears and braids, Lucy said: "You wicked, wicked girl. How can you say these things about that poor dear boy? I demand that you stop at once."

Hedy stopped. Not because this interloper asked her to, but because she was stunned. It had never dawned on her that Lucy would take this attitude. She had imagined words of solace sliding from the red lips, sticky solicitousness oozing everywhere, and then her father banishing Ralph forever. It had, she saw now, been an illusory hope.

"I'm not going to tell your father of your wickedness toward your brother, but I never, never want to hear such filth again. Do you understand?"

What she understood was that Lucy was her arch enemy and that she had to make the witch listen whether she liked it or not. "He puts his pee-pee in my mouth," she said, staring into the blinking eyes.

Lucy shrieked as if she'd been stabbed and ran for the door. Hedy followed her into the hall and they stood at the top of the stairs.

"I think you're possessed," hissed Lucy, her entire body shaking. "I demand that you stop this talk at once."

"He puts his fingers inside my privates."

Lucy slapped her across the face, knocking off Hedy's glasses. And Hedy's vision blurred, as did her memory. Until she found her glasses a few feet away on the green carpet, vision and memory remained out of focus, fuzzy and runny like a specimen on a chemist's slide. When she hooked the glasses over her ears, she was amazed to see she was alone in the hall. And then she heard a faint sound from below.

Lying at the bottom of the stairs was Lucy, her body twisted. Slowly, Hedy descended. When she reached the woman, she bent over and found her breathing shallow and spare. The red mouth tried to speak but succeeded only in twitching. Her eyes, glassless, stared into Hedy's, and clearly begged for help. Hedy stared back. And then Lucy's left eye closed, but the right one remained at half mast. Hedy knew she was dead.

"Good-bye," she said, and left the house to play.

Now that the Lucy-recall was out of the way, Hedy could enjoy the rest of her remaining time alone. She would spend it as she had since Danielle Swann's death: planning everything about her girlbaby's life. First a name. Kathleen? Linda? Nancy? Carol? Beth? Nothing was right, but there was plenty of time. One year to be exact. Nothing would stand in her way.

In the fall of 1956, she would give birth to her baby girl. And if it somehow turned out to be a boy, she would kill it.

Amelia stared at the morning mail on the hall table. Her hands trembled slightly as a sense of disquietude, distinct and pervasive, haunted her skin. When was it that she had looked forward to mail? It seemed a long time ago. Before. Everything had been reduced to Before and After. With quivering fingers, she lifted the mail from the table.

In the dining room she sat down and with her foot pressed the buzzer for Brenda, the new maid. Wallace had left at the beginning of September, unable to withstand the notoriety and desperately and stupidly afraid for her life. Amelia had tried hard to understand Wallace's defection but, finally, she felt betrayed, abandoned.

Brenda materialized, bearing coffee and half a grapefruit, Amelia's quotidian breakfast.

"Thank you, Brenda." She looked up into the young woman's round, plump face, her dome-shaped forehead a shiny tan.

"Anything else?" Brenda asked in her flutey voice.

The exchange was ritualistic, but what could have been an annoyance Amelia found comforting; there was a kind of security in the sameness each day as though if her morning began with these identical questions and answers, the rest of the day must have a natural rhythm, unfettered by surprise.

"No, thank you, Brenda," she said speaking her part. "This is all I'll have today."

"Yes, Madam."

Alone, Amelia glanced down at the mail lying next to her coffee cup. It was almost four months since Danielle had been murdered and still the letters came. Slowly, she sorted the envelopes: bills, advertisements, known sources, strangers. Strangers went into two categories: sane and insane. Pierre had urged her not to read any mail from strangers even if it appeared sane, because occasionally she was fooled. When the envelopes were handwritten (especially in pencil), sprawling or crimped, she had come to know they were the work of lunatics and threw them away. At first, in her innocence, she'd opened them all and been assaulted by a barrage of filth and maniacal accusations. They blamed Danielle for her own death, calling her whore, harlot, hooker, bitch, hag, fury, harpy, hellcat, and other appellations, some of which Amelia had never heard before. Some letters blamed her, as if at Danielle's age Amelia should have been a better mother. And that, playing into her hands, exacerbated the guilt she already endured. The writers also blamed Pierre, accusing him of incest, communism, sorcery. It might have been funny, but it wasn't. Even considering the sources, it hurt. There was a frightening reality to these people and their hatred: some called for more tragedy, others wished her death.

But there were kind strangers, too. She couldn't imagine expressing sympathy to a stranger, yet she found consolation in some of these missives.

She stared at the different piles she'd arranged. There were four obviously insane epistles today and two normal-looking ones. She tore the lunatic letters in half, a feeling of accomplishment infusing her. It was a fitting end to the ravings of sick and evil people.

Looking at the other two letters, she wondered if she should heed Pierre's warnings. At best they would be honest expressions of sympathy or even letters from parents who'd lived through the same experience. At worst, they might contain more scathing accusations. And there was a third category: prose filled with the most shameless treacle; these were almost the worst, causing her to squirm in embarrassment. Perhaps, in the end, they belonged to the lunatic fringe. But the oddest thing, to her, was that in almost all the letters which were meant to comfort, strangers and friends alike wrote about Danielle's *senseless murder* or *senseless death* as though there were *sensible* ones: how, she wondered, could there be sensible murders or deaths? Finally, she decided, it was simply a thoughtless expression meant well. But she was tired of well-meaning people saying the very thing that tore her in two or jolted her from a safe plateau she'd taken days and weeks to achieve. Her instinct was to withdraw and her pervading feeling one of loneliness; her only contact: mail. A full circle of hell.

Mechanically, she lifted her sterling silver grapefruit spoon and drove the tip into the flesh of the fruit, traced the line of the wedge until it was freed from the membrane, and raised it to her lips. She knew she had to take in some nourishment, provide the upkeep of her body like the superintendent of a defective machine. So, joylessly, she ate.

She reached over to open one of the sane-looking letters but stopped as Guy came into the room and, following him, her newest and youngest Persian, Rochelle; she now had five cats to comfort her.

"Morning, Maman," Guy said, and kissed her lightly on the forehead.

"Good morning," she answered, staring at Rochelle.

Guy stood near his mother, his violet eyes gloomy. "Would you ring, please?"

"*Mais, oui.*"

His cheeks jumped as he ground his teeth together.

Brenda arrived with his coffee, poured from a silver pot, and started to leave.

"Can't we just have the pot here?" he asked.

Amelia signaled for Brenda to leave the pot. She stroked the cat and looked at her son. He was very handsome, she thought, and really such a good boy. It had been magnificent for him to decide to stay at home this year with her; his sacrifice, she knew, had cost him a great deal. And he was a comfort even if she didn't see him all that often.

"How's school?"

"Fine."

"It's always fine if one applies oneself," she said.

Guy grunted.

"If one would eat more breakfast, one might smile more."

"What one would that be?"

"Don't be fresh, dear. Oh, just look," she said, isolating a mat on Rochelle's gray coat. "This is very bad. Could you hold her while I——"

"I don't have time. I'm sorry. I have a nine-thirty class." He stood, swallowing the last of his coffee. "See you later, Maman."

"*Adieu.*"

"Good-bye," he said pointedly.

"It's not that I loved her more," she whispered to Rochelle when Guy was gone, "but a daughter . . . you know."

Rochelle, annoyed with the fingering of her mat, jumped from Amelia's lap. It was probably strange, Amelia thought, that she felt closer to Danielle than Guy. Guy was of her own flesh and blood and Danielle had been adopted, a secret until she'd found her birth certificate when she was thirteen. Danielle had chosen to continue the subterfuge, telling no one.

Perhaps Amelia's special feeling for Danielle was because she had chosen her in a sense and Guy had come as a shock, at forty, after she'd been told she would never have children. Oddly, the maternal feelings she'd had for Danielle had been much stronger. Was it age? Was it because of the child's sex? Most women she knew were desperate for sons and, having them, were indulgent, treating them in a sacrosanct manner. But although Amelia loved Guy, he had never aroused the deep set of feelings she had experienced for Danielle.

And now her baby girl had been stolen from her as surely as if an eagle had plucked her from a nest. The image made Amelia shudder. She set down her coffee cup; the Aynsley resonated as it contacted the white saucer and she imagined it chipping as her heart was chipped. Nothing would ever be the same. Especially not her marriage, and she did not understand why. They had been so close, she and Pierre, but since Danielle's death it had all turned sour. There was no comforting each other, as she would have presumed; alone, if they spoke at all, it was to attack, accuse: little things, inadequacies and misdemeanors of married life over the years; a hauling out of soiled linen. She no longer knew who she really was and certainly had no idea who Pierre was: she might as well be living with a stranger. Just as her daughter had been purloined, so had her husband. Only her son was present. And sadly, strangely, he left her untouched.

With an air of defeat, Amelia rose from the table, unopened letter in her hand, and headed toward the library where she had set up a large dollhouse outfitted with miniature furniture and peopled by tiny carved figures. There was a mother, a father, a son, and a daughter. She moved them around within the house and told herself stories about their lives.

This was her new reality and here she was happy, content, fulfilled.

It was definite now: they had solved the mystery of United Airlines flight 629. John Gilbert Graham had blown up an entire plane to kill his mother. Pierre let the paper fall to his knees, where it covered his legs like a laprobe. How much hate would it take to rationalize the slaughter of forty-three innocent people in order to annihilate one? The authorities had focused on money as a motive, but it was clear now that the son loathed the mother, never forgiving her for neglecting him as a child. How had Mrs. Daisy King neglected her son? Had she denied him food, clothing, shelter? Or simply love? *Simply* love? Was love ever simple?

He lit a cigarette and blew a wreath of smoke above his head. If anyone understood neglect, he did, at least from the time of his brother's death until his mother died when he was twenty. But never had Pierre had a negative thought about his mother; one simply did not think that way. Mothers were cherished, revered, venerated. Or at least that was how it had been in his day, with Europeans. America was a new and vulgar country and the people were often the same. Take this Graham person, for instance: it was a vulgar act, the blowing to smithereens of forty-four people. A European, if he had the need to murder a family member, would employ a nice quick poison, keeping the act confined and neat. Pierre shifted in the chair, the paper falling to the floor. What was he thinking? Was he going mad to entertain such gruesome thoughts? But since Danielle's murder, death of a violent nature had become diminished somehow as if the edges of atrocity had frayed. The loss of his daughter, his child, had brutalized him in such a way that he was immune to pain. His heart, although it still pumped blood through his aging arteries, was, for purposes of love, finished.

And he had become like Mrs. Daisy King, culpable; neglecting his son, his wife. Would they blow him to smithereens somehow? Would Guy come into the library one day, swinging a shotgun, and blast his father's brains from his head? "My Papa neglected me," Guy would cry across the pages of newspapers. But no one cared about a father's dereliction, did they? It was *The Mother*. And no one cared much about Papa losing his baby girl. It was *The Maman*. Almost all the sympathy which flooded their house had been directed toward Amelia. Not that he begrudged his beloved wife solace or the beneficial balm of condolence, but if neglect was the subject of the hour, then surely he qualified. Friends and family had been ruthless in their disregard of him. It was as though they believed he hadn't really loved, or was not cognizant of death and loss because of his profession. Or was it the elementary fact of his being male which made them derelict? He was a man and, therefore, strong, superior, omnipotent perhaps? Devoid of needs, in any case. A straightforward *You have my sympathy* sufficed, they thought. But, it wasn't enough; not nearly enough. Then what? What would have comforted him, consoled? Understanding? Acknowledgment of pain? They ignored him, friends and family, and he wanted to blow them to smithereens . . . were there more than forty-four?

Pierre reached for the *Times* and carefully folded it back into its original shape, rose from his chair, and placed it on a shelf with the papers of other days. He was astonished by his feeling of outrage; how could a dead man feel such anger? Perhaps there was some life left in him yet. He glanced around his office where he'd spent the last twenty-five years of his career and wondered how much longer he'd have this refuge, his home away from home? It was unlike any of the other doctors' offices in the hospital, eschewing the usual austere appearance of the professional. He'd early on made it into a comfortable room. Lately he'd spent more and more time here, avoiding home, avoiding Amelia.

Guilt was his constant companion now. He should, he felt, be at home with his wife, encouraging her, but when they were together they hardly spoke and if they did, they fought. Something they'd barely done in all their years of marriage. Standing at the window he looked out on the bleak November day and wondered why he and Amelia could not help each other. Had their intimacy been an illusion? Certainly he'd thought of speaking to her about their drift, but he never could. At each approach it suddenly seemed infelicitous and he succumbed to silence. Perhaps, if the murderer was caught and punished, then he'd have Amelia again.

He wandered over to his desk, sat in the hard wood chair, his eyes resting on the silver-framed picture of Danielle, Cristina, and Claude. A tortured sound escaped his lips. So beautiful. It was impossible to think she was dead, gone forever, his darling girl. Cristina was obviously going to look like her mother and her *real* grandmother.

Her name was Anna Wilson, and she'd been raped. Where was she now? It had been thirty-four years, she'd be fifty-four. Had she read of Danielle's murder? But that wouldn't tell her anything; he'd only promised her to place the child in a good home. From the very first second of that black-haired baby's entry into the world, he'd known she was going to be his.

Something new had transpired at delivery. With other babies he'd had no special feeling other than relief that they were healthy, normal, all toes and fingers intact; with Danielle, the instant he saw her a small sun spilled warm rays throughout his body. All these years later he could remember that time in crystallized detail. *She's mine,* he'd said to himself, gazing at the tiny, rumpled body. *This child is mine.* It had not occurred to him a moment sooner.

In those days it was easy to arrange it all: doctors and nurses turned deaf ears and blind eyes to the situation. Two weeks after the baby was born, he'd brought her home to Amelia and placed her in her arms. Both of them had cried so long and loud the baby finally joined them and their tears had turned to laughter.

Pierre could see that image as clearly as if it had happened that morning. And now that baby, that little girl, teenager, young woman, woman was dead. Somehow he had to put it right. He could not bring her back, he knew, but why did he have to lose his wife as well?

Looking at his watch, Pierre saw that it was almost time. They would arrive soon. Who first? And would Emma Stevenson's findings mean anything at all to Detective Campisi, or would he pooh-pooh them as so much nonsense? The man had agreed to meet the psychic, so he could not be completely cynical. Pierre started at the knock at his door. His nerves, he thought, were rotting.

Campisi entered, his unkempt hair angling out from his head, his face kind, smile sympathetic. Pierre liked him and had from the beginning.

When they were seated, Pierre asked: "Have you ever used a psychic before?"

"No. And if my superior knew anything about this. . . ." He shook his head as if to say he'd be in trouble.

"He will not hear from me."

"Or my partner."

"No. I understand about him."

"Oh?"

"A drunk, yes?"

Loyalty refused to allow Zo a word or gesture of endorsement.

Pierre nodded. "We have our code, too. But it can be very dangerous, you know. I worked once with a Dr. Friedgood who . . . never mind, it doesn't matter. Nothing can be done. Some day Friedgood will kill someone and then he will be stopped. Perhaps."

Zo watched the old man's eyes glaze over in private thought, then return to their sharp blue, settling on his face.

"Do you have any news?" Pierre asked.

"I'm sorry, there's nothing. We're trying. Really." He felt diminished.

Pierre toyed with a loose thread from a button on his gray suit jacket. "Why have you agreed to meet Miss Stevenson?"

Zo shifted uncomfortably in his chair. "I don't know. I'm not sure."

"You do not believe, do you?"

"In psychics? No, not really. I mean, they're mostly charlatans, aren't they? How much is she charging you?"

"Nothing."

"Nothing?" He was openly skeptical.

"That is correct. I, of course, offered to pay her, but she refused." The thread unraveled and offered up the marbleized button, which dropped to Pierre's lap. He slipped it into his pocket. "Miss Stevenson said that she does not do this for money."

"Then why?"

There was a soft tap at the door.

"I will let her tell you herself."

Only when Emma Stevenson entered did Zo realize he'd formed a mental image of what she would look like: sixty or so, buxom, gray hair in a bun, spectacles, cardigan, oxfords.

Taking Miss Stevenson's hand, he smiled and looked down into her large, thickly lashed brown eyes. She was no more than thirty and strangely beautiful. Her black wavy hair looked as if she were wearing a soft cloche hat. Under her eyes were dark smudges like wide brushstrokes, giving her a slightly ruined appearance. The nose was prominent but fit the size of her face and her full mouth was nicely curved and colored with a rose lipstick. When she removed her cloth coat, she revealed large breasts, a small waist, and curvaceous hips; she wore a maroon wool dress, a silver pin below her right shoulder.

When they were seated, Zo observed how nervous the woman was: her hands in her lap rustled like the tops of tall trees in the wind and one leg, which crossed over the other, was in continuous motion, the brown pump tapping a silent message in the air. What was her game? Zo wondered. He stared at her, hoping to increase her anxiety, perhaps to flush out her true motives. She stared back, a disturbance in her rouged cheek.

She smiled at Zo. "Listen," she said, "I don't like this any more than you. I mean, I know what you're thinking."

"Do you?"

"Yeah, I do. That's the trouble. This whole thing makes me sick. In the gut." She sighed, recrossed her shapely legs, the hiss of nylons the only sound in the room. Now her other foot took up the jiggling chore. "Mind if I smoke?" she asked Pierre.

"Please," he said, and as if he were a sorcerer a gold Dunhill lighter materialized in his hand.

Miss Stevenson opened her black leather purse, rummaged inside, and came up with a crushed pack of Old Golds. When the cigarette was lit, she looked back at Zo. "Look, I know you think I'm a phony and maybe I am. I mean, maybe it's all screwy and I'm a crackpot, but stuff comes to me and I can read minds and see into packages and why the hell do you think I'm not married? I'll tell you. Because I always know what they're thinking and it's not nice. Better I didn't know. If I didn't know, I'd be married by now. Helen really wants kids, you know."

Zo's bottom lip fell open as if a button had been pushed.

"Aw, gee, I'm sorry. See what I mean? God! I can't help it, things just pop into my mind and pop out of my mouth. Sometimes I don't even know what they mean, but sometimes I can figure them out. Like that. You don't want kids and Helen does. Right?" she asked meekly.

"Who's Helen?" asked Zo.

Emma Stevenson laughed in short tiny snorts. "You kidding me? Your wife, of course."

Zo looked at Pierre, then realized the doctor didn't know his wife's name. But perhaps there was another explanation. "Did you tell Miss Stevenson my name, Doctor?"

Pierre frowned, his eyebrows forming a straight white line above his eyes. "I do not remember. I am sorry."

"You did," Emma said. "But I didn't go digging into your life, if that's what you think."

"No?" But even if she'd learned Helen's name, how could she know about the conflict over the children?

"No. It just popped into my head, the thing about kids, after I saw the name Helen written on your forehead in blue."

Involuntarily, Zo touched his hand to his forehead and Emma laughed again.

"Sorry, I don't mean to laugh. There's nothing there. Listen, either you're going to believe me or not. I think this thing must come from my Jewish side, because I can't imagine it coming from my Wasp side. I guess that's kind of prejudiced or something. See my mother's a Jew and she married a goy, but it's like that side didn't take. I'm very Jewish, in case you didn't notice." Grinning, her eyes became more luminous. "Can we get serious now?"

"What do you mean?"

"Well, I can do more parlor tricks if you want, or we can talk about the murder and what's been happening to me." She blew a stream of smoke straight out.

The smoke reached Zo and he waved it away. "Yes, I think you'd better tell me what you know."

"The thing of it is, I'm not sure what I know. What it means."

"Let me worry about that."

"Yeah, okay." Emma stubbed out her cigarette and moved forward in her chair so that she sat on the edge, her body tense, both feet on the rug. "I never read the newspapers or listen to the radio or watch television. You can believe it or not. It mixes me up and it's bad enough without all that input, understand?"

"What's bad enough?" Zo asked gently. There was no point in being hostile. Besides, something about Emma Stevenson was getting to him: he liked her. Believing her was another matter.

"This whole thing. Whatever it is. Some people say it's a gift. I'm not sure. Sometimes I think it's a curse. I get nauseous and I can't sleep and it makes me nervous. Anyway, I didn't know about the murder until she told me."

"Who?"

"Mrs. Swann."

"Danielle Swann?" Zo asked.

"Yeah," Emma said, "Danielle."

Zo tried not to let his skepticism filter into his voice. "And how did she tell you?"

130

"Listen, I know how this sounds. You don't have to try to hide your feelings. I don't expect you to believe me. I told Dr. Dudevant here that this would be a waste of time. I mean bringing in the cops to hear this stuff."

"I'm not hiding anything," said Zo, feeling very uncomfortable.

"No?"

"Please go on." He took a cigarette from his pack.

"You were brought up by two women, huh?"

Had he not been lighting his cigarette he might have given himself away, but as it was he was able simply to say no and ask her to continue.

"Well, she came to me, I guess it was a dream even though it seemed much realer than a dream. But it was night and I was in bed. She told me her name and that she'd been killed and that I had to help. That was all. The first time. It scared me. Nothing like that's ever happened to me before. I mean, it's all been sort of like games."

"You've never been involved in a murder case?"

"Never. And I don't want to be now, if you want the truth. But it was like I didn't have a choice. She kept coming to me and interfering with my sleep. I'm a wreck, if you must know. I haven't slept good for a month. Since it started."

The dark marks under her eyes, Zo thought. "Why do you think Mrs. Swann would have picked *you*?"

"I haven't the vaguest."

"It makes you pretty special, doesn't it?"

Emma eyed him carefully, understanding his insinuation. "Special? I guess you could look at it like that. But believe it or not, it doesn't make me feel that way at all." She swallowed, her eyes watering slightly. "It makes me feel like a freak." Quickly, she regained her composure. "I don't know why she picked me, mister, she just did."

"What is it you want, Miss Stevenson? Is it money?"

"Ah, hell," she said disgustedly, standing up. "I told you," she said to Pierre.

"Please, please. It is a natural question. Please sit down, Miss Stevenson."

She looked at Zo, her eyes growing sad, discouraged. "I just want to help if I can and I don't even know what I'm saying, understand?"

He thought this time she might cry. "I'm sorry. Please sit

down." He believed she didn't want money. "Is there anything else?"

"Yeah. Maybe you can make something out of it. I can't."

"Let's hear it."

"It's numbers. One, six, and seven. Over and over." She shrugged.

Zo wrote the numbers in his notebook. He cleared his throat, feeling slightly foolish about how to pose the next question: "Does, uh, Mrs. Swann tell you these numbers?"

"No. I just see them all the time. I mean, maybe they don't have anything to do with this. But I feel in here," she touched her middle with the tips of her fingers, "that they do. I see these numbers on walls, on napkins, on foreheads, everywhere, all the time. And there's something else."

"What's that?"

She shook her head from side to side. "It's crazy." She laughed. "Yeah, I know, you think the whole thing's crazy. But this is *really* nuts. Every once in a while I see this big set of eyes and they're wearing specs and they're looking at me and then all of a sudden one eye winks."

Zo could not hide his shock. His pen fell from his hand. He looked at Pierre.

"No," he said. "I did not tell her. This is why I thought there might be something."

No one except Cristina and the family knew of the murderer's wink. It had purposely not been released to the newspapers. "Which eye, Miss Stevenson? Which eye winks?"

"The right."

Christ. Could there really be something here? "Is there anything else?"

"No. It means something, huh? The eyes? The wink?"

"It might." He stood. "I want you to stay in touch with me, Miss Stevenson. Will you? I mean if any new information comes your way."

"Sure. Listen, I could do a lot better if I had something tangible. Did the murderer leave anything behind? See, if I could touch something she'd touched it would help a lot."

Immediately, Zo thought of the gun Frankie Barnes had used to kill Officer Wickham. He'd have to find a way to get the gun out of Evidence where it was locked up, awaiting Barnes's trial. Then he'd have to meet Emma Stevenson and let her touch the damn thing. He knew he was going to do it; there was no question in his mind.

"There might be something. I'll call you. Dr. Dudevant has your number?"

"Yeah."

Pierre helped Emma on with her coat and escorted her to the door, where she turned and looked at Zo. "Was it your mother who hung herself?" she asked flatly.

"No," he said. "My mother is alive."

"Good. I'm glad. Sometimes it comes in crazy-like."

He nodded.

"And sometimes it doesn't," she added, and smiled as if she knew something more.

When she was gone, the two men stood in the center of the room, looking at each other.

"Well?" Pierre ventured.

"Maybe. I have to go about this very carefully, Doctor. I'd be laughed off the force if anyone got wind of it." Zo extended his hand and promised to be in touch.

Alone, Pierre sat once again in his comfortable chair. In fifteen minutes he would make his rounds. He had not told Amelia about Emma Stevenson and he would not tell her now. If and when the woman helped would be time enough; a false hope would accomplish nothing. He had taken action and now his part was done. There was nothing more to do and that was the problem. What irony, he thought: it has taken sixty-seven years for me to find out what I am. Useless. I cannot comfort my wife at the most tragic time of her life. I could not protect my child. Nor could I help my mother or my father. I have grown from a useless boy into a useless man. It is, after all, pointless.

With these thoughts a final shred of caring, a last spark of wonder, died with him. Doctor Useless quit.

―――

Snow had come in the night, leaving a thin coating like homemade white icing, patchy and sparse. On this, the last day of nineteen fifty-five, gray clouds hung low in the sky, threatening, as if ready to leave a mark for the New Year. And Hedy Somerville left her house at 167 Academy Street early in the morning and headed toward New York City, ready to leave *her* mark.

It was a cold, damp day, but Hedy didn't mind; she was

beyond the reach of weather; she felt only what she desired to feel and cold had no effect on her. During the morning she wandered around the Village, through the empty park, past the Swann apartment house, in and out of stores. She did not fear discovery, having taken care to alter her appearance since June. She had dyed her hair black and wore it in a bun at the nape of her neck. And she had insisted Ralph give her money for new glasses after purposely breaking the old ones; now she wore harlequin frames of black and white. There was nothing she could do about her pouchy cheeks or her pinched expression or the hueless blue of her eyes.

Sometime in mid-morning her right eye began to wink rapidly, her breathing accelerated, and she started to hyperventilate, causing dizziness. By noon she was panicked and stumbled into a luncheonette on West Fourth Street. The waitress, demanding that she order, frightened her and she picked the first thing she saw on the menu, something called Chilichow, and coffee. She sat at a table for two in the middle of the room. Her coffee came and as she lifted the steaming cup to her lips she remembered that it was her mother's birthday. She would have been fifty had she lived.

From a location deep inside her, a yawning space, Hedy felt the rage of abandonment and, with it, a fathomless despair which she was unable to identify. Was it for her mother's life, or lack of it, or was it for herself? Doleful and forlorn, she tried to stem the terrible tide of tears she sensed behind her eyes. She had, in her efforts at disguise, bought and attached false eyelashes, and now she feared for their lives. She told herself that this was the reason she must not cry; also that she was in a public place. Unable to curb the tears, she left her small table and went to the ladies room. Fortunately, it was a one-room affair and she locked the door, sat on the closed seat, and sobbed. Poor Mary, she thought, poor Mary, poor Hedy, poor Mary.

When the crying was done she stood, removed her glasses, and looked in the mirror where she saw, as she had feared, the right eyelash adrift in a sea of tears. Part of it hung down on her cheek, pathetic and hopeless; she savagely pulled it from her lid, lifted the toilet seat, threw it into the water where it floated like an eerie insect until she flushed, and then it whirled and twirled in its watery vortex of death, finally disappearing. This appeased Hedy and she found herself smiling. She slipped her glasses over her ears, blew her nose, wiped her cheeks, and unlocked the door, ready for lunch. It had not occurred to her to remove the other eyelash.

Back at the table she sniffed at the steaming plate of food: one side was a brown chili, the other a greenish facsimile of chow mein on crunchy noodles and rice. She had never seen anything like it, but it smelled good and she was ravenous. First she sampled one, then the other; deciding they tasted the same, she mixed them together, making a brown and green mélange, and rapaciously devoured it.

As she was leaving the luncheonette she almost bumped into two big men who were entering, but they graciously stepped aside, touching their hats, and let her pass. On occasion, she thought, men could be nice, but it was rare.

When they had settled in their usual booth, J.J. said to Zo, "You know I think that odd-lookin' broad at the door gave me the eye."

"Lucky you," Zo said. His partner was getting worse, thinking even the ugliest weirdos were on the make for him. "Chilichow?" he asked.

"Natch," answered J.J.

Outside, Hedy pulled her mother's seal coat tighter and took a brown felt hat from her large purse. As she reached the corner of Jones and Fourth, the snow began again, large, wet flakes instantly dissolving as if the sidewalk were heated. She wondered if the dreary weather would keep the peddlers with their pushcarts from Bleecker Street? The desire for an apple prodded her to investigate and she turned down Cornelia. The street was only one block long, devoid of interesting shops, but it was a shortcut to Bleecker.

The snow thickened, solidified, and Hedy kept her head bent, eyes cast down. A few feet away, coming toward her, she spied large black boots. Lifting her head she was shocked to see an enormous figure approaching. Her astonishment was caused by the person's garments as well as the size. Quickly, she lowered her eyes to avoid any confrontation, but the person blocked her path. Hedy, continuing to gaze downward, stood still, afraid to move or speak. She waited. Finally, unable to endure the unknown, she raised her eyes.

Smiling down at her from inside lumpish flesh were two

red lips. Above them, Hedy saw, were large, flaring nostrils. A tattered gray blanket concealed the head and hid the eyes. The cover was wrapped and twisted around the neck, its two ends flying behind like tails. Still another blanket, torn and dirty, was draped across and over the massive shoulders. And from beneath that shroud drooped remnants of many materials creating a strange but colorful cloak. The smile cracked open and the mouth spoke:

"The person who's responsible is the one to show it to, did you ever notice that? I've noticed that and when I did I said to the man without a head that it was time to knight the one who mentioned it the first time and to play a song on my mother's piano when she came back from the dentist and tried to touch me and. . . ."

Hedy screamed, a strangled, ragged sound, ran into the street, and raced down the center. She turned left at Bleecker, flying past the pushcarts. Slowing down and stopping, she was out of breath when she came to Sixth Avenue. In the distance she saw the marquee of the Waverly Theater. Scampering up the avenue, stabs of pain jabbing her middle, she tried to blot out the image and words of the fat . . . woman? Man? What was it? A beast, she decided.

Blackboard Jungle and *Marty* were playing. It had been a long time since she'd seen a movie and just as movies had been her refuge as a child, they would envelope and rescue her now.

Martin could have kicked himself. He wished he'd canceled all his appointments this afternoon; it was silly to be working on New Year's Eve day. On the other hand, it was a time when some of his patients would be the most desperate; loneliness prevailed over the holidays. Miss Webster, the patient who lay on the couch, for instance, was crying because she was dateless on the big night of the year.

Tonight he would be openly celebrating with Lynn. Their affair was no longer a secret. The police and press had tried to crucify them, advancing the theory, by hint and innuendo, that he and Lynn had been in league to dispose of Danielle. Of course, there was no evidence of this and they had had to drop the matter quickly. Still, the papers had exposed their affair and the Dudevants had turned against him, threatening a custody suit which never came to fruition. Through it all, Lynn had been magnificent, supportive and loving, even when she herself was being maligned. Poor Lynn. The idea that she could have murdered Danielle was absurd. But there had been a moment when that thought flashed across Martin's brain like a Times Square neon ad. It was something he could never tell her; Lynn would never understand, her loyalty to him unwavering; she would, he knew, consider it an enormous betrayal.

What hurt Martin most was the injury to his children; no matter what he did, he could not protect them. The scandal had reached their ears through other children, cruel as always. Cristina was affected more than Claude, the difference of two years shielding him from reality. The best Martin could do was to have his daughter attended to by the best child psychiatrist he knew.

Martin sighed audibly and hoped Miss Webster hadn't heard. The scandal had almost ruined him. He had lost several patients. If it hadn't been for Lynn, he might not have survived it all. His fragile nature could not compensate for the condemnation of others.

He was the stereotypical neurotic psychiatrist and the image sickened him. There were, however, some things which could never be cured or changed, huddling so deep in a person's marrow. His inability to cope with outside disapproval was one of these. But only his intimates knew of this problem; aquaintances and patients had no idea. Life was a series of tricks anyway; sleight of mind, he called it.

"I'm not sure I can stand it," Miss Webster said.

Martin refocused. "I think a prescription is in order. You may sit up now. The session is over."

She did as she was told, large eyes blinking at him, waiting to be saved.

"I'm going to give you a prescription for Miltown."

"What's that?" she asked shyly.

"Oh, just something that will make you feel less upset." He was delighted that these mild tranquilizers had been approved. They were going to be especially helpful with women. Martin wrote out the prescription.

As he walked Miss Webster to the waiting room, it crossed his mind to wish her a Happy New Year, but he decided that under the circumstances it might not be appropriate.

Waiting for him, dour as ever, was Aaron Waldman. What a way to end the year. Well, at least he was the last patient of the day. And then he and Lynn would ring in a new year which had to be better than the last. Almost anything would be.

Hedy had left *Blackboard Jungle* halfway through because she thought it far too violent. The image of the dreadful beast she'd encountered on Cornelia Street remained with her, disturbing and haunting. Again she'd wondered what sex the person had been. Even the voice had disguised the sexual identity. It was all too horrible to think about and she'd refused to let it ruin her day, finally able to banish the odious, corpulent vision to the bottom of her mind.

Now she sat, her coat hung on the wooden coattree, her hands folded in her lap. waiting for Martin Swann's last patient to leave. The dress she'd chosen for the occasion was a silk foulard of brown and black which she felt went well with her new glasses. She had returned her hat to her purse and patted her hair. Finding a strand which had slipped from her bun, she gave it a tap with her finger as if it were a recalcitrant child, then tucked it back in place.

She wondered if Martin would recognize her. Well, if he didn't she'd soon remind him. She smiled, thinking of all the things she had to tell him and to ask of him. Glancing down at the diamond ring, she felt the sense of security it always gave her.

The office door opened and Martin and his patient came into the waiting room. Dr. Swann was wishing the man a Happy New Year, but stopped when he saw her. Quickly, he looked away from Hedy and, limping, escorted the man to the outer door.

When he turned back to her, Martin said: "I'm sorry, did we have an appointment?"

She rose slowly, smiling. "You don't remember me, do you?"

Martin searched his memory. There *was* something familiar about the woman, and a feeling of gloomy kismet dropped over him.

"I'm Hedy Somerville," she announced as if she were his favorite movie star.

"Oh, yes." And just as it was falling into place, the missing piece, the shutter clicking, the recall of his daughter's words, she said:

"I killed your wife," and winked.

PART TWO

Legacies

1965

ONE

"Aren't you a little old for all this?" asked Janet Starkman. She and Guy were lying in his bed.

"For sex?" he asked, grinning.

Janet gave his arm a small slap. "Too old for this decor." With a flourish of her hand she indicated the semidarkened bedroom.

This was Guy's third apartment in the East Village and a palace compared to the others. After two years at Columbia he had quit and moved out of his parents' house. The only apartment he could afford was a two-and-a-half with tub in the kitchen for twenty-five a month on Avenue B. He'd stayed there two years, then moved to a five-room walkup on Sixth Street for seventy-five a month. And now he was on Seventh Street (he'd joked to his mother that he was slowly moving uptown) in a small brownstone, six rooms with a terrace for one hundred fifty a month. This one he shared with an Englishman named Christopher Downing.

"You don't like my interior decorating skills?" he asked.

"It just seems juvenile. Red lights over the bed and burlap on the walls. Incense burning. You're not a beatnik, are you, Guy?"

He laughed and put an arm around her, pulling her into his chest. "I don't know. Maybe I am."

"What's that supposed to mean?"

"It means I haven't bothered to label myself. It's true that my hair is a little below my ears and I don't wear ties and I don't have a nine-to-five job and——"

"Why don't you?"

"Why should I?" He moved away and got his pack of Marlboros from the night table. "Cigarette?"

"Thanks. Seriously, Guy, how come you don't work?"

He handed her the lit cigarette. "I work."

"Doing what?"

"Look, Janet, I think you knew when we met I wasn't like Fred or the others in that crowd." Two weeks before, he'd gone to his old friend Fred Van Iderstine's New Year's Eve party for a lark; a desired change from his usual friends. Besides, he'd been curious to see Fred and some of the others after more than eight years. Janet had been at the party; this was the third time they'd seen each other, the first that they'd gone to bed.

"Yes, I knew. That's why you appealed to me. I'm sick to death of that bunch. God, they're boring. I'm only asking you out of curiosity."

"Really?"

"Sure. What do you think?"

"I think you're beautiful."

She was silent for a moment and then said, "I think you are too."

He kissed the top of her head, hair brown and wavy. There'd been a succession of women over the last eight years, none of them lasting more than a year. He was always enthusiastic in the beginning, believing that each woman was the one; he felt this way about Janet, but he knew better. Finally. Still, it was difficult to be temperate, to restrain his ardor. It was all he could do to resist telling her he loved her. Guy delighted in telling women he was in love with them; saying the words thrilled him. He had a set routine: first he would say that he loved them, shyly; later, a few days between, he'd falteringly say he was falling *in* love, the distinction profound. And he believed it, each and every time. On New Year's he'd sworn to himself that he would be cautious next time. This was the next time.

Janet put out her cigarette and leaned on one elbow, looking down at Guy. The red lights he'd strung up above the bed gave her an eerie look and Guy turned them off with the gold fringed cord, leaving on the muted light by his bed.

"Jesus," he said. "You really *are* gorgeous."

She had dark arched eyebrows on either side of a thin high-bridged nose; the cheekbones were sculptured, prominent, and her mouth was delicate. Deep-set brown eyes looked down at him, the thick lashes blinking slowly. Janet kissed his lips. When she pulled back she said, "I think you're going to be very important to me and I want to know about you."

A quiver of excitement passed through him, or perhaps it was fear. Janet sounded as if she had plans; usually he controlled his affairs, but he had grown tired. He wondered if she could sense that or if she was always in command. "What do you want to know?"

"Where in New York did you grow up?"

"Fifth Avenue . . . in the Sixties," he said, studying the ceiling.

"You're kidding."

"Nope. Serious. My mother still lives there."

"And your father?"

"He's dead."

"Oh. I'm sorry." She stroked his hair, then lay back down facing him.

"He wanted to die, I think."

"Why?"

Guy wasn't sure he could answer. It involved so much explaining, so much history, so many painful memories. There was no way to tell anyone that your sister had been murdered without its evoking questions. He understood the curiosity; most people had never met anyone who'd been close to a murder victim. But he'd grown weary of his own answers. He rolled over on his side and looked into Janet's eyes, his hand touching her soft cheek.

"Janet, will you promise not to ask me a whole lot of questions about what I'm going to tell you? You'll want to and I promise I'll tell you more about it another time, but I just don't want to go into it now."

"Christ, you make it sound so mysterious and intriguing."

"It is. Maybe we should just drop it." He tried to kiss her, but she pulled back.

"Oh, no, you don't. Please, Guy, tell me. I promise I won't ask *anything*."

"Okay. In 1955, my sister was murdered by an unknown woman outside her apartment house on Fifth Avenue in the Village. It's never been solved. I guess you could say it tore my family apart. My parents separated three years later and then my father lived for four more. But I think he really died when Danielle did. Danielle was my sister. That's it."

"I think I remember it," she said.

"You probably do. It was a pretty big case for a while."

"Was your brother-in-law———"

He put his hand over her mouth. "You promised."

"I'm sorry."

She sounded so genuine, he relented. "My brother-in-law was—is—a psychiatrist. They had two children. He married again and they still live in New York. But he doesn't let my mother or me see the kids. He's a bastard. Enough, okay?"

"Okay."

Guy was depressed now. He always was when he reviewed the past, even in so capsulated a form. "How come you're not married?"

"What a question. Maybe nobody ever asked me."

"I don't believe that. Want some wine?"

He had a small refrigerator in his room and a cabinet with a few glasses and plates. He poured two glasses, handed her one. "I answered your question, Janet, now answer mine. Why haven't you married?"

Janet sipped her wine. "I almost did once, but he dumped me and married someone else."

"He must have been nuts." They were sitting up in the bed and Guy reached a hand under the covers stroking Janet's thigh.

"Think so?" she asked, looking at him as if she'd heard it all before, a thin veil of cynicism, like a scrim, over her eyes.

"Know so." He kissed her gently, almost chastely. It was more a reassurance than a declaration of passion.

"You're very nice," she said.

He winced. "That sounds so anemic."

"I don't mean it that way. You'd be surprised how few nice men are around."

Guy started to speak but stopped when he heard the front door open, slap shut. Then he listened to Christopher stumbling around in the hall. "Roommate," he said to Janet.

Suddenly the bedroom door was thrust open and Janet, in an effort to hide herself beneath the sheet, spilled a little wine.

"Hey, Chris," said Guy, "how about some privacy?"

Christopher Downing was a large man, six four and solid. His huge head was topped with blond curls; he wore wire-rimmed glasses behind which his small eyes were almost always squeezed into slits as if he were in pain. Swaying in the doorway for a second, he abruptly made a sweeping bow from the waist, almost toppling over. "Good evening lady and gentleman," he said, his accent cultivated even though he was clearly drunk. "Ah, do I see an open bottle of vino?"

"Chris, this is Janet Starkman." It was ridiculous, but the

only thing Guy felt he could do was make introductions. "Chris Downing."

"How do you do, my dear." He landed heavily on the corner of the bed, narrowly missing Guy's feet.

Seeing his condition, any embarrassment Janet might have felt vanished.

"Lovely, lovely." It was hard to believe he could even see her, the opening in his eyes like two incisions. He turned toward Guy. "I left the pub due to lack of funds."

"A depletion of cash never stopped you before," said Guy.

"Too true, dear boy. However, tonight I found it distasteful to accept libations from strangers, as it were. You, on the other hand, are no stranger." He held out his massive hand and Guy placed his glass of wine within it. "Thank you so much, you're very kind." Draining the glass he held it out to be refilled.

Guy knew Chris needed it and filled the glass again. "Want a loan?"

"Well, if it wouldn't inconvenience you, dear fellow, my check should be arriving by the end of the week." Chris was supposed to be going to graduate school, his father supporting him, but somehow he never managed to get to class.

Guy threw back the sheet, careful not to expose Janet, padded over to his dresser, and got his wallet. "Ten okay?"

"Quite. Thank you." Standing, swaying side to side, Chris took the money. Again he bowed to Janet. "A pleasure and an honor, dear lady. I hope to meet you again. I will be off now, perhaps to that classy watering hole Stanley's. Goodnight friends." He lumbered through the bedroom doorway and crashed into something in the hall. Finally he found the front door and slammed his way out.

Getting back in bed Guy said, "I'm sorry, Janet."

She shook her head. "A new experience."

"They don't cavort this way uptown?"

Laughing, she answered, "Can you just see Fred or Rags or Hale allowing his roommate in when he's got a woman with him? Better than that, can you see Muffy or Bitsy being the woman? God!"

"He's really a nice guy."

"Don't bother, Guy," she snapped, an icy edge frosting her words.

He was surprised at her tone and alerted to another facet of her personality. "What do you mean, don't bother?"

"He's a drunk," she stated flatly.

"Well, yes, I guess he is but——"

"But?" she said, incredulous. "There's no but about it, Guy. Anyone with half an eye can see the man's a disgusting drunk." She reached across him, took the pack of cigarettes from the table, extracted one, and lit it with a vengeance.

"Have you had bad experiences with drunks or something? Your father?"

"My father is the most wonderful man who ever lived and he's never been drunk in his life," she said angrily.

"Okay, okay, take it easy."

"How dare you malign my father. I'm getting out of here." Janet tossed back the sheet and jumped from the bed. Her clothes were draped over a chair; she made a grab for them and got on her underpants before Guy could get out of bed and come around to face her.

"What the hell's going on here?" he demanded. Something told him to let her go, but he ignored the advice.

"Nothing's going on. I've made a mistake, that's all." She hooked her brassiere and reached for her half-slip. Guy grabbed her wrist.

"Me? I'm the mistake?"

"Let go, please."

"Janet, come on. What is this?" He dropped her wrist.

"I just want to go home now."

Softly, almost as if he were praying, he said, "Janet, please."

The tenor of his voice stopped her and she looked up into his violet eyes.

"What happened?" he asked kindly.

Something altered in her eyes, her mouth softened. "Oh, Guy, I don't know."

"Sit down a minute, okay?"

They sat on the edge of the bed. Guy held her hand and stroked the long dark hair which framed her face like a hood.

"I'm tired, I guess," she finally said.

"You can sleep here. In my arms."

"No, I don't mean sleepy. I'm tired of this life, of running around, meeting people, dating."

"I know what you mean." The same thoughts, feelings, had recently occurred to him. As frightening as the idea of settling down and being responsible for himself and someone else was, Guy knew the time was approaching, as inevitable as death, and almost as inviting. He couldn't go on hiding out here, a pretender to the throne of decadence. It really didn't work for him, hadn't ever. Alcohol and drugs were never an answer. He had always been a sort of spy in this world of chemically induced highs and lows and artists manqué: the resident straight, although no one ever said so. As surely as he preferred the songs of Frank Sinatra to those of The Beatles, he knew he was going to end up with wife, two kids, a good job, and a house in Westchester.

"It's what I meant earlier about you being too old for living like this," she went on as if she hadn't heard his agreement.

"Yes, I know. I *am* too old."

"So why do you do it?"

"I don't know. Maybe it's habit, maybe I don't know what else to do."

"What *is* it you do now, Guy?" she asked, genuine interest in her voice. "I mean work."

"Odd jobs. I inherited some money from my father so I really don't have to work much. I paint apartments sometimes, move people, stuff like that."

"Aren't you bored?"

He laughed. "Bored silly."

"So why don't you get a real job?"

"Doing what? I don't have a degree or any experience in anything."

"How about a job in publishing?" She took on an air of solemnity as if she were in conference, head of a Board.

"Publishing? I don't have any qualifications. . . ."

"Does it interest you at all?"

"Well, I don't know, I never thought about it. Hey, what's going on here, Janet? You have something up your sleeve?"

She smiled, kissed him, then turned her back so he could unhook her brassiere.

In a few moments she was undressed and they lay entwined under the sheet. Guy was hard again, but he delayed making love to her, wanting to know what she'd been talking about.

"My father," she said, "is president of Compact Books."

"The paperback company?"

"Yes. I can see you're a book lover," she went on.

His room was lined with bookcases. Women were always asking him if he'd read all those books; he was glad Janet hadn't, a plus for her.

"The point is, Guy, if you're interested I could arrange an interview with Daddy." Her hand drifted from his belly into his pubic hair, circled the base of his penis, teasing.

Why did he have the feeling he was being bribed, blackmailed? He experienced the sensation of spiraling into quicksand.

"You think you might be interested?" Her fingers closed around him.

"Yes," he answered hoarsely. "Interested."

"Great," she said.

He began to lose himself, the keenness of his mind dulled by physical exhilaration. Yet somewhere there was an edge of apprehension, a signal warning him of dire consequences; he ignored it all.

Janet carefully guided his penis inside her. Staring up at him she said, "We could be very good together, Guy."

Completely absorbed in passion he saw his life pass in front of him as it is said to do before death; this was not his past life he saw, but rather the future, and Janet and Daddy had starring roles.

Since the birth of Hedy's child, Ralph Somerville had resolutely stayed away from his sister's bed. There were two factors involved in his decision to relinquish Hedy as a sexual partner: his ignorance of her pregnancy until the baby was born and the fact that the child had one blue and one brown eye. Both of these unusual particulars added up, in Ralph's mind, to a large and definite sign. He was not immune to Catholic superstition even though he'd been, it seemed, unaffected by the tenets of Catholicism. The child, of course, was of his flesh, but she was certainly of the Devil's spirit. As far as Ralph was concerned, her birth, her eyes, told him loud and clear to reform and repent and to stay as far away from his sister as possible. If he ever had a moment's doubt, a flash of longing for Hedy, he had only to look at the child's eyes or remember the night of her birth.

He had been in bed almost asleep when he'd heard the first shriek, a stunning sound. Sitting up, heart volleying in his chest, he heard the second shocking scream, which jolted him from the bed to stand immobile in the center of his room. The scalp under his lank hair prickled as he waited, paralyzed, for the next sound. When it came it was not a scream but his father's unintelligible bleating which set Ralph in motion. He headed toward the old man's room. Snapping on the light, Ralph saw his father hanging over the edge of his bed, the good eye wide with fear. He helped him back onto the bed just as the third horrific howl filled the house.

"What is it?" George asked his son, voice croaky.

Ralph said he would investigate.

Terrified, he eased his way into the hall, hands against the wall as he sidestepped along, bare feet sliding over the cold slick floor. A low moan stopped his progress. Now he could tell where the sounds were emanating from: the bathroom.

He stood in front of the closed door, listening. A mixture of heavy breathing and muted murmurs met his ears. With two knuckles he rapped on the door. There was no reply except the continuing, inexplicable noises. He knocked again.

"Hedy? Is that you in there?" Who else would it be? "Hedy? Answer me. What's going on? Are you sick?"

"Go away," she finally answered, a breathless pained edge to her voice.

Relieved to know absolutely that it was Hedy inside, Ralph tried the door. Locked. "Open up," he commanded.

Her answer this time was a guttural growl. Ralph released the doorknob as if it were hot with sound. Perspiration dampened his light blue pajamas and the cotton clung to his chest and back. He screwed up his embryonic face, wondering what to do next.

"Ralph," came the call from his father.

In the old man's room he told him that the sounds were coming from Hedy, who had locked herself in the bathroom.

"Goddamned stupid bitch," George said from the side of his mouth. "What's wrong with her?"

"She won't say."

Another scream made the two men chill with fear.

"Get her the hell outa there," demanded George.

"Maybe I should call the doctor. Maybe she's sick."

Blood rushed to the old man's face. "I don't want any doctors prowling around here."

"She sounds sick," said Ralph.

George threw back the covers. "Take me out there."

Ralph lifted his father out of the bed and carried him into

the hall, where he set him down on the floor in front of the bathroom door. As George raised his good hand to knock, another stentorian scream shook the men.

"Jesus, Mary, and Joseph," George said, crossing himself.

"You see," said Ralph, as if the scream explained why he was helpless.

Faint droning sounds drifted through the door. George raised his hand again and this time succeeded in knocking before a scream cut him off.

"Hedy, wha' the hell's goin' on in there?"

The only reply was a continuation of dulled tones and heavy breathing.

For the next hour the two men sat in the hall alternately knocking on the door and calling to Hedy, who continued to scream, pant, cry, and ignore their entreaties. Ralph tried several times to get George to agree to call in Dr. Stover, but the old man persisted in his stubborn refusal. They sat, their backs against the wall, waiting for the unknown. When they heard a slap and the crying of a baby, they were dumbfounded.

George's good eye stared into Ralph's eyes. "What is it?"

Ralph opened his mouth to answer but found he could say nothing. His ears told him he was hearing a baby, but his mind rejected the knowledge. It simply could not be. He would not allow it. And yet the crying was insistent, forcing its way through his denial and into his consciousness.

"It's a baby, Ralph, isn't it?"

His father's eye, like that of a Cyclops, bored its accusing center into him and Ralph nodded. He decided then he would deny until his dying breath the paternity of this baby. Who could prove it? It would be his word against Hedy's, and he knew in the long run his father would believe him.

Forty-five minutes after the child had begun to cry they heard the sound of the lock turning and the bathroom door opened. Hedy, pale and wobbly, stood before them with a bundle of towels in her arms. Or so it seemed from the men's vantage point, looking up.

George said, "What d'ya have there, Hedy?"

Hedy managed a feeble smile and leaned against the woodwork. "It's my baby," she said, as if the birth were the most natural event. "Her name is Value." And then she slowly made her way past the two men, went into her bedroom, and closed the door.

Ralph carried his father back to bed. As he was about to leave, George grabbed his wrist with his good hand in a grip so tight Ralph squealed with pain.

"Whose baby is it, Ralph?"

"I don't know," he answered without hesitation.

"What'll we do?"

"Do?"

"Say, tell people, you stupid idiot," said George.

"What people?" The only person who ever visited was Father Frank.

George let go of Ralph's wrist. "Get the hell out of here, you pansy."

This epithet almost pushed Ralph into an admission of his fatherhood, but he decided it wouldn't be worth it. He left his father and walked directly to Hedy's room.

She was lying in her bed, propped against several pillows, the baby in her towel bunting tucked in the angle of Hedy's arm. Ralph stood at the foot of the bed. It had been five months since Hedy had acquiesced to his sexual demands. He'd been surprised by her sudden threats of exposure, but he'd gone along, thinking eventually she'd give in again. A phase, was what he'd chalked it up to and, when he'd asked her if it was a permanent state she'd said no, so he'd been placated. But he'd never guessed the truth.

"I never noticed," he said.

She grinned. "Big skirts."

"Why didn't you tell me?" he asked.

"Why should I?"

"I would have made arrangements."

"I didn't want arrangements," she said.

"I can't believe you did this by yourself, delivered that baby."

"I bit the cord with my teeth," she stated proudly.

Ralph felt sick.

"And I cleaned everything up. There's not a trace in there. Except for the bloody towels and rags I left in the corner. Put them in the hamper and I'll throw them in the machine tomorrow."

"Tomorrow? Shouldn't you rest?"

"Why?"

He shrugged, feeling extremely helpless.

"Don't you want to see her?" Hedy asked pointedly.

He did and he didn't.

She motioned him over, crooking her finger. "Come look at her."

Staring down, he looked for a resemblance, but all he saw was a baby face, reddish and small, eyes closed.

"Do you think she's pretty?" asked Hedy.

"No. I mean, I can't tell. Listen, will she be all right?"

"What do you mean, all right?"

Didn't Hedy know that a child born of brother and sister could be insane? Deformed? "Is she normal looking?"

"Perfect." A look of pride lit her face. "Tomorrow I want you to buy some things for her. Now you can make arrangements. I want a crib and clothes and diapers and bottles and formula."

"But I can't do that," he sputtered, feeling as if he might cry.

"Why not?"

"I don't know how."

"Well, learn."

"Hedy," he begged, "please. Can't you go? I'll pay, of course."

"No. I don't go out, you know that." She hadn't left the house since New Year's Eve day of 1955. This was November 24th, 1956. "You'll have to go," she demanded.

There was no way out. Ralph knew she'd tell their father the truth if he didn't yield to her every request. "All right, I'll do it. I'm going to bed now." When he got to the door, he stopped. "Why are you calling her Value? What kind of a name is that?"

"Don't you like it?"

"It's not a name."

"Anything's a name."

"But why Value?"

She smiled enigmatically. "I had a sign at the moment of her birth. I had other names in mind, but when her head appeared I was given a sign."

"What kind of a sign?"

"That's for me to know and for you to find out," she said, quoting a line from childhood.

"Well, I think it's awful."

"I don't care what you think. Value is her name."

In the bathroom Ralph found the bloody towels and rags.

Looking at them made him gag, then swoon, and he dropped to his knees on the floor. In a few moments he found himself lying on the cool white tiles where his sister had lain delivering their child just hours before. He opened his eyes and stared at the ceiling, the paint peeling and chipping. Slowly he let his eyes wander over the room until they stopped at a shelf on a wall opposite his head. The shelf stored three extra tubes of toothpaste and two rolls of toilet paper held together by a paper band. Two large words were printed on the band: VALUE-PAK.

"Jesus," Ralph whispered, realizing the origin of his daughter's name.

And now Value was eight going on nine. Ralph loathed her. Not one shred of paternal pride or love lived within him. She had ruined everything as far as he was concerned. Since Value had entered the world, his home, she was the center of attention; George doted on her, and Hedy, Value's paternity her weapon against him, never ceased ordering him around. He wished the child would die.

The Somervilles sat at the white enamel kitchen table having breakfast. In the background, music came from the Motorola which ached with static. Simon and Garfunkel were singing "Sounds of Silence." Hedy placed a bowl of puffed wheat in front of Value. George and Ralph watched. Value lifted her spoon from the table and lowered it into the cereal, then raised the spoon and its cargo to her mouth and ate. George sighed, Ralph returned to his eggs, and Hedy sat down.

"Why," Value asked, "do we have pictures of him all over the house?" With her eyes, one blue, one brown, Value indicated the photograph of John Kennedy which hung on the kitchen wall.

George cackled as if his grandchild had asked something wonderful and amazing. "Tell her," he squawked to Hedy.

"Because," she said, quoting her father, "he was a wonderful president cut down in his prime by a madman."

"So what?" said Value.

Ralph looked at the child, his mouth twisting into a sneer. "Do you even know what it means?"

"What what means?" She kept her eyes on her cereal, her thin brown hair hanging straight, shielding her from her uncle's stare.

"Cut down in his prime, for example," Ralph said.

"Shaddup," said George.

Ralph glared at his father. "Why should I? I want to know. Does the kid even understand what she's saying 'so what' to? What's wrong with wanting to know that?"

"I know," Value said, stirring her puffed wheat around in the bowl.

"Value, don't play with your food," Hedy said.

The child ate another bite.

"Pains in the ass," said Ralph, pushing back his chair.

"Wha's that?" asked George.

Ralph stomped from the kitchen and in a few moments they heard the front door slam.

Hedy looked at the wall clock. "Hurry or you'll be late."

Quickly, Value spooned up some more of her cereal. "I need fifty cents for a new notebook," she said.

"I thought you just got a new notebook?"

"No."

"Last week you said——"

"Give it to her," George interrupted. He believed Value, whose birth was a miracle, should have whatever she wanted.

"All right." Hedy, who knew Value's birth was not a miracle but a carefully planned reality, also believed she should have whatever she wanted. From a drawer in the sideboard Hedy took her purse. Although she had not left the house in ten years, she still kept her money in her handbag. "Here you are," she said, handing the child two quarters.

"Thank you, Mother."

Even after all this time, Hedy experienced a tiny thrill whenever Value called her Mother. Perhaps it was because the child used the name so seldom. "You'd better get going."

After Value perfunctorily kissed her grandfather's cheek, turning up her small nose in distaste, Hedy walked her to the front door where she tried to help her on with her coat. But Value pulled away, doing it herself. Hedy leaned down for a kiss and the child gave her one, again her little nose wrinkling as if she were smelling something nasty.

"Don't talk to any strange men," Hedy said as Value walked down the front steps.

"I won't," she called over her shoulder. "Bye." She raised a hand but didn't turn.

Hedy closed the door and ran to the window in the living

room so she could watch the child as she made her way down the block. She liked to observe Value as much as possible. The hours of the day when the child was at school or sleeping were bleak to Hedy. She lived to look at Value. She thought the child was beautiful. Mostly she resembled her, but Hedy could also see Martin Swann in the child. She alone knew the brown eye belonged to him. Value turned the corner and Hedy went back to the kitchen where her father was finishing his breakfast, most of it on his face and the large bib tied around his neck.

"I think she'll be the first woman president," said George.

"Value?"

" 'Course Value," he snarled. "Who else?"

"Why do you think so?" She began clearing the breakfast dishes and stacking them in the sink.

"The interest in Kennedy," he said.

Hedy stopped and stared at him a moment. She thought of pointing out the idiocy of his statement, then abandoned the idea. Let him live with his dreams. Since Value's birth she hadn't grown to love her father or to like him any better, but she had less equity in hating him. And he was good to Value. Ralph, on the other hand, was not particularly good to Value although he did nothing to harm her. Hedy knew this was because he believed he was the father and she had no intention of disabusing him of the idea; that belief kept Ralph in check where she was concerned. It had been almost ten years since she'd had to endure him sexually. Just thinking of those times made her queasy. Value was her savior.

"Let me wipe your face," Hedy said. With some wet paper towel she cleaned his twisted mouth and his chin. She untied the bib and helped him wheel himself from the kitchen to the living room.

"I'll see if the mail and paper are here."

They were. She gave George the paper and took the bills and the envelope with Martin's weekly payment into the kitchen. After finishing up the dishes she went upstairs to her bedroom, opened her closet, and reached into the back for the Kotex box. She brought it to the bed where she sat down with it, removed the one Kotex and peered in at the money. Then she tore open the envelope from Martin, extracted the piece of blank white paper, unfolded it, and took out the fifty dollar bill. Smiling, running her fingers over the green bill, she added it to the rest. There were four hundred and forty-two bills in the box, bringing the total to twenty-two thousand one hundred dollars. Martin believed the payments were for Value's support, but of course Ralph took care of that. Hedy was saving the money for Value's future. By the time she was eighteen there would be more than forty-eight thousand dollars. Hedy replaced the Kotex on top of the bills and returned the box to the closet.

Beginning her daily routine by making her bed, she wondered if Martin Swann ever thought about his daughter other than when he stuffed a fifty into an envelope. He had never even asked Hedy if he could see a picture. Not that they communicated in any way other than the sending and receiving of the money. She had made it clear after she got pregnant (there were three tries) that she never wanted to see him again. Still, one might have thought he would show some curiosity about his own flesh and blood.

She finished her bed and went into Ralph's room. It looked like what she imagined a monk's cell would be. Ralph had changed a great deal since Value's birth. Shortly after she was born, he'd thrown out his bed and put down a thin pallet on the floor. He kept one small dresser and removed all other furniture except for a straight-backed wooden chair. He used a madras spread to cover the pallet and this was all she had to straighten each morning. George's room was easy, too. She made the single bed quickly and went on into Value's room, which she always saved until last; it was like having a sweet in mid-morning.

The room was done in pink and white; Hedy had picked the wallpaper (pink roses on a cream background) from one of the books she'd ordered Ralph to bring home from Bob's Hardware. She'd spent weeks scrutinizing wallpaper patterns, sometimes feeling dizzy from the twists and turns of their designs, but finally she'd found the perfect one.

The rest of the decoration, curtains, spread, rugs, and so on, she'd also picked from books and catalogs; Ralph had done the shopping. It was the room Hedy would have liked herself as a girl and often, in the afternoon before Value came home, Hedy would come here to sit and think and dream and talk with her mother, Mary.

Now that Ralph no longer bothered her and that business in 1955 was long forgotten and she had Value, Hedy felt like a lucky woman. She couldn't have dreamed of a more perfect life.

Value stared at Miss Robbins, her teacher, and pretended she was listening. What she was actually doing was thinking. The man in the car was back again. It had been a while now since she'd seen him; maybe months. But this morning he'd been there waiting when she turned the corner. Sometimes he got out of his car and walked behind her on the other side of the street and sometimes he stayed in the green car and drove it very slowly, following her. Other times he stayed in the car and didn't move. A few times she'd seen him when she'd come out of school, standing against a tree on the other side of the street, or in his parked car. When that happened he'd follow her the other way, toward home, but he always stopped when she turned the corner into her street. Her mother had warned her against speaking to strange men, taking candy from them or going in their cars. But this man never did or said anything so she'd never mentioned it to her mother. And there was another reason she'd never told her.
From the time Value was five years old she'd known her mother was crazy. And her uncle and her grandpa, too. The word *crazy* she'd only learned when she was six, but the feeling she'd had at five was what crazy meant.
"Value Somerville," Miss Robbins said, "can you tell us who the first three presidents of our country were?"
"Yes, Miss Robbins."
"Go ahead, dear."
Value stood. She did not lean her crotch into the corner of the desk as she did during the saluting of the flag, because Miss Robbins was looking at her and Value knew the woman would understand what she was doing. "Our first three presidents were George Washington, John Adams, and Thomas Jefferson." She wondered if any of them had been cut down in their prime.
"Very good."
Value sat down, her face slightly flushed with success. She felt her red barette slipping and adjusted it, then leaned back in her chair and in a moment felt her bare arm being pinched. It surprised and hurt her, but she didn't jump or turn around. Barney Middleton sat behind her and whenever she forgot and leaned back he pinched or pulled at her. She hated him but

would not give him the satisfaction of knowing he bothered her; someday she'd get him.

Moving forward in her seat she concentrated on having given Miss Robbins the right answer, the answer she wanted. Value always tried to give everyone the answers that were wanted. It was, she thought, important to be right, perfect. Sometimes it was hard to know what they wanted to hear, but usually she could figure it out. For instance, she had ended her autobiography for Miss Robbins with the sentence: *I hate war.* The teacher had made a big fuss over that just as Value had thought she would. Value knew war was bad and that you were supposed to hate it, so she'd said she did even though she couldn't have cared less.

"You stink, Value," Barney Middleton whispered at her.

She ignored him. Miss Robbins was talking again and Value, truly safe now from further interruption, allowed herself to think of her favorite topic: her father. Her mother had told her he'd died before she was born, a hero, pushing a woman out of the path of a car and losing his own life. Value didn't believe her. Her horrible Uncle Ralph also told her this same tale. She didn't believe him. Grandpa just said her father was dead, but she didn't believe that either. Value knew her father lived. Sometimes she wondered if he was the man in the green car. In her daydreams she often pretended he was; she liked the way the man looked and thought it would be fine if he was her father. Each time she saw him she swore the next time she was going to speak to him, but she never did.

Value had a plan. When she was old enough (thirteen or fourteen), she was going to run away from home. That meant five more years living with three crazy people who were always staring at her and watching everything she did. Sometimes she thought she would scream from their watching. Before the school had a cafeteria, when she'd had to come home for lunch, her mother sat across the table from her opening and shutting her mouth with each bite that Value took. The worst part was that Value felt she was never alone except when she went to bed at night. And even then, sometimes, she'd hear the door open and know that her mother was standing over her, looking and looking. So when she was fourteen she was going to get out and find her father. Another reason she knew he was alive was because of the fight she'd had with Barney last year in the schoolyard.

"You're nothing but a bastard," said Barney.

"Am not," she answered.

"Are too."

"What do you know about it?" She had no idea what a bastard was but could tell it wasn't something anyone would want to be.

"I know plenty," Barney said.

Value was torn between the impulse to ignore her constant tormentor and her curiosity. Curiosity won. "Like what? What do you know?"

"If you'd've had a real father who was married to your mother, you and her would have a different name from her father and brother."

"That's dumb," she'd said and walked away, having gotten the information she'd needed.

This had never occurred to her before. But when she asked her mother about it, Hedy said:

"What is the point of having a dead person's name?"

"But what *was* his name?"

"It's not important."

Value knew her mother well enough to know that to keep on asking was useless. But Hedy's answers made her know all the more that her father was alive, and her resolve to find him became even stronger. That was when she'd begun with the money. She made up different reasons why she needed money for school (just as she had that morning), went through her uncle's pockets for spare change, and got her Grandpa to give her coins for candy, which she never bought. She was saving for her escape and kept the money in a shoebox buried in the back yard. The last time she'd counted it she had over one hundred dollars. By the time she was fourteen she was sure she'd have five or six hundred, plus she planned to steal her mother's diamond ring and sell it. Hedy was always telling her it was worth lots of money. It comforted Value just to think about it. Her plan made it easier to endure the three nuts she was forced to live with.

The other thing that comforted her was making up stories about Barney Middleton. She started one now. It was an old one, one that she'd "done" many times before. It involved kidnapping and torture. Very slowly, Value pulled out Barney's finger and toe nails, one by one, with the pliers they kept in their basement. It ended with Value taking the garden shears and snipping off Barney's ding-ding. No other images made Value smile more, except perhaps when she imagined plunging the roast beef carving knife right through the heart of Uncle Ralph.

The sun looked like the inside of an overripe melon. To Zo, it seemed too hot for April; he carried his raincoat over his arm, annoyed that the showers he'd anticipated were stuck in the sky. At Avenue B and Tenth Street he entered Tompkins Square Park.

People said this area was going to be upgraded, elevated, but as far as Zo could see the drug scene had escalated; the cheap housing attracted artists and leftover beats and people who didn't seem to fit in either category, like the Dudevant kid. Some kid.

Zo looked at his watch. Three thirty. He'd been on for more than twenty-four hours. Helen wouldn't be home yet and he didn't feel like being alone in the apartment. He sat on a bench and lit a cigarette. All around him there were knots of young men and women lying in the grass. Glancing to his left, Zo watched a couple necking. He wondered if the resentment he felt was because he'd just turned forty. Or was it simply his dislike of public display? The boy's hair was long and dirty-looking and a full beard made it difficult to see what he really looked like. The girl's hair was equally long, hitting her waist, and her jeans were trimmed at the bottom with a decorative border. They were both shoeless, sandals nearby, and their feet were black with accumulated dirt. It made Zo sick.

"What'cha lookin' at, man?" the boy yelled to Zo.

He hadn't realized his staring had been noticed. "Not much," he answered, feeling hostile.

The boy sat up, pulling his arm from beneath the girl. "That's real uncool, man, real uncool."

Zo dropped his Chesterfield stub to the ground and squashed it with his foot. He didn't want trouble or to be forced to show his badge. "Forget it," he said, rising, hoping for an amicable end to this stupid little altercation.

The long-haired boy stood up and planted himself in front of Zo. "You insulted my old lady, man."

"Sorry," said Zo, surprising the boy.

"Yeah, well, okay." He took a step backward, not knowing

what to do; clearly there was no fight here. "You look wiped out, man."

"Tired." He turned to leave and felt the boy's hand on his arm.

"Want a smoke?"

He almost said, "No thanks, I just put one out," but then he registered what the boy meant. He could bust the kid, but what for? "No thanks," he said, and gave the boy a half-hearted salute and walked away. Lucky kid, he thought. Good thing he'd just come away from a double homicide and had nothing left. Besides, murder made marijuana possession look like child's play.

Still not wanting to go home, he decided to pay J.J. a visit. He owned a successful bar on Sullivan Street. It was his second one. The first, in Great Neck, had been a failure. Because of his drunkenness J.J.'d lost the place, but then he'd gotten sober. Zo thought it was a miracle. Sobriety certainly had never been in Kelly's plans, nor had the Village bar, but when he left his wife, he moved into Manhattan and bought this place. Zo had thought a bar would be a terrible spot for J.J., but he said it was good therapy, watching the drunks made him realize how lucky he was. Besides, he'd told Zo, occasionally he was able to help some poor slob and lead him to A.A.

When he reached the bar he looked at his watch again and saw that it was now four fifteen. He'd stay for an hour or so and get home right before Helen.

"Hey there, kiddo," yelled J.J. when Zo entered.

Zo was temporarily blinded by the switch from sunlight to dark. "I can hear you, but I can't see you, Kelly."

"Follow the bouncing ball."

Zo stumbled toward the bar, his eyes slowly adjusting. Crashing into a barstool he said, "Goddammit to hell."

J.J. laughed, reached out a hand over the mahogany bar and helped Zo find his balance. "Long time no see," he said.

"No see now," said Zo, climbing onto a stool.

"You will." He set a beer in front of him.

Zo took his pack of Chesterfields from his pocket, extracted the last one, and crumpled the package. "Double homicide," he said, sighing. He knew J.J. would understand; he was one of two people (Helen was the other) he could say those words to and have them mean paragraphs. It told his friend he'd probably been up all night, that he was sick in body and soul, and that he needed to talk about it.

"Want somethin' to eat?"

"Nope."

"So go."

Zo told him about the two young women who were found in a tenement apartment, their throats slit from ear to ear. When he was finished, J.J. refilled his glass. They exchanged ideas on the murder and then went on to other things. And then J.J. asked him what he always asked him.

"Anything new on it?"

It was the Danielle Swann murder, almost ten years old and as important to Zo as it had always been. He knew he was obsessed; J.J. and Helen had told him often enough. "Not really. I bumped into Emma Stevenson the other day."

"Yeah, and? You get anything?"

Zo shrugged. "What's to get, J.J.? We know who did it, we just don't know why."

"And you ain't got proof, don't forget that little matter."

"Forget? I never forget it for an instant. If I had proof, do you think Swann and that Somerville woman would be free?"

"You still watching the kid?"

Zo nodded.

"What for, Zo? What's that gonna do for your life?"

He looked up into J.J.'s pale blue eyes. He could see him clearly now, and was amazed as ever at how well he looked, younger than he had ten years before, certainly thinner. "Don't know. I keep thinking Somerville will show herself, maybe take the kid somewhere."

"Ah, Zo."

"Bartender?" a voice came from the end of the bar.

"Right back," said J.J.

And what if Hedy Somerville did come out of her house? What would that prove? He thought of Emma; she looked ravaged, her life having been disrupted by her unwanted, unexplained connection with the Swann case. It was Emma who'd led him to Hedy years ago, after touching the gun. He remembered how startled, almost frightened, he'd been when he saw the numbers 167 above the door of the Somerville house. In February of 1956, the third time he'd staked it out, a car pulled away as he drove up. The driver was a man; Zo was able to get the plate number and later determined that it was an Avis car rented by Martin Swann. Four days after he'd traced the rented car to Swann, he knocked on Hedy's door.

It was a long time before it opened and Zo was preparing to go around the back. Then she was there, peering through the partially opened door, her face looking squeezed, squashed.

"Yes? What is it?"

He removed his hat. "Afternoon, missus."

"What do you want? I don't need anything."

"Ain't selling nothing," he said, affecting a hicklike sound. Inside he was quivering. Her hair coloring was different, the eyeglasses, too, but her eye was winking rhythmically, like the arm of a metronome, and Zo knew in his gut that he was face to face with the killer of Danielle Swann. He went on with his planned script. "I was told you had a room to let, missus."

She pursed her lips, then said, "Who told you that?"

The sound of paranoia echoed in Zo's ears. "In town," he answered arcanely.

"What does that mean?"

"Do you, missus? I need a room."

"No, I don't." She tried to close the door, but Zo's foot was in place, ready. She looked down at his scuffed brown oxford, then back up at his face, examining his features.

"Ain't you Mrs. Somerville?"

"I don't have a room. Now go away."

"Well, now, maybe I got the wrong place. Can you tell me where Mrs. Somerville lives?" He knew it was Miss and hoped to get a confirmation this way. He did.

"There is no Mrs. I'm Miss."

"Miss Somerville?"

"Yes. And I don't have a room. Now get your foot out of the door before I call my father."

Zo almost smiled. He'd done his homework and knew that George Somerville was a stroke victim, unable to move around by himself. Nevertheless, he withdrew his foot. She'd slammed the door, leaving him on the stoop hat in hand and thinking excitedly the murder was practically solved.

Here it was, more than nine years later and he was no closer to proving her culpability now than he had been then. Or Martin Swann's. There was no doubt in Zo's mind that Swann had paid or bribed or blackmailed the Somerville woman into killing his wife, but he simply couldn't prove it.

He'd never seen Swann at the Somerville place again, never could connect them in any way. As to the identity of Value's father, he simply couldn't imagine. He was sure it wasn't Swann, convinced there couldn't be any romantic or sexual link between Hedy and Martin. But some instinct told him, against all intelligence, that the child's birth and father did have some relationship to the murder. And that credence kept his obsession blooming.

"Want another beer, Zo?" Kelly asked, returning.

"Thanks."

J.J. filled the glass, foam sliding down the side, forming a puddle on the silky bar.

"How's Audrey?" Zo asked.

Audrey was J.J.'s new wife, twenty years younger, and his eyes widened with pride at the mention of her name. He launched into a rapturous story about how they'd spent the last weekend. Zo listened attentively, glad to be distracted from the Swann case and the double homicide.

When Zo left J.J.'s bar, he felt a bit lightheaded, not drunk, but he'd not had sleep and the three beers had certainly affected him. It was cooler now; gauzy clouds had fallen in front of the sun like a screen but there was still no sign of rain. He walked across Bleecker Street to Thompson. It was eight minutes of six; Helen wouldn't be home yet. But when he opened the door he found her there, sitting in the living room in an easy chair, staring, and looking old.

"You're home," he said stupidly.

She looked at him, her eyes clearly red from crying. "Yes."

"Helen, what is it?" He kicked shut the door and stood still as if his feet had been nailed to the floor.

All around them were packing cases; they were finally moving from the small apartment to another, larger one in a brownstone on Sullivan. Zo knew moving caused stress, but they were all packed, the men coming the next day to move them around the corner.

"Helen, what is it?" he asked again.

"Oh, Zo," she said and began to cry.

Now his feet traversed the bare floor and he knelt by her side. They had lived in this place the entire sixteen years of their marriage; of course she'd feel sad, as if they were losing a part of themselves. "Honey, as soon as we get to the new place you'll be okay. I know you will." He stroked her shoulder-length blond hair and put it behind her ear so he could kiss her cheek.

She shook her head.

"Yes, it'll be fine." He hadn't realized just how attached to the place she'd become. Perhaps it was because they hadn't had children. Everything always came back to that.

"Please, Zo, it's not the apartment."

He felt frightened. Helen didn't cry over nothing. "What then?" he asked, mouth going dry.

"I've come from the doctor."

Doctor? The word sounded idiotic in his mind and he couldn't squeeze it through his lips. Finally he forced himself to ask her. "What doctor?"

"Shiffenhouse."

He was her gynecologist. Rejecting beforehand what he might hear, Zo's mind fastened on a picture of Shiffenhouse, hooded eyes and damp skin.

"Zo? You hear me?"

"Yes. What's wrong?"

Helen put her hand on his cheek, ran her fingers over his burgeoning beard. "Cancer," she said almost inaudibly.

The word socked him in the stomach.

"I have to have a mastectomy." She began to cry again and put her hand on her right breast as if this would protect her from the surgeon's knife.

He could think of nothing to say and got up from his kneeling position, took her hand, and led her into the bedroom where they lay down, she in his arms.

After a few moments he asked, "Did you suspect?"

"I felt a lump."

"Why didn't you tell me?"

"I didn't want to worry you."

A flash of anger seared him and he started to chastize her for not telling him, then realized it was pointless now, and only a diversion, a way to avoid more important issues. "You have to have a second opinion."

"This *was* a second opinion. I went to Mother's doctor first."

"You mean you've known about this and——"

"Oh please, Zo, don't. I wanted to be sure before I involved you."

Involved him. As if he were some distant relative. He could not deny how hurt he felt. They had always shared everything, keeping nothing back, no matter how painful or shattering. And from this, one of the worst moments of their lives, he'd been excluded. It was that woman thing again, he thought, that kind of intimacy and sharing no man could ever be a part of. "But your mother knew?" he said, accusing.

"Yes, she knew. I told you I went to Rupell, Mother's doctor."

He clenched his teeth together. She didn't even realize how slighted he felt. And then he heard himself: was he crazy, he wondered, his focus so self-centered? He held her tighter and put aside his feeling of isolation. It was exhaustion and the brutalization of murder which had made him so selfish.

"It's going to happen Tuesday, Zo. I'm so afraid."

Of course she was and it was up to him to comfort and reassure, but any words that came to mind were empty. All he had to give, he decided, was the strength of his physical grip, the comfort of his arms, and the insuperable depth of his love. It was a great deal. Perhaps, in the end, more important than fatuous words.

Zo's strokings and pettings gave Helen courage to speak. "I'm so afraid you won't want me anymore. I'll only be part woman."

He wanted to laugh, knew Helen would if she weren't the center of the scene, speaking the line. But he had to comment on it. "Helen, that's right out of some awful novel."

She pulled back from him. "How can you, Zo? This is serious."

"Of course it is, darling. Much more serious than thinking about being part woman and junk like that."

"I'm thinking of you."

"If that's true, you should know better. You think I'm going to stop loving you because you've . . . because. . . ."

"See, you can't even say it."

Annoyed, he said, "Okay, so it doesn't roll off my tongue with ease. It's not something I've been living with for years, you know. The point is I love *you*, not your breasts." That sounded wrong; he must pacify her. "You have me nuts. Listen, I love you with all my soul, you know that, and the only thing I care about is you being well. And I love your breasts, too, but if you have to have a mastectomy to save your life, then that's that and I'll want you as much as I ever have. Got it?"

"Got it," she whispered.

"It'll be okay." He wanted to cry. To scream. Maybe it wouldn't be okay. Who could he ask? He'd have to call Shiffenhouse.

As if reading his mind she said, "The doctor says I have an excellent chance of complete recovery. Of course, you don't know for five years."

Zo's lids were heavy, but he mustn't sleep now; she needed him. "Want to go out to dinner like we planned?"

"Guess so, can't cook here."

"Don't be afraid, darling, I'm with you," he said.

"It helps me so much having you."

Sleep threatened and he panicked. "Baby, I . . . I've got to nap first, I. . . ."

"Sure you do. I'm sorry."

"No, no, don't be, it's just that I gotta. . . ."

"Sure. Don't worry. I'm okay now. How long do you want to sleep, Zo?"

There was no answer.

Helen curled further into his arms, trying to accept his absence of the moment, knowing he'd been up for more than twenty-four hours, understanding, as always. But even so she felt abandoned, lonely. Quietly she left the bed, the room. At the phone she dialed her mother.

In Martin Swann's spare time he occupied his mind with thoughts of how to eliminate Hedy Somerville from his life, indeed, from the world. He entertained many plans, never calling any of them murder. *Eradicate, expunge, excise, remove* were the words he used. The desire was especially strong on this day, the tenth anniversary of Danielle's death.

A horrible dissonant sound spilled out of Claude's room, assaulting Martin's ears. It was, he supposed, music. Another one of these awful groups of boys, shouting unintelligible lyrics and torturing guitars, pianos, and drums, their hair in their eyes, their clothing suggestive. He wondered how he would survive the summer with both his children home from school; at best, his condition was precarious. His Valium intake could be increased, of course. He'd been taking it since it had been approved two years earlier, going from Miltown to Librium before that. But Valium was much more effective. Now he was up to fifty milligrams a day. It was essential that he be calm in his work and if he didn't medicate himself his guilt feelings turned immediately into anxiety and then he was ineffective with his patients and that was untenable.

If Hedy Somerville were removed from the world, he reasoned, he would no longer be guilty or anxious and could discontinue his drug therapy. However, if *he* effected her demise, surely he would experience another guilt/anxiety syndrome. It was a conundrum.

"Would you like a cocktail, Martin?" asked Lynn, coming into the living room where he sat, staring.

"That would be nice." He wondered if Lynn knew what day it was. Or if the children knew. Perhaps he should mention it. He couldn't.

At the teak bar in the corner of the living room, Lynn mixed their old-fashioneds, carefully cutting the orange, dividing the thin slice in half. As she measured out the sugar, she said:

"How are you today?"

"Fine, fine," he answered without delay.

"You're sure?"

"Yes, of course," he said. So she did remember. He might as well speak of it; it was obvious that that was what she wanted. "If you mean," he said in an imperious tone, "am I reacting to the date, I am not. Ten years is a very long time." It wouldn't do to let Lynn know his every feeling on the matter; she might become jealous. Besides, it annunciated his vulnerability and this made him uncomfortable.

Lynn handed him his drink and sat opposite, sinking into a comfortable easy chair. When they had moved from their own apartments to this one on East Seventy-seventh, they'd agreed to buy all new furniture, bringing nothing of the past with them except their children.

"It wouldn't be *so* peculiar if you felt *something* today."

"Well, naturally, I feel *something*," he said, trying to recover.

"But you said——"

"I know what I said." He sipped his drink. "I'm aware that it's the tenth anniversary of Danielle's death. I'm aware of the date every year. But I'm not plunged into despair over that fact."

A loud blast of music swept into the room.

"Good Christ, what's that?" he asked.

"If I'm not mistaken, it's The Rolling Stones."

"How can you tell? They all sound the same. Horrible."

"I've been hearing it all day, every day, for the past three weeks."

"Why don't you tell him to stop?"

"I don't really mind. It's nice to have them home. I feel as if there's life here again."

Their eyes met briefly: accusation and loneliness in hers, guilt and denial in his.

She changed the subject. "I got a letter from Ross today."

"How is he?"

"He sounds all right. The letter's on the hall table; you can read it."

Ross was in the army and Lynn always left his letters for Martin to read; he never read them. He didn't like him, never had. To keep peace he took the letters to his study, then returned them to her, unread, saying Ross sounded fine.

"Are you getting along with Cristina?" Martin asked.

Lynn adjusted her glasses, fingers fluttering around the rim. "Yes, I suppose. I try, Martin, I really do. She doesn't like me."

"Nonsense."

From the beginning Cristina had resented Lynn, had made it clear. But Martin refused to see the truth, clinging stubbornly to the idea that it was paranoia on Lynn's part, the natural assumption of the stepmother. Lynn tried to make him see that, perhaps it was the natural reaction of the *stepdaughter* to resent. He wouldn't hear her. It was true, of course, that she was the adult and Cristina the child, but she was not a miraclemaker. Cristina held fast to her dislike of Lynn, perhaps on some irrational level blaming her for her mother's death. In front of Martin, Cristina was civil to her and although she was never openly hostile, she exuded an aloofness which enveloped Lynn as if she were caught in an icy net. But it was always "nonsense" to Martin.

"I'll see about dinner," she said.

Martin sipped his drink and turned his thoughts back to Hedy. It wasn't just the money he sent her every week that plagued him; it was her erroneous idea that the child was his. Of course if she hadn't believed that, who knows where he'd be now?

Cristina, tall and thin, looking like Danielle more each day, came into the living room, book in hand. "Hi, Poppy."

He found it almost painful to look at her, especially today, and only glanced in her direction when he said hello. And hadn't he capitulated in the mad scheme of Hedy's because of this child, both children? Of course he had. It was a form of protection for them, shielding them from any further pain and horror; an act of altruism.

"What are you reading?"

"*Cat's Cradle*," she said.

"What's it about?" he asked, not really interested.

"I can't explain it. It's weird." She sat on the sofa, pulling her legs up under her. She was wearing bell-bottom jeans and a red cotton short-sleeved shirt.

The word *weird* made him think again of Hedy and her child. She had told him she'd named the child Value. Well, what could he have expected? Would someone like Hedy Somerville name her child Joan or Ann or Carol? But where'd the child come from? Her ultimatum to him made it clear that even though she wished for his child, she would not tolerate intercourse. Artificial insemination was the way it had to be done.

"Poppy?"

"Yes?"

"You know what today is?"

"Yes, Cristina, I know." He looked at her now, so young and vulnerable, curled into the pillows, taking refuge. There had been three psychiatrists for her so far. How many more would be necessary? If she'd been his patient, he would have asked how she felt; but she was not, so he changed the subject.

"You're sure you don't want to go to camp this summer?"

"I'm sure." She opened her book, a hurried retreat.

Relieved that she was reading, he finished his drink and rose to make another. It was inadvisable to drink at all with Valium, but Martin believed he could handle it.

Returning to his chair with his drink, he glanced at Cristina, who was still absorbed in her book, then laid back his head, closing his eyes.

Martin's first instinct that day, nine and a half years ago, on hearing "I killed your wife," was to run to the phone and call the police. But something, a presentiment of some sort, had stopped him. He'd invited her into his office and listened to her explain that unless he fulfilled the "contract" she would tell the world that he had asked her to murder his wife. Hedy Somerville was, as he'd diagnosed years ago, psychotic and, as many psychotics were, clever. At least she had been clever enough to elude the police for six months.

"What contract are you referring to?" he'd asked.

"Aha!" she said, raising a stubby forefinger. "Now we come to it."

Martin waited for the explanation as Hedy sat and stared at him, an odd, fixed smile on her face. He wondered if at any moment she would shoot him, almost hoping she would. The presage of something horrible was overpowering and death seemed a viable option. Would the police take her word against his? And what about the press? He'd already been through that particular crucifixion once.

"Tell me what you have in mind. What contract?"

Her chin snapped up, her eye winked madly. "I did your bidding and now——"

"I beg your pardon?" This was insane! Yes, it was. That was the point. Still, he persisted as if he were speaking with a rational person. "What bidding?"

The pale blue eyes narrowed, one heavy and droopy with fake lashes, the pouchy cheeks rising and pressing against the harlequin frames. "Don't pretend you didn't want her dead. I knew, I always knew, how you felt about her. And then when you got the other one I knew what you wanted me to do."

There was no use arguing. She wanted some sort of exchange with him, but how could he possibly make a deal with this madwoman? But it wasn't just him; there were the children. They'd already suffered and if money was what Hedy wanted it would be little enough to protect them from further damage. Besides, Danielle was dead and there was no bringing her back whatever he did or did not do. His first duty now, he reasoned, was to his children.

"How much money do you want?"

"Money?" she said. "You must be insane."

He wondered if he was, and if he was imagining this imitation of Alice's Tea Party.

"What is it you want then?"

"I want to have a baby. A baby is needed. It will restore the balance." She leaned forward, her hands, the fingernails crimped from biting, on his desk. "And it must be your baby."

Astonished, Martin listened while she went on, telling him about the artificial insemination and how she expected the first attempt to take place in one week at her home in Irvington.

The alternative was her confession, implicating him. He had no doubt that she would do it: sacrifice her life to destroy him.

The moment she'd gone, he reached for the phone to call Detective Campisi. But he couldn't go through with it. If Hedy Somerville started even the slightest ripple about his innocence, his life would be ruined. He'd squeaked out of it last time but a second barrage of doubts would finish him; he might lose Lynn. And, again, there were the children. Martin believed that before the meeting took place with Hedy he would think of an alternative action.

"H'lo, Poppy." It was Claude, crashing through his memory.

Martin opened his eyes. The boy was tall, his shaggy, unkempt, blond hair below his ears. Martin hated the look but allowed it, not wanting to make him any more of a maverick than he already was. At fourteen, Claude had not learned to read.

"Hello, Claude," Martin said. "How was your day?"

"Cool." Plopping down on the couch beside his sister, Claude said, "Did you take my Beatles record?"

"No," Cristina answered, not looking up.

"Well, somebody did."

"Maybe it was a ghost." As she said it she lifted her head, eyes looking into Martin's.

He shifted his gaze.

Cristina pressed her lips together in a hard line, then said, "You don't even know what day it is, do you, Claude?"

"It's Thursday."

She clucked her tongue in disgust, eyes back on the book. "You make me sick."

"What's wrong with you, Tina? What're you talking about?"

She didn't answer.

"What's the matter with her, Poppy?"

Martin shrugged and rolled his eyes as if to say, You know girls.

Claude put a hand on her book and pushed it down. "What day is it?"

Cristina let the book fall to her lap, finger marking the place. "It's so typical of you not to know. You live in a dream world," she said, the sound of envy betraying her accusation. Looking at Martin, she ordered, "You tell him, Poppy. Tell him what day it is."

"Why?" Martin pleaded. "What's the point?"
"God," she said.
"Will *somebody* tell me?" begged Claude.
Angrily, Cristina rose and, looking down at her brother, brown eyes growing darker, she said, "It's ten years today that Mommy was killed."
"Oh," he said, shamed, as if he were responsible for his mother's death rather than guilty of forgetfulness.
"Oh," she mimicked. "Is that all you can say?"
"Yes," he answered defiantly.
"You're pathetic," she said, and stormed from the room.
Martin was sure her epithet was meant for him, too.
"You should've told me, Poppy," Claude said. "The thing is . . . the thing is. . . ." He fiddled with the strap of his watch.
Martin took a deep breath. "What is it . . . the thing?" He wished he were far away, on an island perhaps.
"You won't get mad?"
From his pocket Martin withdrew a small yellow pill and surreptitiously popped it into his mouth, washing it down with his drink. "I won't get mad."
The boy's brown eyes were shot through with remorse and an old scar near his left eye grew whiter in the flush of his cheek. "The thing is, Poppy, I don't remember Mommy." His voice cracked.
"You were only four, Claude. It's understandable."
"Tina remembers her."
"Those two years make a difference. Besides, she . . . she saw. . . ."
"Sometimes I think I saw it happen, too." Claude sat on the edge of the couch, his elbows on his knees, chin in his hands. "I know I didn't, but sometimes, I dunno, it sort of comes to me, but I still can't see her face, remember her, you know?"
Martin nodded. "It's all right, Claude."
"You think so?"
"I do."
"Don't tell Tina, okay?"
"I won't."
Claude stood up and stuffed his hands in his pockets, hunching his bony shoulders. "You feel bad today, Poppy?"
He felt bad every day but knew that wasn't what the boy

meant. "A little, yes." His chin fell against his neck and he inspected his drink as if it were extraordinarily interesting.

Claude made a sound of sympathy, then quietly left the room. Martin was relieved. Even the meager exchange he'd had with his son had drained him. He turned back to his memories.

It was Lynn's son, Whitney, who'd solved the problem. Martin knew there was no way he was going to artificially inseminate Hedy; the best he could do was to stall. He feared that, however, because Hedy seemed to have some schedule in mind. But the day before the appointed date, Whitney brought something glutinous and white to the table for his dessert: yoghurt. Martin knew at once that thinned down and placed in a test tube it would resemble sperm, at least to Hedy Somerville's untrained eye. The deception accomplished his purpose.

Hedy's plan was to meet every two weeks until she became pregnant. Martin had no idea what he was going to do when the woman eventually realized that it wasn't working. Increasingly agitated, he took drugs: Miltown during the day, Seconal at night. And then, on visit four, Hedy told him that she *was* pregnant.

"Aren't you going to congratulate me?" she asked.

"Congratulations," he said dully. What he wanted to say was, how is it possible and who is the father?

He had never seen her again after that day, but she was always with him. And so was the thought of the child. The whole idea of Value Somerville growing up in Irvington, New Jersey, horrified him. In his own way, he kept track of her, thinking: now she is two, now she is five. On November twenty-fourth of this year, she would be nine. A little girl like any other? How bad could she be at that age?

Sometimes he toyed with the idea of going to New Jersey to see Value. Sometimes he entertained the thought of calling Detective Campisi and revealing all. Yet, what good would that do? Everything he'd tried to avoid would happen. No, the whole thing was out of his hands and he'd have to let go of it. But he couldn't; day after day he went over the same ground, trying to figure out a way to eradicate, expunge, excise, remove.

The worst thing was that there was no one he could confide in. This was something he had to deal with himself, and so far his only solution was Valium and Seconal and they really never helped. That was why he often contemplated suicide. He doubted that he'd ever have the courage; he prayed that he'd accidentally overdose. It had happened to others; there was no reason to believe it couldn't happen to him.

Cristina lay on her bed, her secret treasure chest opened next to her. She had refused dinner, thinking it disgraceful and disrespectful to eat on the anniversary of her mother's death. There was something especially meaningful about the tenth anniversary; it had more weight somehow than seven or twelve. She felt the same about her age. Everyone had made a huge fuss about "sweet sixteen," but she'd found fifteen infinitely more significant. Perhaps it was the five-year marks. She imagined she'd be much more moved by turning twenty than twenty-one.

Reaching out a hand, she touched the red felt box. The contents were mementoes of Danielle. Cristina had collected the few things when she was seven, so her choices weren't the ones she might have made had she been older. Still, the objects had been her mother's and that was all that mattered. There was a lipstick, Crimson Red; a gold pin with script initials: D.D.S.; a gold locket which held baby pictures of Cristina and Claude; a Zippo lighter; a marbleized fountain pen, blue and yellow; a white lace handkerchief; and, finally, a picture of Danielle taken a year before her death. Cristina lifted the photograph from its coffer. It was easy to see that she was growing more like her mother every day and this fact made her inordinately happy. She reveled in the resemblance because it kept her memory green. Poppy would have liked her to forget. He even wanted her to call Lynn Mother, but she steadfastly refused. Her mother was Danielle. Maybe it was mean to Lynn, but she couldn't help it. Poppy wanted her to pretend that her life with Mommy had never happened. She was sure that was why she never saw her grandparents anymore. Or her Uncle Guy. Cristina touched the photograph, the tip of her forefinger on the dimple in Danielle's chin. Then she touched the hollow in her own chin; it was growing deeper all the time.

Dr. Hess had said she must leave her mother in the past and engage with the present. Cristina thought he was a jerk. They all were. None of them understood. She took the pin from the box, returned the photograph, and fastened the piece of jewelry to her shirt. What would Dr. Hess say if he knew what she had planned for the next day? Smiling, she felt slightly wicked. She couldn't believe she hadn't done it before.

Her plan was to simply knock on the door and say, "Hi, I'm Cristina, your granddaughter." The image made her tingly. Poppy would never have to know. She was very good at keeping secrets. In all these years, she'd never told anyone, not one of those stupid doctors, that the lady with the wink had said: *"This is for. . . ."* She'd still not been able to fill in the end of the sentence, but who cared? Anyway, it proved she was a good secret-keeper. And by this time tomorrow night she would have a grandmother and grandfather again and maybe even an uncle. She could hardly wait.

TWO

Cristina could not remember her heart's beating in this fashion since the time she'd first seen Frank, the boy who cut lawns at Miss Porter's School. But today it was irregular from terror and she wondered if there was any relationship between sex and fear. Toddy Garland claimed she had had sex over Christmas vacation and said there was nothing to fear. Some of the girls had been shocked by Toddy's tale, some repelled, and some enthralled. Cristina was one of the latter. She could hardly wait to experience the sensations firsthand, but had no intention of doing any of it until she was married.

The reason for the wild beating of her heart today was her plan to see her grandparents.

"What's wrong, Cristina? Don't you feel well?" Lynn asked.

"I feel fine," she answered, looking across the breakfast table at her stepmother.

"You have a weird look," said Claude.

"I do not," she answered irritably. She wished everything about Claude didn't annoy her so much.

The boy shrugged his bony shoulders and resumed crunching his toast.

Lynn said, "You do look a bit pale, that's all."

It was a wonderful opening for her. "I've been hanging around the house too much. I need some sun. I'm going over to the park today."

"Please be careful," said Lynn.

"Of what?" she asked contemptuously, and was instantly sorry. She hated the way she spoke to Lynn, but it was automatic. The thought of apologizing sailed through her mind and into the atmosphere.

"Of strangers," Lynn answered.

"Lynn means dirty old men," Claude said, grinning. "Don't you?"

"Well, they aren't always dirty and they aren't always old."

"Honestly," Cristina said, "I'm not a child, you know. I'm not going to take a piece of candy from a stranger. God."

"Of course not. I just meant. . . ." She waved her hand in the air, the long thin fingers making a streak of pink flesh.

"Don't worry, I know how to take care of myself."

"I'm sure you do."

Their eyes locked in ineffable accusation and struggle. Lynn was the first to yield.

As Cristina walked west on Seventy-seventh Street, she felt the anger at Lynn begin to drain away. She loathed it when they had these silent battles, because she didn't really hate Lynn and suspected Lynn didn't hate her. Cristina thought Lynn was a drip but also believed she bore no resemblance to the mythical mean stepmother. It was her drippiness, however, that Cristina resented most. Why, if she had to have a stepmother, couldn't she have had someone neat? Having to contend with a boring stepmother was just awful, and it also made her wonder about her father. Why had he chosen her?

Turning the corner at Third Avenue and Seventy-fourth Street, Cristina, deep in thought, bumped into a woman.

"Watch where you're going," she flared.

"Sorry," said Cristina.

The woman brushed herself off as if Cristina had knocked her down instead of grazing her arm. "You kids," she said, and bristling still, moved on.

Angry and humiliated, Cristina kept her eyes cast downward as she began walking. Then, from somewhere up the block, came a voice which froze her in mid-step.

"You ever notice that Jesus is after us all the time to change the ways we sin, trying always to get us nearer the sandwiches and bring. . . ."

The voice was so familiar that Cristina felt she might have heard it yesterday rather than ten years ago. A snaky ribbon of fear slithered through her and yet she found herself approaching the fat person as if she had no will of her own. A few feet from the mammoth figure she stopped, listening.

". . . it reflects the ideas, you know, a warning more than willpower and understanding, this is why Andy Warhol needs to see a dipthong over and above the. . . ."

This creature had visited Cristina in her dream so often, she would have known it anywhere even though there were changes. Age had touched the face and the clothes were different: the khaki jacket was replaced by a worn madras one,

178

the pants were a shiny blue gabardine. The hair was still long and the fat less firm.

". . . it reflects the expanding population who never reach out to see water under the bridge, did you ever notice that, little girl?"

The question was addressed to Cristina and the piercing eyes riveted her own as if two burning spikes linked them together. Only when the madrased arm, the huge hand, nails long and yellow, reached for her was she able to move.

She ran up Seventy-fourth and when she'd made it to the other side of Lexington, she stopped. Leaning against the side of a building she took long restorative breaths, gulped exhaust-filled air as if it were sweet and pure.

"Need some help, girlie?"

She shook her head.

"Somebody chasin' ya?" The man gave a lubricious smile.

Dirty old man, she thought, and would've laughed if she'd had the breath. Instead, she shook her head again and hoped he'd go away.

"Maybe ya need an escort, huh?" He took a step closer, one hand propped against the brick, leaning over her.

He was extremely vulnerable in this position. It would have been so easy to lift her knee and get him where it hurt most, but she hadn't the heart for it.

"You're a pervert," she said and ducked under his arm, running.

At the corner of Fifth Avenue, she turned downtown feeling, finally, safe; at least from pursuers of any sort. Walking slowly, trying to regain her equanimity, she could not shake a feeling of gloom. As a child she'd been sure that the fat person was a woman, but later she'd lost that certainty. And she was still uncertain now.

Why had she seen it on this day of all days? Should she tell someone about this sighting? But who? And what did it mean, after all? The fat person really had nothing to do with her mother's murder. Still, seeing it today was disconcerting and ominous.

Perhaps she shouldn't go. But that was stupid, like believing in the supernatural. It was coincidence, no more, no less; she wasn't about to let it ruin her day.

Her grandmaman's apartment house was just a block away.

Stopping, she took a surreptitious look beneath her arms to see if sweat had strained her lavender blouse; it had, but was fading now. Should she wait until any evidence of sweat was gone? Dumb, she decided. Everyone had sweat glands and the day was hot. Besides, she couldn't just stand here on Fifth Avenue looking weird, waiting to dry. She began walking again. As she approached the doorman her heart took up its earlier thrumming.

"Help you, miss?"

She smiled, holding her dimpled chin high. "I'm here to see the Dudevants," she said.

"Mrs. D. expecting you?"

Cristina didn't like the man's informality and said, with all the hauteur she could muster, "I'm her granddaughter, Miss Swann."

"Granddaughter, huh?" He pushed back his gray, gold-braided cap so it rested over his brow in a more jaunty fashion. "Didn't know there was a granddaughter."

"Well, there is. I mean, I am."

"I'll announce you," the doorman said.

"No," she said quickly. "I haven't seen them in a while and I want to surprise them."

"*Them?*" He cocked his head to one side, suspicious.

She hadn't counted on anything like this. She mustn't let him see her nervousness. "My grandparents," she stated with a flourish of authority.

"I think you'd better go along, miss. You don't belong here." He motioned, palms out, for her to leave.

The dismissal enraged her. "I do belong! How dare you speak to me this way? I'll get my grandpapa to have you fired."

"And what grandpapa would that be?"

Even through her rage Cristina realized something was terribly wrong. It was evident this man knew something she didn't. Her grandpapa must be dead. She had no idea what to say. Tears filled her eyes.

"Ah, dammit now, miss, don't be cryin' all over the place. Just move along." The tone had softened some.

"Oh, please," she said, the tears breaking over her lashes, "I can explain." And she did, in stumbling, halting phrases. But when she was through, the doorman believed and understood.

He handed her his handkerchief. "It's true, your grandpapa

is dead. And Mrs. D., well, she don't go out much or anything. I mean, she a mite unusual. You don't think I should ring up, prepare her?"

Cristina wiped her cheeks dry. "I really would like to surprise her. I know she'll be happy to see me."

"Sure she will. Okay. It's the tenth floor. It's the maid's day off, so if she don't answer the door come back down and I'll ring up. Okay?" He smiled, kinder now.

"Thank you." She smiled back, returned his handkerchief.

In the elevator she wondered what *a mite unusual* meant. Any bravado she'd had was gone, as if someone had pulled a plug and her courage had gushed out. The great idea seemed limp and she couldn't remember one reason why she was here. The elevator man swayed the lift to a stop and opened the doors. Cristina stepped out into the hall and faced the familiar apartment door. *A mite unusual* sang in her mind with a dissonant ring. "Oh, what the hell," she said out loud and rang the bell.

It seemed a very long time before she heard a shuffling sound and then the tinny scraping of the peephole cover being lifted. Cristina smiled.

"Who is it?" asked the peeper.

She hadn't planned it this way. In her imagination the door just opened and both grandparents awaited her, arms outstretched, no questions. Why was reality always so different, so awful.

"Who's there?" came the voice again.

Identifying herself would ruin the surprise, but how else was she going to gain admittance? "Grandmaman," she said, "it's me, Cristina."

Nothing stirred. Then the metallic clicking and turning of locks rent the quiet. Slowly the door opened. Amelia stared at the child, her gray eyes widening in alarm. "Danielle," she whispered, clutching the door handle for support.

"Oh, no, Grandmaman, it's Cristina."

"Cristina," she repeated.

"Your granddaughter. May I come in?" She was shocked by how her grandmother looked.

There was no light in Amelia's eyes, no signal of recognition or comprehension. She simply stared at the child, bewildered.

Deciding to take charge, Cristina said, "I'd like to come in to visit with you, Grandmaman." She stepped into the apartment, moving slowly, aware that her command of the situation must be gentle.

Amelia watched as Cristina came in and once again felt the keen shock of recognition, as if she were viewing a revenant.

"Grandmaman? Don't you remember me?"

There was no answer.

Carefully, as if she were speaking to a mentally retarded person, Cristina said, "I am Cristina. I am the daughter of Danielle. My father is Martin Swann."

At the mention of Martin's name a shot of hatred exploded across Amelia's face. "Swann," she hissed.

Cristina ignored this and tenderly put an arm through her grandmother's, leading the woman across the marbled floor toward an open door. Three cats dashed in front of them. As they entered the library a sense of remembrance washed over Cristina, at once sad and comforting. She had recalled that the chairs were blue but noted that now they were of a lighter hue as if suffering from anemia. She helped Amelia to a chair and occupied another, facing her.

Cristina had no idea how old her grandmother was, but she looked ancient. Her paper-thin skin was scored with cross-hatchings. From each side of her nose to each side of her mouth were two fluted marks. Above her lip it looked as though someone had taken a tiny rake to the skin and the grooves at the corners of her eyes were so deep one might think her cats had turned against her. Her hair was dyed a burnt ocher but clearly not professionally. It was too dark and it hung in clumps. The use of makeup bordered on the grotesque. Her face seemed drowned in powder, death white, and each cheekbone was rouged like that of a wooden soldier; the carmine lipstick applied as if with a palette knife. And then there was the jewelry: her dress was festooned with necklaces, pearl earrings dripped from her long lobes, bracelets adorned each wrist, and large rings circled eight of her fingers. Perhaps this was what the doorman had meant by a *mite unusual.*

"I've wanted to see you for a long time, Grandmaman." The sentence was the one she'd practiced, but she'd never imagined this kind of awkwardness and strain.

Amelia sat near the edge of her chair, her hands knitted together, squeezing each other so tightly the knuckles showed white. She stared at Cristina intensely as if she were an invention of her imagination.

182

Cristina licked her dry lips. "I'm sorry about Grandpapa. I just found out today."

"He was no good," said Amelia. Her voice sounded scalded. "When Danielle was alive I didn't mind Pierre's affairs, but later it seemed inappropriate somehow. Do you understand?"

"I think so," Cristina answered bravely.

"After I divorced him the new one must have left him because he didn't remarry."

"You *divorced* Grandpapa?"

"Of course," Amelia said, sitting straighter, prouder. "He should have been a comfort to me. My daughter had been killed, you know."

Didn't her grandmother understand who she was? "My mother," she said. "It was my mother who was killed."

"Your mother?"

"Yes. Danielle, your daughter, was my mother. Please understand." Cristina felt on the verge of tears.

Amelia stared. Her spidery legs crossed at the ankles slowly rubbed against each other.

"I'm your granddaughter. Cristina."

"Cristina," she repeated. "Danielle's child. The little girl."

"Yes, yes, that's right."

A broad smile slashed open Amelia's face. "Oh, my dear, my dear, I see now. Come." She extended her arms, waiting to engulf the child, her bracelets jangling.

The last thing Cristina wanted was to be enveloped by her grandmother; even touching her had lost its appeal. But she knew she had no choice; she couldn't hurt her. She crossed to the waiting arms, knelt on the floor, and leaned in against the flabby bosom. As Amelia pressed Cristina closer, she recalled the childhood feeling of suffocation. But then the breasts had been full and soft. Amelia was rocking her, the spindly arms around her back, jewelry tinkling.

"My baby girl, my darling dear, you've come home."

Oh, God, Cristina thought, does she think I'm my mother again? Claustrophobia was overcoming her, her nose hurt, pushed hard against Amelia's chest. Minutes seemed to pass before Cristina felt her grandmother's grip loosen. She took the opportunity to pull back, sitting on her heels.

"It was Martin who kept you away from me, wasn't it?" Amelia asked.

So she did understand who she was. "Yes, I guess so."

"Swann the bastard," said Amelia.

A squiggle of shock zipped through Cristina. She wasn't used to hearing words like *bastard* from the adults she knew. And certainly not applied to her father.

"And the boy, how's the boy, Claude?"

"He's fine."

"How old?"

"Fourteen."

"How old are you?"

"Sixteen."

"Sixteen. My, my." She shook her head in disbelief.

Cristina thought Grandmaman seemed normal now. Perhaps the earlier vagueness had been caused by the shock of seeing her after all these years. She began to relax.

"Martin doesn't know you're here?"

"No."

"Bastard."

Cristina looked away.

"He hired a woman to kill her. Swann's a murderer."

"Oh, no."

"Yes." Amelia reached down and grabbed Cristina's shoulders. "He wanted to marry that whore, so he had my daughter killed. The detective even said so. They all know but they can't prove it. Swann got away with murder."

Cristina began to cry. "No, it's not true." She wrenched away from the talon-like grip.

"They're crazy, these men, only caring about their *things*. The penis is their God. Disgusting. And then Pierre with *his* whore. Emma Stevenson was her name. I found out."

Cristina, on her feet now, stared at Amelia. Her face had reddened to an alarming color and her hands flailed as if she were tearing the air. As her grandmother's voice rose, Cristina backed away.

"You think anyone would listen to the detective? They didn't care . . . I fooled them all, I had my own detective, that's how I know about the slut, Emma Stevenson, and no one can tell me——"

"What's going on here?"

Cristina turned to see a man in the doorway.

"Maman," he said, "what's wrong? Who are *you?*" he asked Cristina.

She knew who he was and wanted to fling herself in his arms for protection.

"My God," he said, "you must be Cristina. You look just like Danielle."

"You're Uncle Guy."

"Yes." He went to his mother, took her hands in his as he kneeled in front of her. "Maman, are you all right?"

Amelia smiled and held tight to Guy's hands. "My detective told me everything."

"Yes, Maman, calm down now. Lean back, rest." Guy helped his mother into a more comfortable position in the chair. He pivoted around and looked back at his niece. "What happened?"

"I don't know exactly. I guess I upset her. My visit was a surprise. I'm sorry."

He rose, smiled. "It's all right."

Cristina thought he was gorgeous. Even his linen suit and pale blue tie were beautiful.

"I can't get over how much you look like Danielle," he said. "It's extraordinary. You must have really shocked Maman. You're very beautiful, as she was."

She could feel the telltale signs of blushing burn her cheeks and neck and found herself studying the floor.

"Don't be embarrassed."

"I'm not."

"Could have fooled me."

Cristina looked up. Her eyes met his violet ones. Something passed between them, she thought: a connection, tangible and electric.

"Swann has kept her from me all these years," Amelia said, "but now I have her back. She'll come visit often, won't you, dear?"

Would she? She was afraid of this woman. "Yes," she answered faintly.

"Maman," Guy said gently, "would you like to have a rest now?"

He helped her from the chair. Amelia looked at Cristina. Cristina, understanding the silent request, went to her grandmother, kissed her cheek. When she looked at the woman's face she saw that her eyes were different now, like two dying stars.

"I'll take her in to lie down," he said.

Watching them shuffle from the room, Cristina was struck by how unrealized her dream was and an emptiness, hollow and dreary, rang through her. She slumped back into the chair. Why was it that nothing ever turned out the way she imagined? Was there something wrong with her or something wrong with life?

"That bad?" Guy asked on his return. "You look as if the world had come to an end."

"I guess I feel like that," she said.

"Let's go have a cup of coffee or something. Maman will sleep for a while."

The coffee shop was indistinguishable from hundreds of others throughout the city. Guy and Cristina sat in a green leather booth, coffee and hamburgers in front of them. She felt self-conscious about eating, as if she were on a date. Picking up a dull knife she cut her hamburger in two, something she never did unless she was nervous. It was dumb to be feeling this way. He was a grown man and he was her uncle. This is my mother's brother, she said to herself.

"Do you remember me?" Guy asked.

"In a way. I mean, I knew you existed. I didn't remember what you looked like." The reference to his looks embarrassed her. She pushed her food around on her plate.

"You were just a baby. When it happened," he added.

"I remember it though." The image of the fat person loomed up. Should she tell her uncle?

"That must be very painful for you."

"Yes. Grandmaman said that she knew who the killer was."

"She imagines a great deal, Cristina."

"She said she'd hired a detective."

He looked thoughtful. "Yes, to follow Papa."

"She said that your father was. . . ." She didn't know how to phrase it.

"Was what?"

"It doesn't matter."

"Sure it does. I know she upset you, Cristina, and if you tell me what she said I'm sure I'll be able to tell you what's true and not true. Did she say Papa had an affair with someone named Emma Stevenson?"

"Yes."

"I think he did. Maman told me about this woman and

I asked him about her once. He admitted there was such a person, but he refused to discuss her with me. It was his business, after all."

"It's funny, whenever I used to think about them, Grandmaman and Grandpapa, I remembered them being in love. Weird what a kid of six thinks, isn't it?"

He shook his head, the curly black hair jiggling. "You were right. They were very much in love. Danielle's death . . . it changed everything. It changed your life, didn't it?"

Sorrow rolled to the surface and Cristina fought back tears.

Guy reached across the Formica table and covered her hand with his. "I know it was awful for you."

She wanted his hand on hers and she also prayed he'd remove it.

"It was awful for everyone," he said, withdrawing his hand. "My mother became unbalanced. My father couldn't comfort her and they drifted apart."

Suddenly she said, "I saw the fat person today."

"Fat person?"

"Don't you remember? The fat woman or man in the park that day? I though it was a woman, but Mommy wasn't sure. You weren't either."

"You mean that obese thing in Washington Square the day . . . the day. . . ."

"Yes."

"You saw her again?"

"I think it *was* a man. Yes, today."

"Where?"

"On the corner of Seventy-fourth and Third Avenue."

"Doing what?"

She told him, described the incident. He slid from the booth, grabbed the check. She followed him to the front where he paid and then he took her arm and hurried her outside. They headed toward Third Avenue, Guy's loping gait causing Cristina to run to keep up with him.

By the time they reached the corner where Cristina had seen the fat person, he/she was gone. Out of breath Guy turned to her.

"You're sure?"

She felt hurt he would doubt her. "I saw with my own eyes and heard with my own ears."

"Sorry. Of course you did. Let's go." He took her arm and they headed down Third Avenue.

They walked in silence for blocks and then Guy led her into a bar where they sat in a booth in the back. It was dark and Cristina felt very grown-up and important. Guy ordered a Rob Roy for himself and a Coke for her. He didn't speak for a long time and she assumed this was how one behaved in a place like this: pensive and mysterious.

At last he spoke. "I don't know why it seemed so important to see that fat woman or man or whatever, it just did. I'm sure you know that yesterday was ten years since she was killed."

Cristina nodded, a sadness mixed with solemnity.

"The coincidence just seemed somehow to be meaningful, even thought I've always known that the fat person had nothing to do with Danielle's death. It's so incredible to think fatso is still around. And that you should see her one day after the anniversary of Danielle's death. I don't know, it just seems wild."

Tentatively, Cristina asked: "You still think it was a woman?" Why didn't she ask him about Grandmaman's accusation about Poppy? That's what really interested her.

He shrugged. "Who knows? It was the long hair in nineteen-fifty-five that made me so sure. Today, I wouldn't jump to that conclusion," Guy said.

"My brother wears his hair sort of long."

"Soon we'll all be wearing it that way. How is Claude?"

"He doesn't know how to read."

"You mean he doesn't like books?"

"No. He really doesn't know how. Can't learn. Or won't."

"Your father must love that."

She couldn't go on like this; she had to ask. "Grandmaman said Poppy had Mommy killed."

Guy sipped his drink. "Yes, I know she says that. She says a lot of things, Cristina. You mustn't pay attention to her . . . in that way, I mean."

As she looked into Guy's eyes and felt she might drown in the beautiful pools of purple, something flashed in her mind. It was that old image of the killer, and Cristina heard her say, *This is for.* . . . As always the last word was muffled by the gun shot, but it had seemed closer this time, the way a dream occasionally did when you tried to recall it and then pieces slid away into a thick fog.

"What is it?"

"Nothing." Should she tell him? She'd never told anyone, never had the least desire to, but for the first time in all these years she was tempted.

Gently Guy said, "It's something. I can see it in your eyes. Tell me."

There was a moment when she thought she would, but it vanished quickly. Those words were hers and she couldn't bear to part with them, not even to Uncle Guy. "Honest," she said, smiling, "it's just seeing the fat person, that's all."

They stayed for another half an hour, filling each other in on the last ten years. Then Guy paid the check and they went out again into the day, sun hitting their eyes like flashbulbs. Walking back toward Fifth Avenue she had to stop herself from putting her arm through his.

"Do you want to come back with me to see Maman?"

She didn't want to leave Guy, but the last thing she wanted to do was to confront that insane woman. "I'll say good-bye here."

Guy took out a long, thin leather wallet from his inside jacket pocket, flipped it open exposing a pad and a gold pencil. He wrote something down, tore out the piece of paper, and handed it to her. "This is my address and phone number if you need me or just want to talk." He handed her the wallet and pencil. "Write down your address at school." As she was writing, he went on: "I'll send you my new address in the fall. I'm getting married in September."

The appropriate response was momentarily lost to her. Inside, she felt as if every piece of her was crying. Then she forced herself to look up from the pad, smiling. "How neat. Who to?"

"Her name is Janet Starkman."

She handed him back the wallet with her address on the pad. More than anything she wanted to get away from him.

"Maybe you can come to the wedding."

"Great," she said, the smile still stamped on her face. She stuck out her hand to shake his. "I'd better go. It was neat seeing you, Uncle Guy."

Ignoring her hand, he leaned down and kissed her lightly

on the lips. "Let's not lose touch. I feel I've found a part of myself."

"I'll call you," she said, knowing she never would, could.

He grabbed her hands, held tight. "I can't tell you how much it means to me to find you again, Cristina. I won't be able to call you at home . . . your father wouldn't like it."

"I know. I'll call you. I'd better go now." She pulled from his grasp.

Their eyes met and held for a fraction of a second, and then Cristina turned and ran. It was a stupid way to leave him, childish, but she couldn't help herself. She knew he was watching her so she put on some speed, the sooner to get to the corner and turn, out of his sight. It wasn't until she'd reached the middle of the block that she allowed herself to slow, resume a walking pace, head toward home.

Later, Cristina lay on her bed, face down into her pillow. She felt devastated. That was Toddy Garland's word, but today it was definitely hers. Bob Dylan twanged his music into her ears, but it didn't help. The day had begun so differently from the way it was ending. Grandpapa was dead. Grandmaman was crazy. And she was in love with her uncle. None of that had been true for her hours earlier. It was better not to know some things. But she'd always wanted to know everything. She remembered her mother saying, "Curiosity killed the cat," and then smiling that delicious way that filled Cristina with warmth as if she'd been lying in the sun. She wished she'd never gone to her grandmother's apartment. It wasn't so much the smashing of her fantasy she regretted: she wished she'd never seen Guy. *Uncle* Guy, she reminded herself.

She knew from history books that cousins often married; did uncles and nieces? But what did it matter? He was getting married to some beast named Janet. What would Dr. Hess say? Did she have to tell him? She hated telling him anything. When she'd hinted she might like to be a writer some day, he'd smiled in that smug way he had and told her she'd have to find a better way to deal with reality, face the fact that she'd undoubtedly marry and find her glory through her husband and children. She knew this was stupid, but in a way, they all—the doctors she'd had—implied the same thing.

Well, she wasn't going to tell Hess anything about her feelings for Uncle Guy. There wasn't any point. It was dumb anyway. You couldn't fall in love with a person in one day. Except in the movies. Even so Cristina knew she mustn't see him again. It would hurt too much and she had no desire to hurt any more than she did. Not that she was in terrible, awful pain; but there was that constant feeling running through her like a tiny cold brook. Allowing herself to continue to think of Guy would be tantamount to creating an ocean inside, and she wanted no part of it. She would never think of him again. Finished.

When she walked to her stereo to change the Dylan record to a Baez, he was already excised from her conscious mind. She was thinking about calling Mary Beth Williams to ask if she wanted to go to see *Dr. Zhivago*. But even as she made her plans and removed herself further from the day's events, Cristina understood that although Guy had been relegated to a safe place, he would be, after all, with her always.

Forlini's Restaurant was on Baxter Street off Canal, near Chinatown and Little Italy. It was a neighborhood place, nothing fancy, but the food was excellent. In the room that housed the long, walnut bar there were seven or eight booths and, in the back, there was a room with regular tables. Zo never ate there; even if it required a wait he bided his time until there was a place in the front. He always felt more comfortable in a booth, especially when there were only two; he could lean and stretch. Besides the room had a more intimate feeling and he loved watching the people at the bar.

There were always a lot of regulars, "characters" his mother had called them the time he'd brought her here. He should have known: Gloria Campisi pursued the straightest course any life could take; it was, he supposed, an antidote to her marriage to his father. But to Zo, the "characters" at the bar were what gave the place its flavor.

"You sneaked in without my seein' ya," Freddy Forlini said, coming to the edge of Zo's booth. Forlini looked dapper, as always, in a baby-blue linen suit, white silk shirt, dark blue tie. "How's Helen?"

"She's better. Weak. The treatments."

Freddy shook his head in sympathy, brown straight hair sprayed in place. "I know, my friend's mother-in-law had the same thing." He leaned in, whispered. "She lose her hair?"

Zo nodded and felt Helen's pain and humiliation at being bald. Wigs were piling up; she couldn't seem to find the right one.

"It'll grow back," said Freddy confidently. "You tell her I said so, okay?" He smiled, showing white, perfect teeth. "Hey, she meetin' you here today?"

"No. This is a business lunch."

"So anything ya want ya don't get, ya call me, okay, Zo?"

Freddy went off to greet other friends; Zo sipped his beer and his mind filled with thoughts of Helen.

It was five months since she'd had the mastectomy and the chemotherapy would continue for another month. Then it would be five years before she was considered in the clear. Even then, who knew? If anyone was familiar with the insecurities of life, it was he. It was odd the way misfortune could bring you to a greater understanding of something; the possibility of the cancer returning made Zo more appreciative of what Helen had lived with all these years: his possible death. Even though it wouldn't be sudden with her if it happened, it amounted to the same thing. Was it really gone, that ugly killing disease, or was it hiding, lurking in her blood ready to strike as soon as they relaxed? That idea hovered in the back of his mind like some wizened doomster ready to pronounce the worst. What in hell would he do if she died?

Life without Helen was unimaginable; no one could take here place. God, he thought, sipping his beer, I'm acting as if her death is imminent, certain. Lately he had begun to pray, to ask God to spare his wife until they were old and could fade out together. He desperately wanted to know what Helen would look like at sixty-five, seventy. Who else could he laugh with the way he laughed with her, dammit. And his work? Who would he share that with? Or see a movie with? Or split a goddamn bowl of cherries with while they watched television, holding hands. There were *not* other fish in the ocean for him. He'd been the luckiest of men to have found Helen, and he knew it couldn't happen twice. He also knew he was thinking only of himself, his loss, and forgetting entirely that she would be losing much more: her life. Jesus, he was selfish. This premature mourning had to stop; he'd make himself sick. If only she would let him make love to her again, get back into some kind of normal life, he felt he could shake his morbid thoughts. Two nights ago they'd had another fight about it.

"Don't tell me nothing's changed," Helen said, "because if you say that one more time I'm leaving you. I hate liars."

"Okay. Okay. You want the truth, here it is. I would prefer you to be the way you were. Two breasts. If I said I liked this better, there would be something wrong with me, wouldn't there? Huh? Wouldn't there, Helen, if I said I liked you better this way?"

Her eyes were wide with shock and she pressed her lips together in a defiant line.

"Sick. I'd be a sick cookie if I liked you better with one goddamned breast."

"I knew it," she whispered.

"You know nothing. What I'm saying is that I'm not some kind of creep who wants his wife to have one breast but—and this is the part you have to listen to, Helen—*but* . . . I love you just as much as I always have, nothing has changed in that department. You hear me?" He was shaking.

Her bottom lip trembled.

His tone became softer, gentler. "Hey, babe, please hear me. I still want to make love to you, just as much. Let me."

She promised when the treatments were over, when she felt stronger, less nauseated, they would make love again. The doctor had said it would take time, but time was the very thing he worried about. How much was left?

"Zo," Emma Stevenson said. She slid into the booth opposite him. "I'm so sorry."

He looked at his watch. "You're not late, I was early."

She waved a hand, dismissing this. "No, I mean about Helen."

That same electric jolt he'd experienced the day he'd met Emma coursed through him now: Emma had no way of knowing about Helen's illness. "How'd you know, Emma?"

Cocking her head to one side she looked at him, imploring, as if to say, how can you ask?

"Was it written on my forehead in blue?" he snapped, the anger at his wife's illness hurled at Emma.

She ignored his tone. "No, it wasn't written in blue. It just came in my mind when I saw you."

Ashamed, he looked into his beer. "I'm sorry, Emma."

"Forget it. Anyway, I'm the one who should apologize, I'm always shooting off my mouth like that. You'd think I would've learned by now. Anyway, how is she?"

"Not so hot. I wish you could see into the future."

"Jesus, *I* don't. This is bad enough. Anyway, would you really want to know?"

Julio came to the table while Zo was contemplating the question and Emma ordered a glass of seltzer.

"No, I wouldn't," he finally answered.

Looking at her carefully now, he saw that the tired look she'd worn so long ago was still there, age accentuating it. She'd lost weight in the last year, deep hollows in her cheeks emphasizing her nose. The hands still fluttered, moving across the tablecloth as if she were playing a keyboard.

"How've you been, Emma?"

"I turned forty last month, so how could I be?"

He wished he could say she didn't look it, knew she'd know he was lying if he did. "Me, too. I'm forty now."

"I met an eighteen-year-old last week didn't know who Luise Rainer was. Very depressing."

"Are you lonely?" he asked.

She was startled. "You getting psychic now?" Quickly she took refuge in the drink the waiter had set before her.

"I shouldn't have asked that."

"Why not? Fair is fair. You bet I'm lonely. Of course I got my mother who calls me six times a day asking me am I engaged yet, like maybe Mr. Right swooped me up at the automat during lunch. You know, sometimes I feel like quitting my job and going into the business of being a psychic."

"Why don't you? Even the police are using them now."

"Yeah, and they're really helpful, huh?" she said sarcastically. "Hurkos did a great job with the Boston Strangler."

"He came close."

"Close. In my book close is close but no cigar. Let's order." She picked up the menu, hid behind it.

After they'd ordered, Emma looked deep into Zo's eyes. "Sometimes I wish I'd die." She pushed up the sleeve of her orange dress and showed him the scars on her wrist. "I couldn't even do that right."

Zo had wondered why she was wearing a long-sleeved dress in August. "Is it that awful, Emma?"

194

She blew a cloud of smoke between them. "Yeah, sometimes. But I'm supposed to live. I know that now."

"How?"

"Oh, I know," she answered enigmatically.

The hot antipasto was placed between them, a small white dish set in front of each. They split the eggplant, clams, mussels, artichoke hearts, stuffed mushrooms, and began to eat, silently.

Then Emma said, "The old man paid me a visit."

"What old man?"

"Dudevant."

His heart quickened as it always did whenever there was news of the Swann case. "What did he say?"

"I've been expecting him for some time. Years, in fact." She held out a speared piece of eggplant on her fork. "This is good. You know, these last ten years have been a nightmare. I don't think I would've minded so much, the gift I mean, if it hadn't been for Danielle. See, the other images I get I can do something with. Kid stuff. Like finding somebody's lost watch or knowing who should marry who, junk like that. But Danielle Swann, Jesus. Oh, Zo, I failed her, you know."

"But Emma, you didn't. Don't forget we found the Somerville woman. We never would've if it hadn't been for you."

"So what good did it do? Can you prove anything? It's still an unsolved case. And she keeps crying."

"Who keeps crying?"

"Danielle. Every night she wakes me up. Crying, like from the gut."

"You never told me," he said dumbly.

"What for? Anyway, she cries every night. She's ruined my life."

"Don't say that," he said sharply.

Her eyes widened, eyebrows arching. "I always knew you were in love with her."

"That's crazy." A feeling of exposure washed over him like the touch of faint sunlight.

"Is it?"

Julio brought the wine and the entrees. Veal marsala for Emma, fettucini Alfredo for Zo.

He ran his hands through either side of his unruly hair as if he were searching for an answer. He'd never been confronted about Danielle before, his concern, his obsession. Even J.J never really pressed him. He'd been able to swindle his own thinking until now.

"Listen," Emma said gently, "it doesn't mean you don't love Helen. One thing has nothing to do with the other. And it's not real anyway."

"How could it be?" He was clinging on to a last shred of deceit, like grasping a piece of refuse in a swirling sea.

"But I'm not wrong, am I, Zo? It's not real but it's there."

"It's there. You think I'm crazy?"

She laughed. *"Me*, think *you're* crazy? That's a hot one. It's taken its toll on you, too, hasn't it? The murder, Danielle, Hedy Somerville."

"It's changed my life, I think. I might have given in about having kids if it hadn't been for Cristina and Claude. Other things, too."

"Yeah, it's like dominoes."

"So what did Dr. Dudevant tell you, Emma?"

"Oh, right. Well, he said Danielle was adopted. It was a secret. Only the three of them knew."

"Who's the real mother?"

"Her name is Anna Wilson." She took a bite of food. "Eat, Zo."

He picked up his fork, expertly twirled the fettucini in a neat twist, no ends dangling. "Emma, why did Dr. Dudevant tell you this?"

"Funny you should ask. He said he wanted you to know."

That frightened him. He didn't like getting messages from the dead. Besides, it made no sense. What difference did it make if Danielle was adopted? And who even knew if it was true?

"You don't believe me," Emma said, smiling.

"Sure I do."

"C'mon, Zo." She went back to her food.

He'd hurt her. "It just gives me the creeps, you know, him giving you a message for me."

They were silent for a while, then Zo asked, "You saw the old man a lot before he died, didn't you?"

"I used to play chess with him. He was a nice man, poor guy. Her murder ruined his life, too. I don't think he ever really knew what happened to him—his wife throwing him out and everything."

"Why *did* she throw him out?"

"He never told me exactly, but he hinted that she thought he was having an affair with someone. God, what a joke. He adored his wife, or at least he had before she went bonkers." Emma finished her lunch, sat back. "So that's my news of the day. Danielle Dudevant Swann was adopted." She shrugged. "Go know."

"Well, it's interesting, I guess, but I can't see that it has any bearing on the case."

"You're disappointed, huh?"

Emma's knowing everything he felt suddenly made him angry. "So what?"

She smiled sadly. "And you ask me if this power I got is that awful?" She flipped her wrist, her metaphor for life.

He wished there was something he could say to her, but there was nothing. Emma Stevenson was a doomed person and they both knew it.

By four o'clock, when Zo went off duty, he'd checked records that indicated Anna Wilson could have been Danielle's mother. It occurred to him to try and find the Wilson woman, but what could that tell him? It would only disrupt the woman's life. He decided to leave it alone.

The subway jolted to a stop and Zo got off. The station smelled hot and he walked quickly to the stairs. Outside, on Seventy-second Street, the air was heavy and wet with humidity. He walked east. The creepy feeling of Dr. Dudevant's sending him a message lingered. But then why should he believe Emma? Perhaps Dudevant had told her about the adoption when he was alive and she'd decided to tell Zo now because she was lonely. All of Emma's information could be explained rationally, couldn't it? Almost all. How did she know the facts about him? That Helen wanted children and he didn't? That his father hung himself, even if she didn't know it was his father? If Emma knew those things, then why doubt her about anything?

When he reached the block the Swanns lived on, he crossed the street to walk back and forth, observing from a distance. This was part of his regular routine, at least once or twice a week. It was unofficial, and he kept up this surveillance on his own time. He told himself he was watching Dr. Swann, but he knew it was a lie. It was Cristina he wanted to see; she looked so much like her now. The obsession for Danielle had drifted over to her child; he straddled feelings for both but more and more he shifted toward the living, which was something, he supposed. Christ almighty, what had he become? If he wasn't watching one young girl, he was watching another. It was almost as if he were a pervert, lusting after children. Cristina and Value. Were they sisters, after all? And was this spying on the girls really police work? He knew the truth: he'd crossed some invisible line of neurosis and he needed help. But the Force wasn't crazy about their members seeing shrinks and, anyway, he didn't believe in it. It was something he could do by himself. He'd just have to stop. Instead of turning around when he reached the corner he crossed the street, heading away from the Swann apartment building. It was going to be simple. He'd leave and never come back, never follow the kid again, never see her again. He stopped. Never? Never. Okay. A deal. But as long as he was here he might as well wait this last time. He turned around and headed back toward the Swann building. Just one more time.

Laura James sat across from Helen at the kitchen table, sipping a martini. She didn't like drinking alone, but Helen's condition precluded a taste for alcohol. Would they ever have a cocktail together again? she wondered. Helen had always been petite, but now she looked to Laura like an effigy of herself, as though she were made of string and matchsticks. Laura wished she could give some of her weight, strength, fiber to Helen: melt herself down and paste it onto her child.

"I know I look like hell, Mother. You don't have to keep staring at me."

"Oh, Helen, I'm sorry. I didn't mean to be." She looked into her glass of gin and vermouth, counting the drops of lemon oil the peel had deposited.

"I suppose I should get used to it," Helen said bitterly. "Zo stares all the time."

Laura said, "If he does, dear, I'm sure it's out of concern and love."

"I doubt it." Helen's wig was cut in a short style; it accentuated her features and gave her a birdlike appearance, the eyes once luminous, now dull and faded.

"There's nothing wrong between you and Zo, is there?"

"Well, it's hardly like we're living under normal circumstances, you know," Helen said snappishly.

"Yes, I understand that. But *besides* your illness, I meant."

"I'm not sure there is a *besides*. Having cancer is all-consuming."

"Well, you don't have it any more," Laura said quickly.

Helen smiled. "We don't know that, do we?"

"We certainly *do* know that. Dr. Shiffenhouse said——"

"Said he *thought* it was all clear but we'd have to wait five years to be sure. Do you have any idea what that's like? I feel as though I'm living with a time bomb inside me."

"You don't have to," Laura said. "You can put it out of your mind."

Helen laughed, a sharp sound of derision.

Was it really such an inadequate suggestion as Helen's sarcastic laugh implied? To Laura it was pragmatic. There wasn't any magic, after all. "That's what I would do," she added, sounding apologetic.

"Yes, well, you're good at that."

Laura knew the snide remark referred to Catherine. But why should she dwell on a daughter who'd run off, leaving two small children to be raised by their father?

"Remember," asked Helen, "when it was a policy in our house to talk about everything?"

"Ideas, dear, ideas. We spoke of ideas, quite different." Laura wrinkled her aquiline nose as if to say that anything else was odious.

Was that true? Helen wondered. Had she, in her mind, rewritten history to suit her present needs? And why was she giving her mother such a difficult time, pushing her further and further away when it was the opposite she desired?

"I can't stand these people who find it necessary to tell every detail of their lives no matter how personal, can you? They just go on and on, telling you far more than you'd ever want to know," Laura said.

Helen stared at her mother, blinking. This hardly sounded like a woman anyone would confide in, yet she was saying that people did. And surely *she* had, otherwise why would she have thought they'd been so close? Had there been a time when it had been true, then changed, narrowed?

"But naturally, Helen, if *you* want to talk to me about something personal, that's different. You're my child, after all."

And you're my mother, Helen thought. What did daughters tell mothers? Where did one draw the line of propriety? Could she say, for instance, I can't let my husband make love to me anymore?

"I want to know anything you want me to know," said Laura. But she didn't really. She wanted to know the nice things: hopes and dreams and good times. Laura's eyes fell to the flat place on the right side of Helen's chest. "When will you be getting the prostheses?" she asked, as though she were inquiring about some illegal acquisition.

"Soon."

Laura smiled, the matter settled. Still, it was clear there was something on Helen's mind. Should she press her?

The ginger ale Helen sipped quelled her nausea. She looked at her mother's face, implacable and barely lined, the eyes cool and reassuring, opposites of her own. What she wanted from her mother was pure, immaculate in its intention, hopeless in its wish: Mommie, make it better. Kiss the bad and make it good.

"Darling," Laura said, "tell me what's bothering you?" She pulled her body away from the table, straightening her back, ready for the horrible onslaught of an honest answer.

"I'm afraid," she said softly. "I'm afraid to die."

"You're not going to die."

"How do you know?" Helen challenged.

The steady humming of the air-conditioner filled the silence. Helen wanted her to say: *I won't let you die, I'll make it all right. Mothers don't let their children die.* Yet, mothers let their children die all the time, couldn't stop it. But surely *her* mother had some final trick up her sleeve.

Eventually Laura answered: "You've got to pull yourself together, Helen. You can't think about death all the time. You're not going to die, so stop thinking about it."

That was it then, was it? Simple. Mother said don't, so you didn't. Why didn't she feel any surer? She wanted Mommie to make it better, but she was too old for it to work.

"You're right," Helen said, "I must pull myself together."

"Good girl," said Laura affably and patted her daughter's hand.

Helen snatched at her mother's fingers, held on with the

little energy she had, and Laura squeezed; it was the best they could do.

After a moment or two, Helen curled into Zo's big waiting arms. She heard him sigh with contentment as he shifted even closer to her in bed. Feeling his naked body pressed against hers, she experienced a sense of sexual desire, the first since the operation. Relief and joy intermingled. Tonight she didn't have the energy, but she would soon.

"Hey, big fella," she said, "I don't think we've met."

Zo laughed. "Well, considering," he said, running a hand over her thigh, "do you really think introductions are necessary?"

"Probably not."

It was the first time she'd talked to him in their old way since she'd discovered she had cancer.

"Zo, I think it won't be long now."

"It's okay, honey."

"You've been so patient."

"I love you."

"I just need a little time to get my strength back."

"It's okay." He kissed her forehead. "Please know it won't make any difference to me. No more than my birthmark meant to you."

She knew it was true. And she also knew that no one could save her if she was going to die. But she was damned if she was going to sabotage whatever time there was. Maybe her mother had given her more than she'd realized. Maybe when she told her to pull herself together, it had been just what she'd needed to hear.

"Zo, I think I've reached a turning point. I can see things differently now."

"I knew you'd come through. You're no quitter."

"No, I'm not. Oh, Zo, I love you so much." She kissed his lips. "I feel so happy," she said.

"Me, too."

What do you know? she thought. Mommie *had* made it better.

Hedy couldn't believe it had happened again. She wondered if she was losing her mind. The first time, four months before, she had turned the house upside down: dumping out drawers, unburdening closets long neglected, flipping things from cabinets as if she were a dog spraying dirt. She had also called Frazer's Grocery (she did all her shopping by phone) and accused the new delivery boy of stealing it. Mr. Frazer had adamantly defended the young man. Hedy ranted and swore she knew the boy had lifted her diamond ring from the windowsill behind the sink where she always put it when doing dishes. Mr. Frazer finally agreed to question Tyrone, but when he called Hedy back he was as inflexible in his defense of the boy as he'd been before. Hedy slammed the phone in his ear.

She had finally found the ring in her jewelry case. It was a small blue leather box with golden fleur de lys around the perimeter of the cover. In the tier, which rose with the opening of the box, was the diamond ring. She wept with joy at her discovery. But how the ring had gotten there remained a mystery and concerned her greatly. Desperately, she tried to trace her movements from the last time she'd seen the ring. Nowhere could she see herself putting it in the case. Could her mother possibly have transported the ring from ledge to box? Eventually, Hedy came to believe that that was what had happened: there could be no other explanation.

But now it had occurred again. The first place she looked was in her jewelry box, but it was not there. Again she combed all the places she had the first time and came up empty. However, it was Halloween and scores of children had come into the Somerville kitchen since three o'clock that afternoon. She and Ralph had handed out bags and bags of candy corn. The last time Hedy had seen the ring was when she'd taken it off to do the dinner dishes; she'd forgotten, for only the second time in her life, to return it to her finger immediately upon finishing. When she'd remembered, two hours later, the ring was gone.

It was eleven o'clock now and the entire household was exhausted from searching. Even Value was begging to go to bed, something she never wanted to do normally.

"Give up the ghost," George said to his daughter. "It's only paste anyway."

"Don't start that," Hedy screeched.

"It's lost, Mother. It's just lost."

"You don't know what you're saying," contradicted Hedy.

"Oh, God," Value sighed and slumped on the couch, her Snow White costume rumpling and bunching.

"I know it was one of those brats," said Hedy. "Value, what were their names?"

"How should I know? I wasn't here." Her blue eye took on a deeper hue; the brown one stayed the same.

"Yeah, you know it was one of them kids just like you knew it was Tyrone," George croaked.

Ralph laughed, agreeing.

"You'd think it was worth something, the way she carries on," said George.

"Can I *please* go to bed?" Value begged.

"Let the child go to bed," demanded George.

Ignoring him, Hedy went on. "Maybe it was that disgusting priest." Father Frank had spent the evening with him. "I wouldn't put it past him."

"What would the Father want with a hunk of junk like that? And it's a sin to accuse a man of the cloth of being a thief. I've half a mind to tell him what you said."

She couldn't have cared less what her father told that repellent priest. All she was concerned with was finding the ring. She had a feeling that this time it was gone for good.

"Carry me up, Ralph."

Crazily Hedy cried, "No one leaves this room until I find that ring!"

All three stared at her, amazed.

Ralph said, "You want to search us?"

She didn't know what she wanted or what she'd meant. Never before in her life could she remember anything as awful as this. "I just want my ring," she said softly.

"Well, it's gone, so face it," said George. "Now we're all goin' to bed. Come on, Val, let's go."

Value slid off the couch. Her rouged cheeks had smudged from the perfect circles she'd begun with into streaks of red. Crimson lipstick stained her teeth and all around her mouth were the signs of sticky candy.

"Make sure you wash, Value," said Hedy. "I don't want that junk on the sheets."

When they had gone, Hedy prayed for a sign from her mother to show her where the ring was. Its loss felt overwhelming even though the truth was she didn't really *need* the ring the way she once had. It no longer represented the one and only barrier between herself and the poorhouse. Still, she felt naked and vulnerable without it. Looking down at her stubby finger, her stomach lurched at the sight of the whitish, wrinkled flesh where the ring had been. This loss, she decided, was a sign; clearly her mother had again participated in the disappearance of the ring as an omen for Hedy, and heed it she must. Laughter trickled from her mouth as the meaning of the missing ring became evident, dazzling in its instruction: something was going to happen to Value unless Hedy was extremely careful. She must never, never let her out of her sight, neither day or night. Watching Value was to be her life's work.

Value had scrubbed as hard as she could, but the rouge just seemed to spread over her face. She left the stained wash cloth on the sink and went to her room.

Lying in her bed she felt extremely happy. Halloween had been a great success. Her costume had been a hit and she'd raked in four dollars and twenty-seven cents. Every little bit helped. But the most important thing was that she'd finally gotten the diamond ring. The last time she'd taken it, she'd done it only to annoy her mother and later regretted putting it in the jewelry box. Since then, she'd been planning another theft, biding her time until Hedy once again forgot to put it back on her finger. The opportunity had finally come and Value swiped the ring as quickly as she could. Now it was safely buried in the shoebox with her money. It was the only way she could ever have gotten it. Even if she waited until she was eighteen, she knew her crazy mother would never hand it over. You had to take what you wanted in this life. And she had.

It was ten after five. Guy looked at Marc Starkman, hoping to get a sign of some sort as to how long the meeting was going to go on, but his face held no clue. They were discussing Guy's idea; he should've been glad it hadn't been repulsed immediately. As Marc's son-in-law, he had made enemies; there were those who resented what they considered nepotism. Still, they should have known better. Starkman was not the kind of man to promote somebody just because he was his son-in-law, even if he *had* hired him because his daughter told him to. Marc's love for Janet was the one thing Guy found objectionable in his father-in-law; it was a passion so powerful it couldn't help but diminish the effect of Guy's love.

"So who shall we try this on first?" Marc asked the assembled group.

The idea had been adopted and now it was only a matter of which author would be the first guinea pig. Guy said, "How about Kate Tyler?"

"A woman?" said Jack Bowyer, horrified.

"Why not?"

Bowyer shook his head as if to say Guy just didn't know the business. "As you know, I'm not *for* this. Putting writers on television to push their books is——"

"Yes, Jack, we know, you've told us," Marc said. "We've passed that point. Let's get on with it." He glanced at his watch.

Guy held back a smile. Marc was amazing. There'd been no vote, no real agreement on the plan; Marc had simply pushed it through in his inimitable style, charming, bulldozing. Guy watched Marc wave his hand for Bowyer to continue but in another vein. It was all there in the gesture, the simple sweep of his thin hand. Starkman was a delicate man; the only exceptions to his slender build were broad shoulders and a large head. The rest of him was slight, spare. When he was behind his desk there was no way to know how tall he was, the head and shoulders creating the illusion of a man over six feet, but he was only five six. His black mustache, full, drooping, gave him another edge: he looked at once beneficent and sagacious.

". . . it's simply a fact that a man would lend more weight, more authority to a scheme like this," Bowyer went on.

Guy didn't see his idea as a *scheme* but he'd learned not to nitpick. They were going to put the plan into action and if it worked he'd be in a terrific position. He couldn't believe he was actually enjoying this job. All his so-called talents for invention seemed to come to fruition here. True, he wasn't working with authors, editing books, as he'd hoped, but in a paperback house which did mostly reprints, that would have been a superfluous job. This, at least, involved creativity. He smiled to himself: it was like inventing and promoting The Moogies.

"William Whalen is my choice," said Bowyer.

"Whalen is an ass," Thomas Brighton said.

Bella Rubinstein, the only woman at the meeting besides Marc's secretary, said, "How about Edgar. . . ."

The lights went out. Guy looked at the luminous dial of his watch. It was five twenty-seven, time to call it a day anyway.

"See what's going on, Sara," Marc said to his secretary.

They could hear her dialing in the dark.

"What were you saying, Bella?" Marc asked.

Guy couldn't believe they were going on; Marc was indefatigable.

"I thought Edgar Tremont might be a good choice if we're going with a man. Personally, I'm with Guy. Kate Taylor has a terrific personality and she's intelligent."

Bowyer, sounding like a whiny ten-year-old, said, "Naturally, she'd think Tyler would be better. Christ almighty."

"What is it, Sara?"

"Nobody knows. It's the whole street. Look out the window."

There was scraping and bumping as they fumbled their way over to the window. They were looking down at Fifth Avenue and it was black, except for some car lights. But traffic wasn't moving. Street and traffic lights were out, too.

The phone rang, Sara answered. There was silence in the room while she spoke. It passed through Guy's mind that it might be some kind of raid, the end of the world perhaps. He found that he wasn't so much frightened as sad. His life had just begun and he very much wanted to find out what was going to happen. He hoped Janet was safe. Then he thought of his mother and felt a few flutters of panic.

"It's all of New York," said Sara, replacing the phone. "A blackout."

"First thing tomorrow we'll finish this up," said Marc. "I want it settled by noon. Now let's get out of here."

The sound of people trying to get their things together filled the room. Guy wanted to get back to his office to call his mother before going to the Starkman house for dinner. He told Marc he'd meet him in the lobby.

Marc had been wonderful about Amelia, understanding, considerate. There'd only been the one meeting, at the wedding, but that had been enough. It had been Marc who'd gone with him, taken her home in the taxi. His embarrassment at Amelia's behavior stayed with Guy even now, two months later.

In his office he slammed his leg against the corner of the

desk and stumbled into his chair. From his pocket he pulled his father's old Dunhill lighter and lit it to see the phone. Amelia's number rang a long time before she answered.

"*Oui,*" she said.

Guy felt the muscles in his stomach tighten. "Maman, are you all right?"

"The lights have gone out, Guy." There was the nascent sound of fear in her voice.

"That's why I'm calling. There's nothing to be afraid of. It's a blackout. All over the city. Do you have candles?" What if she knocked over a lit candle?

"*Oui.*"

"I think you should light some."

Irritated, Amelia replied, "I have."

Sometimes it was hard to remember that she wasn't senile or truly incompetent; she lived in her own world of bitterness and anger, quite another matter.

"Will you be all right?" Why couldn't he ask if she wanted him to come? She might say yes, he admitted.

"Why shouldn't I be all right?"

Now, he felt, it was safe to ask. "Would you like me to come over?"

"What for?"

"I thought you might be afraid." It wasn't that he didn't love her, didn't care; and if he'd had no other plans he would've gone without asking. He felt guilty for his manipulation.

"How could I be afraid of the dark after what I've been through? It's being in the light that's difficult."

She was starting her perpetual plaint and Guy didn't want to hear it. "All right, Maman, as long as you're okay."

Amelia's laugh said she'd never be okay again and wasn't he some sort of idiot not to know it?

Oh, he knew it all right. He knew it and knew it and knew it. "I'd better go now. I'll call you later," he said.

"What for?"

Out of nowhere came the response in his head: *for a while.* When he was a little boy, Danielle would always answer his *what fors* that way. In some way, Danielle was always there, dangling between them, keeping them apart. "I'll call you later to see how you are."

"I'll be the same," she said.

He started to reply, but the sound of the phone being replaced in its cradle stopped him. Sitting there in the dark he could feel himself becoming depressed. For years he hadn't understood the cause of this sinking feeling of despair until he'd finally cut through the web of his emotions: his mother wished he'd been killed instead of Danielle. At least that's what he suspected. He rose from his desk, found his coat and scarf, and groped his way to the door. Slowly, he headed toward the elevator bank, then stopped. They wouldn't be running. He'd have to make his way down fourteen flights. It was only then he became aware of others in the hall. People were talking in whispers as if the dark demanded a special reverence. Guy hoped Marc wouldn't be annoyed with him for taking so long.

By the time he reached the bottom he found himself damp with sweat. In the lobby, crowds of people were milling about in confusion. Guy wondered how the hell he was ever going to find Marc, but Marc found him.

Out on Fifth Avenue, they started uptown. It was eerie in the dark, November street, otherworldly, alien, yet there was something appealing about it, a kind of peacefulness with the absence of traffic noises. People were moving slowly as if they were in a dream.

"Janet's there already," said Marc. "Safe."

Guy hadn't thought of calling her.

"Is your mother all right?"

"Yes, fine. I tried calling your house, but the line was busy. I guess you were talking," Guy lied.

Why the hell should he have to lie, to feel guilty? Janet wasn't a child or an old woman. If her father wanted to check on her every minute, that was his business. Had other husbands called their wives?

"Rachel isn't there yet," Marc said, "I suppose she'll make it okay."

Had it been Janet out on the street, rather than Marc's younger daughter, Guy knew the man would be upset. He wondered if he'd have favorites when he had children. If he had daughters he swore he wouldn't burden them with his love; unknowingly, Janet suffered from her father's devotion.

Guy would have expected Marc to be jealous of him, but

it had never been that way. From the moment they met, Marc showed signs of liking him almost as if he were eager to hand over his precious daughter, perhaps tired of the responsibility, a parental inanition.

"If I were a young man," Marc suddenly said, "I'd get drunk tonight."

His statement surprised Guy.

"My guess is the city will be wonderful tonight. You know how New Yorkers are when there's a crisis . . . everybody friendly and helpful."

"What about crime?" Guy asked.

"Oh, yes, I suppose," said Marc, as if crime were an irritant, a pesty child. He laughed. "I get the feeling this conversation should be reversed. But then, that's why I knew you were right for Janet. You're solid."

Guy knew Marc meant this as a compliment, but it made him feel terrible. The word *solid* filled him with torpor and he found himself lagging behind Marc, hurried to keep up.

They turned into Sixty-sixth Street and were silent for the rest of the walk. There were candles lighting the first floor windows of the Starkman brownstone.

Janet met them at the door, hugging Marc first. Guy tried not to care, but he did.

"Darling," she said, kissing Guy lightly on the lips as if she were embarrassed or doing something she shouldn't be. The three of them went into the living room where Phyllis Starkman waited, sipping a cocktail.

Guy liked Phyllis a great deal. She was an extremely attractive woman, not yet fifty, small and dainty, yet there was nothing fragile about her. She had very little gray in her hair and in the candlelight it appeared black. It was months after Guy first met Phyllis that he learned she was an overeater. One would never have known from looking at her or sharing meals with her that Phyllis had a problem with food. It was her secret, but a secret which her family knew: Phyllis binged and then she vomited.

"It makes me hate her," Janet said when she'd told him about it.

"I'm sure she can't help it," he suggested.

"You're soft, Guy, you know that? It's the same with your roommate."

He'd remembered then her reaction to Christopher. "Don't you have any compassion for your mother?"

"It isn't that. I just think people who don't have willpower are weak. She knows how bad it is for her system. God, she's been hospitalized for it. Still, she does it over and over."

This "pull yourself up by the bootstraps" attitude in Janet worried Guy; it created an icy island within her he couldn't touch.

"I think it's very exciting, don't you?" Phyllis said, kissing Guy's cheek.

He laughed. "You and Marc are kids at heart."

"I can imagine the looting that's going to go on," said Janet.

Hearing a form of his own sentiments from Janet distressed him.

"Is your mother all right?" asked Phyllis.

"She's fine. She'd already lit candles when I called," he said with pride, as if he were talking about someone retarded.

Phyllis smiled kindly, understanding, the scene at the wedding still fresh in everyone's minds. Guy was grateful he'd married into such a sympathetic family.

Amelia had been quiet all through the wedding itself; it had happened later, at the reception. As she was the only member of the Dudevant family to attend (Cristina had rejected his invitation), a Starkman cousin had been assigned to her, but he was a feckless sort of boy and she'd drifted away from him and begun asking anyone, everyone, if they'd seen Danielle. With each negative reply, Amelia had become more panicked, more disoriented, until she was standing in the middle of the parquet dance floor, shouting Danielle's name, tears scoring her powdered cheeks.

Marc and Guy had reached her at the same time, while the other guests, frightened and bewildered, looked on.

"We'll take her home," Marc said.

"She doesn't always. . . ." he started apologetically.

"It's all right, Guy."

It wasn't his mother he hated and resented that day; it was Danielle. She was always there, spoiling his life in one way or another. How much more she affected him in death than she had in life. Had she lived, had she not been murdered, how different would his life be?

Phyllis and Rachel had both comforted him, assured him

that he was blameless. And Janet had slipped her arm through his, offering love and solace. But he wasn't really surprised when she'd turned to face him that night in their suite at The Waldorf.

"Can't something be done about your mother?" she'd said.
"Done?"
"A mental hospital or something."
"She doesn't hurt anyone."
"Oh really? She hurt us. She ruined our wedding, Guy."
"She didn't *ruin* it."
"A woman's wedding day is supposed to be the most important of her life, and now I'll never want to think of mine again because all I'll remember is that woman howling in the middle of the dance floor."

He wanted to hit her but controlled himself. Janet must have seen the look in his eyes because she quickly said:
"Oh, darling, I'm sorry. I shouldn't have said that. She's your mother, I know." Her expression of rectitude faded, giving way to love.

"Janet, you're going to have to understand and put up with my mother from time to time. Her life's been destroyed. She wasn't always like this."

Gently she said, "But other people lose children and don't go . . . go to pieces."

It was true. Had the seeds of strangeness always been there, lying in ambush, ready at the first provocation to consume Amelia? He tried to remember her as she'd been, failed. All he could manage was, "Some do go to pieces."

Janet smoothed his temples, kissed his neck. "It's been so hard on you, I know. I'm sorry I made it worse."
"You didn't," he excused her.
"I'll try to make it easier for you, darling."

Guy watched her now, sipping a whiskey sour, her long shapely legs crossed at the knee, the expensive Italian shoe bobbing her impatience with the subject of his mother's welfare.

"Do you think," Janet said, "we should go over there, Guy?"

It was a specious offer, but his need to believe in her was stronger than his perception. "No, she'll be all right," he answered.

"You're sure?"

"I'm sure." Permission given, Janet smiled at him, engaging, winning. Amelia was relegated to her place in his wife's life: inconsequential, dispensable.

"Don't we have a portable radio somewhere?" asked Marc. "I'd like to know what the hell's going on."

"I think there's one in Janet's room," Phyllis answered. Even though neither daughter lived at home, the rooms were still known as theirs.

"I'll get it, Daddy."

"Take a candle, darling," Marc said to Janet.

"Will do."

Guy watched his wife take the candle proffered by her father, their exchanged smiles making Guy feel like an intruder. He caught Phyllis's eye and as if they'd viewed something obscene, they quickly looked elsewhere.

Rushing his martini to his lips, Guy had the odd sensation that he was at the center of a Henry James novel. He glimpsed then why Marc had accepted him so easily: a marriage for Janet was essential, a cover for the relationship of father and daughter to flourish peaceably. It wouldn't do for Marc Starkman's daughter to be a spinster. Had Marc approved of him because he was "solid," or, more realistically, because he'd present no threat? Guy's marriage was, he realized stunningly, a spurious connection and unlikely to ever become more. He was delighted when Rachel finally arrived, bringing with her the possibility of rising above his slew of doubts and misgivings.

"Some fun, huh, gang?"

Phyllis held out her arms to her younger daughter, the one who belonged to her, and Rachel, accepting her role in the Starkman drama, leaned down and kissed her mother.

"Hi, kid," Rachel said, then cautiously moved toward Marc, touched her cheek to his, kissed the air, quickly withdrew, and made her way across the room to Guy.

They were friends. "How you doing, brother-in-law?" she said in his ear as they hugged.

"Terrific," he answered.

She smiled at him, knowing the response had been facetious. "Where's herself?"

"Looking for a portable radio."

Rachel removed her coat, scarf, and gloves, threw them on

a chair. She was wearing a gray wool Chanel suit, a cloud-gray silk blouse, and a flowered scarf that blossomed at her throat. Neither her figure nor her face measured up to Janet's, but she had an inner splendor which gave her an incandescence, making her shine and sparkle far more than her older sister. Her eyes were blue like her mother's and her nose, slightly large with a small bump in the bridge, was still her own. Guy had been shocked to discover Janet had had her nose altered.

When Janet returned with the radio, the sisters embraced. There was no animosity between them; they freely cared for one another, competition for parents long ago abandoned: each knew her position vis-à-vis every other member of the family.

"Let's hear the radio," Marc requested.

Janet turned it on, but nothing happened.

"Batteries?" asked Rachel.

"Damn," said Janet.

"Oh, great. We have any, honey?" asked Marc.

Phyllis said, "Don't think so. I guess we'll have to remain in the dark."

They laughed, responding to her pun.

Because of the blackout, the three young people had agreed to spend the night. Lying in Janet's bed while she was in the adjoining bathroom, Guy thought of Rachel. More than once it had occurred to him that he had married the wrong sister. In almost every way, Rachel appealed to him. But he simply did not find her sexually attractive. Fortunately, Janet's sexuality consumed him. It was, he knew, what muted other facets of her for him. He could not get beyond the sensual with his wife, and for this he was grateful. It wasn't that he didn't know Janet's defects; it was simply that they didn't matter now. Everything about her paled beside her sexuality. But he knew it was not always going to be like that. His passion was bound to recede, expire. What then? If he no longer saw her in a sexual light, her lack of compassion, her rigidity would almost certainly vitiate what now held them together. He was no ordinary groom, conscious as he was of the shallow love he harbored for his wife.

But he was extremely beholden to Janet. She had given him a new life, in more than one way. The floundering years he'd spent in the East Village, drinking more than he really wanted to, spending time with fools, was over, thanks to her. Now he had a career, a direction, and had found an outlet for his talents, talents he hadn't even understood. Janet had given him this opportunity. But more than that, she'd given him a new family.

When he'd first gone to the Starkmans' for dinner and then spent a weekend with them in their house in the Berkshires, they seemed to be the young mother and father he'd always wanted and Rachel was a new sister. It was obvious to him now that he'd married Janet for her family, as some men marry for money. Janet got a husband who would not make demands, who'd allow her to continue her love affair with her father, and he got a family: an even trade. And both could revel in a free and easy sexual relationship. What would happen in years to come was none of his concern now.

The door of the bathroom opened and for a moment Janet was silhouetted, her body showing full and curvaceous, making Guy fill with desire. Would she, he wondered, make love with him, her father down the hall? She snapped out the light.

In a moment she was lying beside him and had taken his hand. She drew it downward and eased it between her legs. He was astonished at how wet she was. His penis stiffened as he ran his fingers over her moist, silky flesh.

"I'm so excited," Janet whispered, her hips already in motion, undulating as he took her breast in his mouth, teasing the nipple with his tongue.

"God," she said, "I've never felt like this. Don't wait."

Usually they indulged in lengthy foreplay. Surprised, he asked, "Now?"

"Now."

Guy slid over on top of her, their bodies warm to the touch. He tried to kiss her, but she stopped him, urging him to hurry, grabbing his penis roughly, guiding him in.

"Fuck me good," she said huskily.

As he began sliding in and out, Janet moaned deeply, her cries growing louder with every thrust. Embarrassed that his in-laws might hear, Guy put a hand over her mouth. She turned her head to the side, throwing off his hand, continued her groans, even louder now.

"Janet," he whispered, "they'll hear."

She responded with an even deeper moan, a loud grunt. He started to warn her again and then he understood. The overwhelming desire and excitement she'd come to bed with, the sounds more atavistic than he'd ever heard her make before, were all *because* of the proximity of her parents. The message to them was unequivocal: to Phyllis it said *This is sex at its best, this is how to do it*; to Marc, *This is what you are missing*.

Guy's final thrust brought relief to Janet as well, and her last wails of pleasure trailed into sighs. He rolled onto his stomach, his head sunk in the pillow.

"So good," he heard her say.

She didn't know, he realized. She had no idea that her performance had been for a purpose. Janet was an innocent in her own little drama. Perhaps he should tell her. But what would it accomplish? He turned, put an arm around her shoulder as she snuggled into him.

"I love you so," she said.

"I love you, too," he responded. He did. It was a kind of love; limited, but love nonetheless. And that was fair. He was second best to her. Alone, he could never pitch her into the sexual frenzy she'd just exhibited; it had taken the shadow of her father down the hall, listening. Guy had his family; Janet had her surrogate lover. Everybody got what they deserved.

On the last day before Christmas vacation, Cristina had a session with Dr. Tremont (a new one), her last until school resumed in January. Although he was a little better than all the other doctors, she still didn't seem to be getting anywhere. Of course, she wasn't exactly sure where she was supposed to get. Poppy insisted she be in this dumb therapy every minute; had it been up to her she would've chucked the whole thing. Still, it was nice sometimes to have somebody to talk with who didn't criticize all the time. But Dr. Tremont kept harping on her mother and the murder. It wasn't that he wanted her to think about Mommy forever; it was just the opposite: he wanted her to *forget* Mommy, something she felt she could never do, and never wanted to do. Everyone, it seemed, wished her to forget her mother. Even Mommy.

The dream (or whatever it was, she had never been completely sure) had happened only a few months after Mommy died. Even after all these years, her memory of it was vivid. Danielle had come to her. She looked beautiful and she was smiling.

"Cristina?" she'd called. "Cristina?" Her voice was wavy like a badly tuned-in radio station.

"Mommy."

"No. That's why I'm here, dear," she said mysteriously.

"Mommy," Cristina sobbed.

"Don't cry."

"But I miss you, Mommy."

"I understand. I want you to know that I'm all right. You mustn't grieve so."

Cristina kept crying, tears gushing from her eyes. And then Danielle said the strangest thing, the worst thing.

"Cristina, you mustn't grieve so. I'm not your mother anymore."

It was a stunning thing to hear, and before Cristina could respond, the dream, occurrence, phenomenon, was over. When she became truly positive she was awake, she found her cheeks, ears, neck wet with tears. She sat up in bed, turned on the light: she was in her own room. "Mommy," she whispered. There was no one there, of course, but Cristina was absolute in her belief that Danielle *had* been there; she was certain that she smelled her mother's perfume.

A year passed before she stopped telling people about her mother's appearance: no one believed her. Certainly none of the doctors. It was the first thing she told them, a kind of test. They all failed, including Dr. Tremont. Simply a dream, they said. But a good dream. Her unconscious mind was telling her to let go.

Every doctor told her the same thing: forget, let go. Tremont was telling her that now. She watched his big mouth form the inevitable words.

"Cristina, you have to understand that keeping the memory of your mother fresh is your way of trying to tell yourself she's still alive."

His plump cheeks bounced as he spoke; it made her want to laugh. Spikey eyebrows matched his thatch of black hair, which grew low on his forehead, making him seem to be perpetually frowning. But when he smiled he looked completely different within the same features as if the nicer twin had taken his place.

216

"You're actually afraid, Cristina, to let your feelings for your mother recede, become less intense. You feel it would be a betrayal of some sort."

The word *betrayal* spun her into vibrant memories of the murder day. Why should it do that this time? She'd heard the word many times before from doctors. They all used it in one way or another.

"What are you thinking about?" he asked.

"That day."

She thought she heard him sigh. "What about it?"

"The murderer, the woman." Cristina's eyes were closed.

"Yes, what about the woman?"

She heard the woman's voice say: "Mrs. Swann?" She felt herself turn toward the voice. There was the woman: a lady with glasses and a big hat, blouse, ruffled skirt.

"Cristina?" Dr. Tremont said. "Tell me what you're thinking."

"My mother said 'Yes?' and the woman said, 'Are you Mrs. Swann?'"

Tremont had heard this many times before, but he suspected there was something the girl never told. Perhaps today. "Go on, Cristina," he urged gently.

"My mother said, 'Yes, I am. Is there something I can do for you?' and the lady put her hand into her black bag. She brought out something shiny." She stopped, silent.

"The gun," Tremont helped.

"Yes, the gun."

This was where it always started to break down. Nevertheless, Cristina always recalled the shot, her mother on the ground. Still, he was convinced there was another part, something the girl couldn't or wouldn't remember.

"The gun," Cristina said again. "And then she winked and there was a loud bang." Cristina's mind zeroed in like a zoom lens on the murderer's mouth and saw her for the millionth time say "This is for . . ." the gunshot blocking the final word. But no. Not this time. The phrase replayed: "This is for *Martin*." Cristina screamed.

"What is it?" Tremont asked breathlessly.

Her eyes, open, were wide and staring.

"Cristina? You remembered something. Tell me what you remembered. It's very important."

She blinked, focused. "What?"

"What is it you just remembered?"

"Nothing."

"You screamed," he said, accusing.

Cristina shook her head. "It was just the same old thing. The gun, the shot, blood."

"And something else?"

"I . . . I don't know." But she did.

"Try and remember."

She couldn't possibly tell him. He didn't even know about the "This is for . . ." part. No one did. And now she knew it all. Poppy. "It was nothing," she said.

As she walked through the snow toward the bus that would take her back to school, she tried desperately to think of other things, to bury what she'd remembered. But it was useless. What was she going to do?

Why did the Winking Woman say "This is for Martin"? Did she really know Poppy? She couldn't have been Poppy's lover or anything like that because Poppy was already with Lynn. Lynn. She sucked in her breath, cold and dry, biting at her throat. Did Poppy *ask* the Winking Woman to do it? Ask her to *kill* his wife? *Kill* her mother? That was what Grandmaman had said. But it couldn't be. Nothing could make her believe Poppy would do such a thing. Why would he have to? Then why did the woman say, "This is for Martin"?

Cristina wanted to die. Why did she have to remember? Damn Tremont. It was his fault. Well, just because she remembered she didn't have to do anything about it, did she? But how could she look Poppy in the eyes? She knew she couldn't forget; it was too late. The words were clear now, buzzing her brain like a swarm of mosquitoes.

The cold air stung her cheeks, numbing them, equalizing her outer layer with her inner one, the knowledge of what she'd recalled fusing with the knowledge of what she must do. There was no way she could keep it to herself now that the final word had been revealed. Martin. Poppy. This was, finally, a secret she couldn't keep. She must tell that the Winking Woman had said, "This is for Martin." She must tell . . . someone.

PART THREE

Houses Divided

1975

ONE

"You lied to me," Value screamed at Hedy, "you lied and lied and lied." Her face, a duplicate of her mother's except for the one blue and one brown eye, was florid and contorted with fury.

Hedy backed away from her daughter's onslaught and found herself trapped against the kitchen table. She had no idea what Value was talking about. "What?" she managed to ask.

Value, who was taller than Hedy by several inches, bent over her mother, the mismatched eyes flashing hatred. "All these years you've lied about everything. I always knew you were crazy, but I didn't know you were a shit." Speckles of saliva sprayed Hedy's face.

"What is it?" Hedy asked, frightened.

The girl stepped back, dug deep into her jeans pocket, and when she withdrew her hand, she thrust it straight out. In her shaking palm lay Hedy's missing diamond ring.

Astonished, Hedy stared. It took only a moment to recognize the ring, even though it had been ten years since she'd seen it. She raised her eyes to Value's face and sought an explanation. When none came, she said, "You found it."

The laughter which leaped from Value's mouth struck Hedy like a volley of gunfire. The barrage stopped as suddenly as it had begun.

"Found it? You moron. I've always had it," Value said contemptuously.

As Hedy continued to stare, bewildered, George's wheelchair creaked its approach. "Your grandfather," Hedy whispered, as if it were the police.

"So what?"

"What's goin' on here?" he asked, coming into the kitchen. "Can hear you all over the place like goddamn squawkin' hens." Taking in the sight of Hedy backed against the table and Value's arm still outstretched, the good side of his face twisted into a grimace. "What the hell?"

Gingerly, Hedy reached out and tried to push down Value's hand. The girl closed the ring in her fist like a snapping jaw, dropped her arm to her side, then stepped away from Hedy and slowly turned to face her grandfather. Looking down at him she eased into a winning smile.

His amazingly strong heart tripped with love. "Somethin' up, Val?"

"Something's up, all right." She moved closer to him, held out her hand, and unfurled her fingers exposing the ring.

George stared. "What's that?"

"Don't you recognize it, Grandpa?" she asked sweetly, moving her hand closer to him.

Squinting with his one movable eye, he examined it carefully, then sucked in his wheezing breath. "Goddammit to hell, it's that ring."

"She found it," Hedy said proudly.

Value whirled on her. "I didn't *find* it, I've had it all along. Pay attention."

"You took it, Val?" George asked.

"The winner!" Value shouted, tossing the ring in the air and catching it. Her long, light brown hair swung around her face.

The front door slammed. Ralph was home from work.

"Oh, goody," said Value, "the other genius is here, the whole fabulous family gathered together."

"Why'd you lift the ring?" George asked, snickering.

"Because I wanted it."

"Wanted what?" Ralph asked, standing in the doorway, his cheeks and nose red from the January cold.

"Val's got that damn ring," said George.

"What ring?"

"This ring." She shoved it under his nose, causing him to step backward.

"Christ," he said, recognizing it.

George laughed, sounding like a stuck record. "She stole it years ago."

"Why?" Ralph asked.

Value smiled. "Because I thought someday I could cash it in and get the hell out of this hole." She swept her hand in front of her, indicating the house. "But guess what, folks? It's worthless. A worthless piece of glass," she said in an even, measured tone. "The man offered me five bucks for the setting."

A puff of sound came from Hedy, as if she'd been punched in the belly.

"This bitch lied to me," Value accused.

"Don't talk about your mother that way," said Ralph. He ran a hand over the balding dome of his head.

"You went to an appraiser, Val?"

Her hostile eyes still on Ralph, she answered her grandfather. "You got it."

A high and trilling cackle turned all their eyes on George. "I said it, didn't I? I always knew the goddamned thing was paste."

"Glass," said Value.

"Glass, paste, the thing is, old Mary's ring was worth doodly-squat." Squawking and hacking, he continued his terrible laughter.

Hedy continued to hold onto the edge of the table for support. Value's theft of the ring was almost worse than discovering its worthlessness. Why would a child do anything so awful? Finally, she pulled a straight-backed chair away from the table, slumped into it, and looked up at her family: father, brother, daughter were all laughing, a joke at her expense.

George raised his shaking left arm and pointed a finger at Hedy. "There's one born every minute," he croaked.

Wiping tears of laughter from the corners of his eyes, Ralph said, "You always said it, Dad. I gotta hand it to you."

"Fought with Mary about it for fifteen years. Damned woman wouldn't believe me. Royalty, she said she was from. Royalty, my ass. Pig shit was more like it." His guffaw turned into a coughing fit.

"Okay, enough," commanded Value. "We're getting off the subject."

Ralph turned toward the daughter he hated, his cool blue eyes assessing her. "What *is* the subject, then?"

She smiled, lips pulling to the side in contempt. "It's got nothing to do with you." Value turned back to Hedy. "I'm splitting this scene and I need some bread. Unless you want me to steal it from a bank or somewhere, you'd better get me some."

"What about graduation?" Hedy asked as if Value's threat were of a childish nature.

"What about it?"

"Well, you graduate in two weeks." They'd already paid for the rental of the cap and gown.

"You think I care about that?"

"And college?" Hedy asked. Value had been accepted at three schools to begin the following September. She hadn't chosen one yet, but they were all excellent. Ralph had reluctantly agreed to pay.

"College sucks."

They'd spent hours together poring over college catalogs; Hedy was shocked.

"So what's your plan?" asked Ralph.

"Not that it's any of your business, but my plan," she answered, doling out her words carefully, "is to find my father."

Ralph pressed his thin lips together.

Hedy winked her eye.

George grunted.

Looking from one face to another, Value continued: "And one of you is going to tell me who he is, because I know, for a fact, that each one of you knows who he *is*. Not who he *was*. I know, *for a fact*, that he's alive." Mostly she was bluffing. She didn't know anything "for a fact." The man in the green car had stopped following her about a year after Hedy had begun to dog her every move, but she was still convinced that he was her father.

"If you know that," said Ralph, his voice raspy, "then you must know *who* he is."

"Well, I don't. If I knew that, do you think I'd be hanging around this dump?"

"Hold on now, Val," said George.

She ignored him. "I want two things. Money and info."

"You're a fool," Ralph said.

Blood drained from her face leaving two white streaks across her cheeks and a bluish cast, like an aura, around her lips. "Listen, asshole," she began, but was cut off by Ralph's arm lifting to slap her as he moved closer.

"No," Hedy yelled. "Stop it."

He slowly dropped his arm, his eyes flickering with malice.

It was a standoff, like something out of an old Western film, Ralph and Value facing each other, shoulders squared, fists clenched at their sides.

"Jesus, Mary, and Joseph," George said.

Hedy stepped between the adversaries. "I have money for you, Value."

A satisfied but baleful smile spread across Value's face. "How much?"

"Enough," answered Hedy. So the time had come. Value was going to leave her. She had thought there were eight more months.

"Listen, I want to know how much. Exactly."

"What's all this?" screaked George.

Ralph's eyes folded into slits. "What money are you talking about?"

"My savings."

"Ha!" With what he'd given her over the years for household money, he knew there couldn't be much. "Well, Value, you ought to do nicely on a couple of hundred bucks."

"Is that what you're talking about? A few hundred?" she asked Hedy.

"No."

"So how much?"

Hedy licked her lips. Should she say in front of Ralph? Surely he would want to know where it came from. They all would. But no one could make her tell. How could they? "I'll tell you how much if you promise to drop this thing about your father."

Ralph's chest heaved.

"Tell me how much first."

"If I do will you drop it?"

"Depends."

Hedy decided that saying how much wouldn't be the same as handing it over. "All right. Forty-seven thousand, eight hundred dollars."

All three stared at Hedy. George was the first to break the silence, a wheezing, sizzling sound: his laughter. Joining him was Ralph, raucous and discordant. Value followed, her mirth explosive, like the crack of a gun. The dissonance filled the kitchen while Hedy waited. At last it narrowed down and fizzled out.

"It's true," she said simply. "Laugh all you want, but I have forty-seven thousand eight hundred dollars."

"Where the hell would you get that kind of money?" Ralph asked disdainfully.

"That is nobody's business but my own."

Ralph's face twisted with outrage. "The hell it is. You're under my roof. I support you and this brat. It's my business all right."

"The boy's right," said George. A strange small pain had begun in his head and with his good hand he tried to touch it but couldn't really locate the spot.

"I'm not telling," she said adamantly.

"Who cares where she got it," said Value, "if she's telling the truth. Where is it?"

"Oh, Lord," said George, "if Father Frank were alive he'd get it out of her. Grand man, grand." Since the priest's death George had rewritten history and only spoke of him in sanctified terms.

The idea of beating his sister bloody until she told everything whirled through Ralph's mind. "Where'd you get it?"

"Where is it?" asked Value again.

"You rob a bank, Hedy girl?"

Ignoring them all, Hedy said, "I'll give you the money, Value, if you want to go away, but what I've told you about your father is what you'll have to be content with." She removed her glasses and wiped them with the tail of her blouse.

Value weighed this choice and decided against it. She'd have both or else.

Ralph advanced toward Hedy and slammed his fist on the table. "You can't get away with this."

"Oh, shut up, Ralph," said Value. "Where's the money, Mother?" she asked sweetly.

"Don't you tell me to shut up," he screamed. "You shut up."

The pain in George's head was expanding.

"I'll get the money. You all stay here."

Silently they watched as Hedy left the room.

"It's impossible you know," Ralph said.

"Maybe," said Value.

"But if she's got any money, it's mine."

Value put her hands on her shapely hips. "Say's who?"

"Says me, brat. Where else do you think she got it?"

"Well, not from you, asshole."

"Val, Val, don't," said George.

"Then who from?" asked Ralph.

"My God, you're dumb. From my father, of course."

His mouth flew open and he almost said, "I'm your father,"

but the lips slapped closed again, shutting off the words. Could someone else be Value's father? Had he been duped all these years? No, it wasn't possible. Value was his with her one blue and one brown eye. She *must* be.

Hedy, carrying a jumbo-sized Kotex box, came back into the kitchen.

George's face flushed at the sight of her package. His good arm had a prickly feeling in it.

Ralph and Value stared.

She walked across the green and white linoleum floor and placed the box on the table. "There," she said, as if she'd revealed all.

Value and Ralph ran to the box. She reached it first and pulled it down on its side, peered in. Dark as it was, she could see money and reached inside. When she withdrew her hand she was holding a bunch of fifty dollar bills.

Proudly Hedy said, "There are nine hundred fifty-six of them."

"Oh, my God," said Value, sitting down.

Through his teeth, Ralph said, "Where-did-you-get-this-money?"

"Who the hell cares!" Value threw the bills into the air and laughed as they fluttered down.

Ralph grabbed at Hedy's blouse, twisting the collar and choking her.

"Stop," she squealed, her pale skin growing red.

"You had this money and you were going to make me pay for her school?" He shook her by the neck and her head wobbled crazily like a rag doll. "Where'd you get it?" he demanded.

Seeing her mother's crimson face and bulging eyes, Value leaped on Ralph's back, pounding and pulling.

The pain in George's head clouded his vision but he knew what was going on and called out for them to stop, shouting, "Alligators."

Ralph twisted the polyester material tighter. Value sank her teeth into Ralph's hand and as he screamed he heard Hedy rasp out one word.

"Swann."

Turning on Value he slapped her hard across the face, then clutched the bitten hand with his other.

Hedy was choking and gasping for air. Ralph whirled back to face her. "What swan?" he asked.

He heard movement behind him and turned in time to catch Value leaping at him. He grabbed her wrists in both his hands and twisted, easily subduing her. Value sank to her knees as Ralph let go of one wrist and pulled the other arm behind her back where, once more, he bent it at a painful angle.

The pain in George's head was agonizing. He sputtered and squawked and called for help, saying, "Marshmallows." But no one came to his aid.

Breathlessly, Ralph, who was still holding onto Value, asked Hedy again, "Tell me what you mean by swan or I'll break her arm."

Hedy stroked her smarting throat. "Don't."

"Tell me. I'll break her arm, I mean it."

She knew he did. "A man named Swann gave me the money." Desperately she tried to think of a reason she could give for this, but her throat, aching and throbbing, interfered.

"Why?"

"He . . . he wanted to."

Ralph pulled Value's arm higher and she screamed. "Why?" he demanded again.

It was over; Hedy could see this now. Well, what difference did it really make? She must save her child from Ralph. "He's her father."

"But you said *I* was," Ralph blurted, then dropping Value's arm, clapped his hand across his mouth.

"I never did," Hedy said.

"Oh, Jesus," said Ralph. It was true, she never had. He had naturally assumed it.

From the floor, Value, rubbing her arm, looked up at Ralph. "You?" she said horrified.

Hedy went on. "His name is Martin Swann. He's a psychiatrist. A very important man. Your father," she said, looking down at Value. "He has dark brown eyes."

Value had always known they were crazy, all of them, but that her mother did it with her brother had not ever entered her mind. Did her grandfather know? She turned to ask him.

He was staring straight at her, his good eye wide and vacant. The left side of his mouth hung open and white foam streaked his chin.

"I think," said Value, "Grandpa is dead."

Ralph crossed to him and lifted his wrist, feeling for his

pulse. He dropped his father's hand and turned back to Hedy. "Dead. You killed him."

"Oh, shove it," said Value. If anything had caused the stroke, she believed, it was Ralph's admission.

Hedy crossed herself.

A veneer of sweat, like an oily spread, coated Ralph's face. "We have to call a doctor."

"What for? He's dead," said Value.

"That's what you do," Ralph shouted, leaving the room to phone.

Value began to pick up the money she'd tossed in the air; she stacked it neatly on the table. "Got any rubber bands?" she asked.

Hedy rose mechanically and crossed to a drawer at the side of the sink, opened it and reached in a hand, scrabbled around, finally coming up with a bunch of rubber bands, dangling from her fingers like worms. She crossed back, never looking in her father's direction, and dropped the bands on the table.

Lifting up the Kotex box, Value upended it and the rest of the money tumbled out, some gliding to the floor. She picked it up and began to make small piles which she secured with the rubber bands. When Ralph returned, both Value and Hedy were sitting at the table, staring at the stacks of money.

"The doctor's coming," he said.

"Where's my father now?" Value asked.

Hedy's faint blue-eyed gaze drifted in her daughter's direction. "In New York City."

Perfect, thought Value. It was just where she wanted to go. "Do you have his address?"

"If he still has the same one." She tucked some wispy strands of graying hair behind an ear. "What are you planning to do, Value?"

"I want to see him."

"Stop this!" Ralph said.

They looked at him, surprised by the outburst. His face appeared marbleized: red and white.

"Stop what?" asked Hedy.

"These lies," he said. "These terrible, terrible lies. I can't stand it."

"There are no lies," said Hedy.

"You don't know anyone named Martin Swann," he said.

Ralph was jealous, just as he'd been of Father Frank! A

pleasant sensation washed over Hedy; any time she could make Ralph miserable made her feel good. "I do too know Martin Swann. And he's Value's father. Where else would I have gotten all this money?" She indicated the piles on the table with her stubby hand.

"Why did you think you were my father?" Value shouted at him.

"Why do you think?" He spat the words at her like tiny darts.

She looked to Hedy. "Is it true?"

Her daughter's scrutiny made Hedy squirm and a strange feeling she'd never experienced before made her drop her gaze.

"Is it?" Value demanded.

Very softly Hedy replied: "He forced me."

"You loved it," Ralph screeched.

Hedy raised her eyes. "Oh, no. No, I never did."

For just a moment Value felt sorry for her mother, but that emotion was quickly replaced by detestation for Ralph.

"You're a pig," she said to him, then turned back to her mother. "Did you love this Martin Swann?"

Hedy giggled. There was no way to explain without telling the truth, and that was impossible. "Value, you said you wanted money and to know who your father was. You have those things. That's all I can tell you."

It didn't matter. She'd get Swann to tell her. "All right. But just tell me this: was he the man in the green car?"

"What man in what green car?" asked Ralph, feeling left out.

Hedy knew who Value meant. She'd seen him around, recognized him as the man who'd come to the house pretending he wanted a room. Then he'd disappeared and she'd never seen him again. "No, that man wasn't Martin Swann."

"What man?" Ralph insisted, eyes wide with fury.

They continued to ignore him, addressing only each other.

"Who was he then?" asked Value.

"I don't know. I always wondered."

Value didn't believe her mother didn't know. Somehow she'd find out who he'd been even if she had to hire a detective. The thought made her realize again that she was rich; it made her smile.

The bell rang.

"The doctor," Ralph said, and went to answer the door.

Hedy and Value were silent, each planning her next move. And in his wheelchair the corpse of George Somerville had begun to slowly stiffen: a monument to madness.

Hedy sat on her bed. In one day her life had changed drastically: she had lost both father and daughter. In a way, her father's death was a relief; now she would have more time for herself. But if Value was leaving, then she would have to leave too. She had promised her mother . . . then she remembered. The missing ring had *not* been a sign from Mary Somerville, after all. The constant surveillance of her daughter had been pointless; and the ring was worthless, which meant her mother had lied to her.

Moving further back on the bed she propped up her pillows against the headboard. Her feet, encased in heavy gray wool socks, were crossed at the ankles as she stretched out her short legs in front of her. Had her mother known the truth? she wondered. Or had Mary's mother lied to her? Had Mary's mother's mother lied also? The long chain of lies, like links of steel, stretched back into the past. As if she were an alchemist, Hedy reduced the metal nexus to string, then watched it fray, disintegrate. Surely her mother had been duped as she had been; perhaps all the women all the way back to that poor maid in a royal house had been told the fantastic lie. That must have been the way it was. She was glad her mother had never known the truth. The real worth of the ring was not the devastating blow it might once have been; she'd lived for ten years thinking it was lost to her forever. Now that she handed the forty-seven thousand dollars over to Value, however, she was penniless. Not that she had ever intended Swann's money for herself, but having it stashed away in her closet had always been a form of security. Now she was once again entirely dependent on Ralph. She sucked in her breath and her eye winked wildly. Ralph.

As if to protect herself from him she quickly scrambled under the covers, pulling the quilt up around her neck. She reached down and removed her socks, flinging them onto a chair. Her salmon-colored nightgown measured to her ankles, the sleeves to her wrists, the neck high. The defense of gown and covers against Ralph's possible desires was illusory, she knew, but it offered a chimerical comfort. Would her brother begin his assaults on her again now that he knew Value was not his child? Hedy didn't even have the old ace in her deck of telling her father. She was totally without power.

Depressed, she removed her glasses and set them on her night table, then flicked off the light, scrunching further down in the bed, readying herself for sleep.

Then the door of her room burst open. Ralph's spindly form was silhouetted in the doorway by the light from the hall. Clumps of hair stuck out from either side of his head. He kicked the door shut behind him and they were in total darkness.

"Put your light on," he ordered.

Hedy's heart knocked in her chest. She couldn't believe it was starting already.

"I said, put on the light." His voice was pinched and mean.

Unsteadily, she reached out her hand, found the switch, and then her glasses. She supposed she had a better chance in the light. When the room was dimly illuminated she saw that Ralph was wearing his blue flannel pajamas and that in his hand he carried a brown paper bag. He walked toward the bed, his inimical eyes trained on her face, his slice of mouth turned down at the corners.

"What do you want?" she whispered.

He stopped. "Why are you whispering?"

"Value," she said.

"What do I care what that brat thinks." He sat on the foot of the bed. An expression that might, in poorer light, have passed for merriment crossed his face. "What do you think I want?"

Winking her eye, she said, "I wouldn't know."

"Stop that stupid winking," he directed.

It was useless to tell him she couldn't help it; he knew that as well as she. She looked at the paper bag which rested on his knees, still clutched in one bony hand. Although it was an ordinary brown bag it seemed ominous to Hedy, as if it held ugly answers to the rest of her days.

"You've ruined my life," he said. "All these years you've let me believe that goddamned brat was mine. Do you know I went to Mass every morning for the last eighteen years?" His unformed face was creased with lines, like a wrinkled baby's.

She hadn't known and was mildly surprised. "It probably wasn't wasted," she said.

"Shut up!"

She shrugged.

"And I've been celibate all that time. My penance," he said, emitting a cracking laugh as if to underline what an idiot he'd been. "All because of you and what you let me think. You've destroyed the best years of my life."

Hedy thought Ralph's thinking was twisted: hadn't it been the other way around? But before she could point this out he said:

"Now you're going to pay." He hugged the paper bag closer to him.

Was there a gun in the bag? she wondered. A knife? Or something to do with sex? Surely, sex was on his mind. When he started to rise she shouted, "Wait."

He did.

Hedy said, "Whether you're Value's father or not has nothing to do with it. If you do that to me again, it's as big a sin as it ever was."

His mouth slid into a smile and he pointed a finger at her. "You think . . . you think I want to do *that* with *you?* You must be crazy." His laughter, like the whinnying of a horse, fractured the tension in the room.

Hedy was completely dumbfounded. "Isn't that why you're here?" she ventured, shouting over the raucous sound.

"Of course not," he said, as if she'd imagined those nights of long ago.

"Then what. . . ."

"I wouldn't touch you now with a ten-foot pole," he said indignantly. "You're a whore, Hedy Somerville, and I don't sleep with whores."

"A whore?"

"A slut. A tramp. Used goods."

"Because of Martin Swann?" she asked incredulously.

"You're the scum of the earth," he said.

In defense of this defamation, Hedy almost told him the circumstances of Value's conception, but caught herself in time. What did it matter what Ralph thought if it liberated her from his violations?

Again he rose from the bed and walked closer to her. "Value is leaving in the morning. I had a little talk with her a few minutes ago." A satisfied sneer sailed over his lips. "She agreed to share the money." He held out the paper bag a few inches from his narrow chest.

"What did you do to her?" she asked, frightened. Hedy knew her child to some degree: Value would never give up the money voluntarily.

"I convinced her."

Hedy saw the malevolent cast to his eyes, heard the unmistakable enmity in his tone. "How? How did you convince her?"

"With reason, logic. I explained that it had been me all these years who'd supported her. I fed her, bought her clothes, paid her doctor bills. And then I twisted her arm behind her back."

Hedy touched her own arm as if she could feel the pain Value must have suffered.

"I think I've been very generous. And I intend to be generous with you, too. Under the disgusting circumstances." He threw the paper bag onto the bed. It landed on Hedy's legs. "There's five thousand dollars in there. The brat also has five thousand."

"And the rest?" She knew the answer but couldn't believe it.

"Mine."

The word reverberated in the room as their eyes met and locked in loathing.

She would have to kill him, she thought. There was no way she could allow him to steal over thirty thousand dollars from her daughter.

"In the morning," he said, breaking her train of thought, "you'll pack a bag and leave this house forever. I'm not going to live under the same roof with a whore."

Hedy began to plan: when he fell asleep she would. . . .

"I'll be up all night," he went on, as if reading her mind, "so don't try anything. I haven't forgotten Lucy, you know."

Hedy knew he'd always suspected her, occasionally using that threat when she'd resisted his attacks.

"Where will I go?" she asked.

"Go wherever you like."

"But I don't want to go *anywhere*."

"Too bad. You're not staying here. This is *my* house now. Dad left it to me in his will, I've seen it. And his savings, too." His eyes grew smaller as if they were shrinking. "He left you a dollar so there wouldn't be any trouble." The smile that twisted his lips was the most chilling yet. "You getting the picture?"

Five thousand dollars wouldn't last very long, especially if she had to pay rent. "How will I live?"

He pointed at the bag lying on her legs where he'd thrown it. "There's five thousand in there," he said, as if it were a million.

"After it's gone?"

Ralph shrugged. "Get a job. It's about time you did. You've had a soft life up until now."

The urge to jump up and sink her fingers into his throat was almost overwhelming, but the feeling of inertia prevailed. "And what if I refuse to leave?"

"Then I'll beat you every day until you *do* leave," he said evenly.

She knew he meant it. Of course she could insist on staying, and then kill him when he slept; he couldn't remain awake forever. But it seemed complicated. In the end it was simpler to leave.

"Do you understand now?" Ralph asked.

She nodded.

"Good. I want you out by nine, so you'd better get some sleep." He went to the door. "By the way, why does the name Martin Swann sound so familiar to me?"

It could be a disaster if Ralph ever put two and two together. The case had been in all the papers and she remembered Ralph reading about it, discussing it with their father. "He was my doctor when I had those liver problems."

"I thought you said earlier that he was a psychiatrist."

She grinned. A last opportunity to annoy him. "That's right. I told you at the time that it was liver problems. The truth was I saw him because of you, and you paid."

"Tramp," he flashed, "whore." And slammed out of the room.

The smile died on her face as she realized the lack of real satisfaction she'd enjoyed. Yes, it had irritated him, but now it was over and her plight was unchanged. In the morning she would have to leave; there was no choice. Where would she go? She imagined herself taking an apartment somewhere in Irvington; what would she do there? The sudden solitude of that life engulfed her, weighing her down with its implied emptiness. Always before she'd had a purpose to her life. For the last eighteen years that purpose had been Value. Value. Of course. In the morning she would do what she'd been doing for the last ten years. She would follow her. Wherever Value went she would go.

Hedy got out of bed and went to the closet. From the back she pulled out an old suitcase of her mother's. On the lid there was a faded sticker that said: NIAGARA FALLS. She carried the case to her bed and opened it up. The blue lining was still new-looking. She would dress now, pack, and go downstairs to wait so she wouldn't miss Value's departure.

She picked a green woolen skirt, a tan long-sleeved blouse, and a yellow cardigan. She wanted to look especially nice. Bending down to look at her shoes on the closet floor, she deliberated for quite a while. At last she settled on the brown oxfords; they would be most comfortable for walking. She also took out her sneakers and her sandals to pack. The fourth pair of shoes, gray low-heeled pumps, she pushed to a dark corner of the closet. That accomplished, she felt very secure about the adventure that lay ahead of her. It was going to be fine now that she'd dispensed with the gray shoes. She knew by instinct that those gray shoes, had she ever worn them, would have electrocuted her.

Thank God, she was on top of things once again.

The March wind was particularly strong and Zo, who no longer wore a hat, felt it whip through his hair, creating tangles. He missed his old trilby but knew it was an anachronism; he sometimes wondered if he was. Things seemed to be changing so swiftly and he didn't like it. On the other hand, he hated being one of those people who always looked to the past for comfort and authentication; he disliked it in others, often championing the present despite his own feelings.

His neighborhood, for instance. It had a new name: SoHo. And it had a new look: Chic. The old factories were being bought up by artists who were turning them into living and working lofts. The ground floors were becoming art galleries, boutiques (even Helen was in on this), restaurants. Every few months there seemed to be a new one opening. The buildings were being co-oped, some floors selling for as much as thirty thousand. He'd never been inside any of these lofts, but he'd heard some of them were fantastic looking: shiny hardwood floors, gourmet kitchens, saunas, sunken bathtubs, Italian tiles, beamed ceilings. And the space. Some of the places were five thousand square feet. But even the ones half that size could have encompassed his apartment with plenty of room to spare. Was he jealous? he wondered. Was jealousy always at the root of hating change? Or was it fear? Or both? Did he hate this new goddamned disco stuff because he couldn't dance it? Was he jealous of the loose and lascivious movements because at fifty he thought it unseemly for him to try the steps? Or did he really prefer a foxtrot, dancing close to your partner, touching instead of teasing?

At the corner of Prince and Sullivan, Zo went into Vinnie's luncheonette for a cup of coffee. He waved to Vinnie, who was behind the counter, his white T-shirt and apron clean for a new day.

"Usual, Zo?" Vinnie asked.

He nodded. The place was crowded with regulars for breakfast, but Zo found an empty stool at the end of the counter. He loved coming in here; it was still a real neighborhood place with the smell of bacon grease and strong coffee, thirty cents a cup instead of eighty in the new chic cafés. It reminded him of Joe's in the Village, which was gone now, replaced by an Italian restaurant that was lousy. He wondered what had happened to Rosalie and if he would ever see Chilichow on a menu again. Jesus, he thought, it's getting bad if I'm longing for Chilichow!

From the radio behind the counter came the voice of Nat King Cole singing "Golden Earrings." Zo smiled; Vinnie always kept his radio tuned to WNEW, which played the oldies all day long.

"Whatcha smilin'?" Vinnie asked, putting coffee and a bagel down in front of Zo.

"The song."

Vinnie's eyes, two dark caverns in a sculptured face, blazed brighter. "That's music, right?"

"Right." He could always count on Vinnie to be anachronistic too.

He bobbed his head up and down at Zo, as if to say that only they knew what was really good in life, and when. It was that sort of alliance that made Zo uncomfortable. As much as he liked Vinnie, Zo knew the man's affinity for the past was a symptom of his inflexibility. Zo liked to think of himself as mutable and resilient. On one or two occasions Helen had called him stuffy and it had stung. And when she presented him with her idea for a shop, he'd shown she'd been right.

"Why shouldn't I open a boutique?" she asked. "It's my money."

That had made him very angry. "It's not the money, you know that. It's the types you'll be pandering to."

"What do you mean, *types?*"

He pictured half-naked nubile women, sticks of pot drooping from their mouths. "Trash," he said.

"By trash you mean young, trendy people, don't you, Zo?" She knew him so well. "Of course not."

"Yes, you do. You know, sometimes you're like some old man. Honest to God, you're rigid."

The word *rigid* was like a blow to him. "Well, what cop's wife has a boutique?"

"Since when have I ever done anything like a cop's wife?" She laughed, making him angrier, more defensive.

"Well, it's awkward for a cop to have a wife who hangs out with dopers." He immediately wished he hadn't said it, as he saw the look that crossed her face.

"Oh, Zo. Really."

He felt trapped in his own absurd protestations but couldn't stop. "And Mafia, too. Who knows who might come in there."

"My God, Zo, you're right. I never thought of it." She crossed her hands over her heart, mocking him. "We might attract hit men and dealers and who knows, Richard Nixon might come in!"

"It's not funny."

"Yes, it is. You're just being ridiculous, nothing but an old fogey."

Old fogey was too much. He'd slammed out of the house. Within half an hour he'd returned, sheepish and repentant.

"I was stupid," he said, head bowed.

"Yes," she agreed. "Are you afraid for me to go into business on my own?"

"I don't know. What if you lose your savings? What if it fails?"

"I'll get a job again. I need to have something of my own."

Their eyes engaged. He understood. It was the child thing again, although his rules and regulations no longer had anything to do with it. After the mastectomy she'd needed a hysterectomy, but now she was fine. No signs at all.

"You think you and Tess can really weather a partnership?"

"We want to try. We've been friends for a long time, know each other pretty well. I think we can survive it."

"Well, I wish you luck, lady."

"Thanks, big fella."

Helen and Tess had been in business for over a year and True Confessions, their shop, was clearly a success. Even though the place offended Zo aesthetically with its way-out clothes and bizarre accessories, he was enormously proud of Helen.

He finished his coffee. In a moment, Vinnie was there with a refill.

"Catch any crooks lately?"

"Fifty a day, Vin."

"You get under quota you can always make up for it here, ya know." He winked and jutted his chin, like a pointer, over Zo's shoulder, then walked back to his griddle. Zo saw Doodle, the local numbers man. Doodle was in his sixties, with a face like a collapsed soufflé. He still wore a trilby, but it was too small for his head and sat on top, reminding Zo of Ed Wynn. The majority of Doodle's "clients" were the Italian housewives from the neighborhood. Often Zo watched the money change hands, Doodle's dour expression never altering, eyes snapping from right to left as though they were on rubber bands. It was a game, of course; Doodle knew who Zo was, knew Zo knew him. Doodle was small fry and nobody cared, least of all Zo.

Chewing the last bite of bagel, his second breakfast, he thought it seemed that the older he got, the hungrier he got and the harder it was to maintain his weight. The night before, after they'd made love, Helen grabbed his roll of excess flesh in both her small hands and said, "Not good, tough guy, not good at all." So here he was eating a second breakfast after promising her to go on a diet. Tomorrow. He lit a Chesterfield and blew a short puff in the air; the little cloud joined the gray atmosphere, vanished. He thought about the night before, shook his head in proud amazement: after all these years they still made love a few times a week, and it was better than ever. It had been touch and go that year of the mastectomy. He would always remember it as the worst year of their marriage. First, it was getting through the operation, then convincing her he still cared, desired her. And near the end of 1966 another, worse difficulty erupted. It had been more shocking to him than anything else in their lives.

Helen had looked at him across the dining room table, the candles flickering, casting shadows over their faces. "Zo, I can't go on competing."

"Competing?"

"I knew what it was going to be like when I married a cop. I knew you'd be taken away from me lots of the time, preoccupied and all, but this is ridiculous, Zo."

"Would you mind clueing me in on what you're talking about?"

She laid her fork, a piece of steak still speared, on the plate. "It would be difficult enough to compete with a living, breathing woman, but I can't go on competing with a dead one."

Now he understood. They hadn't spoken of the Swann case for a long time.

"You think I don't know you're obsessed, Zo?"

He shrugged, unable to answer.

"I know you put in time when you don't have to."

Finally, he found his voice. "You've been talking to J.J., haven't you?" A small anger, like a pilot light, burned within him.

"It doesn't matter who I've been talking to. The point is, that case is eleven years old and you're simply not going to solve it."

"You don't know that," he said combatively. Hedy Somerville had come out of hiding nearly a year before and he'd been following her, waiting for the mistake she was bound to make.

"Zo, I want you to give it up. It's coming between us."

"That's crazy."

"No. No, it really isn't."

"There's going to be a break in that case, Helen. I can feel it." So far, Hedy had done nothing but follow her daughter wherever she went. Was she waiting for Martin Swann to show up, snatch the kid? He told Helen about this.

"I don't care," she said simply.

He was astonished. Helen had always cared about his cases.

"You don't understand what you've become. You're obsessed, and it's boring."

He felt hurt. "Are you telling me *I'm* boring?"

"Anyone with any obsession is boring. I don't care what the obsession is, it diminishes the person who has it. I'm lonely, Zo."

She'd gone on to give him an ultimatum: either he dropped the Swann case or she would leave him. He could hardly believe what she was saying, but finally he'd had to look at himself and see that it had validity. All these years of watching Somerville's kid, Cristina Swann, Martin Swann, and now Hedy were meaningless. He was no closer to any proof than he'd ever been. His talks with J.J. about the case, his meetings with Emma Stevenson were, in the end, bogus, pointless. The notion of progress was an illusion. Did every detective have one case like this that totally absorbed him? There had been other unsolved crimes over the years and they all nagged at him, making him feel inadequate, but not like the Swann case. Was obsession a smokescreen, a fraudulent focus? Had he used it all these years to avoid something else? It didn't matter what it was: it would have to go. Helen was more important than any unsolved murder, anything at all.

"Hey, Zo," Vinnie said, breaking through his thoughts. "Whatcha think of Charlie Chaplin becomin' a knight?"

"Haven't heard about it."

"Sir Charles, they're gonna call the guy. Can ya beat that? Sir Charles. The guy's an old reperbate and them limeys make him a knight." Vinnie shook his head, clucked his tongue. "More coffee?"

"No." Zo stood up, put his money on the counter.

"See ya tomorrow."

He waved a hand, smiled at Doodle, and went out into the brisk air. It was his day off and he tried to pretend that he was thinking over different things he might do, but he knew it was all planned. Thinking of Helen, a trace of guilt passed through him. How could he possibly ignore what he'd seen two weeks before? Even Helen wouldn't expect him to if she knew about it. He'd considered telling her, but decided what she didn't know wouldn't hurt her. Besides, it wasn't as if he was going off the deep end or anything. And it was *his* day off; he had a right to do with it whatever he wanted.

At the corner of West Broadway and Prince, he turned right. True Confessions was halfway down West Broadway between Prince and Spring. The shop wasn't open this early, but Helen and Tess were there working. He'd say hello before . . . before whatever it was he was going to do with his free day: museum, movie, who knew? He did. Damn!

Turning the back of his hand to the glass door of the shop,

he tapped with the black star sapphire of his ring. Tess opened the door.

She was younger than they were, forty, and exceptionally pretty if you liked tall, thin model types. "Helen's in back."

"Don't bother her."

"Day off?" she asked.

"Yeah."

"Sit down. I'm dressing a mannikin." Tess walked to a half-naked dress model and began to fit a sleeve over the flesh-colored arm.

Zo stared at the garment Tess was working with. "What the hell is that?"

Laughing, Tess said, "A dress, dearie, a dress. Yours for a mere two fifty."

"Hundred?" he asked, graying eyebrows raised.

"Not two dollars and fifty cents, my friend."

"And you'll get it, too, won't you?"

"Of course."

Suddenly he felt like Vinnie, balking and fighting everything new. "Good," he said. "In fact, I think I like it. Maybe I'll buy it."

"Oh, Zo," she said giggling.

"Yeah, I'm going to buy it for my mother."

"Terrific."

When Helen came into the store from the back room, Zo and Tess were laughing helplessly. "What's so funny?"

"Zo's buying this dress for his mother."

Helen smiled, imagining Gloria Campisi in the smock dress with cargo pockets.

"Well," Zo said, "at least it's new. Everybody seems to be wearing these old clothes now."

"And you're right in style," Helen said, kissing his forehead.

He looked down at his pants, ten years old, shoes six, jacket twelve. "That's different."

"Very," Helen said sympathetically. "What's your plan for the day?"

Zo lit a cigarette, shrugged his shoulders. "I don't know. Maybe I'll catch *Funny Lady*."

Helen said, "He loves Barbra Streisand."

"Yuck," said Tess.

He stood up; it was getting uncomfortable. "Well, I'm off."

He kissed them both. "Say hello to Bill for me," he said to Tess.

"I will."

When he'd gone Helen said, "He's up to something."

"What kind of something?"

"Something he doesn't want me to know about."

"Not another woman, Helen?"

"Oh, no. At least I don't think so. God." She thought of their lovemaking the night before. "No, I'm sure not. Some other kind of something. He'll tell me about it sooner or later. He always does."

In the back room, Helen resumed unpacking an order. Zo had that look again; she hadn't seen it for a long time. During the investigation of the Fitzpatrick-"Groovy" murders in 1967, he'd become possessed and fixated for a while, but that had been short-lived, the solution coming in less than a month. And then again in '70 and '73. It was natural, understandable, when there was an outstanding crime, but as far as she knew nothing special was on the fire. No murders. She didn't want to believe what she suspected: the goddamned Swann case again. It took Zo away from her and she could feel it happening again. Yes, even last night. As good as it had been, she'd known he was just slightly removed; a part of him somewhere else. The question was, should she speak up now, nip it in the bud, or wait and see if it died or bloomed? The danger was that if it got going again, this time she might not get him back so easily. Still, she felt there was time. A little more time.

The sun had broken through thick clouds mid-morning and had managed to stay out, warming the air and making it comfortable to lounge around Washington Square Park. Zo had eaten a hot dog and a pretzel for lunch and now, at two thirty, his stomach was protesting again. Well, it would do him good to be hungry, he thought, clasping the roll around his middle, squeezing. He let his jacket fall back over the bulging flesh beneath his shirt and reached in his pocket for a cigarette. He should give these damn things up too, but he loved smoking and had no real motivation to quit. Looking around the park he was struck, as always, by how much the place had changed over the years.

In the fifties it had been a fairly innocent place; the only law broken then was by the occasional beer drinker or litterer. Now the police patroled constantly and it was dangerous to be inside the park at night. Zo watched the hawkers of drugs approach people walking through. He knew their pitch, had heard it often enough. Pills and pot were the hot items: soft drugs only. To Zo, there was nothing *soft* about them; they did the damage nicely. His brother was a pill freak and pothead and the only thing soft was Marius' brain. But nobody bothered these dealers, they were small potatoes, no room for them downtown, and certainly they were not his problem.

When he glanced over at the arch, he saw a woman coming through it who made Zo sit up straight, heart bumping in his chest. Was it she? He couldn't be sure at this distance, but his eyes were trained on her, his body tensed, ready to jump up and follow her if the need arose. This time he wasn't going to let her get away, perhaps disappear for good. She walked to the circle, stopped for a moment as though she were looking for a place to sit, then moved on, coming in his direction. She was wearing a dark, short leather jacket, a blue turtleneck sweater beneath, and purple painter's pants. When she came into focus, he confirmed that it was Cristina Swann. He had no doubt: she could have been Danielle's clone. She found a seat a bench away from him, an elderly man moving over to give her room. She was carrying a green book bag which she set beside her.

So this was it, what he'd been waiting for these past two weeks. Now what? He had to speak to her, find out how she was. Before two weeks ago, the last time he'd seen her she was a teenager, and now she was a beautiful woman, about twenty-six he calculated. Was she married? In love? Did she work? From the corner of his eye he saw her take a book from the bag. In a moment he turned his head to try to read the title. All he could see was the word *Gold* and the author's name, Drabble, unknown to Zo. The old man got up, walked away. The place beside Cristina was free, his for the taking. The moment he said his name, identified himself, it would all come back to her. Did he have the right to rake up old memories she'd probably put to rest years ago? While he weighed the possibilities, the consequences, the last person between them left. The woman's exit attracted Cristina's attention and she looked up, her eyes meeting Zo's. He smiled and she quickly returned to her book.

He felt like a creep, and glanced around to see if anyone had noticed. Was this how the perverts he sometimes arrested felt? He shifted his eyes to the right: she was reading. He had to speak.

Slowly, he rose, dusted imaginary dirt from his pants, stretched. It was seeming more and more difficult to turn her way, walk the few steps to where she sat; forcing himself, he put one foot in front of the other. And then he was standing near her, trembling slightly.

"Excuse me," he said, "I——"

"Buzz off," she said, not looking up from the book.

"No, you don't understand," he faltered.

Still staring at the book, she answered, "I think I do."

He pressed on, despite the growing shaking of his knees. "No, you really don't. We know each other."

She looked up.

He tried a smile, and knew it had come out stupid looking. Suddenly he felt the eyes of the people on the bench beyond her and couldn't help turning to see. There were three of them: two middle-aged men and one old woman. He smiled at them, but they looked at him disapprovingly; he turned back to Cristina.

"I don't know you," she said, "so beat it before I call a cop."

"I *am* a cop." He sat down next to her, shielding himself from the staring eyes. "I . . . we. . . ." He had no idea how to phrase it.

"Who are you?" she asked.

And then it came to him. "Hello, I'm Zo."

"The detective!"

"Yes. I, I just wondered how you were."

"But it's been twenty years. How did you recognize me?"

Could he tell her, remind her further? He shrugged, smiled. "It's all right, I know I look like her."

"Forgive me for reminding you, I had to say hello."

"Reminding me?" She laughed. "Did you think I'd forgotten?"

"Well, not forgotten exactly, but——"

"Not for a day," she interrupted, "not for an hour."

"Oh, Lord," he said, realizing the gravity of what she was saying.

"And you? Surely you'd forgotten until you saw me."

245

How could he explain? And should he? But the words came out as if he had no control. "Not for a day, not for an hour."

Cristina was obviously shaken by his reply. "But you never caught her."

Ashamed, he shook his head. She knew nothing of Hedy Somerville, her father's association with the woman, he was sure. What would be the point of telling her?

"It's hard to believe that that woman got away with murder," Cristina said.

"For me, too."

"I guess that happens a lot, doesn't it?" Cristina asked as if to reassure herself that her mother's case was not an isolated one.

"Sometimes," he said, and saw this wasn't the desired response. "Often," he conceded. "Do you blame *me?*"

"I never thought about that. No, of course not. I'm sure you did your best." She put her book back in the bag. "Want to have coffee?"

As they walked out of the park together, chatting in a desultory way, Zo knew as surely as if he were following a written script that it was all going to start again and that this time, somehow, he had to prove that Hedy Somerville had murdered Danielle Swann.

The motel Claude had booked for them near the Vermont-New Hampshire border was clean and reasonable. Cristina's room was one away from Martin and Lynn's. Claude and his bride-to-be were staying with friends ten miles away; the wedding and reception were to be held on their property the following day.

Cristina desperately wanted a shower and a nap; the ride up from New York with her father and Lynn had been wearing. Poppy was more irritable than usual, snapping and snarling at both women, who took turns driving. Cristina was baffled as to why Lynn continued to put up with her father but supposed it was difficult to end a marriage of almost twenty years. Quite another matter from her own marriage of nine months, if you could even call what she had with Gerry Marsh a marriage.

In the bathroom, she turned on the shower while she disrobed, dropping her pink broadcloth shirt and jeans in a lump on the floor. She stepped into the warm water, the steam creating gauzy clouds. Her head bent, she allowed the hard spray to pelt her neck and shoulders, hoping it would relieve some of the tension which had settled there during the trip. She was seldom with Poppy and Lynn, visiting them infrequently since she'd moved back from San Francisco six months ago, and she was grateful that she would not have to endure another ride with them back to New York. They were going on up to Maine to visit her grandmother, who was in a nursing home. It was odd, she thought, that both of her grandmothers had lived so long; Grandmaman Dudevant was seventy-eight and Elsie Swann, eighty-nine. Although it indicated possible longevity for her, Cristina hoped she wouldn't end her life in a nursing home. At twenty-six that felt remote, almost inconceivable, but even now time seemed to be speeding by. Twenty years had passed since her mother had been murdered; ten years since she had remembered the killer's words: "This is for Martin."

It was Claude she'd chosen to tell. They'd tried to determine what to do with a piece of knowledge so potent it might have shattered their lives once again. She understood now that her choice of confidant had been brilliantly conceived; she'd picked a younger child and one who lived in a world so unreal that he refused, even today, to learn to read, fearing the intrusion of life. And she'd permitted him to convince her that it was unimportant, nonsense, a dream.

But the information she harbored haunted her almost daily and that feeling increased when she spent any time with her father. She had continually to stop herself from confronting him. Marrying Gerry when she was eighteen had been an attempt to avoid this; moving to San Francisco after graduating from Bennington another.

She turned off the shower, stepped out, and reached for the thin towel. After winding it around her long, brown hair she dried herself with a second impoverished towel. Then she slipped on her blue terrycloth robe, left the bathroom, and sat in front of a large mirror above the gilded chest. In the last year she had come to believe she was beautiful; almost everyone she met told her so. "You look like Elizabeth Taylor," they invariably said, "younger, thinner." For years she'd denied the compliments, knowing her protestations were unattractive, causing embarrassment all around. The truth was, Cristina had for so long been unable to endure her own face because of her resemblance to her mother. As much as she still loved Danielle, she detested the idea of being a copy, knowing reproductions were always inferior. But when a man told her she was like Wharton's Lily Bart, she snatched at that comparison, finding it an easier and more acceptable way to come to terms with her own beauty. Being a facsimile of a literary creation was less jarring: imagination was the essential ingredient rather than a flat-out declaration of the beholder's eye.

She dropped the wet, meager towel onto the bureautop and began to brush her hair. There was a knock at the door.

"Who is it?"

"Claude," came the muffled reply.

Jumping up from the chair, she hurried to the door; she hadn't seen him for three years.

"Tina," he said, his arms open for an embrace.

Cristina flung her arms around his neck as he folded her into his chest and held her tightly. She kissed his cheek, then loosened his grip and dragged him into the room.

"Oh, God, let me look at you," she said, standing back from him. "You're gorgeous!"

Claude was tall, almost six feet four inches, his skin like rare porcelain, his lemon-colored hair brushing his shoulders.

"You're not so bad yourself," he said, grinning.

"I look a lot like her, I know."

Staring down at his sneakered feet he said, "Tina, please, let's not talk about her."

"I wasn't *talking* about her, Claude. I merely was pointing out. . . ."

Raising his head, he met her eyes. "You always manage to bring her up."

"What's wrong with that?"

He slapped his thighs with his large hands. "Jesus."

She watched him pace the room, covering its width in a few strides.

Leaning over her, he placed a hand on each shoulder. "I don't want to fight with you, Tina. I feel very happy and I don't want to spoil it."

"I don't want to fight either. But I do think you're being a little sensitive. I was just——"

"Okay, okay. Here's the hard truth. I have no idea if you look like Mother or not because I can't remember what she looked like. I can't remember *her*. I was four fucking years old and I haven't spent my life making a saint out of somebody I never really knew." He walked away from her.

Cristina felt his words hit her as if she were being sprayed with pebbles. She wished she could be like him, pretending it never happened, that there'd been no Danielle.

"I'm sorry I upset you, Claude," she said, moving toward him. "Let's start over." Silently they embraced, her head on his shoulder.

When they parted, she said, "Tell me about your bride."

"Now you're talking."

"What about her name? It's so unusual."

"Is it? I guess. No different from Robin, really."

"I suppose. I've just never heard of anyone called Lark. It's beautiful though." Why, she wondered, did she have the feeling she was talking to a child?

Claude glanced at his watch. "She should be here any minute. Her parents have a room down the row and she's seeing them, but she's going to meet me here and then we'll go see Poppy and Moth . . . Lynn."

From the time he was five, Cristina had badgered him about calling Lynn Mother. They'd had their most horrendous fights over it. Now she was ashamed that this man deferred to her; it made her feel like a bully, overbearing and imperious.

"Claude, please, call Lynn whatever you want." She was struck by her own cruelty: she'd kept her brother from having a mother by her own need to enshrine Danielle. How much had she contributed to his flailing about through life?

Claude showed no sign of having heard her. "You'll love her, Tina, everyone does. She's only twenty, but I think she's really mature for her age. She makes beautiful pottery," he said proudly.

"For a living?"

"Well, she doesn't sell much yet, but we're going to put a little shop in our house when we get it built. Did I tell you we're going to build our own house?"

"You and Lark?"

"And a few friends. Poppy bought me a piece of land in Ellenburg, New York. It's near the Canadian border." He smiled, seeing her look of dismay. "You know Poppy. It was cheap."

"What will you do there?"

"Oh, hell, Tina, what would I do anywhere? Odd jobs. And

I have my trust. We'll make out. Will you come and visit when we have the house built?"

"Of course. But how will you afford to build it?"

"Mr. Benson, Lark's father, is paying for that. Pretty neat, huh?"

"Pretty neat." Claude *was* a child. While circumstances had forced her to mature rapidly, the same set of facts had bound him to late adolescence. Still, he had let go of their mother and she had not. Even if he was less mature, he was certainly freer.

"Hey, what about you, Tina? Poppy says you're going to have a book published. What is it? Will it be a bestseller?"

"No fear of that," she said. "It's for kids. Teenagers."

"Lark's teaching me to read," he said.

"That's wonderful, Claude. Reading will change your life."

"I don't want to change my life," he said ingenuously.

"I mean it'll open whole new worlds to you."

"I guess. Say, are you seeing anyone?"

"No one special."

A knock so timid she barely heard it sounded at the door. Claude jumped to his feet, crossed the room. His large body hid Lark from Cristina's view. With an avuncular arm around the young woman's thin shoulders, Claude ushered her in, introduced them.

Lark's hand lay limp and uninterested in Cristina's strong grip. She hated a flaccid handshake but tried not to let it prejudice her.

The girl had long, ginger-colored hair which was parted in the middle, the way young women had worn it in the sixties. Her green eyes had a dispirited droop to them and Cristina felt there was something uncompromising about the set of her mouth. In total, Lark was frail-looking, as if she were built with kindling.

"Claude tells me you make pottery," was the only thing Cristina could think to say.

Leaning against Claude in the chair they shared, Lark nodded.

Who could blame her, Cristina thought. What, after all, was there to say to that? As the seconds ticked by, her mind raced through topics, discarding them all. A feeling of inadequacy began to overwhelm her.

Claude broke the silence: "How're your parents?"

"Okay," she answered very softly.

Thrilled by the cue, Cristina asked, "Where are you from, Lark?"

She saw the woman's lips move, but she could not hear her. Leaning forward, she said, "I beg your pardon?"

"I'm from Connecticut. Originally from Michigan." The response was barely above a whisper.

Cristina had encountered this before. It was a simple, unconscious technique, causing the listener to bend to the speaker, like a supplicant. She found it very annoying but pressed on. "Did you go to school in Connecticut?"

"Oh, no," she whispered.

All roads, it seemed, were dead ends. For lack of anything better to do, Cristina stood up and crossed to the bureau where her brush lay on its back. "I must brush my hair out," she said stupidly.

"Listen, Tina, Lark and I'll go over to Poppy and . . . Lynn now and we'll see you at dinner, okay?"

She swiveled around, saw that they were both on their feet. "Yes, sure. Nice to meet you, Lark." She didn't offer her hand; she couldn't have stood the feeling of grasping a broken bird again. Kissing Claude, she added, "You look wonderful, honey."

Lark was already outside when Claude murmured, "Isn't she something?" his eyes dappled with lovelight.

"Yes," Cristina answered, "yes, she is."

When she'd closed the door, Cristina stood with her back against it, eyes shut. How could their meeting have been so different from what she'd imagined? A feeling of depression swept over her as she crossed again to the bureau and picked up her brush. She had to laugh when she remembered her fantasies about her reunion with Claude. Even though she hadn't seen him for three years, she should have realized he wouldn't have changed into the sophisticated, witty man she'd created in her mind: that whole meeting had come straight out of a novel. It was absurd. And because she'd invented an alien personality for him the real Claude was a disappointment, leaving her feeling vacant and cheated.

But at least Claude was sweet and sincere; her whole performance had been specious. She wished she could replay the scene. And wasn't that part of the trouble? Everything was a scene to be played rather than time to be lived. And people were who she made them, not who they really were, so that often she was left feeling disillusioned. Which of them, she or Claude, really lived in a dream world?

Hair dry, she went to the bed and lay down, propping the two wilted pillows behind her. She'd been a bitch. Dear Claude, so happy with his awful Lark. But she was *still* being bitchy! Who was she to make such a judgment about Claude's choice? And what was this "dear Claude" crap? Her condescension made her squirm. He'd made her angry because he'd hit on a truth. *I haven't spent my life making a saint out of somebody I really never knew.* But she *had* known her.

She could remember lying in bed waiting for Danielle to come in to kiss her goodnight, hearing the tap-tap of her high heels as she walked down the hall; and then the smell of her perfume as she bent over, cool lips brushing her forehead, her cheeks. Her mother's scent filled her nostrils even now, as if Danielle had entered the room; a combination of ripe peaches and lilacs. Once she'd asked Poppy if he knew the name of Mommy's perfume, but he didn't, saying she should stop thinking about things like that, as though wanting to know was subversive. Eventually, she realized that Danielle's scent had been only partially perfume; the other part had simply been her own essence, impossible to duplicate.

And there were events and activities she could recall: Mommy taking her to see Santa Claus at Macy's; lying in her arms while being read to; helping to bake cookies; playing Go Fish; going to the movies for the first time: *White Christmas* and *Adventures of Robinson Crusoe* (she'd preferred *White Christmas*); eating double-dip chocolate fudge cones together. There were lots of little memories like that, although many had faded like dreams on waking. But even if she could've recalled each moment in sparkling detail, did it mean she *knew* her mother? It did not.

Saint. Claude said she'd made a saint of Danielle and she knew it was true. She *had* spent her life deifying a stranger, someone she hadn't seen in twenty years, someone she'd never see again.

She must dress, find Claude and Lark and apologize. But when she'd finished dressing and was about to leave the room, she realized that to ask for forgiveness might make matters worse. To try and palliate what had happened could serve to accentuate it; perhaps no one had noticed but she. Besides, her feelings of resentment and anger weren't going to be mitigated by an amend; surfacing now was jealousy.

Had she been offered Claude's life in some sort of mystical trade she wouldn't have taken it; still, she was jealous of his happiness, the simplicity of his existence. Her life couldn't have been more different. Between the trust fund Poppy had established for her and the small advance she'd received from the young adult novel, she was comfortable financially, able to pursue writing full time. Her apartment on McDougal Street was small but cozy and only three flights up. She liked living in Greenwich Village after a twenty year hiatus; it was so much more relaxed than the East Seventies. So what was wrong? Why was she jealous of her brother?

Sitting in the green plastic chair she worried the fabric of her taupe slacks between two fingers. The reason was jarring in its ordinariness: she was lonely. Admitting this, even to herself, distressed her: she liked to think of herself as autonomous, self-sufficient, needing no one to feel complete. But it was a lie. She desperately wished to be loved and to feel the kind of love for someone else that she'd read about. There had been three men in her life who qualified as more than casual.

Although for a time she'd thought she was madly in love, her marriage to Gerry Marsh had been a disaster from the beginning. They had spent their "honeymoon" in Las Vegas and out of the seventy-two hours that they were registered at The Sands, she saw him twelve; six of those he slept. He lost every cent they had. Those three days were a preview of the next nine months.

At twenty, she'd become involved with her English professor at Bennington, who was nine years her senior. The affair with Donald Rendell had lasted all of her sophomore year and when she returned to school in September she learned he'd transferred to a college in California. By the middle of her junior year she'd recovered from that blow and for the rest of her college career she kept the men she dated at arm's length.

When she moved to San Francisco it had been in the back of her mind to look up Donald, but she never did. Instead, after a few months of unbearable loneliness, she phoned the only person she had any acquaintance with, Whitney Cunningham, Lynn's son. That had turned out to be an even worse mistake than Gerry or Donald.

The worst part of the whole affair had been betraying Beatrice, Whit's wife, who'd been so marvelous to her in those early months. Somehow, to Cristina, the things that happened between men and women—lies, deceits, betrayals—all seemed a part of heterosexual relationships, acceptable if not admirable; those same things between women who were friends were inexcusable and unforgivable.

She'd seen the Cunninghams often, spent time with the children, shared family expeditions, became Beatrice's confidante. They were older than Cristina by eighteen years, but they treated her as a peer. Her interest in Whit, as more than a friend, had been apparent to her from the beginning, but she'd allocated it to a place where it didn't interfere with the sense of love and family she experienced with them.

When Beatrice's father died, she had had to fly home to Chicago for several weeks. Before she left she asked Cristina to move into the house to help take care of Whit and the children. The first two nights Whit and Cristina stayed up late talking and she had felt an agony of longing for him. On the third night she'd claimed a headache and gone to bed early. She lay awake, staring into the dark, allowing all her feelings that she'd so long repressed to surface. The sound of the door opening startled her and she sat up, the blankets falling to her lap.

"Who is it?" she asked, knowing.

He didn't answer but walked directly to the bed and sat on the edge, his breath warm on her cheek. "I can't stand it another minute."

She saw that his chest was bare and that he wore only his jockey shorts.

Swinging around, he lifted the covers and got into the bed next to her. "You want me too, don't you, Cristina? Oh, God, please say yes."

It had been so easy. The beginning is always easy, especially in the flush of sexual desire. But the middle was tormenting, the end excruciating. Throughout the entire affair, Cristina flagellated herself, and when the end came her crucifixion was complete.

Beatrice arrived at her apartment unannounced and Cristina

knew at once that the affair had been uncovered. The two women had danced around the issue for a while until Beatrice finally said:

"He's a terrific lover, isn't he?"

Cristina was thrown off balance, as if Beatrice had given her a push. She stared into her blue eyes, looking for, but not finding forgiveness. Beatrice's normally soft, rounded features had taken on an angular quality and her mouth was set in two implacable strips. She'd pulled back her straight brown hair into an unaccustomed coil at the nape of her neck. There was little resemblance to the gentle, pretty woman Cristina had known for two years.

"Did you make love every night I was gone?" Beatrice asked.

"Oh, please, Bea."

"Oh, please, Bea," she mimicked. "Don't play Rebecca of Sunnybrook Farm with me, Cristina. Like the man says, the jig's up."

"I don't know what to say."

"I'll bet you don't."

"How did you find out?"

Beatrice's lips twisted into a smile. "The usual way . . . he left one of your love notes in the pocket of a jacket."

The usual way. Cristina felt sick. Whit had told her he'd never cheated on Beatrice before. "It's happened before?"

"You didn't think you were the first, did you?" Beatrice scoffed.

Feeling for Whit poured out of Cristina as if she had a sudden puncture, love leaking away.

"You *did*," said Beatrice, laughing. "Poor dear dope."

"Why did you ask me to move in while you were gone if you knew how he was?" Cristina asked.

"You're kidding?" She looked genuinely surprised.

Cristina was bewildered.

"I trusted *you*. We were friends. I thought."

It was the worst thing Bea could have said. Would it do any good to apologize? Cristina wondered. How could you tell a woman you were sorry for having made love with her husband and sound sincere? The truth was, she wasn't sorry for that. She was sorry for having betrayed Bea. She had to give it a try. "I know this will seem meaningless to you, but I'm sorry I hurt you, I really am. I don't know what more I can say. I have no excuse."

Beatrice looked at Cristina, condemning her, then moved silently out the door.

Cristina had never seen either one of them again.

Since coming back to New York, she had been celibate, a choice. She'd decided to try to find out more about herself: why had she chosen the men she had and why couldn't she let go of her mother? For the first time in her life *she'd* chosen her therapist rather than her father selecting one. Dr. Porcelli was a woman. There had been a number of times over the years when Cristina had timidly suggested to Poppy that she might like to see a woman doctor, but he'd always squashed the idea, saying he didn't know any good ones. Since he was paying, there wasn't much she could do. But now she was paying and Poppy didn't even know about Anne Porcelli. Cristina felt she was moving, although extremely slowly, toward a new understanding of herself. As yet she hadn't told Anne about "This is for Martin," but she knew she would soon. And then she would tell Zo.

She would also, she decided, make it up to Claude and Lark by being warm, friendly, supportive. It wasn't Claude's fault she was so screwed up. It was Mommy's fault, she thought, then quickly left her room as if to lock the sentiment behind the closed door.

The wedding day was clear, a lemon sun swaddling everything in its light. Gauzy clouds occasionally drifted across the sky; the June air was cool, nippy. Lynn drove the car from the motel to the home of the Irvings where the wedding and reception would take place. Martin sat stiffly in the passenger seat, Cristina in the back staring at him. The little hair he had left was white and thin, like used threads. His neck was wrinkled, earlobes long. Sixty-three wasn't really that old, but Poppy looked like a man in his seventies.

"It's a good thing it's not raining. What would they do then?" Martin said.

"They'd simply have the wedding inside," Lynn answered affably.

"Where they should have it anyway," he complained.

"Now, Martin."

Observing Lynn, Cristina noticed again how old she, too, looked. Taking care of Poppy had aged Lynn prematurely. Cristina was surprised that she could feel real sympathy for

Lynn; in past years she'd never allowed anything to surface but the most superficial of feelings: annoyance, impatience, occasionally an anemic sort of fondness.

"Cristina, what did you think of the girl's parents?" He never used Lark's name if he could help it.

"They were all right. I liked her better than him." They had all met at the dinner Martin had arranged the night before.

"A domineering woman, passive man. Classic," he muttered.

"They were both very nice, I thought," said Lynn.

"What the hell do you know about it?" Martin snapped.

Cristina felt herself flash with anger. "There's no need to talk to her like that, Poppy."

Martin's enlarged pupils became larger still. "I beg your pardon?"

She had never interceded on Lynn's behalf before. A touch of fear zig-zagged through her. "I said, you don't have to speak to Lynn like that."

Martin's eyelids slumped as he measured his daughter. He licked dry lips, cheeks twitching. "I'll thank you to mind your own business," he said reproachfully, and turned back to face the front.

For a moment Cristina considered a confrontation, evidential and absolute: *All right, Poppy, tell me in your own words, what did it mean when the woman with the big hat and the wink said, This is for Martin?* But she couldn't do it. He was her father and in the end her desire to protect Poppy was stronger than the one to expose him.

At the Irvings', as they walked up the steps to the restored farmhouse, Lynn took Cristina's arm and squeezed it lightly. Their eyes met briefly and for the first time in twenty years the two women exchanged a look of affection.

The large, open living room, with a beamed ceiling and a huge stone fireplace, was filled with guests. Cristina surveyed the room, looking for Claude and Lark, finally spotting them near the bottom of the staircase.

He was wearing a brown three-piece suit, white shirt, and a silk paisley tie. Cristina couldn't remember the last time she'd seen him dressed in anything but jeans. Lark was in a long white cotton dress with a high ruffled neck and ruffles at the wrists. In her ginger hair, which was twisted and piled on top of her head, she'd twined a delicate rope of flowers like a tiara. Her normally pale lips were touched with an apricot color to blend with her hair; it was the only makeup she wore. Cristina found herself admiring Lark, able to see an ethereal quality to her she hadn't noticed before. She watched them make their way around the room, greeting friends and relatives. At last they came to her.

"We're so happy you're with us to share this moment in our lives, Tina. It's especially meaningful to us."

Claude took Cristina's right hand in his and nodded to Lark to take her other hand, forming a small circle.

"This is a chain of love," he said, "that won't be broken."

Claude's eyes clouded with sentiment as he leaned down to kiss his sister on her cheek. Lark's lips brushed the other. But before Cristina could kiss either of them, or say a word, they had disengaged their hands and moved on as if on silent castors. Then Doug Irving rang a cow bell for quiet and announced that Claude had something to say.

Claude, a beneficent smile on his face, stepped forward. "I want to thank everyone for coming today and for sharing with us this special occasion. Lark and I are going to make our marriage vows at the top of this mountain behind us. There are cars ready to drive anyone who wants to go that way, but there's a path that Lark and I are going to take. It's all uphill and a little rough," he laughed. "I hope you all wore good walking shoes like we told you on the invitation."

Cristina realized she'd forgotten, but her pumps were comfortable, the heel of medium height.

"Anyway, it's about a half-hour walk. It'd make us very happy if you'd join us. Well, that's all. We're going to start now. See you at the top."

Martin appeared next to Cristina. "He's insane. What the hell is the point of this goddamned procession?"

"Go by car, Poppy."

"Damn right. You coming?"

"No, I'm walking."

Outside, those people who were going to be in the wedding procession drifted into twos and threes and began the climb. Cristina, walking with Amy and Doug Irving, noticed a young woman ahead of them who kept turning around and looking in their direction.

"Who's that girl?" asked Cristina, "the one in the jeans and sweater up ahead?"

"Where?"

"About six ahead of us. Long dark hair, yellow workboots."

"She doesn't look familiar. Amy?"

"Well, I can't see her face."

At that moment the girl looked around again, then instantly turned back when she saw that all three of them were looking at her.

Amy said, "I never saw her before, but there are quite a few people here I don't know."

Something about the girl bothered Cristina. There were others who were dressed in a rather casual way, jeans and shirts and sweaters, but this girl's outfit was less than casual; it was sloppy, defiant. And her long brown hair looked uncombed. Most likely, though, the girl's glances had nothing to do with her.

When they reached their destination, they saw that chairs had been arranged in a semicircle; a flat rock a few yards away had been decorated with dried flowers in pots. The view was breathtaking and Cristina could understand why they'd picked this spot. But a brisk wind was lashing out, causing people to turn up coat collars and to stuff their hands in pockets. Then the sun disappeared behind a gray quilt of clouds, the air turning colder still.

The sound of the cars coming up the other side of the mountain turned their attention in that direction. Cristina watched Martin limping across the meadow, Lynn following, her hand reaching out and continuously missing the fabric of his jacket sleeve. The picture of the two of them touched Cristina in a new way; they appeared so old and fragile she wanted to forget everything and tuck each one under a protective arm. They were seated in the front row and she joined them.

"Look at that, just look," Martin said. "I can see my damn breath it's so cold."

"Martin, please," Lynn implored.

He blew out another puff of frosty breath in answer. The bride and groom took their places on the rock. They had written their own service, inserting more equal pledges and adding commentary on nature, love, and art. Cristina found it incredibly youthful and almost unbearably beautiful. Tears fell onto her cheeks as she listened. Lynn pressed a tissue into her hand and they exchanged a smile when Cristina saw that she, too, was crying. Glancing past Lynn, she was shocked to see that

Martin was wiping away his own tears. As she was about to turn back toward the wedding couple her eyes caught sight of the girl in the jeans and sweater. She stood against a tree, staring toward Cristina. Who the hell is she? Cristina wondered, and why is she looking at me? At that moment the minister pronounced Claude and Lark husband and wife; they kissed and the assembled group broke into spontaneous applause.

Back at the farmhouse a yellow and white striped tent had been erected behind the house, sheltering tables and chairs for the wedding dinner. A five-piece band had begun to play and hors d'oeuvres covered two tables facing the outdoor bar. Feeling the cold, Cristina plucked a stuffed mushroom from the table and made her way inside the house where she ordered a vodka martini.

"Hello," a male voice said behind her.

She looked up into the blue eyes of a tall, muscular man; a thick gold chain circled his strong neck and a patch of black, curly hair sprouted from his bare chest in the vee of his open silk shirt. Cristina knew the type. But this was her brother's wedding, his friends, and it wouldn't kill her to be pleasant; she smiled and said hello.

"I'm a friend of Claude's. He tells me you're a writer."

It was finally sinking in that Claude was proud of her. She nodded.

"I've wanted to write myself, never seem to find the time," he said, as if writing were a hobby.

She'd heard that before and was almost sure she knew what was coming next, in one form or another.

"I'm a mystery fan. When I get some time, I'm going to write one. I think it's time I gave something back after all the pleasure I've received." He smiled, flashing perfect white teeth as if they were signal cards saying what a swell, decent guy he was.

Cristina smiled back at him, letting him think she was going to listen. His posturing permitted her to look around the room without it registering on this arrogant man. Past his right shoulder she saw the girl again. There could be no doubt this time that she was staring at her, even though she immediately averted her face.

"Excuse me," she said to the man and headed toward the

girl in the yellow workboots. As she approached, the girl turned toward her and Cristina was chilled.

She felt her arm grasped from behind; it was Claude. "That girl," she whispered, "who is she?"

"What girl?"

"The one against the wall in the jeans and red sweater."

He looked over her head. "I don't see any girl like that."

Cristina spun around. The girl was gone. She scanned the room, but there was no sign of her.

"C'mon, I want you to meet our minister." Claude began to guide her toward the double doors that opened to the tent.

"Wait. Do you remember seeing a girl in jeans and a red sweater and yellow workboots? She had long, sort of scruffy looking hair." The fear she'd felt when she looked into the girl's eyes continued.

"Oh, yeah, I think I saw her."

"Who is she?"

He shrugged.

"Is she a friend of Lark's?"

"Hey, what's the matter with you, Tina? You look like you've seen a ghost."

"Let's find Lark and ask her."

When Cristina described the girl to Lark, it didn't get her any closer to an identification. Later, she questioned others, but no one knew who the girl had been.

During dinner, the cutting of the cake, the dancing, Cristina tried to forget about the girl, but her image kept intruding. Where had she seen her before? She looked familiar. Yet try as she might, Cristina could not place her. But that in itself was not what she found so disturbing. The girl's eyes were what haunted her: they were incredibly cold, devoid of any emotion, and one was brown and the other blue.

TWO

Sunlight, like an interloper, crept between the slats of the blue Levelor blinds and across Guy's face, waking him. His eyes focused on the ceiling, papered in a rosebud pattern. Would he wake to this view for the rest of his life? Five years ago, when they'd bought this house, that prospect had seemed tolerable. But since Marc had died and Janet had become remote and peculiar, he was unsure how long he could endure this marriage.

Carefully, so that he would not wake Janet, he swung his long legs to the floor and slipped into his rubber thongs. From the bureau he took a pair of shorts and a T-shirt; the sound of the drawer opening and closing was muffled by the drone of the air-conditioner.

As he left the cooled air of the bedroom and entered the already humid atmosphere of the hall, he wondered if Rachel was awake. Her visit would help make the long Fourth of July weekend bearable. In the bathroom Guy changed into his clothes, then made his way downstairs.

Rachel was drinking coffee at the counter when he entered the kitchen. "Hi, sport," she said. "What the hell is that you're wearing?"

Stenciled on his T-shirt in silver glitter was: EAT A DUCK TODAY, the best-selling novel Compact had published six months earlier.

He brought his mug of coffee to the counter and sat across from her. "You didn't read *Eat a Duck Today?*"

"I am happy to say, I didn't."

"Now don't tell me you never heard of it?"

"Okay, I won't tell you. Was it a good book?"

"Awful. Number one on the best-seller list for fifteen weeks."

"Figures. How can you stand it?" she asked.

"I'm not sure I can."

"Meaning?"

"Meaning, pushing trash is getting to me." He ran a hand through his long, curly black hair.

"Well, hell, you're president now, can't you do something about it?"

"Not if I want to stay president."

"And do you?" she asked.

"I wish I knew. Some days I'm convinced that I have to carry out what Marc started. Other days it all seems like a bunch of crap. I mean, Christ, I can't even remember the last book we did that I even liked, let alone one that had any merit. I might as well be producing television shows, sit-coms and cops and robbers."

Guy was suddenly aware that this was a conversation he should have had with his wife, but Janet had no interest in his work. She said it was too depressing because it made her think of her father. As if she didn't think of him all the time anyway.

"Sometimes I'd like to chuck it all," he said to Rachel. "Everything."

"You mean this?" gesturing around the kitchen. "This house, Janet, the kids?"

"Yes," he said softly.

"I think you should." She stubbed out her cigarette.

Guy was startled and sat back in the high stool. "You do?"

"Are you surprised because Janet's my sister? I love her, but she's gone bananas. It's been three years since Daddy died. I think that's long enough to get over the death of a parent, don't you? Their relationship was sick when he was alive and death's made it worse."

"I've tried to get her to see a psychiatrist, but she won't."

"I think she likes it this way."

This wasn't a new idea to Guy but one which he'd tried not to dwell on.

Rachel took a blue ribbon from the pocket of her terry cloth robe and tied her hair into a pony tail. "The point is, Guy, she doesn't seem to be getting any better. Frankly, I don't see how she will."

"Don't you think she'd get worse if I were to leave?"

"She probably will anyway. Untreated, these things don't improve. Oh, hell. The truth is, I don't think Janet would even notice if you left her." She lit a cigarette and blew a gust of smoke between them, then, seeing Guy's face, reached out to touch his cheek. "I'm sorry if that hurt."

A stillness settled in the kitchen. Guy, toying with his spoon, felt stuck in the silence.

"Don't be an ass, Guy," Rachel said. "Get out of the marriage and leave the job. You're not Daddy and you owe him nothing. Before you know it you'll be fifty and it won't be so easy then."

"I'm thirty-eight and it doesn't feel easy now."

"It's never easy. You think it was a breeze for me to leave David? I thought I'd die. But I had to do it or I might have died. Inside. How about you, kid? Got any life left in there?" She poked his chest with her finger.

"Not much," he admitted. "But the kids, Rachel. They're so young." Hilary was eight, Marc six.

"They'll survive. Plenty do."

"Do you think . . . do you think she's competent?"

"Why don't *you* take the children?" she suggested.

"I've thought of that. There's so much to——"

"Ah, look who's here," Rachel said, cutting him off.

Guy turned and saw the children. "Awful quiet."

"We were trying to be good," said Hilary. "We didn't know anyone was up." She stood on tip-toe as Guy leaned down for a kiss.

"Can we go swimming, Daddy?" Marc asked.

"You have to have breakfast first," he said.

"Why?"

"Good question," said Rachel.

"You're a big help," Guy said affably.

"There's nothing like an invigorating swim before breakfast, Guy. And I think you should join us."

"Not me." He wanted to talk to Janet, perhaps venture into the idea of divorce.

"Oh, Daddy, please," begged Hilary.

"Daddy's chicken," Marc said.

"You're right," Guy said.

Rachel said, "Well, at least let the kids go."

"I'll make a deal. If they swim now, you make breakfast later."

Rachel cocked her head to one side. "Somehow I think I'm getting the short end of the stick here."

"Say yes, Aunt Rachel, say yes," Hilary demanded.

"Okay," Rachel said. "Some deal."

The children, cheering, dragged Rachel from the kitchen.

As Guy listened to their excited shouts, a profound sense of loss enveloped him. Glancing at his watch he saw that it was a quarter to nine. In the last three years, Janet had been sleeping in the mornings, sometimes until ten. During the week they had a housekeeper who made breakfast and generally took care of them all, but weekends Guy ran the house.

If he took the children, he mused, it really wouldn't be so different from the way things were now. But what about a custody suit, which could be harmful to them? He'd been so careful to create a safe place for Hilary and Marc. It would be ironic if he were the one to destroy their security.

Guy went up the twisting back stairs to the second floor and crossed the hall to the bathroom. He would shave first, he decided, as if scraping away the shadowy look on his cheeks and chin would gain him a clarity of mind, a fresh, clean approach. Lathering his face, he noticed a splash of gray in his hair, like seafoam. Gray was nothing new; it had begun around his thirtieth birthday. But the rate at which it was turning lately had started to alarm him: he wasn't eager to obtain a distinguished appearance before forty.

Guy made a path through the lather on his cheek. If Marc had lived, would his marriage to Janet have changed? But he hadn't; he'd died and Janet had vanished, leaving Guy alone and lonely for adult company. Those first seven years had been good, better than he'd anticipated. Sex continued to be fulfilling and the friendship between them increased, creating a satisfying if never very thrilling union. It seemed to Guy to be the kind of relationship most people had, and much better than some. But death had transformed a modest marriage into one that was as stale as old bridal cake.

After carefully trimming his drooping, black mustache, he left the bathroom, suddenly wishing for a cigarette. It had been ten months since he'd quit and the desire still overtook him with swift surprise. He took a deep breath and the moment passed.

Janet was awake, her head slumped against two pillows, eyes staring ahead. She did not turn when he came in or when the mattress dipped as he sat next to her.

"How did you sleep?" he asked.

"The same." She continued to stare.

Guy knew her answer meant badly. This probably wasn't a good time, but he knew there never would be one. How could there be? "Rachel and the children are swimming."

"Mmmmm."

Should he try once more, be sure he'd given them every chance? "Janet, you can't go on like this."

She turned, her dazed brown eyes meeting his. "Why?"

"Because it's sick." He'd never been quite so direct about her behavior before.

"You don't understand."

He pressed his lips together. She was always telling him he didn't understand. "I do though, that's the trouble. I understand that you can't seem to recover from your father's death and you won't do anything to help yourself." It annoyed him that Janet still flinched at the words "father's death."

"There's nothing I can do," said Janet gloomily.

"Oh, Christ. Of course there is. You could get help."

Her mouth turned down in distaste. "There is no help."

Guy had no arguments left; his desire to reason was exhausted. "I want a divorce," he said.

Janet was so still he was convinced she hadn't heard and he grabbed her wrist and forced her to look at him. "Janet, I said, I want a divorce."

"I heard."

"Then why don't you say something?"

She smiled in an enigmatic way.

Exasperated, he said, "Oh, fuck it. There's no talking to you."

"You're not talking to me, Guy. You're telling me you're leaving. I always knew you'd dump me."

"I'm not dumping you, Janet. I just can't go on like this anymore. There's no point. We don't even have a sex life." It had been over a year since they'd made love.

"I told you why."

"You certainly did." She had come to believe that Marc Sr. was watching them. "Another good reason for you to get help."

"Stop saying that," she demanded.

"I will. It's over, Janet. I'm leaving you. And . . . and I want the children." His words surprised him, but he knew they were right, knew he really did want them.

"Yes," she said.

"What does that mean?"

"It means," she said compliantly, "you can have them."

Guy was astonished. "You don't care?"

She took a cigarette from the crushed box of Marlboros on

her night table. Then, she said evenly, "I don't want them. They're yours, and I don't want anything that belongs to you."

He'd had no idea that Janet hated him so much, assuming only that she no longer felt anything for him. Her loathing was startling, inexplicable. "They're your children, too."

"I don't like them," she said as if she were speaking about shoes or draperies.

"You're very sick," he said, rising and moving away from her.

She went on: "The sooner you all get the hell out of here, the better."

He felt he was watching a film instead of being a participant in this dialogue; it made it easier to continue. "When did you begin to hate me?"

"Three years ago, and the reason should be obvious."

"You mean when Marc died?"

"Yes," she said.

"What did his death have to do with me, Janet?"

"You lived and he died," she said simply.

A sense of *déjà vu* stole over Guy. He felt he'd heard that before, although he hadn't. "Thanks a lot," he said, and left the room, quietly closing the door.

Protectively, his mind whirled away from Janet's hurtful words and focused on his children, unloved by their mother. As soon as possible, he'd get them all out of this house. And he would love and cherish them and make them feel wanted.

He went outside, walked across the tessellated brick patio, and stood at the edge of the pool, watching. As if he were on automatic, he responded to the children's calls, bantering easily. Then he walked to the far end of the pool and knelt next to the skimmer. When he lifted the lid to get the basket, he sucked in his breath, startled by the dead bird which lay in the container. It had happened before: birds, mice, once a snake. But finding these dead animals never ceased to shock him. Guy bent his body sideways to shield the children from the sight of the dead bird as he scooped it up in his hands. A starling. The eyes were open, beady now as in life, and its neck was curved in an unaccustomed angle. He got to his feet and walked slowly to the back of the yard where he laid the sopping bird behind a pile of bricks and sand he'd never bothered to clear. By morning the bird would be gone, eaten by wild things.

Back at the second skimmer, he almost lost his balance as he uncovered another starling. It was too much. Again the eyes were open, glassy, like toy eyes, and the neck bent to fit inside the basket. Leaves and dead bugs clung to the feathers. Carefully, as if to prevent further damage to the corpse, he removed the bird from its watery grave, carried it to the back of the yard, and gently laid it next to the other one. Guy knelt, sat back on his heels, and staring down at the two wet, black birds, he wept.

The apartment Hedy and Value shared was on Avenue B between Eleventh and Twelfth streets, in a small building owned by Mr. and Mrs. Stein who lived in the third floor front. The Somerville apartment was on the second floor rear and all of the sounds from other buildings were clear and resonant, an assault on Hedy after the relative quiet of Irvington. The hardest sound for her to bear was the yelling that came almost every night, between two and three in the morning: a woman began shouting *"God Love You"* in an anguished intonation. And then, of course, there were the ravings of Mrs. Stein herself. Fortunately, her yammering took place during the day and was only audible as she made her way up or down the stairs. What Mrs. Stein said was indecipherable with the exception of one word: *"Fire!"* The first time Hedy and Value heard it they'd run into the hall clutching their brown paper bags filled with money. There they had confronted the mad Mrs. Stein, her thin brown hair released from a dangling rubber band, the strands flying around her shrunken face like long insect legs.

"Fire, fire," she squawked.

"Where?" asked Value.

The woman's eyes skidded off Value's as she continued down the stairs, a barrage of words, incomprehensible, fluttering behind her. Before Value or Hedy could decide what to do, Mr. Stein appeared on the second floor landing.

"Pay no attention to her," he ordered. "She doesn't know what she's saying. If you don't like it, you can move." He hurried past them, then shouted over his shoulder, "She was in a fire once."

By now, eight months after taking the apartment, Hedy had become quite used to Mrs. Stein, but the God-Love-You lady still disturbed her sleep.

The apartment itself was small, three rooms and a water closet. The tub was in the kitchen. A previous tenant had painted it red and Hedy found this lovely. She also liked the claw feet of the tub, as they reminded her of her bathtub in Irvington. The rent was one hundred and fifteen dollars. Value had agreed to share an apartment with Hedy if she promised not to follow her when she went out. Reluctantly, Hedy had agreed; it was better than being without Value altogether. Sometimes Hedy saw her daughter by accident. Occasionally, she sat in Tompkins Square Park and saw Value talking with other young men and women. She was glad Value was making friends, but one thing she hated was when she came home at four or five in the morning or not at all. Still, she said nothing because she knew if she raised objections Value would force her to leave.

The worst time had been the previous June, when Value disappeared for three days. When she returned, she told Hedy she'd been in New Hampshire.

"I went to a wedding."

"Whose wedding?"

"My brother's."

At first this confused Hedy, but when Value went on she understood perfectly.

"They were all there. My sister, my father, my stepmother. My brother and sister are very good-looking. Why did I have to get your looks? And they're rich. You should've gotten more out of him. Never mind, I will."

"I think you should forget about them," Hedy said.

"I don't care what you think. When the time's right, I'll make my move."

Hedy didn't know what Value's move would be and didn't want to know. She hoped whatever her daughter did would not inflame Martin Swann too much. She had written him a note at his office telling him to send the fifty dollars to the new address. Value knew nothing of this, as Hedy always got the mail. Another sixteen hundred dollars was hidden in the back of her bureau drawer. When they ran out of money, Hedy knew she'd have to ask Swann for a raise; it was a prospect she didn't look forward to. She wished Value would get a job, but whenever she suggested it Value laughed in her face.

"I don't need to work. Nobody needs to work if they're

smart. You'd think you of all people would know that. I have my connections with men just like you had yours."

Hedy didn't want to think about Value's connections or what that meant. Another thing she didn't like about sharing the apartment with Value was the ever-present sweetish smell of the cigarettes Value had started smoking. In the beginning she had complained about it, but Value just laughed and continued smoking the thin, smelly cigarettes.

Most of Hedy's days were spent walking around the city. She had her perimeters: she never went above Fourteenth Street or below Canal, but she did go as far east and west as she could. Hedy discovered there was a great deal to do on the streets and many items of worth to salvage. Often Value threw out what Hedy dragged home, causing some of their worst fights.

"What the hell is that?"

"It's a mirror. We need a mirror," Hedy said.

"Maybe you do, I don't. Let me see. My God. It's all scratched," Value snarled. "Get it out of here."

"I like it," Hedy said.

"Out."

"But——"

"Either *it* goes or you go."

It went. But Hedy managed to squirrel away other treasures. Someone had built a huge closet on one wall of the bedroom alcove where Value slept and it was divided into two parts. Value had made Hedy promise not to look in her section and swore, in exchange, she would leave Hedy's closet alone. At the back of her half, Hedy kept her "things."

She had just returned a small wooden footstool with a missing leg to the back of the closet when Value, who'd been out all night, returned to the apartment.

"Is that you, Value?"

"No, it's Martin Swann." She mentioned his name as often as possible.

Hedy came into the living room where Value was slumped on the couch which also served as Hedy's bed. It was eleven in the morning and although Hedy wanted desperately to know where her child, who looked drawn and yellowish, had been, she knew to ask would avail her nothing.

Peeking up from beneath scraggly eyebrows, Value looked at her mother. "Guess who I saw last night?"

Hedy's heart plunked in her chest. "Saw?" she asked timidly. She was terrified of the day when Value would speak to Martin Swann.

"Yeah, saw. Guess." Value lifted one long hank of hair and tucked it behind her ear.

"I can't guess."

"It was outside. Practically in front. I was coming home about three this morning and there she was."

She, Hedy thought. Who did they know in common? In fact, who did they know? Well, Value knew people, but Hedy knew no one. "Who?"

"The-God-Love-You lady."

Hedy was astounded. She never thought of the God-Love-You lady being out on the street.

Value took a pack of cigarettes from her jean jacket pocket and tapped one into her hand. "You want to know what she looks like?" she asked.

She didn't. Hedy didn't want to know anything about the God-Love-You lady, not ever. But if she told Value that the girl would tell her and tell her, over and over. So instead she shrugged, hoping Value wouldn't go into too much detail.

"She's pretty tall, about five ten, I think. Of course everybody looks tall to me," she said accusatorily, as if Hedy had purposely passed on her lack of height. "Anyway, she's tall. She was dressed all in black. A long black skirt to her black shoes, and a big, long, black cape. Her hair was black, too. Even though it was three in the morning, I could see that her hair was that awful black color. That dyed black color that nobody has naturally. And big, black eyebrows."

Hedy didn't like picturing this. Now, when the God-Love-You lady started her ritual screaming, she would have to see her as well as hear her.

"And," Value said, blowing a cloud of smoke in front of her, "her mouth was covered in a thick red lipstick. Blood red. It looked like she'd put it on with a knife or something, it was so thick. And so red. Like blood."

Hedy winced at the image.

"Her skin was white. White white. Maybe it was the blood-like lipstick that made her skin so white, I don't know. Anyway, she was standing there on the sidewalk in her black clothes with the bloody-looking lipstick and the white white skin and howling her usual. God Love You," Value shouted.

"Shhhhh," Hedy warned.

"Then she looked right at me. Her black eyes looked at me and the bloody lips moved and she said, 'God Love You.' It was horrible." Value took a deep drag of her cigarette. "So I turned right around and got the hell out of there."

"I'm glad you did," said Hedy, shivering.

"There is no God, is there?" Value asked.

They had never discussed the existence of God, and her daughter's question frightened Hedy. "Why are you asking *me*?"

"Who else should I ask? You're my mother."

Tears filled Hedy's eyes. She was deeply touched by Value's words.

"Oh, shit," Value said, breaking the mood. "What are you crying about?"

"Connections," Hedy answered.

"Connections to God?"

"Might be."

"Then you think there *is* a God?"

Hedy's eye winked in answer.

"Don't do that," Value commanded.

"I can't help it."

Value's small mouth slipped into a smile. "Does God make you do that winking?" she taunted.

"Yes," Hedy answered, thrilled at the idea. "Yes, I believe so."

"You *believe* so. But you have no proof."

Warming to the subject now, Hedy said, "I have no proof that God makes me wink my eye, but I have proof that there *is* a God."

Value moved forward on the sagging couch, her feet flat on the floor. "What? What's your proof?"

"It's embarrassing to speak about." She raised her stubby fingers to her cheek, stroking.

"I'm your daughter. You can tell me anything."

Hedy could feel a warmth spreading over her neck and face. Value watched her mother's cheeks turn pink.

"I know," said Hedy, "that there is a God because my arm is just the right length to wipe myself." She dropped her gaze to the worn linoleum of the living room floor.

A feeling of rage, beginning in her toes, slowly crept up

Value's limbs and centered in her stomach, exploding there. For the first time in her life she had tried to have a serious conversation with her mother and this is what she got! She imagined leaping on Hedy and knocking her to the floor. Instead, she rose from the couch and said, "I'm going to bed."

Hedy watched her daughter go into her bedroom. There were no windows in the room and it was extremely dark, but Hedy had trained her eyes to see in there. She had been surprised that Value hadn't hung a curtain to separate the rooms, because from her couch-bed Hedy was able to watch Value when she was in her alcove. Now she curled herself into a corner and faced Value's room. The girl would sleep for a long time and Hedy would stay where she was, watching. These were her happiest hours.

Value pulled the covers up around her neck. From where she lay, she could see the outline of her mother sitting on the couch. Although it was impossible in this light to see Hedy's eyes, Value had no doubt about where her mother was looking. She despised the constant surveillance, yet she'd been unable to do anything to alter it. It was odd, but on the rare occasion when Hedy was not watching her, Value found it much harder to fall asleep.

But today Value was so excited about the plans made earlier, that she couldn't calm down: she and three others were going to hit a Greenwich Village bank. They would be rich. And then she could dump her mother, take an apartment near the Swann home, buy some good clothes, and present herself to her father. It had occurred to her some time ago that if she went to Martin Swann well turned out and living in a decent place, he'd be much more likely to accept her than if she presented herself as she was now. So when The Sphinx asked her if she wanted to participate in the holdup, she was not only honored she was ecstatic. She was honored because she was the only female included. The other two were Jackie and Bino.

The Sphinx said the job would be a piece of cake. Value had no reason not to believe him; The Sphinx had never lied to her. In her estimation he was a great man; a man with vision. The Sphinx gave so much and asked so little in return. Cooking his meals and cleaning his apartment seemed a pittance compared to the thoughts and knowledge which he shared with her. Even the sexual arrangement seemed fair under the circumstances. If The Sphinx wanted to be sucked off two or three times a day because it made him think better, who was she to deny him? Occasionally, he had Jackie or Bino fuck her while he watched and, although she would rather have been fucked by The Sphinx, she felt it would be ungrateful to complain. Besides, The Sphinx never fucked. Fucking, he said, was for the masses. And clearly he was not one of the masses. They all knew he was special, maybe even a saint.

The holdup was going to happen right before Thanksgiving. The Sphinx was making arrangements for their guns. Three guns were needed for the three of them who would go into the bank. The Sphinx would stay at home, guiding them with his thoughts. Just imagining pointing a gun at those capitalist bastards filled Value with joy. She scrunched further down under the covers and turned onto her side. A smile drifted across her lips. When she presented herself to the Swann family, dressed in her new clothes, she conjured up the face of her half sister. The snotty bitch would probably have a fit. Good. Value had hated her on sight. If she could work things out just the way she'd been imagining them for the last few months, she would become Martin Swann's *only* daughter. It was a matter of careful planning, and she had always been good at that.

Zo thought it was strange how the mind made connections. Last July, when he'd first read the news reports about Dr. Charles Friedgood, he knew the name was familiar but he couldn't place where he'd heard it. It made no sense that he should know anything about this doctor from Nassau County who had been accused of murdering his wife. Only now, four months later, as he sat waiting for Cristina Swann, did Pierre Dudevant's words come back to him.

"I once worked with a Dr. Friedgood who . . . never mind. Nothing can be done. Some day Friedgood will kill someone. . . ."

Why had he remembered Dudevant's words about Friedgood? Was it true that the brain stored everything it ever heard or saw? Now he wondered what it was that the doctor had known about Friedgood so long ago. And if Dudevant had told what he knew, would Sophie Friedgood be alive today?

Tomorrow was Thanksgiving and Zo had the day off. What worried him was that Cristina was going to give him information so important that he wouldn't be able to wait until Friday to act.

"I have something to tell you that I should have told you twenty years ago," she'd said. "I hope you'll forgive me, Zo." Who wouldn't be excited by those words? So why in hell was she late?

The waitress refilled his cup of coffee. Looking through the plate glass window, Zo viewed Sheridan Square. There had been many changes in the past years: the worst one to him was the demise of Jim Atkins, a greasy spoon but a Village landmark. In its place was a branch of the Emigrant Savings Bank. Street musicians, dancers, magicians, mimes performed in front, a relatively new innovation on Village streets. Now he could see a mime, in traditional whiteface, going through his paces. A few people watched but most gave a cursory glance and passed by. Zo had always hated mimes, finding them intrinsically dull.

He shifted his gaze toward the Riviera, a bar that had occupied the same site for years. Nothing special was going on there; a girl and two boys stood on the Seventh Avenue side talking. He watched as a huge rag-covered bum hit them up for some change. One of the boys searched a pants' pocket, found some change, and gave it to the bum. Then the big guy slowly lumbered up the avenue.

Zo looked at his wristwatch. Cristina was now twenty-five minutes late. He'd met with her often enough to know that she was not a chronically late person. A feeling of foreboding slipped over him like another skin. Could someone have found out Cristina was about to give him important information? Jesus, he was beginning to think like the detectives on television. Or was it more like George Smiley? He laughed to himself and took a sip of his cooling coffee. When he looked up again, Cristina was coming toward him.

She reached for his hand. "Please forgive me, Zo. I'm really sorry to be so late."

"Don't worry about it," he said, shaking her hand. "I didn't even realize."

"Just as I was leaving my brother called to say he was—I mean, his wife is pregnant. God, he was so happy."

"Then why do you sound so sad?"

"Do I? Maybe I'm jealous. Not because I want a baby. Believe me, if I did I'd have one. But because his life seems so simple and ordinary in the best sense."

"I see. Want something to eat?"

"Just coffee, thanks."

Zo signaled the waitress and gave her the order. "So," he said, turning back to Cristina, "you'd like a simple life, huh?"

"I'd probably hate it if I had it. Life just seems so easy for him. Everything's all laid out."

"And it's complicated for you?"

"Maybe."

"Are you unhappy?"

The waitress slapped the coffee on the table, jarring the cup in the saucer so that some of the liquid sloshed up and over the rim. When the watiress was gone, Cristina said, "*That's* unhappy."

"Angry," Zo said.

"Yes, but because she's unhappy. Probably unhappy with her job. See, that's when I know how lucky I am. I love my work."

"Me, too."

"Which brings us to why we're here," she said.

"Not if you're not ready."

"My God, Zo. I've taken twenty years to get ready, twenty years of withholding one piece of information."

One piece of information. He could feel the tingle of anticipation dancing down his arms. *One piece.* Would it be *the* piece? Had everything, all this time, hinged on what Cristina was going to tell him? Probably closer to a solution than he'd ever been before, a perverseness in him wished to delay the answer: it was like staving off an orgasm. "I thought you were pretty forthcoming at age six."

"But there was something you didn't know."

"I knew," he said. He recalled the feeling, at the time, of knowing the child had remembered something but wouldn't or couldn't reveal it.

"You knew and you didn't force me to tell?"

"I couldn't force you, Cristina. Anyway, you'd been so helpful. You gave me a terrific description of the murderer."

She smiled. "Maybe I made the whole thing up."

"You didn't," he stated.

"Maybe I wanted attention. Maybe I. . . ." Cristina's face registered Zo's words. "How do you know I didn't make it up?"

Now he was sorry he'd diverted her. "Tell me what you've withheld, Cristina." Until he could evaluate her information, he didn't wish her to know how much he'd uncovered. These past months he'd kept her in the dark about Hedy Somerville's identity and her connection with Swann. A moment ago he'd almost blown it by his need to live on the edge.

"You know something, don't you, Zo?"

He reached across the table and touched the cuff of her blue sweater. "Please tell me," he said gently.

"But you know something. You've kept something from me."

"Then we're even."

"Oh, hell, you sound like a goddamn parent." She moved away from his fingers, resting her hand in her lap.

"I'm not a parent, I'm a detective, and if I have information I've withheld from you it's because I've decided that that's best for the case. Now please tell me what you know."

"I thought we were friends."

"We are."

After a moment she said, "She said something else. The woman who killed my mother said something else. Right before she pulled the trigger she said: 'This is for Martin.' Oh, God." Cristina's head drooped on her neck as if she'd begun to pray.

Zo couldn't help feeling disappointed: the information merely corroborated what he already knew.

Slowly she raised her eyes, meeting his. "For years I could only hear her say, 'This is for . . .' and there was a blank because the sound of the gun going off had covered her last word. Or I thought it had. Anyway, finally it came to me. I'll never really know if I read her lips or I actually heard it, but I'm dead sure she said Martin."

"When did you realize the word was Martin?"

"A while ago."

Zo raised his eyebrows, questioning.

"About ten years ago. I'm sorry."

"It doesn't matter. I understand. He's your father." He thought of his own father and how he'd wished to protect him.

"Would it have made any difference if I'd told you then?"

He ignored the question, asked her one instead. "What do you think it means that the woman said it was for your father?"

"I'm not sure, but I suppose it means he knew her."

This was a crucial moment. Should he tell her everything he knew?

As they stared at one another, the waitress filled their cups, this time being careful to get every drop within. "Anythin' else?" she asked truculently.

"Not right now," answered Zo.

She made a disapproving, clucking sound as she left their booth.

Zo said, "You look angry."

"I am. I'm damn angry."

"At me?"

"Yes, at you. Jesus, Zo." Lifting her coffee to her lips, she was surprised to see that her hand was trembling and quickly replaced the cup in the saucer without drinking. "Okay. I'll tell you why I'm mad. If it was my brother sitting here, you'd tell him everything you know without a moment's hesitation."

"Your brother? I don't even know him."

"That's not the point." She ran a hand through her dark hair, fluffing it out from the side of her head as if she were airing her thoughts. "Why are you protecting me, Zo?"

"I'm not protecting you."

"Oh, the hell you're not. My God, I'm sick of men treating me like I'm going to break or get hysterical should I suffer the slightest discomfort."

Cristina's challenging tone pushed Zo further back into the booth. "I don't know what you're talking about."

"It's simple, Zo. You're trying to protect me because I'm a woman. If I were a man, you'd tell me what you know; you would have long ago." She held up a hand as he opened his mouth to speak. "Don't bother defending yourself, I know everything you want to say. Arrogant, huh? I don't care. I've heard it all before."

After a moment, Zo said, "May I speak now?"

"Sure, go ahead."

"Thanks. I think you're right. I think I have been trying to protect you and I wouldn't have done that if you were a man. I didn't realize that, though. I'm sorry."

"Okay. And now? Will you tell me what you know now?"

"Yes." Zo was convinced that once he told her, nothing would ever be the same for her. But he had no right to assume she couldn't handle the information. "The name of the woman who killed your mother is Hedy Somerville."

"You know her name?" she asked astounded. "You know who she is and you've done nothing?"

Zo felt angry and tired of being attacked. "Don't judge me, Cristina."

"I'm sorry. Go on."

It took him only about ten minutes to tell her what he knew. The paltry amount of information he'd acquired over twenty years was, in a way, embarrassing, particularly when the crucial connections had been made by a psychic.

When he was finished she said, "Well, it's clear enough. My father refused to marry this Hedy and she killed my mother. The worst thing is, he obviously slept with her afterward. The girl's age would indicate that. He must have known from my description that it was she, and the bastard said nothing."

"It's almost impossible to imagine your father involved in any way, especially sexually, with her."

"But you saw him leaving her house in New Jersey. And she said 'This is for Martin.' It must be true. I want you to take me to see Hedy."

"What in hell for?"

"I want to ask her if——"

"If she killed your mother, if she slept with your father? Don't be a child, Cristina. You think she's going to tell you because you ask?"

"Why does that make you so angry?"

He was feeling protective again. Well, what in hell was wrong with that? He was a cop, for God's sake! "It makes me angry because it's so damn stupid and irresponsible. We're talking about a killer, and you want to go and introduce yourself to her as if you're the daughter of an old college chum or something."

"If you don't take me, I'll go myself. Somerville. Irvington. It shouldn't be hard to find her," she said.

He knew she meant it. A calm, rational approach was best, and he took a deep breath, trying to marshal his thoughts. The sound of a car backfiring distracted him and then he immediately knew it was a gunshot. Another shot was fired as he looked through the window. People were running out of the bank. Zo jumped up, slamming against the edge of the table, overturning his cup.

"What is it?" she asked.

"Trouble. Don't do anything on your own." He was running toward the door.

"Will you take me?" she shouted.

"Yes," he answered, pushing through the door.

Zigzagging across Seventh Avenue to avoid the oncoming traffic, Zo managed to draw his gun. By the time he reached the bank the shooting had ceased. Inside, two bodies lay on the floor, blood oozing from their wounds. A uniformed cop, gun drawn, held a girl at bay. Zo went to the girl and, taking his handcuffs from his belt, he replaced his gun and showed the cop his shield. The cop nodded as Zo went behind the girl, cuffing her wrists. It was then that Zo realized the girl was the one he'd seen standing on the street near the Riviera. He shifted his gaze to the floor. They were the boys she'd been with. Other policemen were arriving and Zo walked over to the bodies where a cop was bending over them.

"What's the story?" Zo asked.

The cop, who couldn't have been much older than the boys on the floor, looked up, his face pale as if it had just been laundered.

"Dead," he said. "I did it. Christ, I did it."

"It's okay."

"It was me or them," the rookie said.

"You did the right thing. Don't worry about it." Zo hoped the poor kid wouldn't be brought up on charges: some group, some asshole, claiming he should've shot at their legs or something. "It's all right, anyone would've done the same."

Unsteadily, the young cop rose. "It was automatic, aiming for the heart. It was so fast, it all happened so fast, ya know. Me or them. Jesus. I feel sick."

Zo patted him on the shoulder. "Go get some air." The cop nodded and headed for the door. When Zo turned around, he saw they were taking out the girl. As she passed him she looked his way and skidded to a halt.

A frightened expression came over her face and she said, "You."

"Get goin'," said the cop who held her arm, and pushed her forward.

Zo watched as she was taken away. The girl kept turning

around, trying to look at him again. He was certain he'd never seen her before, but the way she'd said *"You"* indicated she'd seen him, knew him. Of course the sunglasses and the long hair which shielded much of her face made a true identification impossible. Maybe he'd busted her; it was getting more difficult to keep track of these kids. He hadn't at all liked the way she'd said, *"You."* There'd been something threatening in the tone. Puzzled, he decided to go to the Charles Street station where he knew they'd taken her. He could never let a loose end go.

He'd been waiting around the station, drinking one cup of coffee after another, for an hour and a half when Solly Marcus came out of the holding room where he'd been interrogating the girl. By the look on Solly's face, Zo could tell things weren't going well.

"Solly," he called.

"Son of a bitch," the tall, lean detective said, offering his hand to Zo. "Haven't seen you in a dog's age. Where ya been?"

"Around. You look good. How are you?"

Immediately Solly's hand went to his middle, pressing inward. "The gut, ya know. Ulcer. What can ya do?" He arched his thick, black eyebrows. "So whatcha doin' here, Zo?"

"The girl," he answered, jutting his head toward the door Solly had exited from.

"Ya know this twat, Zo?" Solly asked excitedly.

Zo hated the way most of the cops talked about women, but he said nothing. "Maybe. I think she might know me." He told him what had happened in the bank.

"So join the party," Solly said. "Maybe you can get somethin' out of this douche bag. She won't even tell us her name and there was no I.D. on her. Just sits there starin' at us with those weird eyes. Ya ever see a broad with one blue eye and one brown eye, Zo?"

"No." He was really puzzled now. If he'd ever busted anyone with that description, he'd remember. "She give you a make on the boys?"

"Just first names. Says that's all she knew. It's probably true. Lemme get a cup a coffee and then I'll take ya in, okay?"

Zo wished he had time to call Cristina again; he'd tried her number a few times, but there was no answer. He wanted her to swear to him she wouldn't try and see Hedy Somerville without him.

"Let's go," Solly said.

Inside the room the girl sat with her back to the door. Facing her was a detective Zo knew in passing. His name was Bill Grant and his nickname was Cruncher, for good reason. Zo loathed him and Cruncher, he knew, had little use for him. He thought Zo was soft. The two men nodded to each other.

"Hey, tiger," Solly said, moving around in front of the girl, "I brung someone to see ya. Don't move," he ordered as the girl started to turn. In an instant, Solly's face changed from affable clown to menacing, dangerous enemy. "We're fed up wit you and we brung you an old friend who wants to chit-chat. Now, you're gonna tell this here old friend who the fuck you are, got it?" He motioned for Zo to come around.

When Zo stepped in front of the girl she stiffened, frightened. Looking down at her he could see now that there was something familiar, but he couldn't place her.

"So?" Solly asked. "Ya gonna tell Detective Campisi here your name?"

"No."

Cruncher said, "You are some ugly bitch. I seen a lot a dog's dinners in my time, but you are Alpo personified."

As Zo studied the lower half of her face, the cheeks jowl-like, something in his memory was jogged. "Wait a minute," he said aloud.

"You got a make?" asked Solly.

Zo tried to see the nine-year-old in this angry face. He could barely believe it, but he found the child, Value Somerville, lurking there. And Hedy, too. Never having gotten really close to the kid when he was watching her, he'd had no idea about the two different colored eyes. Jesus, he thought, while she was holding up the bank he and Cristina had been talking about her mother.

He took Solly by the arm and led him to a corner of the room. "Let me talk to this kid alone, will ya, Solly?"

"Ya know her?"

"Maybe. I think so."

"Ya got a name?"

"No," he lied. If he gave Solly that, they wouldn't let him talk with her. "Let me have a shot at her alone. I think I can get some info."

Solly shrugged his bony shoulders. "It's okay wit me. I gotta

282

take a piss anyways. C'mon, Grant," he said to the other detective.

"Ya sure, Sol?" Cruncher said, his tone meant to deprecate Zo.

"C'mon," Solly answered, understanding the nuances, refusing to play. "Twenty minutes," he said to Zo.

When the two men left, Zo took a chair and sat facing the girl. He smiled but she didn't. He could feel his insides shaking. Everything seemed to be converging. All his life he'd believed that there was no such thing as coincidence, but what else could this be? There was no time now to analyze that: he had twenty minutes, a minute for every year that had passed since the death of Danielle Swann.

"So you know me, huh?" he said.

She stared at him but said nothing.

"You made that clear in the bank. That was dumb."

Nothing.

"You've grown up," he tried.

Her eyes responded, squinting.

"Why don't you talk to me, Value?"

Her lips parted when he used her name. "Who the fuck *are* you?"

"I'm Lorenzo Campisi, Detective First Class."

She gave a small, dry laugh. "I thought you were my father. You know, back then."

Bingo! It was a definite make. There had been the smallest doubt; there always was until confirmation. "In Irvington?"

"Yeah. You're not my father, are you?"

"No."

"She said you weren't, but who knows with her."

"Your mother? Hedy?"

"Yeah. She finally told me who my father is. But back then, when you were always there, I was sure it was you. Why were you following me, anyway?"

Hedy had told the girl who her father was. He had to be careful now not to blow it. "Will you tell me who your father is?"

She looked at him suspiciously. "What do you want to know for?"

"I'll tell you why I followed you when you were little if you tell me who your father is."

283

"Fuck you."

"I don't have to tell you anything, Value."

"So don't."

It was time for threats. "Let me explain something to you. You know the detective who was just in here, the big mean-looking one? His nickname's Cruncher. Can you guess why?"

She tried a defiant look, but the almost imperceptible tremble in her pouchy cheeks betrayed her. "What do I win if I guess?"

"Cruncher is a very mean guy. You'll do a lot better with me."

"You got a cig?"

From his jacket pocket Zo took his pack of Chesterfields and offered her one.

"You smoke these?"

"What's wrong with them?" He lit the cigarette for her.

"Strong."

It made him laugh, thinking about what she probably put into her system. "Let's get on with it, okay?"

"This is what I think," she said, blowing a puff of smoke his way. "I think that Cruncher isn't going to give a shit who my father is."

She was right, but Zo couldn't let her know that. "You don't know that guy. Cruncher likes to know everything. And the funny thing is, sooner or later he does." Making these veiled threats went against the grain; it simply wasn't his modus operandi.

"You know my mother, huh?"

"A bit."

"You promise you'll tell me why you used to follow me if I tell you who my father is?"

"I promise." He'd never told a child that her mother was a murderer, and even though this child seemed to be going in the same direction, he didn't relish the task.

She took a drag deep into her lungs as if the smoke was going to give her courage. "She . . . my mother . . . says his name is Martin Swann. He's a shrink."

Zo kept his face impassive, but inside his body all systems were alert. Nothing about Value resembled Swann. He tried to see her as Cristina's half sister, but that was impossible. So now what he'd suspected all these years was confirmed and still it did no legal good unless he could enlist Value's help.

"Okay, so why were you following me?"

There was always the smallest hope that the shock of what he had to tell her would make her compliant. But would it be a shock? Maybe she knew the truth. "What else did your mother tell you about Swann?"

"Nothing. But I've done my own research. I've seen them all. My half brother and my half sister, and Mrs. Swann, too. I guess she's my stepmother."

It frightened Zo to think of Value looking at Cristina. "But you've never spoken to any of them, have you?"

"I'm going to. I'm waiting for the right time. I'll do it when. . . ."

A frown creased the narrow forehead. Zo thought the girl was comprehending her circumstances.

"I got time," she said. "So now you tell me. Why'd you follow me?"

"Did you know that Mrs. Swann is Martin Swann's second wife?"

"Sure I did. What do you think?"

He could tell she'd never heard this before. "Do you know what happened to the first Mrs. Swann?"

Defensively she answered, "No, so what?"

"She was murdered. She was gunned down in front of her apartment house in nineteen fifty-five."

"I wasn't even born yet."

Zo smiled. He wasn't sure if her response had been out of fear, as though he were somehow accusing her of the act, or if it was simply ego: an overwhelming self-involvement in which nothing existed or mattered unless it directly related to her. "I know you weren't born yet. Anyway, Mrs. Swann was murdered. Her assailant, although never apprehended, was described by an eyewitness. One of the most interesting and telling pieces of description was that the woman—oh, yes, I almost forgot, the murderer was a woman—anyway, the thing that was most outstanding was that the woman winked when she fired the fatal shots. Familiar?"

The little color which had been giving her sallow skin a tiny touch of life drained suddenly, as if a stopper had been lifted and her blood had gushed away. Zo wondered if she might faint and reached toward her. She pulled back at once.

"You all right?" he asked.

"Sure. Why wouldn't I be?"

"I thought maybe you recognized the description. Your mother has a wink that's a tic, doesn't she?"

"Are you trying to say my mother killed this woman, this first Mrs. Swann?"

He nodded.

There was a moment of silence and then Value threw back her head, the scraggly hair falling limply behind her ears, and laughed an ugly, cackling sound.

Astonished, Zo listened to the continuous staccato laughter. Eventually, it began to diminish, coming in short spurts like the barking of a dog, and then it died, leaving in its wake a tear-stained face.

"You are loony tunes, man." With the sleeve of her work shirt, she wiped the tears of laughter from her cheeks. "My mother wouldn't hurt a fly. She's a pain in the ass sometimes, but . . . oh, wow, you're crazy."

"You're wrong. Your mother killed Danielle Swann."

"You're full of shit. So that's why you followed me? 'Cause you thought my mother was a killer? And what were you gonna get out of following *me*, a kid? You know what? I think you're bonkers. If you know my mother killed somebody, how come you never arrested her?"

How could he tell her that the only proof he had was the word of a six-year-old and the feelings of a psychic? Carefully, he said, "Sometimes the kind of evidence we have isn't the right kind for legal action, but we know all the same."

"Ha!"

"I think Martin Swann somehow got your mother to kill his first wife so he could marry Lynn Cunningham. Maybe he promised your mother money, I don't know about that. Or maybe it was you he offered in exchange."

"Me?"

"He could've promised a baby in return for the murder of his wife. I've seen your mother and I doubt very much if the union which took place between her and Swann was based on passion."

Value moved so quickly Zo had not time to react. Her hand slashed across his face, stinging his cheek, and then she fell back into her chair. "You just shut up about my mother, you pig."

Zo touched his hand to his cheek. His other hand had gone

to his gun, but now that she had reseated herself he released it. "You really must love your mother," he said.

She said nothing, shrugged, looked embarrassed.

"I might have shot you."

"No," she said confidently, "you wouldn't. Maybe the other guys, but not you. Anyway, I didn't think about it. You just pissed me off."

"Because I implied your mother was . . . was not a great beauty?"

"Oh, go fuck yourself." She stood up, turned her chair around, and sat down with her back to him.

Zo rose from his chair. "If I were you, Value, I'd stay away from the Swanns."

"You're not me," she said to the wall.

"Well, you'll be going to jail for a while, but when you get out, don't try and contact them, because I'll be there to stop you. Is your mother still in Irvington?"

She didn't answer.

Zo knew there was no way he was going to get her to talk anymore. It didn't matter; he'd gotten what he wanted to know from her. "So long, kid," he said.

Outside the room, Solly and Cruncher waited for him. "Her name's Value Somerville."

"What kind of a name's that?" Grant asked as if Zo were making it up.

"I don't know what kind, but it's her name. V-a-l-u-e," he spelled.

"Where'd the bitch know you from, Zo?"

"Oh, just around Tompkins Square Park. It was nothing. So thanks, Solly. I'll see you around. So long, Grant."

"See ya, Zo," Solly said. Grant nodded.

Zo went down the stairs and passed the front desk where two transvestites were being booked and giving a performance.

"You just ax anyone, honey, and you'll find out I give glorious head. Just ax anyone, sweet tits."

"Ax me lover, I'll tell ya. She is lou-zay. Blows instead of sucks!"

"Shut up, bitch."

"Douche bag!"

"Shut the fuck up, boata youse," the cop behind the desk yelled.

Zo quickened his pace, not wanting to hear the rest of what the sergeant had to say. He knew how it would go. The kind of epithets that would be hurled at the two queens would depress him. There was enough to think about now, without thoughts of his father intruding.

He walked down Charles toward Seventh Avenue. His stomach was grumbling from lack of lunch. It was three twenty; a snack from Smiler's would do the trick. But he had to try Cristina again.

The first booth on Seventh Avenue was occupied, the second had the receiver ripped from the box, but the third was usable even though it reeked of urine. Holding his breath, he dialed: no answer after ten rings; reluctantly he replaced the receiver. There was no need for panic, he assured himself. She could be anywhere. It was insane to think she'd gone to New Jersey on her own. He'd said he'd take her; surely she knew he was a man of his word.

Opening the glass door to Smiler's, he was convinced he'd get Cristina later. Then what? Even as his eyes perused the sandwich board behind the counter, debating over baloney or liverwurst, Zo knew that he and Cristina would be going to Irvington the day after Thanksgiving.

Helen slammed the front door behind her and faced her husband. It had been a trying day; first with her own family and then Zo's. She felt worn out, depleted, and now he'd hit her with this.

"The day after Thanksgiving can be the biggest retail day of the season and so I go and make arrangements for extra help so I can go to the movies with you, like you've been begging me to do, and now you tell me you have to work? You've got to be kidding, Zo."

"I'm not kidding," he said softly.

"I don't get it. Is there some big murder or something? I didn't hear of anything. You'd've had to work today if something big had broken. Zo, you're lying to me."

It was no use. He had to tell her the truth and hope she'd understand. "Come here." He took her by the hand and led her to the flowered couch. Putting his arm around her, he said, "I have something to tell you."

"Ah, Zo," she said, "I know."

"You do?"

She shook her head despairingly. "I've been trying to ignore it, to pretend I didn't see or notice. I knew months ago, but I shoved it aside."

His arm slid from her shoulders and he turned to face her. How could she possibly know? "What? What do you know?"

"I know it's the Swann case again. I know that."

He stared at her, marveling at her perception. Finally he said, "You'd make a helluva detective."

She didn't even smile. "Yeah, sure."

"Helen, please let me explain."

"It doesn't matter, Zo."

"But it does. There've been new developments."

"You're sick," she said flatly. "I wish I understood it better. If it were the only unsolved murder in your career, maybe then I'd get it."

"Please let me tell you what's happened," he pleaded.

"Go ahead," she said, but her tone implied a lack of interest as if she were defeated.

Zo stood up, lit a cigarette, and began his tale. He told her every new development from the time he'd met Cristina again through the day before with Value. "You see now, don't you? You see why we have to go to New Jersey tomorrow?"

"No, I don't."

"Oh, Helen, come on, be fair."

"Fair? *Me* be fair?"

"Well, Jesus, Helen."

"Zo, you haven't told me a single thing that's really new. Okay, so now you know for sure what you always suspected. So what? You still can't prove a damn thing. You think Cristina Swann is going to get a confession, after all these years, just by asking?"

"She might, you never know." But he did know. His expectations for the confrontation were very low.

"Who is this girl to you?" she asked suddenly.

The question made him acutely uncomfortable. "What do you mean?"

Helen rose from the couch and walked to a window, where she stared out at the street. "I think it's plain enough."

"You're jealous," he said, trying to divert her.

"Yes, but not the way you mean."

He watched Helen's shoulders square, as if she were making her back a shield against him.

"Zo, is Cristina Swann the child you never had?"

He was shocked by his visceral reaction. Was that, after all, what it was all about? It was stunning to realize he knew himself so little. Was it possible that Helen understood him better than he understood himself?

"You hear me, Zo?"

"I heard."

"Well?" She turned to look at him sitting stiffly on the couch.

"I never wanted children, have you forgotten? No, I guess you haven't," he said.

Slowly Helen approached, then stood in front of him, her arms folded across her chest, hands clutching her arms. "You know what I think? I think you really didn't want kids in the beginning and then you did. I think you changed your mind about ten years ago."

"I don't know what you're saying."

"I'm saying, by the time you wanted them it was too late, big fella. And I'm saying that you resent me for it."

Zo jumped up and reached for his wife, but she stepped backward.

"No, don't, Zo. Let me finish."

"But it's crazy what you're saying."

"I don't think so. The truth is, I think you changed your mind twenty years ago, and it started with this Swann kid, Cristina, only you didn't know it."

"And you did?"

"No, not then. But I've thought about this a lot, God knows."

"A few minutes ago you said you didn't get it; you said you didn't understand it."

She smiled, her mouth like a slice of lemon rind. "I'm capable of self-deception, too. You think I like what I know?"

Zo wanted to run. His mind focused on the streets below, beckoning to him, sprawling with freedom from his wife's accusations. But he could no more run from the apartment than he could move now to the right or left, back or front. He felt literally nailed.

"All along," she said, "your obsession has been with the girl. The little girl you never had. The little girl you finally wanted but then your wife couldn't have any. Your wife let you down."

"Stop," he said hoarsely. "That's not true, Helen. I never felt that."

"Somewhere you did, Zo. And the thing is, somewhere I always knew it. That's why I made you stop the whole damn thing. You promised and then——"

"I kept my promise. I did."

"Until last March, huh?"

"Yes," he said ashamed.

"I couldn't compete ten years ago, and I can't compete now. It's me or her, Zo. I mean it."

"What are you talking about?"

"I'm talking about choice. If you go to New Jersey with that girl tomorrow, it's over between us."

He was frightened, as if he'd suddenly walked into a net of cobwebs, clinging, creepy.

"We've had a pretty good marriage, Zo, but this thing has always been there between us. Twenty years. Even during the time you supposedly weren't involved in the case, you were still, in your head, always a little bit there, with the Swanns, the Somervilles."

"So if that's true, what makes you think it will be different this time? Even if I stop seeing Cristina, let the whole thing go again, how can I stop my mind?"

"You probably can't, but I can live with that. This I can't live with."

He reached for her with both hands and before she could duck his grasp he held her arms and brought her close against him. "But if we confront Hedy Somerville tomorrow and she confesses, the whole thing could be over once and for all."

"So, let Cristina Swann go herself."

"Too dangerous. Besides, she'd need a proper witness."

"Then send her with another cop."

They stared at one another and slowly Zo's hands slipped from Helen's arms. She moved away from him, shook her head sadly, then headed toward the bedroom. Zo watched her disappear beyond the doorway.

THREE

They ceased speaking as they entered the Holland Tunnel, and the radio died as well. Cristina's mind was on another day after Thanksgiving in 1953 when her mother had taken her to see Santa Claus at Macy's. They'd stood together on a long line, for hours it seemed, and by the time it was her turn she'd felt cranky and just a little bit frightened on the lap of the rosy-faced man with the silky white beard. The moment he'd opened his mouth, rolling out a sonorous _ho-ho-ho_, she'd burst into tears and wails of protest. Danielle had scooped her from Santa's lap and held her close, stroking her hair. Another woman on line behind them with her little boy said: "I'd give mine a good wallop if he pulled a stunt like that after waitin' on the line all this while." And Danielle had replied softly: "Then I'm awfully glad your little boy isn't going to cry."

The next year they'd tried again and Cristina had been unafraid, enjoyed it thoroughly. And the next year her mother was dead. Now she was on her way to see the woman who'd effected that end. Zo had told her about Value's arrest, and now she knew who the girl at the wedding had been.

Yesterday, as she'd sat at the Thanksgiving table with her family, she'd been unable to look at her father. The struggle to refrain from confronting him had been almost unendurable. But she believed she must forgo any accusations until she'd spoken to Hedy Somerville. Chances of a full confession were slim, but even a few sentences exchanged would give her a sense of the truth, she was sure.

Emerging from the tunnel, she noticed the sky here was gray and sickly looking, puffs of smoke staining the few patches of blue.

"I hate tunnels," Zo said.

"Do you know what my father would make of that?" she asked.

"What?"

"He'd say you had a fear of women."

"Well, he'd be wrong."

"You've been married a long time, haven't you?"

"Yes. A long time." Zo felt despairing.

"Has it been a happy marriage?" she asked.

Had it? he wondered. Oh, God, it had. "Very." He couldn't talk about this anymore. "You know, the brother might be there, since this is a holiday weekend. It might make things tough. Impossible."

"Are you trying to get me to tell you to turn back?"

"I'm just going over possibilities."

"Sure you are, Zo."

"No, really. It's important to know the odds and be aware of possible liabilities. I wish I'd thought about him before. I would have put this off to Monday.'

"Would you?" she asked.

"No."

For the rest of the trip to the Somerville house, neither of them spoke. They parked the car in front of number 167. A smell of burning leaves filled the air. Zo came around to the passenger side and stood with Cristina staring at the house.

"I'm scared," she said.

"We can still turn back."

"No. It's just that . . . I can't believe I'm going to see her again. I have an image in my mind and . . . well, she won't look like that. She'll have aged, as I have."

"And that frightens you?"

"I don't know. Maybe the truth frightens me."

"Sometimes there's nothing scarier," he said, thinking of Helen's words of the night before.

"Well, we're not going to get anywhere standing here. Let's go."

She put her arm through his as they walked up the path to the door.

"Ring," she said.

"Sure?"

"Yes."

There was a long silence after Zo pushed the bell and then they heard someone coming. Inside, the person opened the door just wide enough to peer out but not enough to reveal himself completely.

"Yes?" came the wary question.

"Is Hedy Somerville in?"

"Who wants her?"

"I'm Detective Campisi," Zo answered, flashing his gold shield.

Slowly the door opened wider and the man, dressed in a pair of brown polyester slacks and a green rayon shirt with brown piping, showed himself. Thin gray hair, like violin strings, lay across his balding scalp. "What do want her for?"

"Is she in?" Zo asked.

"No. She doesn't live here."

Zo and Cristina looked at each other. Neither of them had anticipated that.

Zo asked, "Are you Ralph Somerville?"

He took a frightened step backward. "What is this?"

"Are you Ralph Somerville?" Zo repeated, a more authoritarian sound to his voice.

"Yes. Why do you want my sister?"

"Do you have her new address?"

Ralph glanced at Cristina. "You a policewoman?"

Before Cristina could answer, Zo said, "Mr. Somerville, I need your sister's address."

"I don't have it. She moved out of here last January and never bothered to let me know her address." He shook his head. "After all I'd done for her, too. Some people have no gratitude."

Zo was perplexed. He couldn't imagine Hedy out in the world. "Did she go with her daughter?"

Again Ralph showed signs of fear. "They moved out on the same day, but I don't think they went anywhere together. So what's this about? Don't I have a right to know?"

"Your niece has been arrested in a bank holdup."

Ralph's mouth spread into a wide grin. "Well, I'll be damned. I'm not surprised. I always knew that brat would get into trouble someday." He let go of the door and stood freely in the doorway, his arms folded across his chest, taking pride in his early vision of his niece's future.

"If you'd like to post bail, you can———"

"Bail? You must be kidding. That bitch can rot in jail for the rest of her life as far as I'm concerned. Bail," he scoffed.

"Maybe her grandfather would feel differently." Zo thought George Somerville might have an address for Hedy.

"My father's dead." He put his hand on the door, ready to close it. "Anything else?"

294

"One more thing. Do you know the name of your niece's father?" Zo had decided there was nothing to lose by this question, and perhaps everything to gain. Finding Hedy was not going to be easy.

"You think he's going to put up bail? Well, maybe he would. He's been paying through the nose for years."

"You know him?" Cristina asked, trying to suppress her excitement.

Shifting his gaze to Cristina, Ralph said, "I thought you were a mute."

There was a lascivious look on Ralph's face, Zo thought, and he wanted desperately to wipe it away with the flat of his hand. Instead he said, "Would you answer the question, please? Do you know the man?"

"Never had the pleasure of meeting him, no."

"But you know who he is," prompted Zo.

"I know," Ralph said smugly.

At his sides, Zo's hand curled into tight, hard fists. "Name?"

"Martin Swann. According to my sister, he's one of those head doctors in New York."

At the sound of her father's name, Cristina ran for the car. Zo followed. When he caught up with her he said, "I have to ask him a few more questions. Will you be all right?"

"Yes, yes, go ahead. I'll wait in the car."

Cristina slowly opened the door and got in. Until the very last second, when the man had spoken Martin's name, she'd held out hope that her father had no connection with her mother's murderer. And now that she knew the worst was true, it was still almost impossible to believe. But it was a game she was playing, useless and stupid. There was no way to deny what she'd heard; if it wasn't true, how else would this man know her father's name? Her thoughts disintegrated with the opening of the car door.

"You all right?" Zo asked her.

"Yes, I guess."

"Listen, it may not even be true. He only heard your father's name for the first time last January. You know, we're talking about a nut when we talk about Hedy. She could be making the whole thing up."

"What're you doing, Zo? He said Poppy had been paying for years. What was he paying for?"

"He also said he'd never really seen any money. It was just something Hedy told him."

Cristina reached across the space between them and put her hand on Zo's arm. "I have to face it. My father either had my mother murdered or else went along with it once it was done. And that strange-looking girl I saw at the wedding is my half sister. Please, don't try and help me circumvent the truth."

"We still don't have any real proof." He put his hand over hers, patting gently.

"Perhaps not for your purposes."

"Are you going to confront your father?"

Absently, Cristina laced her fingers through Zo's. "I don't know. It's odd; I thought if I got this kind of confirmation, I'd blast him so hard and fast he wouldn't know what hit him. I thought I'd be in a rage. But I don't even feel angry. I think I'm numb."

"Shock."

"Maybe." She withdrew her hand. "Let's go."

Zo wished to say more, to comfort her somehow, but there was nothing to say. Cristina would have to decide her own course of action. And so would he.

The sight of the Christmas lights distressed Guy. Walking to his mother's apartment, reminders of the holiday filled him with a profound sense of despair. He'd always loved Christmas, but this year was very different. Now he lived alone with his children and Janet had refused to participate in any part of the holidays. He'd not been able to tell Marc and Hilary they wouldn't be seeing their mother, but he knew he must within the next few days; Christmas was less than a week away. If only there were someone he could discuss this with, but no one seemed right. Guy's sense of isolation had begun to feel alarming.

In the past four months almost everything about his life had changed. He'd left his wife, taken on the sole responsibility of his children, and become editor and publisher in a new company. On the stress scale his points must have been high, he thought. And then there was the move back to the city and buying a loft in SoHo. Still more points.

When he reached his mother's building he tried to suppress these feelings; it was difficult enough dealing with her. Eight months earlier, Guy had moved Amelia from Fifth Avenue to this three-room apartment on Park. Although she sometimes lived in the past, she was still able to manage on her own. A maid came in once a week, which kept the apartment clean, but things which required daily care Amelia found difficult to contend with.

He used his key to let himself in. "Maman," he called, then immediately began to cough as the acrid smell of cat urine assaulted his nostrils. Changing the litter was one of the chores she neglected. Guy had tried to get her to relinquish some of the cats, but she refused. Now the small apartment housed twelve.

Four of the cats nuzzled around his ankles as he shouted a second time to his mother, whose hearing was not as keen as it once had been.

The weak response came from the kitchen. "In here, *mon chéri.*"

She was sitting at the small table, a cat on her lap. Seasons no longer meant anything to Amelia and she was inappropriately attired. Her yellow summer dress was sleeveless, and as she stroked the Siamese, the flesh on the underside of her arms, which hung down like the wings of a bat, wobbled. "Ah, Guy," she said, as always giving his name the French pronunciation.

"Maman." He kissed her cheek, his lips sinking down into the toneless skin. "How are you today?"

"Very well, very well. Would you like some coffee or tea?"

"All right. I'll make it."

"No, no. I will." She stood, the cat jumping from her lap. Carefully, her unsteady hands in front of her like antennae, she made her almost blind way to the sink.

Guy would have preferred to make the coffee himself, but he knew it was a matter of pride for her. So even though it was almost always too weak or impossibly strong, he allowed her to make it. "Coffee," he said.

"*Oui.*"

"While you do that," he said, "I'll change the litter."

It took him fifteen minutes to empty out old litter and refill with new after scrubbing the pans. When he returned to the kitchen, Amelia was back at the table, a cup of coffee in front of her and one at his place. As he lifted the steaming cup to his lips he looked down and saw on the inside of the rim a small roach making its way up over the lip. Filled with revulsion, Guy set the cup back on the table.

"Do you want something to eat?" Amelia asked.

"No thanks."

It was extraordinarily difficult to have a conversation with her; her world was confined to her cats and her memories. She saw no one but him and the maid. Friends had long ago either died or abandoned her. There were no questions to ask her beyond those about her health, so he spent his time with her telling her things about his life and hoping what he said wouldn't jettison her into the past.

"The children are doing well in their new school."

"Hilary and Marc," she said, as if to assure herself of who they were.

"Yes."

"Why didn't you name her Danielle?" Amelia asked.

They had been through this many times before. "I didn't want to be reminded every time I said her name, Maman. I've told you."

"She doesn't look like Danielle. But she wouldn't."

She often said cryptic things of this nature, but Guy ignored them, preferring to try to get her off the subject of his sister. "Marc is showing a definite talent for drawing. I'll have to bring you one of his paintings next time."

"Yes, bring me one."

"Are you sure you won't change your mind and have Christmas dinner with us?" He really wished she would.

"I will have the day with my dears," she said, waving a liver-spotted hand to indicate the cats. "It's just another day to me, Guy."

He wouldn't push her further, or ask again. Some time on Christmas day he would call her, check to see that she was all right.

"Perhaps Danielle and the children will stop by," she said, her eyes glazing over as she focused just beyond him. "Cristina is growing so. The other day she cut her knee and made such a fuss, but Grandmaman took care of it."

There was almost never a visit when she didn't return to that moment in time, to the last day she had seen her daughter alive.

"I wonder," Amelia said, "if Pierre will be late tonight."

She was getting worse, Guy thought, but for the time being he could see no valid reason to put her in a nursing home. Things might not be as sanitary as he would like them, but she wasn't a danger to herself or others at this point. Smiling and making appropriate sounds, he drifted to thoughts of the new writer he'd taken on that morning, while Amelia continued her ode to the past.

He was much happier as an editor, and although he still had to deal with some third-rate stuff, he was developing a line of serious, well-written fiction. The gimmicks of promotion he could now leave to others and this gave him a real sense of freedom. He'd been surprised when the job was offered to him, having no experience as an editor, but decided if Praxis Publishing felt he had the qualifications he wasn't going to argue. The only thing missing in his life was a woman, but he found his interest in sex eclipsed by his job and the care of the children. Whether he would ever marry again was something he couldn't even contemplate.

Guy waited for a break in Amelia's monologue and then rose, carrying his untouched cup of coffee to the sink where he surreptitiously dumped the cold liquid down the drain. The roach had long since escaped and traversed the table onto the wall and down to the floor, where Guy had squashed it with his shoe; all this unseen by his mother.

He said his good-byes and left her in the kitchen, where she continued speaking about Danielle to a large gray Persian. Out on Park Avenue he started to hail a cab, then changed his mind, deciding to walk. The usual depression he felt after visiting Amelia engulfed him; he wanted desperately to get into the Christmas spirit, perhaps the party he was going to would help. Earlier, he'd decided to skip it, but now it seemed like the perfect thing to do.

Turning away from the bar, drink in hand, Guy viewed the legion of people somewhat apprehensively. Although he knew many of them by name, he had few intimate relationships in the publishing business, and making small talk was not his long suit. He swore at himself for coming here and thinking this would make him feel better. The martini he sipped burned his throat and hit his empty stomach with a sting.

"Guy!" a woman's voice said from behind him.

When he turned, he saw the voice belonged to Peggy Gold,

the editor-in-chief of a major house. He said hello, returned her kiss, although he didn't particularly like her and had no respect for her as an editor.

"I hear you're taking on Richard Moffat," she said, fiddling with her glass of tomato juice. Peggy never drank; her addiction was food, and Guy could see by the way her white silk blouse pulled across her breasts that she was, once again, on the way up.

"How do you know, Peg? I just signed him this morning."

"Oh, I have my ways. He won't make you a cent, you know."

Money and deals were the only things Peggy cared about, and after the failure of Moffat's last book to bring in a hefty paperback sale, she'd dropped him as if he'd literally begun to smell. "He did all right by you with his first book," Guy said.

Peggy kept looking around to see who else was there. "A fluke," she answered. "The man can write, I'll admit that, but what's that got to do with anything if he won't write things people want to read about."

Guy knew she was serious. Fine writing meant nothing to her; reaching the "subway reader" was her only interest. She had no idea how she'd hurt Moffat, promising the world, then tossing him away with no regard for his feelings, unable even to call him when the first bad review appeared in *Publishers Weekly*. "I think," said Guy evenly, "his new book is excellent."

"I saw the first two hundred pages, of course. Bizarre. I mean who the hell wants to read about stuff like that? I love Richard, but he's never going to make it if he keeps writing such depressing stuff."

Guy started to defend Moffat but then saw that her eyes had gone out of focus, a look which he'd seen on her before: Peggy Gold had made her point and now she was no longer interested in this conversation or in him.

"Oh, there's André and Phyllis just coming in. Excuse me, Guy, nice talking with you."

She moved away so quickly Guy didn't have a chance to respond, for which he was grateful. He watched while she made her waddling way toward her top money-making author and his wife. André Mahlar was Peggy's kind of writer: facile, derivative, dull. But his books sold, the atrocious writing overlooked, escape their only value.

A set of sloping shoulders appeared in front of him; a thin neck erupting from a brown sweater held up a narrow head, hair springing from the sides like cotton batting from a chair. "Hiya, Guy."

Breaking into a smile, Guy grasped the extended hand. "Turner! Am I glad to see you."

Turner Easton was one of the few people in the business Guy genuinely liked and respected. An honest agent who cared about his clients, Turner made his way in a vicious world with remarkable sweetness. "What are you doing here?" Guy asked.

"Same as you."

"You don't usually come to these things."

Turner shrugged, his slender body seeming to bang around inside his clothes. "Christmas spirit, I guess. Besides, I have a client who's never been to one of these wingdings, so I thought I'd show her what the big time is like." He laughed, showing small, childish teeth. "Don't know where she's gotten to." He looked around, then gestured toward a group of people on the other side of the room. "Oh, there she is. Seems happy."

Guy glanced at the group and saw a woman and two men engaged in conversation. "Novelist?" he asked.

"She's written a children's book. A young adult. Really good. I'm trying to get her to write an adult novel, but she's resisting. I think she's afraid."

"What's her name?" Guy asked perfunctorily.

"Cristina Swann."

"What?"

Turner, who had returned his gaze to Guy, saw that he seemed disturbed and gently put a hand on Guy's arm. "Hey, you all right?"

"I suppose there could be two," Guy said to himself. "How old is she, Turner?" Cristina would be twenty-five or -six.

"I don't know. Young. In her twenties. What's this about?"

"I think she might be my niece."

"You *think?*"

"It's a long story."

Turner took Guy's arm with his bony hand and began to pull him toward Cristina.

"No," Guy said, standing firm.

"Don't you want to know?"

"In a minute." He finished his drink as if it were water and set the empty glass on a table. It had been ten years since he'd seen her and something about that meeting lingered, making him uncomfortable at the thought of confronting her again.

"She's coming over here," Turner warned.

Guy looked up. Had Turner not told him who she was, he would have known. There was no question as she approached that she was his niece; although taller, her likeness to his dead sister was almost overwhelming.

Turner put his arm around Cristina's shoulders, drawing her in to face Guy. "Cristina, this is——"

"Guy," she said.

"Yes." He took both her hands in his.

"Old purple eyes," she said. "I'd know them anywhere."

"And I'd know you."

"Well," Turner said, "you didn't know her across the room."

"Sure I did," Guy said, continuing to look at Cristina. "Pay no attention to this bum."

"I never do," she said.

"In that case," said Turner, "I'm getting a drink. Don't miss me too much."

"I didn't know you were a writer," said Guy, his knees feeling strangely weak. "I don't know anything about juvenile books."

"I wouldn't expect you to."

This was not the conversation either of them wished to be having, Guy knew, but his mouth kept moving, saying things, as if he had no control over his words. "I'm an editor at Praxis," he said.

"Yes, I know. I read about you."

He felt inexplicably delighted, as if she'd told him she was keeping a scrapbook of his life.

"If you get around to writing an adult novel, I'd like to see it."

She smiled sadly. "No chance of that."

"Why not?"

"Nothing to say."

"I doubt that."

A look passed between them, an unspoken agreement that this wouldn't be pursued now.

"How's Grandmaman?" she asked.

"I just came from seeing her. She's all right."

"I feel so guilty about not visiting her, but she lives so in the past. Or does she?"

"She does."

Cristina laughed, a self-deprecatory sound. "There are those who would accuse me of doing the same; those who have. I'm a phony. The truth is, Guy, she frightened me the last time I saw her, but I was sixteen then. I have no excuse for not seeing her and I'll make up for it before I leave."

"Leave?" He felt panicky.

"I'm going to live in England for a while. Right after the new year."

He wanted to tell her she couldn't. Instead he said, "You're beautiful, Cristina."

"Thank you," she said, "but it's only because you remember my mother."

"That's not the only reason. You're beautiful on your own."

"Thank you again."

When she looked into his eyes, he remembered why the last meeting with her had left him feeling disquieted: he'd been attracted to her then, a child, and he was attracted to her now, a woman.

"Listen," he said, "would you like to have dinner with me, catch up on the last ten years?" He knew it was a terrible mistake; he should go home, forget he'd ever seen her. She was his niece, his sister's daughter, his mother's grandchild.

"Yes," she answered, "I'd like that very much."

When they were out on the street, walking toward Fifth to get a cab, he looked down at her and asked, "Are you married?"

"No," she said. "But you are."

The "but" made him think she might feel the same as he. He could have kept silent about his marital status, using it as a last shield between them, but he hadn't a shred of desire to do so. "I'm separated from my wife. We're getting a divorce."

"Oh," she said, looking up into his eyes and putting her arm through his. "You'll have to tell me about it."

"I'll tell you everything," he said, and felt an enormous sense of relief.

"So will I," she said. "Everything."

The ball began to drop from its perch atop the Allied Chemical building, signaling the end of 1975 and heralding the beginning of 1976, the long-awaited bicentennial year. The crowd below screamed and shouted and some picked pockets while others groped crotches. On Forty-second Street between Seventh and Eighth avenues, a massive figure dressed in browns and blacks, woolens and corduroys, stepped out of a doorway.

A navy blue, wide-brimmed hat was pulled low over the forehead, obscuring the eyes. Hands, ungloved, were fleshy, the nails long, cracked, yellow; they gestured in the air as if they were clawing at an unseen assailant. At first, only unintelligible sounds issued and then the brays and squawks turned to words.

"The smallness changes into bigness but you carry it with you always, did you ever notice that? I've noticed it a lot. They say they love you but it isn't true because lies are everywhere. Hubert says we must always repel the central themes and truth will be at the forefront, but I've found this to be only correct for Johnny Carson. Archie Bunker has a different approach, of course, as does Jimmy Hoffa. Excuse me, miss, but have you met Patty Hearst? Oh, well, as long as you know Squeaky Fromme everything will be coming up roses I've noticed. Have you noticed that? The time we have which isn't time at all is for Martha Mitchell to begin seeing that man with no head and offer some friendship to Karen Ann Quinlan who could use a friend as couldn't we all and Betty Ford might remember that streaking isn't that much fun unless you do it with Farrah Fawcett in the lead, as I've noticed. Excuse me, sir, have you noticed that?"

"What? Oh, Happy New Year."

The ball on the Allied Chemical building reached the bottom of its descent and the Guy Lombardo band, at the Waldorf Astoria, struck up a rousing "Auld Lang Syne," while the obese person on Forty-second Street stepped back into the doorway, saying softly:

"Happy New Year to you, too, Ronald McDonald."

PART FOUR
Revelations

1980

ONE

C. P. Snow's novel, *A Coat of Varnish,* lay closed on Cristina's lap. She had read half of it but really had no idea what the book was about. Her eyes had taken in page after page but her mind had not; her thinking was absorbed by life rather than fiction.

She turned away from the book and looked out the window. There was nothing to see but sky, atmosphere. The continuous thrum of the airplane's jets had a lulling effect on her, but she'd been unable to sleep. And now she was almost home.

The occasion for her return to the States, after five years, was so removed from any fantasies she'd entertained about it that it was almost impossible to digest the reality. Almost, but not quite. The reason for her homecoming managed to intrude just often enough to keep her anxious: hands cold, head achy and tight, stomach churning. The specter of a death in the family hovered, whirling her into the past, then tossing her into the present with a freezing ferocity.

When Cristina tucked the book into her L.L. Bean bag, she spotted the crumpled cable. She opened it, smoothed it out on her knees.

CLAUDE IN ACCIDENT STOP NEAR DEATH STOP
PLEASE COME HOME
LYNN

Staring at the message, she remembered seeing it for the first time. Was it only yesterday? She'd been sitting at her desk, looking through the mullioned cottage window at the bleak landscape, trying to start the third chapter of her fourth young adult book, when there'd been a knock at her study door. Grateful for the interruption, she swiveled around in her chair.

It was Desmond, looking disheveled as always: hair tousled, beard unshaved, plaid shirt wrinkled. His blue eyes were blinking rapidly, as if he were tapping out a message, and his usual ruddy complexion had a sallow, unhealthy look to it.

"What's wrong?" she asked.

He shrugged, the square, wide shoulders hugging his sturdy

neck. "Don't know. Maybe not a thing, love." He forced a smile.

"Meaning?"

"Cable. For you." He slowly lifted his arm and revealed the yellow paper clutched in his huge hand. "Perhaps one of your novels has been sold to the films."

"Fat chance," she said, holding out her hand for the cable. She had no feeling of alarm and asked why Des did.

"I've never had a good one, that's all. Idiotic, I know." He handed over the envelope.

"Well, I have." She opened the cable and read the contents.

"Cristina, what is it?" He knelt at her feet, hands on her knees. When she didn't respond, he took the cable from her. "Oh, Christ," he said.

Desmond had taken over in his wonderfully capable way. He'd tried to get through to Lynn and Martin, but never reached them. So she'd left England knowing no more than what was in the cable. Des had booked her flight, sent a cable to Poppy and Lynn, packed her bag, and driven her the two hours to the airport. While she was waiting to board, he'd said:

"You're sure you want to go alone, love? I could still come, the plane's not full."

She shook her head. As helpful and supportive as he was here, he'd be a burden there. That realization, like a chink of light through drawn blinds, illuminated a suspicion she'd had for some time. But there was no time to examine it then.

And there was no time for it now. Her mind was blurred, unable to cope with the vicissitudes of her love affair; Desmond Yorke had only been in her consciousness for two years, while Claude had been there thirty-one. No contest. Again she looked at the creased paper on her knees. Signed Lynn. Why had Lynn sent it? Why not Poppy? An absurd question. It was impossible to picture Poppy going to the phone, dialing Western Union, relaying a message. But, of course, it was always the wife who sent cables. The odd note wasn't that Lynn had sent it, but that she hadn't signed it Poppy. Perhaps she'd become less self-effacing in the last five years. It was unfair to believe that change was exclusively the province of the young. Lynn, in her mid-sixties, might have made enormous changes for all Cristina knew. But Poppy, almost seventy and drugged night and day, was, she was sure, the same as always.

Seeing him again, would she be able to remain silent as she had those last months before she'd gone to England? Would Claude's accident (what had it been?) obliterate the need to confront her father finally?

Near death, the cable said. But that didn't mean he *would* die. People could rally from the brink of death, fight back, come around. Was Claude a fighter? He'd survived the murder of their mother much better than she had. He'd even learned to read. Two years ago she'd received a short note from him.

> Dear Tina,
> I wanted you to know that now I've read both your books for kids and I think they're super. Keep up the good work. Lark and Hazel are doing great and send their love. Me too.
> Claude

She'd not heard from him about book number three, and decided either he hadn't read it or he disliked it. It was, after all, about a boy who refused to learn to read. She hoped the book hadn't hurt him in any way. Why hadn't she written him about it? Well, she'd talk with him, reassure him . . . *Near death*. What if it was too late? Well, what if it was? Would it matter then? Another issue she hadn't resolved. Still, she hadn't forgotten her mother's afterdeath visit. Christ, she hadn't forgotten a thing. Least of all Guy.

As they approached Kennedy Airport the red light came on and Cristina buckled her seat belt.

She'd run from Guy as much as she'd run from all the rest; perhaps even more. They'd been like teenagers in the fifties, those two weeks before she'd bolted: staring into each others eyes, holding hands, kissing, but nothing more. Did they feel they were in love because of the strictures, or in spite of them? And how much did it have to do with her mother? In the end, none of the reasons really mattered; the result was incest. Even when they kissed, the thrill was pushed aside by guilt.

"We can go away," Guy had said. "No one needs to know."

"But *we'll* know."

"What I know, Cristina, is that I'm desperately in love with you and I'm not going to give you up."

"Where would we go, anyway?"

"I'll come to England with you."

"And the children?"

"Don't you like them?"

"Oh, yes, it's not that. But what will they think? They know who I am."

"I shouldn't have told them," he said.

"But you did, Guy. It's too late now." And then she asked him a most disturbing question for her. "Has it ever occurred to you that our attraction for each other is because of my mother . . . your sister?"

"No, it never has," he answered, dismissing the idea. "But what has occurred to me is that I want to make love with you." He reached for her, but she moved away.

"I've got to think. Please."

"All right," he said, resigned. "But just know this: I've never been in love before. There was a time, early on in my marriage, that I knew that I wasn't in love with Janet, and then I buried that knowledge. I made myself believe I was in love. But it was something else."

"Maybe *this* is something else."

"No. I'm in love with you, Cristina." He'd said it with so much conviction she believed him.

That conversation had decided her: she must go to England. She'd left without seeing him again, but she'd written him a letter telling him that she loved him, too, and that he must not follow her. She said she couldn't handle the situation; that she'd lived most of her life in the shadow of her mother's murder and now she must find out who *she* was. There was no way to do that as the lover of her mother's brother.

Guy had been kind and respected her wishes. But she hadn't forgotten him. Desmond had helped dull the angles of her pain and she honestly liked him, but she was not in love with him. At the airport when he'd offered to come along and she said no, she'd known that with absolute clarity.

The plane touched down and Cristina gripped the arm rest. Rolling down the runway she felt herself moving away from Desmond, toward Guy; the airplane was in control but she was not.

When Cristina cleared customs and came out into the waiting room, a man called her name. He looked familiar, but she couldn't quite place him.

"Ross," he said, smiling. "Lynn's son."

"Of course." She hadn't seen him for fifteen years; he'd been twenty-one then.

"I've changed, I know." He touched a hand to his balding head. "But you look the same."

"Well, not quite. Claude?" she asked.

"It's very bad."

The relief she felt made her slump and he caught her arm. "I was afraid he might be dead," she said.

Ross shook his head. "No, but don't get your hopes up."

"What happened?" she asked as they walked toward an exit.

"Motorcycle accident. Lark was lucky, but she lost the baby."

"Hazel?" she asked, shocked.

"Oh, no. She was pregnant again. Didn't you know?"

"No. I haven't been a good correspondent." It was easier to take the blame than admit that no one ever wrote her.

"I've been staying with Mother and Martin for about a month now. Since Karen and I separated."

Karen, Cristina thought. Yes, she'd heard that Ross had married. Did he have children?

"That's how I happened to get your cable. Listen, do you want to go to the apartment first for anything?"

"No. Let's go right to the hospital."

Ross unlocked the car door for her. "I keep forgetting you don't know anything. We have to drive to *Vermont*. He's in a hospital there."

Cristina was exhausted, and the idea of driving five hours made her want to weep.

Ross touched her arm. "You must be tired."

She nodded.

"You can sleep in the car."

By the time he got into the driver's seat, she was crying.

"Maybe he'll live," Ross said.

"Maybe," she managed, and cried harder. Cristina wasn't totally sure where her tears belonged. Most of them were for Claude, but she suspected that some were for herself: because she was driving out of New York, away from Guy.

She did sleep during a good part of the drive, but at one point she and Ross stopped for something to eat.

Sitting in a booth across from him, Cristina suddenly remembered the early years when she'd lived with Ross, before he'd been sent to boarding school.

"My God, I hated you," she said.

Spots of crimson flushed his cheeks. "I don't blame you, but I hoped you'd forgotten."

"I had. It just came back."

"I hated you, too, you know. You and Claude were interlopers, ruining everything between my mother and me." He tried an awkward smile, intended as a plea for understanding.

Cristina did not smile back. "But Claude and I were so fragile."

"I was twelve," he said.

"You seemed so old to me. Twelve. God." She took a bite of her egg salad sandwich. It felt as if it would stick in her throat and she quickly swallowed some coffee.

"I was a terrible brat," he said apologetically.

Cristina stared at the T-shirt he was wearing under his open flannel one. It said MAY THE FORCE BE WITH YOU and she wondered what it meant but was too tired to ask.

"I'd lost my father," he said, then realized the insensitivity of the statement. "I'm sorry. I didn't understand then, or rather, I was only concerned with me. I was only twelve," he said again, begging.

She remembered Ross telling her that a wolf lived in the toilet and if you sat too long it would bite your behind. She smiled.

"What is it?" he asked.

"Do you remember the wolf in the toilet?" she asked, laughing.

"Oh, God. You didn't think it was funny then."

"No, indeed I didn't. I was constantly jumping up and peeing on my legs. You gave me a lot of Indian burns, too."

"Jesus," he said, ashamed.

"The happiest day of my life was when you went off to boarding school."

"It was my worst day."

She'd never considered that. Why would she? "I didn't know that. I was only ten."

He nodded, getting her point. "Do you hate me now?"

Did she? she wondered. "I thought I'd hate you forever."

"And?" He lit a cigarette, blew out the match.

"You tortured us for several years."

"Yes."

"Isn't it amazing what we can let go of? At least with some

312

hurts, some pain. Then there are other wounds that never seem to heal."

"Only if you keep pulling off the scab," he said.

"But there are some things you have to understand before they're finished."

"No, I don't agree. You can just let God take it."

"What if you don't believe in God?"

He shrugged. "I guess then you continue to hurt."

Back in the car, before she dozed off again, she touched the sleeve of his shirt. "I don't hate you now, Ross."

"I'm glad. I'm also sorry . . . for then."

"Thanks."

"And, Cristina, I'm sorry about your mother, too. I never told you that."

She squeezed his arm, turned away, prepared to sleep.

They hadn't made it in time; Claude was dead before they'd even reached the New England Thruway. Now they were all gathered in the funeral parlor in New York. Martin had insisted on bringing Claude back, even though his friends were all upstate. Lark was too weak and distraught to give Martin any sort of struggle over arrangements. The funeral was to be wholly Martin's production. Cristina had to keep reminding herself that Claude was Martin's son and that it must be horrendous to lose a child, no matter what his age. She thought of Grandmaman and her mother. Grandmaman had lost *her* child: Danielle was only six years older than Claude when she died. Was the old woman still alive? She would be in her eighties. It was certainly possible. Perhaps she would visit her. A wave of guilt engulfed her; her treatment of her grandmother had been shabby, cowardly.

Looking across the subtly lit room, Cristina watched Lark tending to Hazel. The child shouldn't be here, she thought, then wondered if she was wrong. She and Claude had not attended their mother's wake or funeral. Cristina had last seen her mother bleeding on the ground. Still alive. She'd never seen her dead. Nor had Claude. A finality had been obscured for them. If they had seen their mother in a satin-lined casket, as Hazel had seen her father, would it have changed anything? Would Claude be alive today? Cristina recalled the conversation she'd had with Lark and Ross as they drove back from Vermont.

In the back seat Hazel, hair a dazzling yellow, slept, curled in her mother's lap. The child's small round face so resembled Claude's that Cristina felt her first wrench of death, absolute. Until that moment it was as if she'd been given a shot of novacaine numbing her entire body. She had, unfortunately, learned how to truncate feeling, shut down completely. Partly, she believed, this was because she saw things through a writer's eyes: taking in life as material, sifting it until she found the nuggets of fiction, storing them away. When she did this on a subway or in a restaurant and the characters were unknown to her, it was a pleasing skill. But when it removed her from her own life, reducing loved ones to words in her head, she experienced a sense of shame. Cristina felt that, looking at mother and child.

Lark had always seemed fragile, giving the illusion of weightlessness, transparency, as if she were a kite. Now her face, whiter, thinner, the bruise on her cheek where she'd hit the pavement large and shocking in its purplish hues, had taken on a different appearance: a definition that suggested anger. This surprised Cristina. It was then she decided that she could no longer go on hiding from the facts. No one had told her what happened; she hadn't asked.

"Lark," she said, their eyes meeting, "I'd like to know about the accident. Do you mind?"

The narrow shoulders shrugged and one thin hand touched her daughter's hair, gently stroked. "It was the usual," she said, her voice dim, as always, so that Cristina had to turn further around, undoing her seat belt.

"The usual?" If she'd heard correctly, she didn't comprehend.

"The speeding thing," Lark whispered. "But Haze and I were with him, that's the part I'll never understand." Her mouth twisted downward and, as clearly as if she'd spoken the words, her expression said: "And the part I'll never forgive."

Ignoring Lark's look, Cristina persisted. "You mean he'd done this before? Had accidents?"

Lark's sharp shard of laughter was jarring. "Accidents?" she said sarcastically. She shook her head from side to side, her hair brushing her cheeks. "Don't you know about him, Tina?"

Hearing the diminutive of her name, Cristina stifled a cry she felt pushing for release: only Claude had called her that. "No, I guess I don't know about him. Tell me."

"He's been trying to kill himself for years." Lark's voice had risen to a normal pitch but was dull and hard like unshined silver.

Cristina turned away from Lark to stare through the windshield at the flakes of snow which were making progress slow and precarious. She felt Ross looking at her, and glanced his way. He smiled sadly, then had to look back at the road. She couldn't believe what she'd seen in his face.

"Did you know, Ross?"

"Yes. Mother told me," he said apologetically.

"But why wasn't *I* told? Did Poppy know?" He must have.

Ross cleared his throat, stalling, searching for the best way to explain this flagrant exclusion of Cristina from the family's life. "I think . . . I think they wanted to protect you. I think they thought you had enough troubles of your own."

The rage which filled her made her feel swollen, ready to explode, but she controlled herself. She turned back to Lark.

"Are you telling me that there have been other incidents?"

"Dozens," she said simply.

"And you let him continue to ride that goddamn motorcycle?"

Lark ignored the accusation, choosing instead to retaliate with facts. "The bike stuff was only half of it."

"Meaning?"

"Slit wrists, pills . . . once I found him with the shotgun in his mouth." Even her thin, reedy tone could not mitigate her words.

"How long had he been doing that?" Cristina felt numb with shock.

"I think," said Ross, "he'd been doing destructive things for a very long time."

She reached back into the past, trying to recall anything of that nature. She could think of nothing. "How long?" she repeated.

"You'd gone to college," he said.

"Well, what did they do about it? Surely Poppy would have sent him to a psychiatrist."

"He never saw a shrink," said Lark.

"But I was sent the moment I showed. . . ." Cristina let her sentence die and no one asked her to finish it. Who could say why she'd been attended to and Claude had not? The variables were numerous. What was most dismaying to her now was that she hadn't known anything at all about him. She remembered being jealous of what she thought was his serenity, his simple, uncomplicated life. The arrogance of her assumptions sickened her.

Cristina crossed to the casket and looked down at her dead brother. Oddly, his head and face had been spared from any mark; only his body had been broken and shredded. Only. His blond hair lay across his head, neatly combed. He wore a new blue suit, ordered by Martin, as he'd owned only the suit he'd been married in. The tie was a simple subdued stripe, the shirt white. He rested on gray satin. Again, she assessed his face. There was nothing in it. But he was dead; what could she expect? Dead faces didn't betray agony or joy. She'd never seen a dead face before, only the dying face of her mother. But that was different: life leaving was still not life gone.

It was several moments before Cristina recognized that she was writing in her mind: a detailed portrait of the dead man who lay in the casket; the sickening odor of flowers mingling with perfume; snippets of conversation, a peal of nervous laughter. Her cool detachment overwhelmed her with guilt and she forced herself to be present, in the moment, as she once again looked down at Claude's waxen face.

This time she felt a violent pull inside her. Oh, Claude, she thought, I can't believe it. Sorrow surfaced, then was shunted aside by anger. She pivoted away from the coffin and stalked across the room toward her father. He'd killed Claude. By ignoring his pain, he'd killed him as surely as he'd killed their mother.

But when she saw Martin sitting slumped in his chair, as if he were a soft puppet whose strings had been cut, she stopped. The anger which had propelled her diminished, died. Her eyes filled. This was no time to confront her father on any issue. And perhaps her impulse had been to divert, to obfuscate her own culpability.

She felt a gentle tap on her shoulder. When she turned, she looked up into the face of Zo Campisi. She hadn't seen him since the day they'd gone to New Jersey, more than five years ago. He'd aged, his eyes seeming dimmer, although his hair was still more black than gray.

"How did you know?" she asked.

"I read it in the *Times*."

Cristina was surprised to notice that Zo's shirt was frayed at the collar, his black overcoat missing a button.

"I used to read the *Post*, but no more. Trash. I started reading the *Times* and. . . ." A discomfitted smile crossed his lips. "Christ, I don't know why I'm going on and on like this. I wanted you to know how sorry I am about Claude."

"Thank you, Zo." She was struck, as she always had been, by what a kind man he was. "How are you?"

"Oh," he said, shrugging, his eyes skidding away from her face, "I'm all right."

She didn't believe him. There was a hollowness in his words. "Are you sure?"

Zo ran his tongue over his slightly protruding teeth and then he spoke haltingly. "My wife died. Cancer. We thought she had it licked, but it came back. Boy, did it come back!"

Cristina saw that his brown eyes were watery and she put her hand on his arm. "When did she die?"

"Let's see . . . ten months ago. I really loved her," he said, his voice cracking.

"I'm so sorry, Zo." She remembered his telling her he'd had a happy marriage.

"Oh, Lord, *you're* comforting *me*." He swallowed, blinked away incipient tears. "I'm supposed to be comforting you. I think it's being in this place. The last time it was *her* funeral."

"It's all right," she said.

"I'm acting strange, I know. I don't want you to think I don't know."

"God forbid," she kidded.

He tried to laugh, but it came out like a cough. "Are you all right? I mean, aside from this?"

"Yes, I guess." She had no idea how she was.

"Are you going back soon . . . to England, isn't it? Emma Stevenson told me you live in England now."

"The psychic?"

"Yes. You're leaving pretty soon, aren't you?"

His question seemed urgent. "I imagine I'll go back in a few weeks. Why? Shouldn't I?" Cristina asked.

He looked around the room as if searching for spies, but when he turned back to her she saw he'd only been checking to see if he could smoke. The crumpled pack of Chesterfields was small in his big hand. Sticking the unfiltered cigarette in his mouth, he answered her. "Value Somerville is going to be released from jail next month. Early February."

Cristina heard his words, her eyes trained on the bobbing unlit cigarette as if it were a pointer. "And?" she asked.

"It makes me nervous. For you. Emma says that. . . ." He blushed suddenly, hung his head.

"What does Emma say? Tell me."

"Cristina, Emma's never been wrong in this case."

"Oh, Zo, is it still a *case* for you?" Her empathy was strong, but his involvement amazed her nevertheless.

"Not still. Again. I gave it up for Helen right after you left——"

"I'm sorry," she said, cutting in, "I should've said good-bye."

"You didn't owe me anything."

"I should've said good-bye," she insisted. "There were reasons. Nothing to do with you."

"Sure. I know how it goes."

"You were saying you gave up the case."

"It's a long story. I almost lost Helen because of it, but then, when you left——I'm not blaming you, Cristina, in fact, I guess you could say you sort of saved my marriage——when you left, I realized if you could stop, so could I. Thank God she took me back."

"Took you back?"

"We'd separated for a while. It's too complicated to explain. But we were happy those years before. Really."

"I believe you, Zo," she said. Why did he seem so desperate?

"Anyway, we had a really good year and a half before she got sick again. Now she's dead and it doesn't hurt her anymore. My connection to you, the case, I mean."

Cristina felt helpless. Should she lead him toward another topic or urge him to go on, explain further? Before she could decide he'd picked it up again.

"I know Emma's only a psychic, but I think it's important to listen to her. She's gotten a warning."

"What kind of a warning?"

"Value is going to kill someone."

"And you think it's me," Cristina said.

"Yes. You or him." He jutted his chin in Martin's direction.

"Why? Why would she kill either one of us? Oh, Zo, you've

got me talking about this as if it were a fact," she said, verging on anger.

Zo blew a cloud of smoke between them, then looked down at his black scuffed shoes.

"Let's drop it, okay?" It was too much. Everything was crowding her: Zo's painful loss, Emma's warning, Martin's negligence, and, of course, her brother's death.

"Sure. We'll drop it. But you *will* go back to England soon?"

"I can't imagine why not. Don't worry, Zo, I'll be all right." But suddenly she didn't care if she was all right or not.

"I know you will." He patted her shoulder, his hand eventually sliding down her arm and trailing off. "Well," he said, "I'd better go."

"Let's have a drink before I go back," she said, and was immediately regretful. He might ask if she'd talked to Martin about Hedy and Value, urge her to do so. Associating with Zo could be extremely painful, but the words were out.

"I'd like that," he said. "Call me."

She wished he'd go, because she knew now she wouldn't call and believed he knew too; it was as if they were standing in a triangle: embarrassment the third party.

For a moment it appeared as if he were going to say something else but then, instead, he smiled, touched her cheek with his fingertips, and headed toward the door. She watched him go, shoulders slumped, his hatless head thrust forward, his step tentative, unsure. Maybe she would call after all, surprise him. Surely she could withstand any suggestions he might make, memories he might raise. She felt terrible that she'd hurt him and considered running after him to apologize. But as she deliberated, Zo was swallowed up by a new crowd of people pushing through the double doors and when they dispersed toward members of the family, he was gone. In his place, standing with his tweed overcoat thrown over one arm, his short black curly hair wet with snow, was Guy. Spotting her, he started in her direction.

The time, the place, the circumstances had all served to make Cristina and Guy cautious with one another. Each having established that the other hadn't married seemed to relax them to a degree; she hadn't referred to Desmond and wondered if Guy was also not mentioning someone in his life. For her, nothing had changed. It was as if it was January 1976 instead of 1980. But nothing else had changed either: they were still related by blood.

She watched Guy cross to the casket, head bowed as he viewed Claude. Then he closed his eyes. She wondered if he was praying.

When he returned to her side he said, "I saw him last when he was a tiny little boy, five or so, I think. What a shame that a stupid accident should snuff out——"

"He killed himself," she said bluntly.

"But the paper said. . . ."

"Oh, yes, that's true. But he was suicidal. It was something I never knew about him. He might as well have been a stranger. I thought his only problem was he wouldn't learn to read. What a joke. I suppose I believed that I owned despair and grief."

"He must've given you the impression he was okay."

She thought a moment. "Yes, that's true. He certainly did that. But I know better than to accept the surface of a situation. I don't do that with strangers. Why did I do it with my own brother?"

"You must have felt too fragile to deal with it. Don't be so hard on yourself," Guy said gently.

"Thanks for trying to let me off the hook, but no thanks. I was too wrapped up in myself and he never grieved the way I wanted him to. He replaced my mother with Lynn—*his* mother with Lynn—and I simply couldn't tolerate it. I wanted him to do it *my* way and when he wouldn't, I dismissed him."

"If that's true, you've answered your question as to why you didn't dig deeper. Can't you forgive yourself?"

"I hope so."

"Will you take me over to Martin now? I'd like to offer my sympathy," he said.

"You really want to talk with him?" She knew Guy had hated Martin for his affair with Lynn.

"It's water under the bridge now. I see him only as a man who's lost his child. If anything happened to Hilary or Marc, I don't know what I'd do."

Cristina put her arm through his and guided him across the room.

"Poppy?" she said.

Martin looked up. Cristina was used to the man in front of her, but now she saw him through Guy's eyes. The skin on his face was yellowish and the lines that had once given him a craggy handsomeness were so deep, so abundant, they made him appear scored like a piece of meat. From his nostrils and ears, white hairs grew unattended. His brown eyes were glazed, unfeeling, almost unseeing. His head and hands were in constant motion with tiny tremors. Cristina saw once again how pathetic he was, so far from the dragon she sometimes believed she must slay.

"What is it?" Martin asked, his voice cracked and wavery.

"This is Guy," she said.

"Who?" He squinted at the middle-aged man who stood above him.

"Mommy's brother." She felt Guy stiffen at her words.

Martin bit at his dry, lower lip. "Brother," Martin said.

"Hello, Martin," Guy said. "Don't you remember me?"

"No. I don't know." He kept staring, trying to recall the man.

"I'm Guy Dudevant. Amelia and Pierre's son. I wanted to tell you how sorry I am about Claude."

Martin's lower lip began to tremble. Cristina thought he'd understand who Guy was, but in a moment, when the squawking sound started, it was clear that Martin was crying. Everyone became still, except Hazel, who squirmed off her mother's lap and ran to Martin, hugging his knees.

"What's wrong, Granpoppy?" she asked innocently. "What's wrong?"

He reached out a shaking hand to touch the child's hair. "All dead," he said, "everyone's dead."

"Not everyone," Hazel said. "Not me, Granpoppy."

"It wasn't my fault," Martin said, looking from Hazel to Cristina. "It wasn't me." And then his eyes shifted to Guy. "Things elude you, you must know that."

"Yes," Guy said.

"Control," said Martin. "Control is only . . . an illusion."

Cristina thought she was going to be sick. What was Poppy saying? Was this to be it, the moment she'd dreamed about, the denouement of her life? Would revelations come in a funeral parlor from a drugged, sick old man? What wasn't his fault? Claude's death? Danielle's? Both? Or perhaps he wasn't even talking about them. Perhaps he was in another place in his destroyed mind and his words had little or nothing to do with what she was thinking. In any case, she had to get out, get some air.

"Guy," she whispered, "I'll see you outside."

"I'll be right there."

When Guy joined her on the street he said, "I can't believe that's Martin."

They began to walk. "I told you he was a drug addict," she said.

"Oh, it's not just that. What the hell was he talking about?"

"I don't know," she said quickly. "It might be anything." She'd never told him what she knew.

"For a minute there I thought he meant Danielle. That it wasn't his fault she was murdered. It felt as if that's what he meant. I suppose his mind's a little disturbed," he said cautiously.

"Lynn told me that he goes to his office every day and stays there for hours by himself."

"What do you mean?"

"He doesn't have any patients anymore, hasn't for four years, but he goes just the same."

"It's all so awful, isn't it?" He stopped, took her arm, and turned her toward him. "Do you realize that we were all victims of that insane murder? How different our lives would be now if Danielle had lived."

"I don't think we'd be standing here together, for one thing," she said.

"No, I suppose not," he said thoughtfully. "But where did it start? I mean, we're all each other's victims, aren't we? You and I, Cristina, we're the victims of the woman who murdered Danielle, but whose victim was she? You see what I mean? Whoever created her, that's who we're really connected to."

"Then we're not responsible for anything we do?"

He started walking again, she with him. "I didn't say that. Of course we're responsible. But in some ways our destiny, our walking along this street right now, was predetermined by the ancestors of a woman we've never met."

"Do you think that's what Poppy meant when he said control was an illusion?"

"Doubtful. But who knows? It fits."

Cristina wanted desperately to tell him everything. But if Guy knew, she was afraid he would act. All she wanted now was to understand and let go.

322

"Where are we going?" she asked, trying to change the subject.

"I don't know."

Again they stopped and looked at one another. Cristina knew her defenses were almost absent, and she felt frightened.

"I'm not going to let you go this time," he said.

"Please don't say that," she begged.

"Why not? I know you still feel the same way about me."

She had one last guard against him but knew, even as she spoke, that the barrier was ephemeral. "I live with a man in England named Desmond Yorke."

"Fascinating. The woman who lives with me is named Diane Shields. Perhaps we should introduce them."

The stab of jealousy she felt almost made Cristina laugh. "We can't do this,'" she said weakly.

"We can. I love you. Do you love me, Cristina?"

"We can never be married," she said.

"I think we can live with that. Do you love me?" he persisted, moving closer to her.

She was vaguely aware that people were staring at them as they passed, but she didn't care about that or anything else. She only cared about Guy. "Yes, I love you."

He almost kissed her but then drew back, squeezed her arms gently, and led her to the curb where he hailed a cab.

"The Plaza," he said to the driver.

As the taxi pulled away and Cristina laid her head on Guy's shoulder, eyes closed, she began to form a vision of the ancestors of Hedy Somerville who had arranged this moment and, presumably, the rest of her life. It was easier than blaming Poppy.

Freezing weather stalked the streets. The temperature was in the teens, but the wind chill factor made it feel way below zero. In a faded green cloth coat and white cotton gloves, bought at a thrift shop, Value Somerville walked up and down Park Avenue between Eighty-third and Eighty-fourth streets. The weather, keeping pedestrians to a minimum, allowed her to go unnoticed. She took her hands from her pockets and tugged on the blue wool cap, pulling it down over her ears. Brown hair stuck out from beneath the hat. In jail she'd been issued glasses; she wore them now, one lens cracked in the plain black frames. On her feet she wore old black loafers, the right one sprung at the toe. A piece of once-white sock peeped through.

There was nowhere she could huddle out of the cold on this fancy block, so she had to keep moving, occasionally jogging or running in place. This had been her routine for the past ten days, every afternoon, beginning at two. Two o'clock was when Martin Swann came back from wherever it was he went. At four o'clock the doormen changed shifts and they always walked to the back of the lobby to confer. When that happened today she was going to make her move.

Her breath plumed in front of her and seemed to freeze in midair. She began to jog, the very wide, out-of-date bottoms of her jeans flapping around her ankles. It was hard to believe this day had finally come; she'd spent almost every moment of the four and a half years in jail planning it. She believed it was the only thing that had kept her going, allowed her to remain sane. Value was determined she would not fail. The first part of her plan had already been thwarted.

When she'd been released from prison two weeks earlier, she'd gone directly to her old place on Avenue B to find her mother. Not only was her mother missing, the building was missing as well. In it's place was an empty lot, charred remains strewn over the area telling her the obvious: there'd been a fire. Down the block, in a fast-food place, she questioned the counterman.

"Fuckin' thing went up like paper."

"When?" she asked.

"Long time now."

"There's still burned bits there."

"So what's new? Ya think this is Park Avenue?"

"Well, how long ago did it happen?"

"Hey, gimme a break, huh?" He wiped his greasy hands across his T-shirt that said SATURDAY NIGHT FEVER in faded blue letters. "Whatcha wanna know for?"

She had no desire to tell this man anything, but she suspected if she didn't, she'd learn nothing. "I used to live there."

"Yeah, so?"

If she had a knife, Value thought, she'd stick it in his belly, which spilled over the brown leather belt like a sack of sugar. "So, I'd like to know what happened," she said reasonably.

"Yeah?" Suspicion clouded his drooping brown eyes. "Why?"

She shrugged. "Curious."

"Yeah? Curiosity killed the cat, ya know." He laughed, showing yellow teeth.

In her pockets, Value dug her nails into her palms. "I'm not a cat."

"But yer a pussy," he said, and doubled over with laughter.

Value stood there unsmiling, enduring the idiotic guffawing that went on and on. When it ceased and the counterman stood up straight again, there were small tears at the corner of each of his eyes.

"Whasamatter? You ain't got no sense of humor?"

"No," she said, "I don't."

This admission seemed to sober him and he stared at her for a moment, not knowing what to say next. Then he swiped at his eyes with the back of his thick wrist. "So, whatcha wanna know?"

Patiently, Value repeated her question.

"I think it was three, four years ago," he said.

"How'd it happen?"

He shrugged. "Nobody knew for sure. Everybody died."

A shocking bolt ran through her. "What do you mean?"

"Ya don't unnerstan' English? They all croaked. Burned to crisps. Like bacon." He grinned sadistically.

She couldn't believe what she was hearing. Recalling the mad ravings of Mrs. Stein, she said, "Was it the landlady who did it?"

"Prolly. She was crazy as hell, they tole me, and always yellin' about fire anyways."

"And everyone . . . every single person died?"

"Guess so."

"What do you mean you *guess so*?"

"Hey," he said, "enough already, girlie. Whadaya think anyways, I got all day to fart around wit you? I tole ya what I know. Now ya want somethin' to eat, or what?"

She'd checked out a few more employees of other stores in the neighborhood, but most of them didn't know anything, hadn't worked there when the fire had happened, or had nothing to add to what she'd been told.

Some days Value was convinced her mother had died in the fire and other days she was sure she was alive. It occurred to her that Ralph might have been informed, but she didn't want to deal with him. Maybe her father would help her to sort this out. He looked pretty old, even though she'd only seen

325

him from a distance, but that didn't mean he was senile or anything. He still went to work every day.

Stopping across from Swann's building, Value saw that the evening doorman was arriving. Slowly, she crossed the street. As she reached the building, the two men disappeared. She had about thirty seconds to enter and find the stairs. At the rear of the small lobby, she turned to the left. She prayed the stairs would be there and they were. Pulling open the heavy gray metal door she ducked into the stairwell. She'd made it. A wonderful sense of accomplishment came over her and she knew that the task that lay ahead, finding his office, would be achieved as well. Taking the stairs two at a time, she made her way to the first floor.

Value was lucky; Swann's office was on the second floor so it only took her a short time to find it. Now she stood facing the door, unable to decide whether to ring or just walk in. At last she tried the handle, found it open, and went into Dr. Swann's waiting room.

She was shocked by what she saw. The walls were dingy gray, years of unattended dirt causing the discoloration. Beneath her feet lay carpet so filthy that it was impossible to know the real color. The two chairs and small couch were haggard, worn, pathetic. A wooden clothes tree was unadorned by garments. Two doors, besides the one to the hall, led off the waiting room. Value went to each one and put her ear to it, listening. Behind one door she could hear the sound of heat rising, knocking pipes, the hiss of steam; behind the other was total silence. Pulling that one open she saw it was a closet. His overcoat hung there, his hat sat on the shelf, and a pair of black rubbers, like dead animals, lay on their sides on the floor. She closed the closet and returned to stand in front of the other door. Still the only sound was steam filling the radiators.

Should she knock or just open the door? She chose to knock. There was no response so she knocked again. Then she heard the squeaking of a chair and the dull sound of someone walking. She stepped back, away from the door. When it opened she was startled to see how really old her father was.

Martin blinked his eyes. "Yes?" he asked.

"Dr. Swann?" she said, trying to sound demure.

"What is it? Who are you?" Martin stepped backward as if he were afraid.

Value smiled, then with a sweeping gesture removed her glasses and, with her other hand, took off her wool cap, her hair tumbling to her shoulders like overdone spaghetti. "I am," she said, "your daughter."

He stared, the nerves around his eyes twitching. "Who?"

Value licked her chapped lips. This wasn't going at all as she'd imagined it. And there was something definitely wrong with her father. It wasn't just that he appeared ancient and feeble; he was trembling and twitching as if he had some nervous disorder. Even so, she must go on. Clearing her throat, she said again, "*I* am your daughter."

Martin narrowed his eyes to a squint. "Get out of here before I call the police." He started to close the door.

Value stepped forward, blocking it. "Wait a minute. My mother's Hedy Somerville. Remember?"

Martin reeled, knees buckling. For an instant she thought he might fall to the floor, but he held onto the doorknob. She crossed past him into his office and sat down on the couch. Slowly, Martin closed the door and limped across the room to his chair behind the big mahogany desk.

Value removed her coat, letting it slide from her shoulders to the couch. She wore a light blue sweatshirt with the face of Virginia Woolf imprinted on it, purchased at the thrift shop for a quarter. She had no idea who Woolf was.

Martin stared at the image on Value's chest as if it might reveal something to him.

"Aren't you glad to see me, Daddy?" Value asked.

Slowly, he raised his eyes from the sweatshirt to her face. "I'm not your daddy," he said.

She went on as if she hadn't heard. "I'm twenty-three now. It's time I got my rights. I want to live with you." She returned her glasses to her eyes.

Martin reached into his pocket, then brought his hand up to his mouth, put something in, and swallowed.

"I've been away," she went on, "or else I would've come to see you sooner. I went to Claude's wedding, of course. I should've talked to you then, but——"

"Stop it," he said. "You're not my daughter. I only have one living child."

"Oh, no," she said brightly, "you have three. Cristina, Claude, and Value, that's me."

"Claude is dead."

She hadn't known, but now was not the time to discuss the others. "My mother told me all about you—that you're my father and that you sent us money all those years and——"

"Your mother is insane. I don't know who your father is, but it's not me. I think you should go."

The cheery attitude Value had been trying to maintain began to fail her. An odd feeling, beginning in her belly, leaked into her veins. "I have nowhere to go," she said flatly.

Martin stared, head bobbing. "Where's that woman? Your mother?"

"Dead."

"When did she die?"

"About four years ago."

His eyebrows, thick and white, shot up. "But I've been sending money for years to a place on Avenue B."

They sat in silence, each wondering where the money had gone. To a dead-letter office? Did some postal employee open it, find the money, and forever after watch for the weekly envelope? Or were dead letters shredded, burned?

"I just sent more yesterday," Martin said, appalled.

Her mother hadn't told her Martin was sending money when they moved into New York. The bitch had obviously kept it for herself. Value was feeling terrible. Nothing was going right; nothing ever did. She had to make her father see that she was now his responsibility, no matter what had happened to the money or her mother. Just as she was about to speak the door flew open.

Looking in the direction of the intruder, Martin saw a strange man; Value saw that damned detective.

"What's this?" Martin asked, hands splayed on his desk as if he were about to rise.

Moving into the room, Zo said to Value, "What are you doing here?"

"I've come to see my father. But it's none of your business."

"Is this true?" Zo asked Martin.

Martin shook his head. "I'm not her father. Who are *you?*"

"Detective Campisi. Don't you remember? I'm the detective on the case."

"What case?" asked Martin.

"The murder of your wife . . . your first wife, Dr. Swann," Zo answered softly.

"Danielle," Martin said, staring at the green, frayed blotter on his desk.

"You'd better tell me everything, Dr. Swann. I think it's time."

"Make him tell you he's my father."

"I'm not her father."

"He's lying," Value wailed.

"You keep quiet," said Zo. "Let's have it, Swann. The truth."

Martin raised his head, the long, lined face defeated. Tears threatened to spill down his seamed cheeks, but he brushed them away with a trembling hand. At last he spoke:

"She came here, that woman, exactly like this child today. I'd treated her for a short time. Long before. She said she killed Danielle. I was afraid. For the children . . . for me. She wanted a baby, she said. She wanted me to father it. Oh, Jesus, God."

After a moment, Zo encouraged him to go on.

"She didn't want . . . intimacy. Artificial insemination instead. I couldn't possibly. I was stalling for time. I made a fake solution. And then she became pregnant. Of course she slept with someone, but I never knew who."

"That bastard," Value said.

The two men looked in her direction.

"Goddamn, fucking bastard."

"Who?" asked Zo.

Value looked at him, defiance in her eyes.

Zo knew she wouldn't answer and turned back to Martin. "And that was it? You never had anything to do with her again?"

"I sent money. For the last twenty-three years I've sent money every week. She thought the child was mine. I let her think it. It was what I had to do for silence."

"But why didn't you turn her in? Why didn't you tell me?"

"My children," Martin said. "No . . . no it was me. *I* was afraid. It would've been so awful. Publicity. She said she'd pretend I was in collusion."

"No one would've believed her," Zo said. "You must've known that."

"I was swept away, and then it was too late."

Value said, "Maybe he did plan it with her. Maybe he got her to kill his wife for him. Why would she kill her otherwise?" The words rolled off her tongue with ease. She wanted Swann to pay. That creep Ralph, her uncle/father, would pay, too. Nobody was going to get off easy. She'd see to that.

"I had nothing to do with Danielle's murder," Martin said. "Hedy Somerville decided to do it for reasons of her own. But I've paid for it all these years. Not the money . . . no. Not the money." He laughed a wheezy snort. "She might as well have killed me, too."

Value thought she'd be glad to put him out of his misery, but she had other fish to fry. She stood up and put on her coat. Suddenly it occurred to her that Campisi had known her whereabouts. "Were you following me?"

"Yes."

"Since I got out?"

"Yes."

"You gonna keep following me?"

Zo deliberated a moment, then said, "Where's your mother?"

"Dead." It felt funny to keep saying this.

Zo was shaken. "When?"

Value told him about the fire.

"Then you're not really sure?"

She shrugged.

"We can check it out."

Maybe she should go along with this moron and find out what she wanted to know. Afterward, she'd convince him she was okay and then he'd leave her alone. "All right."

"What about me?" asked Martin. "Are you going to arrest me?"

"No. But I'd like to know where Cristina is."

"England."

Zo asked for her address and Martin gave it to him.

"Will you be all right?" Zo asked.

"Never," he answered. "Are you going to tell Cristina I knew?"

"She's always suspected. When Hedy killed your wife, she said, 'This is for Martin,' and Cristina heard. She didn't remember it for a long time, but eventually she did. She'll be happy to know you didn't actually have Danielle killed."

"Cristina thought that?" He was horrified.

"She didn't know what to think," Zo said.

"Nor did I."

"Would you like me to take you home, Dr. Swann?"

"No . . . leave me alone." He dismissed them with a flapping hand, an old man swatting flies.

Closing the office door behind them, Zo and Value crossed the waiting room to the outer door. While they waited for the elevator a woman with a small dog approached and stood with them. After a moment of appraising them, she backed away a few feet. When the elevator came the woman went into a corner holding the dog in her arms. She was going to complain to the management as soon as possible: lunatics were overrunning the building.

Zo took Value downtown to J.J.'s bar. He was an old man now, in his late seventies, but still sober, he looked much younger. He continued to run the place and tended bar during the early-evening shift. Zo and Value took a booth in the back.

"What do you want?" he asked.

"A beer."

"Aren't you on parole? You shouldn't even be in here. I'll get you a ginger ale," he said and walked to the bar.

Value stared after him. There was something different about him since she'd seen him last. It wasn't just that he was thinner, shirt collar too big, jacket hanging on him; it was his face. The slanting brown eyes had a weird look to them, as if he was afraid of something, and the dark sunken circles under them looked almost like he'd been punched. Well, who the hell cared what this dumbass cop looked like? Not her. Now he was rapping with this old guy behind the bar. Value wished he'd get on with it. He'd told her that he would call someone and they'd have the answer about Hedy within the hour.

She looked at her watch. It was the one her grandfather had given her on her sixteenth birthday. Almost six o'clock. Well, there was still plenty of time to put her plan into effect.

Zo ambled back to the table and put their drinks down. "My friend is going to make the call now."

"That old geezer?" she said.

He sat down on the red and green leather bench seat across from her. "Now what's that supposed to mean?"

"Why aren't you making the call? What's he got to do with it?"

"What difference does it make as long as we find out what we want to know?" He sipped his beer.

"Why do you care?" she asked warily.
"Whether she's dead or not, you mean?"
"Yeah."
He made a sound that might have been a laugh, but Value couldn't be sure. Then he slowly shook his head from side to side. "I wish I knew, I wish I really knew."
"You really believe she killed Mrs. Swann?"
"No doubt about that," said Zo.
"But why?"
Zo searched the girl's eyes. Was it possible she honestly didn't understand? "Because," he answered, choosing his words carefully, "she's very sick. Or was."
"You mean she's nuts," Value stated unequivocally.
"Well, yes, that's right."
Value stared into the glass of ginger ale, the little bubbles popping and snapping in miniature explosions. Why were his words so alarming, just as they had been the last time they spoke? Hadn't she always known about her mother, grandfather, uncle . . . father? All her life in Irvington she'd believed she lived in a house of maniacs, and that to keep herself from joining them she must be constantly vigilant. So why, when this man told her her mother was "sick," did she recoil from the truth as if she'd never entertained the thought herself?
"What're your plans?" Zo asked.
Value almost laughed. Wouldn't you just love to know! She told him what she thought he wanted to hear, what she knew she was supposed to say to cops. "I'll get a job and a place to stay."
"You're living at the Y now, right?"
Bastard, she thought. Watching her every move. Looking and looking. "Yeah, I'm living there for now."
"Do you know who your father is, Value?" he asked solicitously. Foam dotted his upper lip, then died.
"No," she lied.
"I think you do."
"What if I do? It's none of your business, is it?"
He thought a moment. "No, I guess it isn't. Even so, I think you know."
"Think what you want." Her lips slowly curled into a smile.
Looking at the growing grin on Value's face, Zo felt cold, as if his clothes had been stripped away; he shivered.

Silence hung between them, finally broken by J.J.'s shout for Zo. While he was gone, Value continued her planning. She checked her old set of keys and counted her money. When Zo returned to the table, she looked up expectantly.

"There's no record of her death," he said simply.

Something jumped inside her. "What does that mean?"

He sat down. "It means just that. And they didn't find any unidentified remains in the fire."

"So she's probably alive?" Was it happiness she felt?

"Maybe. Are you going to look for her?"

If she said yes, he'd continue to follow her, she was sure. "No. What for? Are you going to look for her?"

Zo considered the question for a long time.

"You hear me?" she asked impatiently. She wanted to get away from him now; get started.

"I heard you. No, I don't think I will. Needle in a haystack. Anyway, like you said, what for?"

She shrugged. "I'm going now."

"Where?"

"Do I really have to tell you everything?"

"No. You don't. Aren't you freezing in that coat?" he asked as if he'd just noticed it.

"Can't afford anything else."

"You have any money at all?"

"A little." She had fifty dollars.

Zo reached into his pocket and pulled out some bills. He counted out twenty dollars. "Here. Buy a down coat. You can get a used one on Bleecker, corner of Leroy."

"If I take this money, are you going to haunt me?"

"Haunt you?"

"Follow me and watch me," she said.

"No. It's all over now," he said sadly.

Value took the money. "Thanks. So long."

"So long. And Value, try to be good, huh?"

She didn't answer him; she didn't know what to say. Instead, she pulled on her wool hat, then waved. Out on the street she let herself smile. Now she had seventy dollars. It was a breeze getting money from men.

As she crossed Washington Square Park she was offered a range of chemicals for reasonable prices, but she knew now was not the time for that. She needed her wits about her. Putting her hand in her pocket, she clutched her set of keys and walked determinedly toward Ninth Street and the Path train station.

Ralph Somerville lay in the double bed which had once belonged to his mother and father. The room also had been theirs. He'd moved in here when the others had gone; when he'd finally gotten rid of the trash he'd been forced to live with for so many years.

Lately, life had been very much to his liking. He still had lots of money left, which he kept in a safe deposit box. Occasionally, he went to the Jersey shore for his holiday, spending some of the money there. Or sometimes he dipped into his cache for a new suit. His everyday life required very little money. Eventually he planned to leave his job, sell this house, and go to Mount Desert Island in Maine, where he would buy another house. He'd never been there, but he'd read about it and it seemed suitable for him. He imagined himself, in the summer, living on lobsters and steamers and, in the winter, hanging around a pot-bellied stove in the local grocery with some other men. Maybe this summer he'd go there, see what it was like.

Suddenly frightened by a noise from below, he dropped *Time* magazine to his knees. He sat up straighter, head cocked like a listening dog. There was nothing now, only the ordinary sounds of his house. Had he imagined it? He must have. Relaxing, he went back to his magazine. He'd been reading an article about ABSCAM. While looking for his place, he jumped again. Another unfamiliar noise. Then nothing.

He pulled back the quilt and carefully swung his skinny legs over the side. With his toes he searched for his slippers and then the noise came again. Now the sounds were unmistakable: someone was on the stairs. But it was impossible. Paralyzed, he felt sweat popping out all over his body as if he'd been pricked by pins. Someone was on the stairs. Stopped. Crossed the landing. Up one . . . two . . . stopped. Ralph looked around wildly for a weapon. Another sound, another stair, the last one. The fall of feet crossed slowly toward his door and in a final desperate panic he reached for the glass lamp by his bed just as it opened. He screamed, dropping the lamp on the floor where it shattered.

She smiled and said, "Hiya, Daddy."

TWO

Mt. St. Helens volcano had erupted. Zo watched the reports on television, then decided to go out for coffee. But there really wasn't any place to go; not any place he liked. Vinnie's Luncheonette was gone. It seemed to happen overnight: one day the place was there, the next it wasn't. There were dozens of rumors as to why, after years, Vinnie had closed up his place. Some said he owed people money, others said he had cancer, and it was even suggested he'd gone to jail for some elusive crime. But Zo was sure it was nothing more than what was happening to all the neighborhood shops in SoHo. The rent had gone up too high for Vinnie to make it. Every few months another small business folded and was replaced by a boutique or fancy food shop. So now there wasn't a down-to-earth coffee place in his own neighborhood. Idly Zo wondered where Doodle was conducting his business these days.

He decided to walk up to the Village. Maybe he should get a daytime job, Zo thought. At first, since he had trouble sleeping anyway, working nights seemed like a good idea. But it hadn't solved the problem. When his bartending shift at J.J.'s was over at three or four A.M., he couldn't go right to sleep and by the time he did, at seven or eight in the morning, he felt guilty for sleeping during the day and allowed himself only a few hours. Last night he'd been off so he'd slept between one and six. Five hours wasn't bad. If he could do that every night there was no reason why he couldn't hold down a daytime job. But what would it be? What, after all, did he know how to do? He knew how to be a policeman and J.J. had kindly taught him to tend bar, and that was it. They wouldn't let him be a policeman anymore, so why waste time thinking about jobs he couldn't do?

The dealers were in full force as he entered the park, but no one offered him anything because he still looked like a cop. He decided to sit on a bench for a while and make the punks nervous, disrupt their routine. The ground around him was still brown; in another few weeks grass seedlings would do their damnedest to grow and some would survive, giving the park the illusion of spring.

April fifth would be one year since Helen died. Last year at this time he'd been tending her at home. They'd made the decision together to do it that way; neither of them wished her to die in the hospital. But he hadn't had any idea what it would be like. Had he known, he wondered, would he have done it any differently? Probably not. As exhausting and painful as it was, it had given him something: it was the one period in their marriage when he'd been totally hers. Helen never knew that, in the end, the Swann case brought him back to her. Perhaps it all would've happened anyway; he'd never know.

He and Helen had lived apart for six months, until she read in the paper that he'd killed an innocent bystander during a shootout on Mercer Street and that he was under investigation. She came to the room where he'd been staying on West Eleventh Street and wasted no time asking him what had happened.

"It was an accident," he said.

"Well, of course. I know that, Zo. I didn't think you purposely killed an innocent eighteen-year-old boy. But it's not like you to have accidents."

"An accident's an accident," he said defensively.

"Brilliant."

"Ah, Helen," he said, "it happened, that's all. I feel . . . I feel like hell about it. I don't know if I'll ever get over it." He'd begun to cry then, thinking of Mike Walters, the boy he'd killed, walking to his freshman French class at NYU. He put his head down on the Formica table and Helen stroked his hair.

"Poor baby, poor Zo."

"You don't understand," he said, the words muffled as he spoke them into his sleeve.

"Why does everybody always say that when they're in pain?" she asked.

But Zo really meant it. He couldn't tell Helen, of all people, why he'd had the accident. He couldn't tell anyone, but certainly not his wife.

He'd been crouched at the side of a building, aiming his gun at a piece of scum who'd killed two children, when a figure across the street came into his peripheral vision. For a split second, less perhaps, he'd looked that way because he'd thought that it was Hedy Somerville. When he looked back toward his prey, who was running now, he didn't take the time to make sure the street was clear. He fired, killing Mike Walters. Zo didn't know if it had been Hedy or not. There hadn't been time to determine the woman's identity, and when it was all over, she'd vanished.

"I think you should come home with me, Zo."

He raised his head, tears streaking his face. "Is it pity?"

"Yes, I think so," she said matter-of-factly.

"Christ."

"And because I love you, you dope. This is no good, Zo. For you to have had that kind of accident could only mean one thing."

Could she know? The idea terrified him.

"You had to be distracted," she said.

Still apprehensive, he waited for her to go on.

"Was it because of me, Zo? Were you distracted because you were worrying about me . . . us?"

Oh, God it was tempting. How he had to fight the impulse to say yes, to lay the whole thing at her feet. It would have been extremely easy; it was what Helen wanted to believe. The requirement for admission was very small: a faint nod, a sigh, a blinking of his eyes. But he couldn't do it; it would have been too monstrous and, certainly, too cowardly. He was compelled to continue his lie.

"I don't know what happened," he said gloomily.

A wisp of disappointment fluttered in Helen's eyes but didn't settle there. "Well, no matter. Whatever it was, I still want you to come home."

"I'm through with the Swann thing. I mean it, Helen, I really am." And he was sure he was this time. Any connection to it was clearly poison to him. He'd taken a life because of it, and that was the final tally.

"Don't make promises you can't keep, Zo."

"But I really mean it. Believe me. You'll see."

"Then you'll come home?" she asked, as if it had been in doubt.

"Of course I will," he said. "Life's no good without you."

"For me either."

He'd had no defense at his inquiry; "I don't know what happened," was what he'd said there as well. That was unacceptable and he'd been dismissed. But, having served more than twenty years, he had his pension. Between that and Helen's money (made from the sale of her half of True Confessions) and the bartending job, he was doing all right financially.

A blast of music from a huge radio carried on a young man's shoulder rattled his thoughts for a moment.

He had kept his promise to Helen. The first year and a half they were totally devoted to one another, as if they'd fallen in love all over again. And then the cancer had come back in devastating force, and all their energies were concentrated there.

They hadn't let a stone go unturned: healers, laetrile, elixirs of undetermined mixture, novenas, and acupuncture. All this after the conventional treatment had proved ineffective. But nothing worked.

In the end, Zo was powerless, as he knew he would be, and had to watch Helen writhe in agony and listen to her screams of pain. He prayed for her death as much as she begged for it. When it was over, he felt relief for a while but when that passed and a kind of numbness wore off, a constant ache in his chest set in. It was as if his heart had shrunk in the wash.

And then, morbidly, he'd been brought to a semblance of life by Emma's call about an impending murder. The Swann case had raised its dreadful head again. Then there was Claude's death, the confrontation with Value and Swann, learning that Hedy probably was somewhere in the city (he was sure now he'd seen her the day of the Walters tragedy), and finally the clipping J.J. had given him. He took it from the faded wallet in his inside breast pocket and read it once again.

> *Irvington, N.J.* It was discovered today that Ralph Somerville, the murder victim whose body was discovered in his home here two weeks ago, had cash totaling more than $31,000 in a safe deposit box at the Independent Bank & Trust.
>
> Police speculated that the money may have been what Somerville's killer was searching for. The house was ransacked at the time of the murder.
>
> The case has baffled police ever since they were called in to investigate Somerville's absence from his job and

found his remains in the bedroom of his home. He had been dead for nearly a week.

Police described the murder as particularly brutal; the body was mutilated. The house had been thoroughly searched, but police were unable to say if anything was missing or not.

Somerville, 57, lived alone and apparently had few friends in the neighborhood or at his place of work. Police are attempting to locate the dead man's sister, who shared the home with him until several years ago.

When he'd called Emma about this, she said she was sure Ralph's murder was the one she'd been warned of. Zo had gone to the library and looked up the original story. The murder had happened the day he'd seen Value. There was no doubt in his mind that she had done it. She believed Ralph Somerville was her father. And so did Zo. It would explain so much. He wondered if Hedy had engaged willingly in the incest or if Ralph had forced her. Would he ever know? Not unless he found Hedy; even then, she might not tell him anything. Must he know? What difference did it actually make to his life? Loose ends agitated him and there were still those few in the Swann case. But were there really? He knew Hedy had killed Danielle; that was absolutely corroborated by Martin. And he knew she'd done it because she was mad. She might have fixated on someone else, but she hadn't. And he also knew that Swann hadn't fathered Value. What more did he need to know?

"Hey, man?" said a male voice.

Zo turned and saw a boy, around eighteen, bare-chested, standing behind him. "Yeah?"

"You got any soap?"

"Soap?" Zo saw that the boy's blue eyes were unfocused and his hair was stiff with dirt.

"I wanna take a bath."

Zo couldn't deny that it was a good idea as he could smell the stale odor of sweat and urine emanating from the boy.

"I don't have any soap on me," Zo said. "Aren't you cold?"

"Cold?"

He reached into his pocket and handed the boy a dollar bill. "You can buy some soap."

The boy looked at him a moment, curled the bill into his fist, said, "Fuck you," and walked away.

339

Shocked, Zo jumped to his feet and started after him, then stopped. What was he going to do, demand his money back because the boy wasn't properly grateful? But why had he said that? Zo recognized that he was hurt and had to laugh at himself. He needed to get out of this park; it was no longer an oasis from anything; it was a hellhole all its own.

He headed out of the park toward McDougal, thinking of the two Somerville women again. Where were they, mother and daughter, both murderers? Were they together? And what if he found them? Hedy Somerville had ruined his life. But he'd allowed it, participated in his own destruction. Another cop would have let go. J.J. hadn't let it get to him.

At Eighth, he turned left. The street was a disaster: punks and junkies; shoe stores and fast-food joints, the squawks and beeps of electronic games filling the air. The Eighth Street Book Shop was gone and so were the quality stores that had been there for years. Next to the movie theater, a man in a porkpie hat held eight to ten people spellbound while he duped them with his three-card-monte game. It was a scam, and people had been warned over and over again, but they continued to play, believing they could beat it even though they lost consistently. Why were people such idiots? But was he any different: the game he played and lost was with people instead of cards.

He walked on. At the corner of Eighth and Sixth Avenue, where Nathan's Restaurant was now boarded up, an enormous mound of rags was heaped against the side of the building. It made Zo furious that the Village he loved was allowed to deteriorate this way. Where the hell was the sanitation department? But when he got closer he saw the bundle move and, thinking it was rat-infested, stopped and stared, alarmed. Slowly the pile of rags unfurled and Zo realized that inside that filthy hill of material was a person. Standing to the side he saw a huge fat hand creep out from beneath the putrid heap of refuse and make its way up to where the face must have been. Then the top of the moldy mass moved again and turned in his direction, revealing part of a face: eyes, nostrils, mouth. The cheeks, chin, and forehead were concealed by drapes of fabric, shredded and dirty. The eyes stared past him, unseeing, and then the lips began to move.

"Don't bother to look for me closer to the sun because I noticed I'm gone for good. Have you noticed that?" the androgynous voice asked.

Zo knew this person was not speaking to him but still the words, even though they made no sense, frightened him. He wanted to go on, pass by, cross the street, but found himself rooted to the spot.

"Miss Ellie and J.R. haven't a ghost of a chance with those Muppets who're in cahoots with Ronald Reagan," it said, looking directly at him now.

The thing heaped on the sidewalk, the words that spewed forth, made him feel sick. He had to move. Taking a step toward the curb, he heard it start talking again and he ran, a car almost hitting him. From a distance he could still hear the disconnected drone, but the only words he understood were *Brooke Shields* and *Khomeni*.

A few minutes later, Zo stumbled into The Peacock Café on Greenwich Avenue. Although he liked the place better when it was on West Fourth Street years ago, he was in no condition to be choosy. He walked through the main room to the back, near the gilded statue, and sat down. The place was fairly empty so Virginia waited on him right away.

Sweat covered his body, making him feel clammy and depressed. Strains of an opera he couldn't identify amplified his sadness. He hadn't felt so shaken since Helen died. He couldn't understand it. Encountering weirdos and derelicts had been part of his life for years; and even as a civilian he was used to seeing them around the city. Was he on such emotionally shaky ground that an everyday occurrence could unnerve him so?

Virginia placed the cup of cappuccino in front of him. He dribbled in some sugar and stirred. Suddenly, he understood his unusual reaction: he'd identified with that human bundle of rags. He'd been drifting, sliding slowly down into his own form of madness. Looking at his jacket, he saw that the material was shiny with age, the cuffs of his shirt frayed. And then he scrutinized his hands, the nails long, ungroomed, unclean. He touched his face and felt the two-day growth of beard. His trousers, he noted, were spotted with grease, dirt, who knew what else. Zo's eyes filled with tears. Quickly he checked them; he couldn't bear to feel sorry for himself. Other men recovered from their wives' deaths. Why couldn't he?

A bubble of something akin to joy burst inside him. He

knew the answer: he was a man who needed purpose, who must have a goal. No matter how difficult or how impossible it seemed, he must resume his pursuit of Hedy. It was the only sensible thing for him to do.

He thought of his apartment and its disarray. For the first time in months, he had the desire to clean it. He wanted to put things right, to lead an orderly life again. The first thing he'd do was write that letter to Cristina in England, tell her all he knew. And then he'd map out a plan and foot by foot, inch by inch, he'd search the city of New York until he found Hedy Somerville. Lifting the cup to his lips, he acknowledged that it might take a very long time: perhaps the rest of his life.

The oppressive August weather, wet with humidity, airless, as if a huge vacuum were sucking the life's breath out of New York City, was almost as hard on Hedy as was the killing cold of winter. Still, finding places to sleep was easier, although not less dangerous, and the heat was not going to annihilate her. Most of the winter she'd spent in the ladies room at Penn Station and for two weeks, at the end of April, she'd shared a Kelvinator refrigerator box with another woman somewhere near Eleventh Avenue under the highway. But that didn't work out because they didn't get along and Hedy was asked to leave.

This was her fourth or fifth year on the streets (she couldn't remember how long), and she'd discovered ways of surviving. One of the biggest dangers was the attacks from men. Early on in her street life Hedy had learned that filth and repellent odors were her best defense: she'd resisted this method for quite a while, but after the second time she'd been raped she gave in. Now the men stayed away, but she still wasn't immune to theft. She always tried to sleep on top of her capacious yellow plastic bag which held her belongings: two sweaters, a bamboo fan, socks, her collection of Tab bottle tops, a light cotton blanket, and way at the bottom, wrapped in a piece of scrap material, the diamond ring. In her first week on the street she'd worn the ring, but more than once she'd been awakened by someone trying to pull it off her finger so she hid it. Besides, it no longer fit and kept slipping off. Also in her bag was a lidded jar of water for those occasions when she did wash; sometimes it got too bad to live with herself. Water was not always easy to come by, so she'd learned to keep a jar with her.

Some days she couldn't remember how she'd come to live this way; other times she had glimpses of the past like a speedy slide show. She recalled that a place she'd lived in had burned and with it had gone her belongings, including packs of money. But where those bills came from remained a total mystery. There was a block of time, from about the age of ten until a few years ago, that eluded her entirely. But it didn't bother Hedy; her life was occupied with two pursuits: survival and finding her mother.

Waking around six, beneath a bench in Union Square Park, Hedy rolled out and sat up, her bag's handles around one wrist. This was a dangerous place, but her stench was as protective as two burly bodyguards. Even at this hour, wet heat permeated her clothing and she felt as if she were in a bath. Underneath the acetate dress, which once had had a background of pink, a foreground of large white and green flowers now very indistinct, she wore a pair of faded purple polyester pants. She wriggled out of them, bouncing her bottom against the pavement, exposing emaciated legs festooned with scabs and sores. Carefully folding her pants, she tucked them into her bag. On her feet she wore a pair of Adidas sneakers she'd found that almost fit when she stuffed the toes with paper. While she was arranging her socks, caked with spots of black grease, she saw over the tips of her sneakers that someone was standing nearby. Slowly she looked up. Hedy no longer owned glasses, so it took a moment to focus. A man, bearded and red-eyed, wearing trousers cut off at the knees and a T-shirt which said something about a bicycle and a fish (it was too faded for Hedy to read), smiled down at her, showing black holes where teeth once lived. She regarded him with skepticism, waited for him to speak.

"Nice day," he said finally.

Hedy did not reply.

"Whatcha got in there, huh?"

She pulled her yellow bag closer to her. "Nothing you'd want."

"Wine?" he asked.

Clucking her tongue and shaking her head, the gray hair unmoving in its sticky strings, she pushed herself up onto the bench. "I don't drink," she said to the man, pride in her voice. "And you shouldn't either."

"Don't tell me what to do, ya filthy cunt," he said, his smile gone now, despair and anger in its place. "I oughta cut yer throat."

Hedy doubted if he possessed a knife, you could almost always tell who did or didn't, but sometimes you could be fooled, so she held herself still and waited. After a moment the man shuffled toward a group of ragged men several benches away.

She reached into her bag, scrabbled around, and eventually located the heel of bread she'd found the night before in a garbage can. In the last year or so she'd lost many teeth and the ones which remained were shaky in their sockets, so chewing the stale bread was difficult. She had to do it tiny bite by tiny bite. This breakfast would take at least an hour to devour.

While she ate she tried to think of her plan for the day. What part of the city should she search? Yesterday she'd combed the area between the FDR Drive and Broadway and Thirty-fourth and Fourteenth streets. Hedy supposed to continue on downtown would be the most sensible thing she could do.

Suddenly, as so often happened, she was struck with a word. This time it was *Ralph*. She'd never known anyone called Ralph. Still, when the name hit her mind, like instant graffiti, it gave her a sickly feeling in her belly. She shook it away and immediately felt better.

By seven o'clock she'd finished her breakfast and rose from the bench to begin her sojourn south. As she left the park she passed a man and woman who were sharing a hotdog roll and Hedy called out to them: "Have a good day."

The walk downtown was slow and tedious as there were many litter baskets which required her attention. It was almost nine thirty when she reached the corner of Ninth Street and Fifth Avenue, where she turned south. Partway down the block she crossed the avenue and stopped in front of a red brick apartment house. Two new words slammed into her brain. *Danielle* and *swan*. Staring at the building, she was sure she'd been there before. Maybe she'd noticed it in the last years as she covered Manhattan inch by inch. *Danielle* and *swan*. What could it possibly mean? Maybe Danielle knew Mary? A friend?

"Okay, okay, move along."

Hedy looked in the direction of the voice. It was a man in

uniform standing near the doorway of the brick building. She was used to being told to "move along," "get lost," "beat it"; it didn't faze her at all.

The man, pulling down his cap so that the shiny black visor tipped further over his brow, took a few steps toward her. "I said get going."

"Swan," Hedy said, her eye winking rapidly.

"What?" Crazy bitch. "Get going before I call the cops."

"Swan," she said again.

The doorman advanced, coming very close to her. He held up a large fist, hair sprouting from his knuckles. "I'm not against using this on you, you know." And then he whirled backward as if he'd been slapped. "Jesus H. Christ, you stink! Get the hell outta here."

Hedy spit a gob of saliva, yellowish and thick, at the man's feet, then headed down the avenue.

It was all Mary's fault, she thought, everything was Mary's fault. Mary was a very bad girl to leave her. The bad boys had gotten her when Mary left. When Mary had gone . . . gone . . . gone . . . when Mary had gone. All alone for the boys to hurt. Mary was very, very bad and that was why she'd shot her. But now Mary would be good again and when Hedy found her Mary would hold her and keep the bad boys away. It was all very simple if you gave yourself time to understand.

Hedy walked through the arch into Washington Square Park. Bad boys roller skating with big black things on their ears almost knocked her down. Bad boys.

"Mary," she said aloud, but no one heard.

It was time to rest. She found a spot on a bench. Soon the people on either side of her got up and left. She put her yellow bag between her sneakered feet. The word *value-pak* floated into her mind. *Value-pak, value-pak, value, value, value-pak.* It was stupid. What did it mean? These words that came into her mind tormented her with their repetition. Something must be wrong with her brain, she thought. Once she'd asked Francine, a street woman, if that ever happened to her and Francine said that Hedy must be very intelligent because she'd read that repetition was a sign of superior intellect. But the answer didn't really satisfy Hedy. When she found Mary, it would be the first thing she'd ask her. The second was where she'd been and why she'd gone and if she understood why Hedy'd had to shoot her?

A man sat down on the bench, glanced over at Hedy, then moved to the end, his nostrils twitching. It was her habit to ask people if they'd seen Mary and she did this now.

"What?" he said.

"I wondered if you'd seen Mary?" she asked again.

Zo smiled, his kind brown eyes creasing at the corners. "No," he said, "I haven't. I'm sorry."

"It's all right," she said, and turned away.

The sun rolled over the tops of the trees and beat down on Hedy, causing her odor to become even more horrendous. When the smell reached Zo, he got up and walked away.

For a second or two Hedy watched him and then she lost interest. From the corner of her eye she saw a policeman walking down the path. Immediately she picked up her bag, rose, and started off in the direction of McDougal Street. The policemen never let her sit in this park. Anyway, it was time she was on her way; there was much work to be done. In her bones, Hedy felt that today was her lucky day and by the time night fell again she would be reunited with her mother as all good girls should be.

THREE

They awoke to another murder, another assassination day. But this time it wasn't a political figure; it was a star. John Lennon had been gunned down in front of his home. The killer had called Lennon by name and then he'd shot him.

Cristina and Guy sat up in their king-size bed, holding cups of coffee, staring at the television screen and listening to Tom Brokaw tell them what had happened. For each of them the news was numbing, the memories they brought to the event inflating sorrow.

There was a knock at the bedroom door and Hilary, dressed for school, stepped inside.

"I guess you heard," she said.

"Yes, we did. Come here." Guy gestured to his daughter to join them.

Almost grudgingly, Hilary crossed the large room and tentatively sat on the edge of the bed near Guy.

"Where's Marc?" he asked.

"I don't know, dressing, I guess." She looked over at Cristina and saw that there were tears in her eyes. "I didn't know you liked John Lennon that much," she said suspiciously.

Cristina turned away from the screen. At thirteen, Hilary was a formidable enemy, causing Cristina considerable discomfiture. She understood the girl's position, it echoed what hers had been with Lynn. But as an adult, Cristina made efforts to conciliate, while Hilary, as a child, could or would not. Her question was a challenge, a test rather than honest inquiry, and Cristina was careful how she answered it.

"I did like him . . . but, even if I hadn't, I'd be sad. He was a human being killed by an insane person."

"Do you think," Hilary said, playing with a barette in her long brown hair and attempting a nonchalant air, "that it has anything to do with the fact that your mother, my *aunt*, was gunned down like that?" She never missed an opportunity to stress Guy's and Cristina's relationship.

Cristina ignored the reference. "Yes, I think it probably does," she answered candidly.

Guy, cognizant of the quiet battle, interrupted. "Did you have breakfast, honey?"

"I couldn't eat anything, Daddy. Gross!"

"No, of course not," said Guy, patting her hand. He understood that at Hilary's age, drama was of the essence; he also understood that his affair with Cristina caused his daughter embarrassment and pain.

"Isn't it time for you to go, Hilary?" Cristina asked. "You don't want to be late for school again."

"Honestly, Cristina, I don't see how anyone could go to school today," she said, as if Cristina was an idiot.

With nine months' experience in dodging the child's censoriousness, Cristina said mildly, "Well, I think you should try."

Hilary pressed her lips together in a tight angry line, then nestled her head between Guy's chin and shoulder. "I couldn't possibly go to school today, Daddy. It just wouldn't be right."

Guy and Cristina exchanged a look; he smiled at her but she remained solemn.

"I think," said Guy, "since school is in session you'd better go. I understand how you feel, honestly I do, but I don't think that's your decision to make."

"Oh, Daddy," she whined.

Guy sat up straighter and pushed her gently from his shoulder. "Sorry, toots. Get going now."

Hilary looked at her father, an expression of betrayal reflected in her eyes. "I'll bet no one else goes."

"If you're the only one who shows up, they'll send you home, don't worry."

"I'll look like a nerd if I go. You just don't understand," she said.

Guy kissed her cheek. "Bye, bye."

Hilary rose from the bed and flounced across the room. At the door she stopped and turned back to them, a hand on one hip. "Tell me, when my aunt was shot, killed by an insane person, did you both go to school?" She didn't wait for an answer but slammed the door shut behind her.

"What a little bitch she can be," Cristina said.

"Don't."

"I'm sorry, but she gets to me sometimes."

Guy moved closer and drew her to him. "I know. I'm sorry."

348

The door slapped open and Marc, already in his parka and wool hat, ran over to the bed.

"It's gross, isn't it?" he said. "I mean about John Lennon."

"Awful," said Guy.

"Yes, Marc, horrible." Cristina tucked an end of his hair under the hat. He'd run directly to her, flinging his arms around her neck. Marc loved Cristina, choosing to ignore any ignominy in her connection to his father. He desperately needed a mother: his own had abandoned him and Diane had been parsimonious with her affection. But Cristina adored him and showed it.

"Who could do something like that?"

"A crazy person," Guy answered.

"Yeah, must be," Marc said. He moved around the bed to kiss his father. "What will they do to him? The guy who killed Lennon?"

"It depends. He'll either go to jail or a mental hospital."

"Well, if he's crazy, shouldn't he go to a mental hospital? Why should he go to jail?"

"Good question," Guy said.

"It's complicated, sweetie," Cristina said to Marc.

"Seems simple to me. If you're bad, you go to jail. If you're nuts, you go to a nuthouse." He shrugged. "Gotta go. See you later."

When he'd gone, they went back to watching the television. Aside from the inescapable depression this murder awakened in him, Guy felt forlorn about the situation between Cristina and Hilary. His daughter's continuous assaults on Cristina were wearing. Guy believed Cristina's love for him was invincible, but her acceptance of the situation was not. And with Hilary constantly throwing the morality of their affair in Cristina's face, Guy knew the relationship was in jeopardy.

"Darling," he said, reaching for her again, "don't let Hilary come between us."

Looking up at him, she said, "I'm trying not to. But it's not just her persistent goading about who we are to each other, it's other things as well."

"Like what?"

"She arouses other guilts in me because she treats me an awful lot like I treated Lynn. And I want to be friends, you know, just the way Lynn wanted to be friends with me. More than friends. And then there's Marc, who accepts and loves me as Claude did Lynn. The whole thing is so damned reminiscent. Now this," she said, sweeping her hand out toward the television set. "I don't know, Guy, even though we know everything now, it still hangs on, plagues me."

Zo's letter, sent to her English address in April, had finally caught up with them in July.

"That reminds me, you never called Campisi, did you?"

"No."

"Why not?"

She shrugged. "Just haven't gotten around to it, I guess."

"Cristina," he said, "it's been five months."

"Why are you bringing this up now?"

"I suppose because of the Lennon murder. As you said, it's reminiscent." He kissed her brow.

She changed the subject. "Are you going to work today?"

"Sure." Going to work meant walking to his office in their four-thousand-square-foot loft. Guy had become an agent two years earlier, deciding he'd rather sell the work of an author he liked than buy it. As an editor he'd had to justify his existence; being an agent allowed him to retain his dignity as well as his autonomy. Sometimes finances were shaky because he wouldn't handle a book he didn't really like, no matter how commercial it might be. Many of his colleagues thought he was foolish, but he preferred his self-respect to a fat bank account.

"Are *you* going to work?" he asked.

"I don't feel much like writing today." She was almost finished with her latest young adult book.

"Then why don't you call Campisi, meet him for a cup of coffee. The man lives right in the neighborhood."

"Guy," she said, facing him, "what's this push for me to see Zo?"

"I think it might be good for you, darling. But you think he's going to urge you to confront your father, don't you?"

"Oh, God," she said, and slid down in the bed, pulling the covers up around her neck.

Guy slipped down next to her, throwing one leg over hers. "It's your decision, you know. Campisi can't make you do anything."

"So why should I see him?"

"For one thing, it's rude not to. For another, I think it'll finish things for you."

"It won't finish my feeling about Poppy, Guy." She'd refused to have anything to do with Martin since receiving the letter telling her he'd let the murderer go free.

"I think if you talk to Campisi you'll get a better understanding of the whole affair."

"You think I should see Poppy, don't you?"

"I think as long as you hold onto old stuff, you're simply not going to move ahead. Seeing Campisi might be a step in that direction."

She was silent for a few moments. "All right. I'll call Zo today. Of course he might not be there," she said hopefully.

Smiling, his violet eyes shining beneath the long black eyelashes, Guy said, "Then again, he might."

Before she could respond, he bent his head and kissed her. Aroused, he could feel she was also. In the beginning with Janet, he'd believed the sexual heights they'd scaled would be impossible to exceed. Now he knew he'd been wrong. And he understood that love made the difference.

Cristina's arms sailed over his shoulders and coasted down his back as she drew him over on top of her. Moving slightly to the side, Guy reached beneath her nightgown and engulfed her breast. She moaned softly and began to move under him.

As they drifted further from reality, their bodies merging, they became oblivious to their surroundings. From the television the voices of the mourners in front of the Lennon apartment house rose in unison: "All we are saying is, give peace a chance."

Almost every day, Guy had lunch uptown with different editors who were courting him, another plus in being an agent. Today, however, he had no lunch date and ate a sandwich at his desk. It was just as well, as the Lennon murder had taken its toll on him. The similarity between the two murderers calling the victims' names and then shooting them was, he supposed, enough to sink him into this feeling of lassitude. Except when he visited his mother or Cristina brought it up, he no longer thought much about his sister's murder. Even though Cristina was Danielle's daughter, he'd managed to separate them. Perhaps it was repression but, if so, he didn't care; it made life easier. Still, there were those times he couldn't avoid retrospection. After their lovemaking, when he had looked into Cristina's eyes, he'd seen signs of shame, stigmata he could not obliterate by word or action: he was uncle, she was niece. As much as they loved one another, that relationship was always there, undermining them, threatening destruction.

Finishing his sandwich he polished off a glass of milk and turned to a manuscript he'd been reading. Almost at once he drifted, recalling his accidental meeting in Bloomingdale's the week before with Susan Phillips, his teenage sweetheart. They had recognized each other at once. She'd aged, of course, but he thought she was lovelier than she'd ever been.

"I often think of that last night I spent with you, Guy," Susan had said, laughing. "My God, what babies we were."

"Yes, we were," he said, laughing with her, his mirth undercut as he remembered his adolescent suffering.

"What a lot of sturm and drang," she said lightly.

"Everything seems so real, so important at that age," he agreed.

She opened her mouth to speak but was stopped by the appearance of a teenage girl who materialized at her side. "My daughter Alexis," Susan said, introducing them.

The girl was pretty, too, her mouth and eyes Susan's. Guy smiled and took her hand.

"Mother's spoken of you," Alexis said.

"Really?" He was surprised to learn this and wondered what Susan had told the girl.

"I also have a ten-year-old son," said Susan.

"I have a girl and boy too," he said.

An uncomfortable moment followed and they fiddled with coats, gloves, scarves. Susan broke the silence.

"I know your sister was killed that day. It must've been a terrible time for you."

"It was. Terrible."

"I'm sorry I never wrote you or anything. I didn't know what to say."

"I understand," he said.

"I wanted to call, but. . . ." she trailed off, still disconcerted after all this time. "Did they ever catch the murderer?"

"No, they never did," he answered, astounded as always that this was so.

"Random violence. People think it's something new. Well, at least in your sister's case no one else was hurt."

"At least," he said softly.

They had dutifully exchanged phone numbers, though they'd probably never use them. Seeing Susan again made Guy feel that his life had come full circle. He'd always had a sense of unfinished business with her which dovetailed with the unsolved mystery of that day. If only Cristina could experience a similar sense of resolution. He wished desperately that he could help her. When he'd urged her to write about it, she'd steadfastly refused, even though she claimed she wanted to write adult fiction. Guy was sure, until she wrote her own story, she wouldn't be able to do that. He wondered how her meeting with Zo Campisi was going; perhaps he would be helpful, after all.

Guy forced himself once again to turn back to the manuscript that lay on his desk. When he'd read two pages more, he knew the novel was not for him and packed it back into its box. He reached for another manuscript, then changed his mind. He was simply no good today, his concentration impaired by the awful murder of Lennon. Instead, he'd make some calls, he decided. As he lifted the receiver his office door swung open, revealing Cristina and Campisi.

"What is it?" Guy asked, replacing the phone.

"You're not my uncle," she said. "We're not related at all."

It was almost impossible for Guy to believe that Danielle was not his sister. If it were true, surely he would have been told; if not by his parents, then certainly by Danielle. They had been friends. Or was that an illusion? Perhaps he'd assumed they were friends when, in reality, she thought of him as her pesty kid brother. And not even her blood brother. Was there some stigma attached to her heritage?

Cristina was equally shaken. Why hadn't she been told? Did Poppy know? Had Claude? Lynn? Maybe her mother hadn't even known. The possible freedom of not being related to Guy was overshadowed, for the moment, by other implications. It was a shocking thing to discover that you were not exactly who you thought you were. If her mother had been adopted, Cristina was not really a Dudevant. And what did that mean?

The cab Cristina and Guy shared as they headed toward Amelia's apartment was caught in traffic and creeping uptown at an infuriatingly slow pace.

"I could scream," she said.

Guy took her hand. "I know, but there's nothing we can do unless you want to get out and walk. We've endured this long, a little longer won't kill us."

"But we didn't know then."

"We don't *know* now. Let's not forget who told Zo about Anna Wilson," Guy said. At least the mystery of who Emma Stevenson had been was solved. Poor Papa, totally misunderstood by Maman.

"But it was your father who told Emma Stevenson, don't forget that."

Guy looked at her, surprised. "You believe all that?"

"Why not? She's been right about other things. Anyway, what about the birth certificate?"

"All that proves is that a child was born to someone named Anna Wilson at the same time Danielle was born. Darling, we shouldn't get our hopes up."

"They are up, I can't help it," she said.

"Just don't count on Maman too much."

"God, she's not even my grandmother . . . my real grandmother. Anna Wilson is."

"Maybe."

A cacophony of horns caused Cristina to shrink further down in her seat. Covering her ears with her hands she said, "Nerves are shot."

"Frayed," he suggested.

"Frayed." She sat up again. "Do you know that in three years I'll be as old as my mother was when she was killed? It gives me an odd feeling." She shivered as if a cold wind had blown across her neck.

At eighty-three, Amelia's health was fair, her blindness her only physical impairment. She shared her apartment with a paid companion, Elizabeth Blackstone. Elizabeth admitted them now, surprised to see them as they ordinarily called ahead.

"We didn't expect you," she said cheerfully. "Amelia's napping."

"I'm sorry we didn't let you know," said Guy. "Something important's come up and we just hopped a cab."

Elizabeth, tall and angular, swept a bony hand to the side, ushering them in. As they walked down the short hall, Guy felt a surge of gratitude to Elizabeth, noting the absence of odor and filth. Amelia had outlived all her cats but one, a gray Persian named Sebastian. He darted in front of Guy now, almost tripping him.

In the living room Amelia, small and frail, sat in her Windsor chair, asleep. A woven blanket of reds and purples was tucked around her waist and it draped her lap and legs, black oxfords peeping from beneath it. Her hair, although thin enough to show her pink scalp, retained a sheen, giving it the color of highly polished bone. Amelia lived in her loosely hanging skin as if it were an old dress, far too large but too familiar to throw away.

Gently, Elizabeth touched her tiny shoulder. "Amelia? Wake up, dear. The children are here to see you."

Her lids fluttered open, revealing eyes like bruised grapes. She moved her mouth as if to speak, but she was only tasting the aftermath of sleep.

"Maman," Guy said, leaning over and kissing her forehead.

"Guy."

Cristina touched Amelia's hand, then kissed her cheek. "Hello, Grandmaman." Quickly, she looked at Guy, unsure, embarrassed by the name she'd used.

He smiled at her reassuringly.

"Maman, how are you today?"

Her unseeing eyes looked in the direction of his voice. "You brought the child again. Very lovely, very nice."

"I have to ask you about something very important, Maman. I must ask you something about Danielle."

"Who?" Amelia asked.

"Danielle," he repeated.

A puzzled look came over Amelia's face and she shook her head from side to side.

Guy had known he couldn't count on his mother's memory or lucidity. There were days, times, when she was extremely coherent, remembering things accurately, recalling moments he'd forgotten. But most of the time Amelia lived in a world of her own devising, creating a place where no one suffered and, certainly, where no one was ever murdered. He felt extremely cruel having to force his mother to reenter reality. There was a small hassock at her feet where he sat.

"Maman," he said gently, "try to remember. Danielle. Your daughter."

Slowly Amelia's mouth twisted sideways, her chin trembled. "Ah, Danielle," she sighed.

What was the least hurtful way to phrase the question? Guy wondered. Was there any good way to ask a woman if the child she claimed was hers was not? Glancing at Cristina, he saw she understood his dilemma.

She reached out and touched his hand. "You simply have to ask. It'll be all right."

"Maman," he went on, "I have to ask you something that may upset you, but I want you to try and remember. It's very important. Was Danielle your *real* daughter? Did you give birth to her?"

The wrinkled face furrowed as if she were trying to remember. "My baby girl," she said finally.

"Maman, was Danielle adopted?" he asked, stroking his mother's dry hand.

"Adopted?"

"Yes. Did you and Papa adopt Danielle?"

"We cried when we saw her," Amelia said. "We were so happy we just cried and cried."

"I don't think we're going to get anywhere, darling," Guy said to Cristina.

Elizabeth, sitting against the wall, pursed her lips, appalled by the term of endearment. Seeing this, Guy said, "We have to find out if we're related or not. We've fallen in love."

Trying to take this in stride, Elizabeth nodded and smiled stiffly.

Guy turned back to his mother. "Maman, have you ever heard of anyone named Anna Wilson? Please try to remember."

"Anna Wilson," Amelia repeated. "Anna Wilson."

They were all quiet while they waited for Amelia to make a connection.

"I think," Amelia said, "she was a silent screen star."

"Did you know her?" Guy asked, still hoping.

"Oh no, dear, I never knew any of those people."

Guy felt defeated.

Cristina said, "Try asking her directly."

"Maman, was Anna Wilson the real mother of Danielle?" It seemed extremely cruel to him, but he knew it was the only way, the last chance.

"Who's to say what's real and what isn't," Amelia said.

356

The Persian cat, who'd entered the room like an inspector of something extremely important, jumped into Amelia's lap.

"Sebastian," she said smiling, "my baby boy."

Guy stood up and put an arm around Cristina. "I think it's a dead end here. Maybe we can try to find Anna Wilson."

"Yes," Cristina said, hiding her disappointment, "maybe Zo will help."

"Sure. We won't give up."

"Guy," Amelia called.

"Yes, Maman?"

"We love you, you know. Pierre and I love you, dear," she said as if time had stopped twenty-five years before. "But a daughter, you know, a daughter is different somehow."

Something caught in Guy's chest. "Yes," he whispered.

"It was all so strange," Amelia continued, "I never understood the reason."

Guy knew she meant the reason for Danielle's murder. "There was no reason, Maman."

"Oh, no," she said, "you're wrong. There's always a reason. But we don't always understand it. There's always a reason, Guy."

"Yes, Maman." Could she be right? he wondered. If she was, would he ever know why? And did it matter anymore? He thought not. "We have to go now."

"Guy," she said, "when you see Danielle, will you give her a message for me?"

Cristina took his hand in hers and squeezed hard.

"Yes," he said.

"Tell her that we don't blame her. Tell her that no one blames her. Will you say that, dear?"

"I will," he said, "I promise."

Cristina had called Zo to ask for his help in finding Anna Wilson; it was their only hope. But before he'd come up with anything, Elizabeth Blackstone phoned.

"I hope you won't think I'm being intrusive," she said, "but I think I've found something that might interest you and Mr. Dudevant. On the other hand, it might be meaningless."

"What is it?" Cristina asked, trying to keep the impatience from her voice.

"I was cleaning out a closet I hadn't gotten around to before and I came upon a box of papers and old notebooks. Well,

I had to look through them to see what could be kept and what could be thrown out. I wasn't being a nosy parker or anything like that."

"I'm sure you weren't."

"There are seven rather thick notebooks with your mother's name on them. They look like diaries."

Whether the diaries would reveal anything about her mother's heritage was almost immaterial to Cristina. The idea that she was going to learn something new about her mother was thrilling.

They sent a messenger for the notebooks and when they arrived, began to read immediately. The diaries started when Danielle was twelve and went to the last week of her life, although there were not daily entries for all those years. They found what they were looking for near the end of the first diary.

"Here it is," Cristina said. She began to read, her voice trembling. " 'Today I found out something incredible. Maman and Papa aren't my real parents and Guy isn't my real brother. My mother's name is Anna Wilson and my father is unknown. I guess that makes me a bastard. Oh, well, Maman says nobody ever has to know. Robert Simpson looked at me in school today and. . . .' " Cristina stopped. "That's all," she said incredulously. "Imagine finding something out like that and not giving it any more importance than . . . than. . . ."

"She was only thirteen," he said.

"Yes, that's true. Guy, do you realize, this is all we need?"

"I realize," he said, "it's all we need."

Cristina took the rest of the diaries and closeted herself in her study with them. She read them slowly, savoring the mundane details her mother had recorded, as well as her flights of fancy, making the acquaintance, at last, of this shadowy woman who'd been always at the center of her life. She discovered that Danielle was intelligent, kind, that she'd been ambitious, afraid of her husband, that she could laugh at herself, was easily hurt. But perhaps the most important thing Cristina learned was that her mother was an ordinary woman. Only her death was extraordinary, the most remarkable fact of her life.

As for her father, his transgressions so far in the past, he now seemed simply weak and pathetic. She'd lost her need to boycott him. She would see him because he was her father. That would have to be enough.

It was all nearly finished now. When she awoke on the last day of 1980, she skipped breakfast and went immediately to her study. The pages of the young adult novel were stacked up beside her typewriter and she carefully put them into a box. Eventually she would finish it, but now there was something else she had to write.

She rolled a piece of paper into the machine and numbered it one. Halfway down the page, in the center, she typed ONE. And then she began to write:

The Checker taxicab was new; a smell of fresh leather was unmistakable. Danielle Swann tasted this essence on the back of her tongue as though she had sampled a bite of the sleek, burnished interior. She swallowed, trying to chase away the flavor; she could not help thinking of the animals who had furnished their skins to create this environment. Yet she ate meat, wore leather belts and shoes, carried handbags made from hides. Never, however, would she wear a fur coat: it was one principle she still embraced.

When Cristina read it over, she knew it was the right way, the only way, to begin.